Praise for THE

"Hilarious, touching, romping fun… Ibbotson is one of the three greatest children's writers of our time, and if you have not yet discovered her, you're in for a treat"
Amanda Craig, THE TIMES

"An outlandish and very funny adventure told with vivacity and warmth"
GUARDIAN

"Another gem … up there with her finest work"
Lorna Bradbury, TELEGRAPH

"Touching, exciting and funny"
SPECTATOR

"One final gift… A poignant reminder of why its author was so loved, The Abominables brims with character and wit… A charming story from a much-missed author"
INDEPENDENT ON SUNDAY

"This novel is an unexpected bonus … a classic Ibbotson story – with humour, brave children and miraculous creatures… This lost treasure is a joy"
THE SUNDAY TIMES

"Ibbotson's last book is a typically delightful invention"
TELEGRAPH

Also by Eva Ibbotson

THE ABOMINABLES
&
One Dog and His Boy

EVA IBBOTSON

Illustrated by Sharon Rentta

mlb
MARION LLOYD BOOKS

Scholastic Children's Books
A division of Scholastic Ltd
Euston House, 24 Eversholt Street
London, NW1 1DB, UK
Registered office: Westfield Road, Southam, Warwickshire, CV47 0RA
SCHOLASTIC and associated logos are trademarks and/or registered
trademarks of Scholastic Inc.

The Abominables
First published in the UK by Marion Lloyd Books, 2012
Text Copyright © Eva Ibbotson 2012
Illustration Copyright © Sharon Rentta, 2012

One Dog and His Boy
First published in the UK by Marion Lloyd Books, 2011
Text Copyright © Eva Ibbotson 2011
Illustration Copyright © Sharon Rentta, 2011

This edition published by Scholastic Ltd, 2013

The rights of Eva Ibbotson and Sharon Rentta to be identified as
the author and illustrator has been asserted by them.

ISBN 978 1407 14312 5

British Library Cataloguing-in-Publication Data.
A CIP catalogue record for this book is available from the British Library.

Printed in the UK by CPI Group (UK) Ltd, Croydon, CR0 4YY
Papers used by Scholastic Children's Books are made from wood grown in
sustainable forests.

1 3 5 7 9 10 8 6 4 2

THE ABOMINABLES

Contents

1

Kidnap

About a hundred years ago something dreadful happened in the mountains near Tibet.

A beautiful young girl called Lady Agatha Farlingham was sleeping peacefully in a tent pitched on a ledge below the summit of a mountain known as Nanvi Dar. Beside her, wearing a green woolly nightcap against the bitter cold, slept her father, the Earl of Farley, and in another tent close by slept their three porters, tough natives of the Himalayas, who carried their baggage and looked after them.

The Earl had come to the roof of the world to search for rare and unknown plants which grew only in these high and dangerous places. He was a famous plant hunter and he liked his daughter Agatha too much to leave her at home in England doing all the boring things that girls had to do in those days, like painting pictures of ruins, or taking walks with their governess, or visiting the poor, who often preferred to be left alone.

Soon after midnight on that awful night, Lady Agatha was woken by a most strange and unearthly

sound – an
eerie and mournful noise like a
train with indigestion.

She sat up, pulled her father's heavy tweed jacket around her shoulders and bravely stepped outside. And then it happened. Out of the blackness and the snow there loomed a ghastly, gigantic, hairy THING. Before she could even scream, a pair of huge brown arms grasped the terrified girl and then the foul beast turned and, leaping swiftly back up the sheer side of the mountain, vanished out of sight.

The poor Earl and his porters searched and searched for many days, risking death in the cruel blizzards and the raging wind, but it was useless. The fresh snow had wiped out all possible tracks.

Only a blue
bedsock, kicked off by
the struggling girl, remained to Lady
Agatha's distraught father. He took it back to
England, to his ancestral home at Farley Towers,
and slept with it under his pillow for the rest of
his life. And when people asked him what had
happened to his lovely daughter, he always said
she must have lost her memory and wandered
away and been buried by an avalanche. Because he
simply wouldn't believe what all the porters told
him: that his daughter had been carried away by a
yeti – that vile monster who can tear a human being
limb from limb, or crunch one up in a single bite. A
creature so terrible and fearsome that it is known as
The Abominable Snowman.

But of course the porters were right. Agatha *had*
been carried away by a yeti. He had run with her
high over the sacred mountain of Nanvi Dar, and all

her kicks and struggles and screams felt no more to his brute strength than the hiccuping of a flea. Until at last the thin air, the bitter cold and blind terror brought release and the poor girl mercifully fainted.

When she came round she knew at once where she was. There could only be one place as beautiful as this: heaven. The sky above her head was a marvellous rich, royal blue with little fleecy clouds. The grass on which she lay was soft and sweet-smelling and studded with beautiful flowers: tiny blue gentians, golden primulas, scarlet lilies. Agatha sat up. She felt sore and bruised but that was understandable. You couldn't die and go to heaven without feeling a little bit uncomfortable.

She looked around. The air was warm, and she saw trees covered in red and white and cream blossoms as big as plates. There was a stream, crystal clear and bubbly, with kingfishers darting about its banks. Far above her an eagle circled lazily. She was in a broad valley, surrounded on every side by sheer, jagged cliffs and escarpments. And then to her surprise, beyond the steep ridges which surrounded the valley, she saw the unmistakable outline of the peak of Nanvi Dar, glittering white in the early morning sun.

"Perhaps I haven't died after all," said Lady Agatha.

And there was something else that didn't go with the idea of heaven in the least. A few metres away from her, sitting so quietly that she had taken it for a boulder or the stump of a huge tree, was an absolutely enormous dark brown beast. It wasn't a bear; it was much, much bigger than a bear. It wasn't a man; it was much, much hairier than any man. And then she remembered. A yeti. She had been carried away by a yeti over mountains so dangerous that she could never make her way back alone. She was trapped here in this secret valley, perhaps for ever.

"I should feel terribly frightened," thought Agatha.

But feeling frightened is an odd thing. You either feel it or you don't, and Agatha didn't. Instead she got up and walked quietly towards the yeti. Then she leaned forward and put her hand on the yeti's arm. At once she was buried up to the elbow in long, cool, silky, tickly hair, masses and masses of it.

The yeti leaned forward. He blew softly with his lower lip to clear away his hair – and then Lady Agatha Farlingham became the first human ever to see a yeti's face.

She thought it a most interesting and distinguished face. Yetis have huge, round, intelligent eyes as big as saucers. If you stop and look into a yeti's eyes, instead of just running away and screaming, you can't be afraid. Yetis also have snub noses and big ears and the ears have a most useful flap on them, an ear *lid*, which they can close. This saves them from getting earache in the fierce Himalayan winds, and is also useful when they don't want to hear what people are saying. Their mouths are big and generous-looking.

Best of all are their smiles. "Before I had seen a yeti smile," Lady Agatha used to say, "I didn't know what a smile was." Not only was the yeti's smile beautiful, it was very, very comforting to anyone who might be worrying about being eaten. If you want to know what a person eats, look at his teeth. The yeti's teeth were white and even and quite flat, like the teeth of a very clean sheep, and Agatha understood immediately not only that the yeti *wouldn't* eat her but that he *couldn't* eat her. And in fact, as she found out later, yetis are the strictest and most careful vegetarians.

"Oh, I *like* you," said Agatha, holding out her hand.

A great burden seemed to fall off the yeti's back. He got up and stood there, waiting, with his head on one side, till Agatha got up too, and then he began to lead her along the floor of the valley towards a little copse of slender Himalayan birches where some yaks were peacefully grazing. And as he walked, Agatha saw that his enormous feet – each about the size of a well-fed dachshund – had eight toes and were put on back to front. And this, of course, was why later when people tried to track yetis in the snow they never found them. Yetis who seem to be going are really coming, and yetis who seem to be coming are really going. It is as simple as that.

Suddenly the yeti stopped, bent down to a little hollow by the bank of the stream and began to clear away the dried grass and sticks which covered it. When he had finished he grunted in a pleased sort of way and then he moved aside so that Agatha could see what he had uncovered.

"Oh!" said Agatha. Sleeping peacefully, curled up in each other's arms, were two fat, furry baby yetis. She bent down to touch the one nearest to her. Its silly, big feet were pulled round its plump stomach and when it opened its eyes and looked at her, they were a deep and lovely blue.

Then she tickled the other yeti and it twitched in its sleep and woke too, and *its* eyes were a rich and serious brown.

But the yeti father had begun to look anxious.

Something wasn't right. He began to stir the babies round, prodding and digging and turning them over like underdone sausages. And then he pounced, and with a proud grunt, held something out to Agatha.

It was another baby yeti – but so small and squashed and funny-looking that it might just as well have been an old glove or a tea cosy or a run-over cat. And when it opened its eyes and looked at her, Agatha got a shock. One of its eyes was a bright and piercing blue, the other was a deep and serious brown.

"A wall-eyed yeti," said Agatha in amazement.

Later she called him Ambrose.

2

The Trouble with Yetis

As soon as she saw the orphaned yetis, Agatha gave up all idea of escaping from the secret valley. No, she would stay and bring the babies up to be God-fearing creatures and give them a mother's love. For she realized at once that the big yeti who had kidnapped her must be a widower who had lost his wife in some tragic accident and that he wanted her to care for his children.

And care for them she did. The very fat, blue-eyed baby was a girl and Agatha called her Lucy, after the kennelmaid who had been her best friend at Farley Towers. The brown-eyed yeti, who was a boy, she called Clarence. And of course there was Ambrose, with his mad eyes and his squashed face – Ambrose who was always being sat on by the others, or falling into mouse-hare holes, or getting lost.

The first thing Agatha did, naturally, was to teach all the yetis to talk. Father learnt to speak quite quickly even though he was over three hundred years old by the time Agatha came to the valley and it is not so easy to learn things as you get older. And of course the children learnt as easily as they breathed.

After that, Agatha taught them all the things that her governess had taught her, like the importance of good manners: not burping after meals, not scratching under the armpits however much one itched, and *never* closing one's ear lids when people were speaking to one. She taught them how to clean between their teeth with a sharpened stick, and how to wash their eight-toed, backward-pointing feet in the stream after they'd been running because smelly feet are *not* polite. She taught them sums and their alphabet and how to sing hymns. Best of all, she used to tell them stories. Soon after she arrived in the valley, Father had realized that a well-bred English girl needed somewhere to call home, and he had gathered stones and built her a little house, no more than a hut really, roofing it with branches and grass. In the evenings, Agatha would sit outside with the yetis around her. "Once upon a time..." she would begin.

The yetis were *mad* about stories. *Puss in Boots*, *Jack and the Beanstalk*, *The Three Bears* – all day they followed her about, begging for more. As for Ambrose, long before dawn Agatha could hear him sitting and *breathing* outside the entrance to her hut (by the time he was two years old he was much too big to get through it), waiting and waiting to hear about Ali Baba, or poor Cinderella, or Dick Whittington's cat.

At first Lady Agatha was surprised by how easily the yetis took to a civilized English upbringing, but she soon realized that they were truly kind and considerate by nature, not only to each other, but to every living thing. In the mornings, when she combed them, they would cup their huge hands to catch the little spiders and beetles that had crept into their hair during the night, and release them carefully on to the ground. They always looked where they were putting their huge feet, avoiding worm casts and spiders' nests and molehills, in case someone was at home. So they were particularly pleased when Agatha taught them to say sorry, for you should Always Apologize for Any Inconvenience You Have Caused.

But when they began to apologize to everything they ate (and yetis eat a lot), saying "Sorry, mango," "Sorry, flower," "Sorry, yak-milk pancake," Lady Agatha thought that this was going too far – Moderation In All Things – and taught them to say grace. "For what we are about to receive may the Lord make us truly thankful." It was not a great improvement. They did say grace politely when they sat down to a meal together. But yetis graze quite a lot, on grass or fruit or young tree shoots, and they went on apologizing as they wandered about, so that there was an almost constant murmuring in the hidden valley, rather like a swarm of contented bees. Agatha tried to persuade them that saying sorry to every nut and berry was not the English Way, but although she was a remarkably good governess, in this she failed. The yetis continued to apologize to every blade of grass.

*

This doesn't mean, of course, that they were perfect. Perfect yetis, like perfect people, would have been dull. Lucy's little problem was food. She really loved eating. All day one could hear Lucy wandering up and down the valley saying, "Sorry," before she cropped a mouthful of grass or, "Sorry, tree," before she chewed up a branch. The result of this, of course, was that she became very fat, and the hair on her stomach looked as though it was growing on an enormous kettledrum. And because her stomach was always full, Lucy slept badly. Or rather she *slept* all right but she walked in her sleep. When you heard a terrible crash or a fearful rumbling noise in the mountains of Nanvi Dar, it wasn't necessarily a rock fall or an avalanche. It was just as likely to be Lucy falling over a tree stump as she blundered with unseeing eyes out of her bed.

Clarence had a problem too. With him it was his brain. When he was small, Clarence had been naughty and left the valley without telling Lady Agatha and gone climbing on his own, and a gigantic boulder had come loose and hit him on the head. After that Clarence's brain did not work too well, so that while he was as strong as the others and could pick a fir-tree as easily as a daisy, he was really not very bright and could only say one word at a time and that was usually wrong.

As for Ambrose, he started life as a little mewling thing, all eyes and feet and not much in between, and Agatha had some very worrying moments, sitting up with him when he was teething or running a temperature. Once, when he had had a runny nose for a full month, she said, half-joking, "Ambrose, you really are an abominable snowman." The name stuck and he was Ambrose the Abominable from then on. Because of all the trouble he had caused her as a baby, and the times when she seriously thought he might not survive, he had a special place in Agatha's heart. This sometimes happens to mothers, however hard they try to love all their children absolutely equally. But at last the worst was over, and Ambrose grew fast, and he grew strong. When he was nineteen, before he lost his milk teeth, he pushed over the biggest pine tree in the valley looking for woodlice to play with, and he would cheerfully lift boulders the size of telephone boxes to help Lucy make a Wendy house. If anyone had happened to catch sight of Ambrose, with his wall-eye and enormous strength, their knees would have started to tremble and sweat would have broken out on their brow. He really did look like people imagined yetis to be –

abominable. In actual fact, however, he was the soppiest yeti ever, forever making daisy chains for Lady Agatha, or lying beside her asking if there were fairies in the stars, or begging for another story. He always gave things away – food to Lucy, or pretty stones to Clarence, and sometimes Lady Agatha thought it might be a good thing if he really was a tiny little bit abominable. She would never have called him wet, exactly, or soft (he never complained when he hurt himself), but was he just a little bit too kind for his own good?

When Agatha had been in the valley about thirty years and Ambrose, Clarence and Lucy were already children rather than babies, a very old and stringy female yeti tottered into the valley from a range of mountains to the east. They called her Grandma, and just sometimes after she had taught her to speak, Agatha wished she hadn't, because all Grandma did was grumble. She grumbled about her rheumatism, she grumbled about her teeth. She grumbled about her share of juniper berries at lunchtime and about how careless Ambrose was, bouncing on her corns. But the yetis knew one had to be kind and gentle to the old and they behaved beautifully to Grandma. The only thing they wouldn't do, even for Lady Agatha, was to keep their ear lids open when she sang. And really, you couldn't blame them. Grandma singing "Onward Christian Soldiers" as she milked the yaks didn't just sound like a road drill. It sounded like a road drill with tonsillitis.

Even after Grandma came, Agatha's family was not complete. A few years later, Father, who sometimes went exploring in the High Places, came back with a rather shy and nervous yeti a few years younger than himself.

When he was young, Uncle Otto (as they called him) had had a Dreadful Experience. He was standing on a pinnacle of rock admiring a most beautiful and uplifting sunrise, when two Sherpa porters, carrying the baggage for a party of mountaineers, had come round the corner and seen him. Uncle Otto had smiled most politely, showing all his beautiful white teeth in welcome, but the porters had just screamed and gibbered and, throwing down their packs, had rushed down the mountain so fast that one of them had fallen into a crevasse and been killed.

After this, Uncle Otto had always felt shy and unwanted, and soon afterwards a bald patch had appeared on his high, domed forehead. There is nothing like worry for making your hair fall out. But when Agatha taught him to speak, and to read, she was amazed at his intelligence. In the pocket of her father's jacket, which she had slipped on before she was carried away, had been a copy of the Bible, and Uncle Otto used to spend hours sitting under his favourite rhododendron tree and reading. What's more he never skipped like the others did but even read the bits where Ahaz begat Jehoadah and Jehoadah begat Alameth. Not that he was conceited – far from it. It was the others who were so proud of him.

And so the years passed peacefully and happily for Agatha and her yetis in the secret valley of Nanvi Dar. Because there was no smoke to get into her lungs, or petrol fumes to give her headaches, or chemicals to mess up her food, Agatha grew old only very, very slowly. Nearly a hundred years after she had come to the valley she was still healthy and strong.

But in the meantime the world outside was changing. More and more mountaineers came to climb the high peaks with newer and shinier tents and ropes and ice axes and stood about on the top of them being photographed and quarrelling about who had got there first. And then one day Clarence said, "'ook! 'ook!" and when they had looked up to where he was pointing they saw, far away, a strange red bird in the sky – a helicopter – which quite amazed Lady Agatha, who'd left England when there weren't even any motor cars.

After that came the hotel.

It was a huge, luxury hotel – the Hotel Himalaya, they called it

– built just across the border in the province of Bukhim, so that wealthy people who were too lazy to walk anywhere could sit in their rooms and watch the sun go down on the peaks of Nanvi Dar. The hotel meant new roads, and plane loads of tourists. It meant litter on the snowy slopes, and monasteries serving egg and chips and rubbishy souvenirs. It also meant new kinds of people: property developers and speculators, people who thought of the mountains not as beautiful places to be respected but as something that might make them rich.

Lady Agatha wasn't a worrier, but she began to worry now. It seemed to her only a matter of time before someone discovered the valley. And she knew enough about the cruel and terrible things that might happen to her yetis if the wrong people found them. They could be put in zoos behind bars with people poking them with umbrellas and throwing toffee papers into their cages. They could be put in a circus or a funfair and treated like freaks. Or – but this was so awful that Agatha began to shiver even as

19

she thought of it – they could be hunted and killed for sport as the great mammals of Africa had been hunted and killed when man first set eyes on them.

"Now listen, my dears," she said to her yetis, gathering them around her. "I must ask you to stay safely hidden in the valley. No climbing in the High Places. No exploring."

"But I want to meet humans," said Ambrose. "You're a human. They could be our friends and tell us stories, like you do. And we could help them lift things."

Lady Agatha sighed. She blamed herself, of course, for not having been more honest about the world from which she came. But how could she explain about human wickedness to the yetis? They would simply never understand it. She could only hope that the yetis would obey her.

And the yetis did. Ambrose, in any case, was busy taming his pet yak, an animal called Hubert. Yaks (which are a sort of small and very shaggy cow) are stubborn and hardy animals. But they are not very clever at the best of times. They don't need to be because all they do is eat grass at one end and give milk at the other. All the same, there had probably never before been a yak as stupid as Hubert.

He was about the size of a folding pram, with

a sad, boot-shaped face, a crumpled left horn and
knees which knocked together when he walked.
Hubert knew he had a mother, but he was never
quite sure which of the yaks was her, and when he
did find her he would suddenly get the idea that he
was supposed to be back with Ambrose. Sometimes
he would get so muddled that he would just bury
his head in a hollow tree or a hole in the ground and
give up; there were Hubert Holes like that all over
the valley. Ambrose, however, wouldn't hear a word
against him, and as he said, Hubert was probably the
only potholing yak in the world.

But though all the yetis were as good and careful as could be, something dreadful did happen after all.

In a way it was Lady Agatha's fault for cooking such a lovely yak-milk pudding for their supper. Father and Uncle Otto had three helpings each; Grandma and Clarence and Ambrose had two. But Lucy said, "May the Lord make us truly thankful," to the yak-milk pudding no less than *five* times. Nobody can have five helpings of pudding and sleep soundly. And that night, Lucy rose from the bed of leaves in which she slept beside her brothers, and with her blue eyes wide open and her arms stretched out in front of her she walked – sightless and fast asleep – across the meadows, scaled apparently without effort the ferocious cliffs surrounding the valley, and stepped out on to the eternal snows.

3

Footprints in the Snow

Lucy got back safely to the valley – sleepwalkers usually seem to get back to their beds. But the glacier she had walked across had just had a new fall of snow. And right across it, from end to end, she left a row of footprints. Huge, clear, dachshund-sized prints: eight toes, rounded heels and all. There is nothing like a portly yeti with flat feet for making marks which even a nitwit could identify.

If only it had snowed, then things might have gone on as before. But it didn't snow, not the next day or the next. And on the third day a couple of climbers came across the prints.

Within a week photographs of Lucy's footprints were on the front page of newspapers all over the world. All the old stories about Abominable Snowmen were dragged out again: how fierce they were, how huge... How they could swallow three goats at a gulp, how just to *see* one was to die within the week.

The owners of the Hotel Himalaya, who knew all about how to make money, set to work at once. The day after the climbers had burst breathlessly into

the hotel dining room with their news, people were sent out to find the footprints and preserve them, by roping them off, putting up signs, and covering them with tarpaulins in case it snowed. And a few days later full-page advertisements appeared in all the travel magazines and brochures, saying, *Enjoy the Experience of a Lifetime! A week at the luxury Hotel Himalaya with guided Yeti Safari to the famous footprints!* And underneath a picture of a hairy monster with fangs and blood dripping down its chin were the words *Who will be the first to meet the Abominable Snowman Face to Face? IT COULD BE YOU!*

But it wasn't a photographer or a journalist or a thrill-seeking tourist who found the secret valley of Nanvi Dar. It was a boy; quite a young one. And his name was Con.

Con was a pageboy at the Hotel Himalaya in Bukhim. He was, perhaps, the smallest pageboy in the world and in Britain he would not have been allowed to work at all because he was far too young.

When Con's father, who ran a restaurant in London, had been offered the job of chef in the new hotel in Bukhim, he had tried to leave Con and his sister Ellen behind at nice boarding schools in England. But Con had dug in his heels. He was not, he said, going to spend his time rushing about on cricket pitches in silly white pants, or letting idiot boys hit him on the head with pillows in the dorm, when he could be living in one of the most exciting places in the world.

"And anyway," he'd said to his father, "I might see a yeti."

Con's father didn't believe in yetis but he believed in Con. And when Con and Ellen both promised to work very hard at their lessons, he agreed to take them along.

And the children kept their promise, and worked very hard indeed. Even so, because they didn't have to stand about in Assembly having headmasters make speeches to them, or hang around in draughty schoolyards waiting for whistles to blow, or fight for their school dinners, they had lots of spare time. So in the afternoons Con put on a red uniform with silver buttons and helped to look after the visitors, and Ellen, who was very domesticated and liked to be busy, worked with the maids. The children's mother had been killed in a car crash two years earlier and it helped Ellen to do the things she'd done with her.

When Con had told his father that he might see a yeti he hadn't been joking. Ever since he'd first read about yetis, he'd had a special feeling about them. When people had scoffed and said there weren't any such things, Con had just shrugged. He just *knew* there were and that one day he would see one.

So when Lucy's footsteps had first been seen on the slopes of Nanvi Dar, Con had been incredibly happy and excited. He longed to join the parties of visitors on the trek up to the glacier. For the Yeti Safari was a huge success. People arrived at the Hotel Himalaya from all over the world. But soon Con stopped being happy and began to feel quite sick. The hotel manager did everything he could to cash in on the yetis, selling yeti pyjama cases and yeti headscarves and yeti postcards which made them look like dim-witted baboons. And finally, when Con had spent some time helping groups of tourists get ready for their trek, running backwards and forwards with Thermos flasks they had left in their rooms, tying their bootlaces, polishing their snow goggles, pulling on their padded mittens and smearing suncream on their noses, he stopped feeling sick and began to be frightened.

In one of the parties there was a couple of beetroot-faced army officers drinking rum out of silver hip flasks who talked about "getting a potshot at the brutes, eh?" In another there was a very thin woman wearing boots which Con was absolutely sure were made from the skin of the terribly rare snow leopard. She kept laughing like a hyena and telling her husband that she "*must* have a yeti-skin coat, daah-ling". When a third group departed which included a fat little man who seemed to think a yeti was a kind of elephant because he did nothing except wonder how much one could get for a pair of tusks, Con had had enough.

That night he couldn't get to sleep. He was just too horribly angry. He knew what would happen if one of those rich, bored, stupid people really did stumble across a yeti. Nobody who cared deeply about those mysterious creatures could even afford to buy a cup of tea in the Hotel Himalaya, let alone go on the ridiculously expensive Yeti Safari. So it was only a question of time.

"I wish they had never found those footprints," he said to himself. And then he knew what he had to do.

He woke an hour before dawn, dressed quickly in the warmest things he had and began carefully and methodically to pack his rucksack. He had been out hiking many times, and knew what he would need. But he also knew that he was planning something very dangerous, and probably very foolish. He left a note for Ellen and his father. Then he slipped out of the hotel.

The route up to the glacier was not hard to follow. It had been well trampled the last few weeks, there were fixed ropes at the more difficult places, and it was certainly no harder for Con than for the little fat man. He reckoned on cutting the time the guided parties took by several hours, because they moved very slowly, with frequent stops for tea and titbits. And in the early afternoon they stopped at a specially prepared campsite with fires blazing and servants rushing about with hot meals and drinks. Even so, Con was expecting to spend at least one night well above the treeline at a dangerously high altitude.

By mid-afternoon, exhausted and breathing with difficulty in the thin air, Con was standing on the glacier in the shadow of the huge, towering rock face which made up the eastern shoulder of Nanvi Dar. It was easy to find the footprints. Already hundreds of tourists had shuffled around them. But now it was over. When he was finished, the mountains and their secret inhabitants could find peace again.

He had to hurry. If he did not get off the glacier and find some kind of shelter before nightfall then he would die, no doubt about it. All he needed to do was remove the protective covering, and let the snow clouds which were gathering in the west do the rest. He pulled the heavy tarpaulins aside and then, to be absolutely sure, he started kicking snow into the prints, tramping in them, so that they were completely obliterated. He followed the prints, kicking and stamping, all the way to where the snow of the glacier ended and the footprints (if you followed them the right way, letting the *heels* lead you) stopped. Over this great cliff of rock the yeti must have clambered, but a human being could not hope to follow. No less than three mountaineering expeditions, with the newest equipment, had tried to conquer the eastern ramparts of Nanvi Dar and failed.

Afterwards, Grandma said it was the will of God, because why should Con have come to the sheer rock face just at that moment? The moment when there burst out of the space between two boulders at the base of the cliff a most extraordinary THING.

A sort of molehill it seemed to be. But were molehills hairy? And did they *bleat*?

Completely puzzled, Con scrambled up to have a closer look.

The THING was a head. The small, earth-covered head of a very worried baby yak.

Hubert had had a dreadful day. First he'd gone up to someone who he was absolutely certain was his mother but she hadn't been, and had been rude about it. Then he'd trotted back to find Ambrose but Ambrose was helping Lady Agatha to pick bamboo shoots and he wasn't there. By this time Hubert was so muddled that he'd gone and buried his head in a hole, meaning to wait till things got clearer inside his

head. But the hole hadn't been like his usual holes. It had gone on and on and on. And now he had come out in this strange place and his back end was stuck in the mountain and it was all very difficult and very hopeless and very sad.

"Don't worry, little Bootface," said Con, patting the yak on the nose, "I'll soon get you clear."

He took hold of Hubert's shoulders and began tugging and pulling – carefully but with all his strength. For a while nothing happened except that Hubert's bleats got more and more frantic. Then suddenly there was a popping noise and in a shower of small stones, Hubert's backside came out of the mountain and fell across Con's feet.

"A *tunnel*?" said Con, peering across Hubert into the deep, black hole from which the yak had come. "It can't be!"

But it was: a narrow channel through the side of the mountain which had once been the bed of an underground river.

"You must have come from the other side," said Con wonderingly. "And if I lie down I'm smaller than you are..."

He dropped on to his hands and knees and began to edge his way into the tunnel. The sunshine turned to grey twilight, then to darkness: pitch darkness as

Hubert, terrified of being left alone, turned back and followed him.

It was a fearful journey and agonizingly slow. Water trickled down the sides of the rock, jagged daggers of ice hung from the roof; Con had never been so cold. Often he wanted to stop and go back but behind him, blocking off all retreat, puffing, dribbling, butting with his crumpled horn – came Hubert.

"I ... can't do it," gasped Con. The passage was getting narrower now. It was like being in an endless, ice-cold grave. "I can't..."

And then he saw it. A narrow chink of light. Golden light. *Sunlight*.

The chink grew bigger. It had grass in it; flowers; the flash of water... And something else...

"No," breathed Con, "I don't believe it."

But it was true. On a tussock of grass sat a little old lady wearing a long, white flannel nightdress. Beside her, his armchair-sized head within reach of her hand, lay an enormous chocolate-coloured creature whose left ear she was gently scratching. Another huge beast – with a dreamy look and the largest stomach Con had ever seen – was sitting nearby, peacefully combing out her elbows. Three more of them were paddling in the stream or picking flowers and one – his bald patch gleaming in the sunlight – was leaning against a tree and reading a book.

"Tell it again," came the voice of the chocolate-coloured yeti. "Tell where the Ugly Sisters tried to cut off their toes to get them in the glass slipper?"

"That's enough for today." The old lady's voice was firm. The creature lifted his head and began reluctantly to get up. Then he let out a great yell.

"Look, Lady Agatha! Look, everybody! It's a funny sort of human dwarf thing. And it's come out of Hubert's hole!"

4

A Plan

An hour later, as the shadows lengthened and the sun began to set behind the eastern escarpments of the secret valley, Con was sitting on a grassy bank beside the stream, drinking the warm yak's milk that Lady Agatha had heated for him on a charcoal fire.

"So it's the crater of an extinct volcano?"

"Well so I believe," said Lady Agatha. "There are some marvellous hot springs over there. I don't know what I would have done without hot water when the children were small. And the soil is wonderfully fertile, even better than Hampshire. But are you sure," Lady Agatha broke off, "that your father won't be worried about you?"

"Well, I did leave a note," said Con, "so he won't be *too* worried until tomorrow evening. Anyway," he went on contentedly, "I can't leave tonight, can I?"

All around him sat the yetis, as close to him as they could get, but trying very hard not to stare because they knew it was rude.

"I don't *mind* him having no hair on his face," whispered Ambrose to his sister. "I just know we are going to be friends."

"He's very *thin*," murmured Lucy worriedly. "Shall I go and say sorry to some grass for him?"

"Now run along, all of you," said Lady Agatha, when Con had finished drinking. "I want to talk to this boy alone before bedtime."

"But he hasn't told me a *story*," wailed Ambrose.

"He knows a new one, about a chicken called Donald!"

"Not a chicken, Ambrose," said Con. "A duck."

"Later, dear," said Lady Agatha, and Ambrose ambled off after the others to investigate Hubert's hole, which had turned out to be a tunnel to the world outside.

When they had gone, Lady Agatha looked at Con's serious, thoughtful face, and sighed.

"If you'd been grown up," she said, "not still a child, I'd have thought you'd been sent in answer to my prayers."

Con was sitting on the grass at her feet, his hands round his knees.

"Why?" he said.

For a moment she didn't answer. Then she said: "For some time now, I have thought that my yetis ought to leave the valley. That they ought to be taken to a place where they will be absolutely safe. I am an extremely old woman, you see. How old you might not believe. And if anyone found them here in the wilds after my death ... well, anything could happen."

Con was silent. He knew only too well how right she was. Those dreadful people in the hotel...

"Father would always be safe," Lady Agatha went on. "He knows every rock, every crevasse; he's wise and he can be cunning. But the children ... they're so trusting. And Grandma is old, and Uncle Otto ... well, he's a scholar and they're never very good at looking after themselves."

"But where would they go, Lady Agatha? Where would you take them?"

A dreamy look came into her face. "To my old home. To Farley Towers, in Hampshire."

"All the way to Britain!" Con was amazed. It was a journey half across the world, through the burning plains of India, the stony wastes of Afghanistan, across Iran and Turkey, and almost the whole length of Europe. How could the yetis ever manage that?

"It's such a beautiful place, Farley. Soft, mellow brick terraces with peacocks, a deer park, a lake... My Little Ones would be safe there, I know, and it's just the life for them. Drawing Room Tea, Church on Sundays, Croquet..."

"But, Lady Agatha, it's years since you left. Anything could have happened to Farley Towers."

But Lady Agatha said she was certain that her old home was just as she had left it and still in the charge of some dear member of her family who would welcome and care for the yetis just as she had done. "After all," she said, "An Englishman's Home is Still His Castle."

Con was beginning to understand. "Was that why you wanted me to be grown up? So that I could help you to take your yetis to England?"

"So that you could take them *for* me. I'm far too old to travel. I shall die here in this valley where I have lived so happily."

Con's mind was racing ahead, thinking out the yetis' journey.

"It would have to be a secret, I suppose?"

"Indeed, yes," said Lady Agatha. "The *strictest* secret. It would be most dangerous if anyone came upon them before they were safe at Farley Towers."

Con was silent, his forehead furrowed. "Do yetis hibernate?" he said at last. "Go to sleep through the winter, I mean, like bears?"

"Not hibernate, exactly," said Lady Agatha, "but in severe weather conditions with extreme cold they can go into a sort of coma. Their heartbeat slows down, and they don't need food or drink. They can survive almost anything. No yeti has ever died of exposure."

"Well, in that case," said Con, "I think I can see how to get them to England without anyone knowing."

And he told her his plan. Once a week, said Con, huge, refrigerated lorries came all the way from Britain to the Hotel Himalaya, bringing frozen meat for the visitors who were too picky to try the local delicacies – sour cheese smoked in yak dung, or tea with rancid butter floating in it. Usually these lorries returned with a load of spices, or cloth, or goatskins which the Bukhimese wanted to sell in Britain. "But just once," said Con, "if I can square it with the driver, I reckon it could return with yetis."

Lady Agatha stared at him. Then: "I have something which might help to persuade the driver," she said.

She disappeared into her stone hut and came back with a little bag made out of the hem of her flannel nightdress. "Open it!" she commanded.

Con took the bag, which was surprisingly heavy, and undid the string. The metal inside, catching the sunlight, was unmistakable.

"Gold," he said, wonderingly.

"I dredged it up from the river," said Lady Agatha. "It's silly stuff but I thought it might come in useful. I need hardly tell you that no one must ever know where it came from." She closed the bag and sat down again on her tussock. "There's one thing you've forgotten," she said. "Where would you hide the yetis till the lorry came?"

Con grinned. "In the last place that anyone would look for them. In the Bridal Suite of the hotel. It's a terribly grand set of rooms on the top floor, quite cut off from the rest of the hotel, with its own lift and everything. The Prince of Pettelsdorf booked it this week for his honeymoon but he's cancelled. My sister knows where the keys are; she'd help me smuggle them in."

Lady Agatha was silent. "It's quite impossible, of course. Quite out of the question that I could let a child as young as you take on the responsibility of such a journey."

But Con wasn't so easily beaten. "How old were you when you came to the valley?" he asked innocently.

Lady Agatha blushed. "Older than you." There was a pause. "Well, not much older... Oh, dear, I don't know what to say."

"Then say yes," begged Con.

This time the pause seemed endless. "All right," said Lady Agatha at last. "You can take my yetis for me. I'll say it. Yes."

Over breakfast the next day Lady Agatha broke the news to the yetis, and they spent the rest of the morning crying.

When yetis cry, just as when they smile, they do not hold back. They do not sniffle or hiccup or gulp. They weep rivers. Now

they cried so hard that their fur became all dark and wet, so that they looked more like huge walruses or seals than Abominable Snowmen.

They cried because they were leaving Lady Agatha whom they loved so dearly, and the beautiful valley of Nanvi Dar where they had lived all their lives. They cried because they were leaving the trees and the birds and the flowers, and they cried because the yaks would be sad without them.

"I will be able to take Hubert?" Ambrose asked anxiously.

"Now, Ambrose," said Lady Agatha gently, "I've told you time and time again that this is going to be a difficult and dangerous journey. How do you think Con can take a yak? Especially a yak that doesn't even know its own mother."

So that of course started Ambrose off again. But when they had cried so much that there was hardly a tear left in any of them, the yetis secretly began to get rather excited about their journey.

"Tell us again about Farley Towers," Ambrose begged. And Lady Agatha closed her eyes and in a dreamy voice she told them about the great vine that grew on the south wall, about the yew trees clipped into the most beautiful shapes, about the big peaceful library with over five thousand books bound in rich, dark leather and the carved four-poster bed in which Queen Elizabeth had slept and in which Ambrose might be allowed to sleep too if only he was a good yeti and stopped *crying*.

While the yetis went up and down the valley saying, "Goodbye, juniper bush", "Goodbye, bird's nest", "Goodbye, beetles", Lady Agatha told Con some of the things she thought he ought to know, like what to do when Grandma's knees went under her and about Clarence not having a brain and about Lucy's sleepwalking. She told him that Uncle Otto liked having something rubbed into his bald patch once a day ("Anything will do," she said. "It's just to show you care") and that Ambrose, although he looked abominable, definitely was not – quite the opposite.

Above all she warned Con to be very careful because the yetis, though the gentlest of creatures, did not always know their own strength and could easily break someone's arm while just shaking hands with them. And she showed him some scars she had got in the early days before the yetis had understood that people were so frail and breakable.

Then she called all the yetis together and made a speech. She said how painful it was for her to part with them, but that she knew Con would be like a father to them and that they would be happy at Farley Towers. She reminded them how wrong it was to use Bad Language, or Forget To Do To Others As They Would Be Done By, and that they were to be sure to chew everything they ate thirty-two times so as not to get Lumps In The Stomach. "And now," she said, "I'm going to give each of you a present to take away."

"'esent," said Clarence excitedly. "'esent, 'esent!" He always seemed to understand things like that.

Lady Agatha turned and went into the little stone hut which had been her home since she first came to the valley. There she kept some of the things she had been wearing when Father carried her away and which were the only treasures she had.

"Grandma first," said Lady Agatha when she came out. And she gave Grandma the delicate, fleecy white shawl that had been round her shoulders when she slept.

Grandma really loved it. It was far too small to wrap around her shoulders, but she could use it as a headscarf and tie it under her chin. It was a crochet shawl with big open-work holes so that little tufts of grey and ginger hair sprouted out of the centre of each rosette, giving her a most distinguished look. To Uncle Otto she gave the woolly nightcap

she had been wearing when she was carried away. With a couple of hairpins, she fastened it with her own hands over Otto's bald patch – a most tactful present, because even if the bald patch *did* grow bigger, no one, now, would ever know.

For Lucy, Lady Agatha had kept a golden locket with a picture of Queen Victoria and all her nine children on it. She had made an extra long cord of plaited yak's hair for it and when Lucy put it on everybody agreed that nothing more beautiful than Queen Victoria and all her children nestling against the furry dome of Lucy's stomach had ever been seen in Nanvi Dar.

Clarence got the brass compass which had been in the pocket of the Earl's jacket. He wandered about with a blissful look on his face saying "'ick-'ock, 'ick-'ock," because he thought it was a watch. And from then on, whenever someone wanted to know the time, he always studied his compass with an important look on his face.

For Father, Lady Agatha had kept the Earl's cigar case. It was very valuable – pure gold studded with rubies – and there was a moment of silence as the yetis took in this costly present.

Father took it in his huge, gentle hands. He turned it over, admired the workmanship and the glitter of the rubies. Then he handed it back to Lady Agatha.

"I don't need a farewell present," he said in his deep, serious voice.

"But—"

"I don't need it," Father went on, "because I'm not going away."

Everyone looked at him, thunderstruck.

"Aren't you going with us, Father?" asked Ambrose in a trembly voice.

Father shook his head. "A hundred years ago I brought the Lady Farlingham to this valley. She cared for my children, she gave us speech, she taught us everything she knew. If I left her now to die alone, I should bring shame for ever to the name of yeti."

When he had finished there was a long and solemn silence. Then all the yetis slowly nodded their enormous heads. What Father had said was almost unbearably sad, but it was *right*.

"I'm not in the least afraid of dying," said Lady Agatha briskly. "After all, everyone enjoys going to sleep. So why not going to sleep for good?"

But nothing could shift Father. He said he was staying with her and anyone who wanted to move him from the valley was welcome to try. Since Father was far and away the strongest of all the yetis, that was the end of that.

But of course after that everybody began to cry again because Father was behaving so beautifully and because they would have to go without him and because Lady Agatha wasn't going to live for ever and ever, which was what Ambrose wanted her to do.

"Come, come," said Lady Agatha, though she was secretly very moved by Father's words, "this won't do. Ambrose hasn't had his present yet."

Ambrose's present was the most special one of all. It was one of the blue bedsocks that Lady Agatha had worn when she was carried away, and it still had a name tag inside saying: *Agatha Emily Farlingham, Farley Towers, Hants.*

"So when you arrive, Ambrose, and show them

this sock, my family will know that you really come from me."

"It's like a sort of password," said Con.

Ambrose was incredibly pleased. He tried the sock on his foot but it would only cover about three of his eight enormous toes. Then he tried it on his left ear, but it kept slipping off. So Lady Agatha plaited a cord for him, like Lucy's, and he wore the bedsock across his chest like a medal.

And then the dreaded moment could be postponed no longer. The yetis kissed Lady Agatha over and over again, they hugged Father, and they cried and cried till Con thought they would never get away. But at last they were ready and with a stout stick to help Grandma they made their way to the head of the valley.

Con could have sworn that Ambrose simply didn't have any tears left. But just as he started the steep ascent up the scree, a last wail broke from him. "My yak! I never said goodbye to my yak!"

But Con knew that he had to be firm. "Look, Ambrose," he said, "you don't want to upset Hubert, do you? You know how sensitive he is."

"He'll think I don't love him," said Ambrose, and his brown eye, which felt things more than his blue one, began to fill up again.

But here the other yetis came to Con's rescue. "Now, Ambrose," said Grandma firmly, "you know that that animal hasn't had a thought in his head since the day he was born."

"And maybe when you're safe at Farley Towers you can send for him," said Con.

"Really?" said Ambrose.

"Really," said Con.

There was no more to say. They had come to the foot of the towering cliff wall that had protected the secret valley for thousands of years. Otto picked up Con, tucked him under his arm, and began swarming up the unclimbable rock face like an enormous hairy spider.

And then one by one the yetis filed in behind him and left for ever the lovely valley of Nanvi Dar.

5

The Bridal Suite

For Con the journey across the High Peaks was a dreadful one. As darkness fell they came across the eastern shoulder of Nanvi Dar, and though Con rode on Uncle Otto's shoulders, the thin air and the biting wind were almost more than he could bear. For the yetis, of course, it was not much worse than an evening stroll, even though they were at times wading through waist-high snow, leaping over crevasses or scrambling down hair-raising icefalls. Con burrowed as deep as he could into Uncle Otto's thick coat, and gritted his teeth.

Ambrose on the other hand had recovered from his sorrow about Hubert, and was in high spirits.

"Will there be proper beds, like in 'The Princess and the Pea'? What's a suite … is it sweet like fruit, or sweet like baby squirrels?" Con was too stiff and frozen to answer.

But at last they were below the snowline and walking down a broad river valley, sheltered from the wind. Scrub and grassland gave way to majestic cedars and pines, and the lights of the hotel appeared shining through the trees.

"Oh, oh, oh," said Ambrose, "it's like in a story!"

Otto lifted Con from his shoulders, and placed him carefully on the ground.

"We will have to be very quiet," said Con. "You must wait outside, and stay out of sight until I have been in and talked to my sister." Then he went on alone.

Ellen wasn't really asleep. She had been a bit worried the night before, in spite of Con's note. Now it was the middle of the second night, and she knew that in the morning she must raise the alarm and start expecting the worst.

So when her door opened silently and Con crept in she was up in an instant.

"Thank goodness you're back, I was getting really scared."

"I'm fine. Just be quiet and listen to me."

Con explained.

Some people, if they were told in the middle of the night that there were five Abominable Snowmen outside who needed to be smuggled into the bridal suite of a luxury hotel, might have asked a lot of questions, or made a fuss. But Ellen was not some people.

"I'll get the keys and wait for you up there," said Ellen. "Are yetis very big?"

Con said yes he could honestly say that they were on the large side.

"Then they'll have to come up one by one. It's going to take a while. We'll wait for you up there." And Ellen pulled on a dressing gown and went to get the keys. Con went back outside.

Yetis are absolute experts at being quiet. In the moonlight, five great shadows flitted across the perfectly mown lawn towards the hotel. The only sound was an almost inaudible "sorry" from Lucy, who was feeling peckish after her walk and happened to pass a bed of Himalayan poppies.

"Right," whispered Con, "Grandma can come first." And while the others made themselves as small as possible, crouching against the wall, he led the way into the hotel.

The entrance to the private lift was in the lobby. In a little room behind the reception desk, the receptionist snored softly. Otherwise, it was deserted. Grandma followed Con across the lobby to the lift, but when she saw it she stopped dead.

The lift was the old-fashioned kind, with a folding metal grate that you pulled shut across the entrance.

"That's a cage. I'm not going into a cage, you horrid boy." She was still whispering, but at any moment her whisper would turn into a screech.

"Please, Grandma," whispered Con, "I'll come with you."

Reluctantly, Grandma went in, and Con squeezed in beside her.

Things went better with Ambrose, and Uncle Otto, and Clarence. Ambrose was nervous, but he trusted Con completely. Uncle Otto was brave, and Clarence really enjoyed it, saying "'igher, 'igher" happily until Con shushed him. One by one the yetis were delivered safely to the top floor and introduced to Ellen, shaking hands with her very carefully as they had been taught to do, so as not to break her arm.

At last it was Lucy's turn. But it was horribly difficult to get her into the lift. She really didn't fit. Con pushed and heaved. Finally he got her wedged in sideways, because she was slightly less fat that way than front-to-back, while Con had to crawl in after her and sit on the floor under her stomach. The lift moaned and clanked and squeaked, and Con was sure that they would wake the whole hotel. But they made it to the top, and Ambrose and Clarence

heaved her out with their brute strength. Then they all walked quietly along the corridor, and gathered at the doors of the bridal suite. Con unlocked them and threw them open.

The yetis gasped. There, on the floor in front of them, was an enormous bear-skin rug! It was a very bad moment. The yetis' ear lids turned pale, and Lucy stumbled, almost as if she might faint.

"Bears are our *brothers*, you see," explained Ambrose.

Con and Ellen felt dreadful. After all, how would *they* have felt if they'd been shown into a room and found a child-skin lying on the floor? But when they had apologized and rolled up the rug and put it in a cupboard, the yetis really began to enjoy themselves.

The rooms were splendid; they were very big rooms, which was a good thing, because five yetis take up a lot of space. And all the furniture – the beds, the bath, the sofas and divans – was king-size.

Clarence started turning the electric light on and off, off and on, with a blissful smile on his face. Grandma tried the beds, bouncing up and down, her fur flying. As yetis go, she was a lightweight, only

about twenty-three stone, but it was touch and go whether the beds would survive. Luckily, they were built to take the weight of rajahs and billionaires, who often eat too much and get too little exercise.

Lucy stared in amazement at the dressing-table mirror and said, "Oh, look, everybody! It's me! It's me so clear and beautiful!"

Ambrose, meanwhile, had found the bathroom. "Ooh! What's that? Isn't it *white*! Is it made of snow? Is it for washing your feet in? I can get both feet into it! Ow! Something hot hit me. What's a shower? Uncle Otto, I'm going to have a shower!"

But Otto did not reply. He stood gazing in wonder at a shelf beside the ornate fireplace. "Books," he whispered, "those are books." It is true that the Bible is a wonderful and interesting book, but if you have had nothing else to read for a hundred years or so then even the exciting bits, like Daniel in the Lion's Den or The Witch of Endor, can get a little bit *too* familiar. Now, before his very eyes, were *Flora and Fauna of the Hindu Kush*, *Excitements at the Chalet School*, *How to Win Friends and Influence People*, *The Compleat Angler*, *Nicholas Nickleby*, *The Tatler* (1925-37), *Finn Family Moomintroll* and many, many more. Otto's vast hairy hand wandered lovingly across their spines, and after hesitating for a moment over *The*

Jungle Book settled firmly on *Grimm's Fairy Tales*. Otto sank on to the largest divan and was lost to the world.

Con and Ellen thought they'd never get the yetis to settle for the night – or what was left of it. After Ambrose had had his shower, the bathroom looked like a disaster area and had to be mopped from top to bottom. Then Lucy wanted Ellen to comb the hair on her stomach into a centre parting and make two plaits on either side.

"Like yours," she said.

"But, Lucy, people don't wear plaits on their stomach," said Ellen.

"*People* don't. But yetis might," said Lucy. "It's for Queen Victoria and her children, so they can see out better."

But even when Ellen had made two fat plaits on either side of Lucy's stomach and tied them with the ribbons from her own hair, and they had all found somewhere to sleep – Lucy and Grandma in the two double beds, Ambrose on the sofa, Uncle Otto and Clarence on the Persian carpet – there was still the bedtime story.

"Tell about the Man Bat," begged Ambrose.

"You mean Batman, Ambrose," said Ellen.

Batman and his faithful friend Robin had not

been invented when Lady Agatha came to the valley and the yetis couldn't get enough of him. But even when the children had told them no less than three Batman adventures they weren't through because Clarence started yelling, "'im, 'im," and the others explained that he was saying "hymn" because Lady Agatha had taught the yetis always to end the day with a beautiful song to God. So they all got up again and sang "We Plough the Fields and Scatter", which didn't fit particularly well but was their favourite.

"Do you know what I thought I heard?" said Ambrose drowsily, when he was back on the sofa. "As we came down the mountain?"

"No," said Con. "What?"

"Footsteps," said Ambrose, smiling. He was half asleep. "Following us."

"What sort of footsteps, Ambrose?" asked Ellen.

"Lovely ... ones," murmured Ambrose. "Hoof steps ... and bleating."

Con gazed at him in horror. Not Hubert! It couldn't be! He walked over to the window and drew aside the curtains. In the moonlight, the grass round the hotel was empty, the woods silent and dark.

"There's nothing there," said Con, sighing with relief. And then at last the children tiptoed out, locking the door in case Lucy should walk in her sleep, and went to bed, feeling as tired as they'd ever felt in their lives.

The following morning, Ellen brought the yetis their breakfast and they all said grace. While she explained to Lucy that usually one ate just the cornflakes and not the packet, and told Uncle Otto about marmalade, which was not mentioned in the Bible, and rubbed toothpaste into his bald patch and tied Ambrose's bedsock on again, Con was down in the kitchens explaining things to his father.

Mr Bellamy, the children's father, was a very great chef. His salmon in aspic had been served at the Lord Mayor's Banquet, his peaches in marzipan had been photographed for the cover of a glossy magazine, and society ladies fell over each other, begging him to bake their daughters' wedding cakes.

But like so many great artists, Mr Bellamy was a little

bit *excitable*. When his son (after playing truant the day before) told him that he had hidden five yetis in the Bridal Suite and was going to go with them to England, Mr Bellamy reacted rather strongly. But the egg whisk that he threw whizzed past Con's left ear, the bag of flour exploded in mid-air, and as for the wooden spoon – well, Con had had so many wooden spoons thrown at him in his short life that it might have been a raindrop for all he noticed it. And when he had got his father to agree that the yetis couldn't stay in the Bridal Suite, and that they might as well go to England as anywhere else, he went off to the garage to wait for the lorry.

There were one or two very tough characters who brought the lorries, and no wonder. It was a punishing journey, and towards the end the roads were unspeakable. But when the lorry came at last, a gigantic, articulated vehicle with eighteen wheels, the driver who stepped out, blinking with exhaustion, was one Con had never seen before. A big, burly man with a ginger beard and bright ginger curls – the kind you could have stuck a pencil in and it would have stayed there. But what struck Con most, was what was tattooed on to the man's freckled forearm. Not an anchor or a sailing ship or a heart with "I Love Daisy" in it but ... a *pig*.

Somehow as soon as Con saw that, he knew that he could trust him. A man with a sensible thing like a pig tattooed on his arm *had* to be all right.

"Excuse me," Con said, getting off the pile of tarpaulins on which he'd been sitting, "I know you're tired but could I talk to you? It's important."

"Sure," said the ginger-haired man, whose name was Perry, short for Perrington, which his mother had believed to be a Christian name. "Let's hear it."

"Actually," said Con, "I think you'd better *see* it. Only it's a secret and I mean that." And he led Perry up to the Bridal Suite and knocked in the way that he and Ellen had arranged.

"They're making themselves beautiful for the journey," whispered Ellen, as she opened the door.

They certainly were. Grandma had found some scissors and was cutting her sixteen enormous toenails, bits of which were charging across the room like shrapnel. Lucy had vanished under a pink cloud of talcum powder and, in the bathroom, Uncle Otto, who was a very hygienic yeti, was gargling.

"We had a lovely sleep," said Ambrose, bounding up to Con. "Is this another friend for us? Does he know about that bear called Winnie?"

Perry did not go through the business of pinching himself to see if he was awake. He just wasn't a person who *dreamed* about yetis with blue bedsocks round their necks wanting to know about Winnie the Pooh. Perry's dreams were quite ordinary ones like missing trains or having to play the piano to a huge audience wearing only his underpants.

"All right," he said to Con. "Describe. Explain. Tell."

So Con told him about the secret valley of Nanvi Dar and about Lady Agatha and how he had promised to get the yetis safely to Farley Towers.

"And I want you to take them back in your lorry, instead of whatever you were going to take. It'll be all sealed up: they'll hibernate. No one'll see them."

"Oh, yes? And when I've dropped them off and get back to my bosses with an empty lorry, what then?"

Con fished in his pocket and handed Perry the

little bag which Lady Agatha had made out of the hem of her nightgown.

"Wow!" said Perry when he had opened it. "The real stuff. You mean I can give them the price of the goods. The lorry, too, if it comes to that. And there'd still be money over."

"For you," said Con. "A reward for taking us."

"Us?" said Perry. "Are you coming too?"

"I promised I'd deliver them. And I'd like Ellen to come too if I can square it with my father. I really *can't* go making plaits on people's stomachs."

Perry nodded. "There's room in the cab, just about."

He stood looking down into the little flannel bag.

Perry had done a lot of things since the day he'd said "Open wide" to a lady called Gladys Girtlestone and decided he wasn't cut out to be a dentist. He'd been a dishwasher, a road-mender, a lumberjack, and now he was driving lorries.

But not for ever. Perry had a dream and it was a dream to do with pigs.

Perry loved pigs. He loved their fatness and their slowness and their little, suspicious eyes and their disgusting habits. He loved Gloucester Old Spots, which look as though someone has spilt paint on them, and he loved Large Whites, which aren't white but the pink of apple blossom in the spring. He loved Tamworths, which fatten like a dream, and

he loved Saddlebacks and Windsors and those black, square, hairy pigs that come from Suffolk. And what Perry wanted more than anything was to have a pig farm and to breed a completely new pig, the Perrington Porker, which would be a pig to end all pigs, the best pig in the world.

Only, of course, to start a pig farm you need money...

"I'd have taken those crazy animals of yours anyway," said Perry, "because I like them. But if there's a reward I'll have it. Now I'm going to sleep for twenty-four hours. Then I'll go down to Jalpaigun and pick up the load I was supposed to take back. It's mostly dry goods – spices and suchlike, and cloth. I'll drop it at the nunnery – they'll make sure it gets handed out to the poor. Then I'll fix the customs forms and the bumph one needs to get across the borders and change some of the gold into cash for the journey. So ... let's see ... I ought to be ready to leave again by Thursday night. Can you have the yetis in the hotel garage just after midnight? There shouldn't be anyone around then."

Con nodded. "Thanks," he said, holding out his hand. He'd have liked to say more but just then Lucy said, "Sorry!" and began to choke horribly on the talcum powder. You could say a lot about looking after yetis, thought Con, as Ellen climbed on to a chair to thump Lucy on the back, but not that it was *easy*.

It was midnight on the following Thursday. It had taken the yetis a long time to leave the Bridal Suite because they had to say goodbye to everything: "Goodbye, bathroom", "Goodbye, toothpaste", "Goodbye, electric light", and that of course had made them sad and so they'd cried. But now they stood in the hotel garage, staring at the huge, eighteen-wheeled, canary yellow vehicle which was to take them to Britain. On the trailer was an enormous metal container almost as big as a railway carriage. It, too, was painted yellow and on it, in big, black letters, were the words: COLD CARCASSES, INC.

"What's a carcass?" said Grandma suspiciously.

Con and Ellen exchanged glances in the light of the lorry's headlights.

"Well, er, it's sort of ... a cow after it's been ... you know ... ready for eating."

"I thought as much," said Grandma grimly. "Well if anyone thinks I'm travelling halfway round the world labelled a cold carcass – let alone a cold carcass with ink on it – then they can think again."

"Cows are our brothers, you see," explained Ambrose, and the children sighed because they had a feeling that *everybody* was going to be the yetis' brother and though they approved of this and knew it was right, it did seem to make things rather complicated. But fortunately at that point Clarence, who hadn't understood about the carcasses, said, "'ox," which turned out to be "Box" and started climbing into the back of the lorry. After that, the other yetis got in too. There was a big, wide rack for each of them, a bit like a ship's bunk, and a passage down the middle, and a tiny peephole at the end through which they could see into the cab of the lorry and the people in the cab of the lorry could see them. Lucy oozed over the edge of her rack a bit but on the whole they admitted that it was very snug and comfortable.

"When we wake up shall we really be at Farley Towers?" asked Ambrose.

"Really," said Con. "All you have to do is hibernate and leave it to us."

"Only of course we can't hibernate just like *that*," said Ambrose craftily, putting his head on one side and gazing at Ellen. "You'll have to tell us a cold story. The coldest story *ever*."

So while Con turned the freezer to "maximum",

Ellen told them about the Snow Queen in her palace of glittering ice, and about little Kay whom she carried away in her sledge and kept a prisoner, and the yetis thought it was very beautiful and very sad and just about as cold as you could expect a story to be.

And the yetis were just getting very limp and drowsy, and Ellen had just kissed them all goodnight when from the patch of darkness outside the garage door there came a trembly, bleating sound – a sound which turned Con's heart to stone.

"What is it, Con?" asked Ellen.

But there was no need for anybody to tell her. Tottering into the headlights of the lorry, his idiot head waving from side to side, his left horn even more crumpled than it had been in Nanvi Dar, came Hubert.

In a second, Ambrose, his drowsiness forgotten, tumbled from the rack and leaped out of the lorry.

"It's my yak! It's my pet! It's Hubert! It *was* him I heard on the mountain. Oh, Hubert, you'll be able to come to England with us!"

"No!" The words burst from Con. "I can't do it! You've got to tell him to go home."

The other yetis had followed Ambrose out of the lorry. Now they looked rather pityingly at Con. "We *could* say, 'Go home,'" explained Uncle Otto. "We could say, 'Go home' three or four hundred times. But you may perhaps have noticed that Hubert is not a very *clever* yak."

Con said bitterly that it had crossed his mind. "But we *can't* take him. Ellen, you'll have to get the maids to look after him."

Ellen gave him a worried look. "Con, it's going to take them three days to get the Bridal Suite cleaned up. And you know what a state Dad's in about us going. I just don't think he'll *wear* a yak."

"Oh, please, *please* can't he come? He loves us so much," said Ambrose, and his brown eye started up again.

"Don't you see," said Con. "Yaks don't hibernate. At the other end you'd find him frozen solid. *Dead.*"

There was a pause while the yetis took this in and Hubert tried two steps, skidded on a patch of oil and fell flat on his face.

"Couldn't we stay awake? Not be refrigerated?" asked Ambrose.

"Actually, I've a fancy to see a bit of the countryside myself," said Grandma. "Seems a shame to go all that way asleep."

Con bit his lip, thinking hard. Yetis peacefully hibernating were one thing. Yetis awake, needing food, needing exercise, were quite another. There was real danger there.

Hubert gave another plaintive bleat and tottered forward.

"Oh, all right, get the wretched animal in," said Con, making up his mind.

And while Ellen ran back for some powdered milk and a feeding bottle, Con turned off the freezer and slammed the door. Then Perry came from the hotel kitchens carrying a crate of beer and his guitar, and, with a last hug for Mr Bellamy, they got into the cab of the lorry and the long, long journey to Farley Towers began.

6

Aslerfan

The yellow lorry drove on, day after day, down through the foothills of the Himalayas, across the burning plains of India and Pakistan, across Afghanistan with its stony mountains and wild goats and poplar trees, and through the deserts of Iran where the sand got into the yetis' nostrils and between their toes and into their food...

It was not an easy journey. The yetis had to be sealed up inside the lorry until night-time, when they found a deserted place to stop and they could come out and stretch their legs and get some air. The lorry was bumpy and every so often Clarence said "'ick, 'ick," and then Perry would have to quickly try and find a place in which a yeti could be sick without anybody seeing, which was not so easy at all. And, of course, Hubert, who had to be fed from a bottle every four hours, and then turned upside down because he'd swallowed the teat, was just as much of a nuisance as Con had foreseen.

But after a while, the yetis got a taste for travelling. Sitting round the campfire at the end of the day, listening to Perry strum his guitar and pushing Hubert's hooves out of the butter, they felt that this really was life. But when they had said sorry to the last of their condensed milk tins and lay down under the stars to sleep, Con and Ellen always took it in turns to stay awake so that no one should come on the yetis unexpectedly. Nor would they ever let Perry take his turn, however much he grumbled, because they knew that driving a lorry for great distances is the most exhausting thing in the world and that he needed his sleep.

And in this way they travelled very happily until they came to the city of Aslerfan, the capital of the state of Aslerfan, which is wedged like a slice of melon between Iran and Turkey.

Although the yetis couldn't see out, they began to feel queer almost as soon as they crossed the border. Grandma said her corns were shooting and she didn't like the way her liver was carrying on. Lucy kept nervously twisting Queen Victoria and her nine children in her long, blonde fingers; Uncle Otto's face was set and stern.

"I don't *like* this place. It feels funny," said Ambrose the Abominable.

Con and Ellen, sitting in the cab in front, liked it even less. They were approaching the city now. There were beggars everywhere; the people had grey faces; half-starved mongrel dogs dodged in and out of the traffic. It was dusty and hot and suddenly Ellen drew in her breath because an old man had just crossed the road leading a poor, mangy, limping bear on a chain so tight that he looked as though he must choke.

"It's a dancing bear," Perry explained, while Con made sure that the peephole to the back was tightly shut. "On the way to the palace, I expect. They jab them and put hot coals in their mouth and make them dance for money. Aslerfan's the only place left in the world where you're allowed to do that."

And he explained to the children that Aslerfan was ruled by a cruel and greedy sultan, who lived in luxury in his palace with a fleet of cars and aeroplanes and yachts. The Sultan Midul had five hundred embroidered shirts and twelve hundred pairs of trousers and three fat wives covered from top to toe in diamonds, but his people lived in poverty and squalor. Instead of building schools and hospitals, the Sultan had huge feasts in which everybody gorged themselves till they were sick and began again. Instead of looking after the old and the needy, he organized great hunts in which hundreds of beautiful gazelles and antelopes were cruelly slaughtered. Everybody hated him, but nobody dared to protest because they would just have been put in jail or shot.

"All I ever want to do in Aslerfan," said Perry, "is get through it as quickly as possible."

But Perry reckoned without the lorry.

Perry's lorry looked all right from the outside, but its inside was more like that of an ailing old lady than a twenty-tonne truck. Its carburettor got choked up as soon as you breathed on it, its exhaust pipe hung on by willpower and string and the engine sounded like an old hen with the croup. And now, just when they wanted to get through Aslerfan quickly, the wretched lorry began to boil.

"Oh, Lord!" said Perry. "Not the water pump."

But it was. "We'll have to spend the night here, I'm afraid, while I get this thing fixed," said Perry worriedly. "I'll find as quiet a place to park as I can but for goodness' sake don't let the yetis out. You saw that bear..."

So he parked in a quiet street not far from the Sultan's palace. Beside it was a little park, with a few dusty date palms, a tobacco kiosk and a public lavatory. And at the far side, something else. A zoo.

The yetis had never before had to spend a night in a town, let alone a town like Aslerfan. It meant that they couldn't get out and say, "Sorry, grass," and build a campfire and stretch their legs, but had to stay cooped up in the lorry, which was stiflingly hot because Perry had disabled the refrigeration system to get at the water pump. But the yetis understood that it was necessary and they were very good.

While Perry went to find a garage and Con went shopping for some fruit, Ellen slipped into the little park to buy some lemonade for the yetis from a kiosk. When she came back, she was very quiet and pale.

"Are you sad?" said Ambrose, and his brown eye got ready in case there was any crying to be done.

But Ellen just shook her head and said it was nothing, or perhaps the heat. And then Con returned and they had a picnic in the back and they were just getting ready for the bedtime story when the noises began.

They were bad noises: howls of misery; roars of loneliness; whimpers of pain.

Even by the light of his torch, Con could see the yetis' ear lids turn pale and Lucy, who had just taken her seventh banana, put it down untouched.

"That was a poor lion who's got no meat to say

'sorry' to," she said, as an ear-splitting roar filled the night.

"That elephant has got a pain in his trunk," said Uncle Otto worriedly.

"And listen to those poor seals coughing their lungs out," said Grandma.

Con was amazed. "How do you know which animals are which and what they're saying?" he asked. "You've never seen lions or seals or elephants, have you?"

Ambrose turned his wall eyes reproachfully on Con. "But they're our *brothers*," he said.

Con sighed. He'd asked for that one. "Look, it's

just a zoo. All animals make noises at night in a zoo—"

But Ellen, usually so quiet and gentle, interrupted him. "No, Con, it's an awful place, this. I saw it when I was getting the lemonade. The cages are filthy and far too small; there are flies everywhere; the monkeys are full of sores and the antelopes have got foot rot... And there's a ghastly sort of dungeon place where they throw the dancing bears that are too old to work."

It was true. The Aslerfan Zoo was a disgrace. But it was the Sultan's private zoo and when people in the city complained, he just laughed. As for the head keeper, a man called Mr Bullaby, he took the money he was paid for the animals and used it for himself. So the animals were sick and cramped and underfed, and hundreds died every year from loneliness or bad feeding or disease.

Con bit his lip, frowning. Cruelty to animals always made him feel completely sick and hollow. But he'd given his word that he'd get the yetis to Farley Towers and that meant keeping them cheerful and keeping them safe. So he began to tell them "Rumpelstiltskin", making up such funny names for the Queen to guess that Ambrose nearly fell off his bunk laughing, and after they had *whispered*, "Lead,

Kindly Light" (because there were still strollers about in the streets who might have thought it odd if a load of Cold Carcasses had started singing hymns) the children slipped to the front and curled up in the cab and fell asleep.

But the yetis couldn't sleep. Even when they shut their ear lids they could still *feel* the noises from that dreadful zoo.

And presently Ambrose leaned down from his bunk and said "Grandma?"

"What is it?" said Grandma, opening her ear lids.

"I was thinking ... Ellen was sad about that zoo, wasn't she?"

Grandma nodded. "And no wonder."

"Con was sad too," said Lucy. "He didn't say anything but his face was all screwed up and tight."

"So we could give them a surprise," said Ambrose. "Con and Ellen, I mean. Because they've been so good to us."

"'urprise," said Clarence happily, nodding.

"What sort of a surprise, Ambrose?" asked Lucy.

"A lovely one," said Ambrose, his blue eye beaming. "We could let all the animals out of their cages. Now, while it's dark. And in the morning they'd all be happy and free."

There was a pause while the yetis considered this.

"Do As You Would Be Done By," said Grandma presently, "that's what Lady Agatha said. Only God said it first. How would we like to be shut up in filthy cages?"

And then they all turned their enormous heads towards Uncle Otto, who was really the head of the family now that Father was no longer with them.

Uncle Otto hesitated. He understood perhaps better than the others how important it was for the yetis to keep out of people's way. But just then there came a sound more terrible than any they had heard yet: the wings of the thirst-maddened birds of prey beating against the wire of their appalling cages.

Uncle Otto made up his mind. And a few moments later, leaving Hubert tied to one of the bunks, the yetis had pushed aside the iron bar which closed the back of the lorry and were climbing over the high barbed wire which surrounded the zoo.

As soon as they dropped down inside the enclosure, the noises stopped. It was as though the animals knew that their time of torture was over. The lions stopped their restless pacing and stood silent and golden-eyed, waiting. The giraffes hung their poor, stiff necks over the bars of their pen and blew softly and hopefully through their velvet lips. The weary old bears got up on their hind legs and danced of their own free will.

"Right," said Uncle Otto. He had left his woolly hat in the lorry and in the moonlight his bald patch shone like the shield of St George. "Let us begin."

The next two hours were the busiest of the yetis' lives. When Lady Agatha had warned Con about the yetis' strength, she hadn't been exaggerating. They bent iron bars like plasticine, broke locks with a couple of fingers, uprooted railings as if they were dandelions...

Uncle Otto freed the big cats: the lions and tigers a n d

panthers and jaguars, and they rubbed themselves, soft as kittens, against his legs before loping off joyfully into the night. Clarence helped out the poor, rheumaticky old hippopotamuses and rhinoceroses, who had almost forgotten how to walk, and led the elephants, with their sore trunks and runny eyes, into a clump of palm trees where they could feed. Lucy let out the little things that had huddled sadly on the concrete floors of their smelly runs for years: opossums like old handbags, scruffy little moonrats and dik-diks and bushbabies, which she shook out and sat gently on their feet before they scampered gratefully away.

Grandma, meanwhile, had got hold of a hose and was washing down the sea lions and walruses and alligators, who were covered in green slime from their disgusting, sludgy ponds. "Now off you go, and get down to the river quickly," she scolded a crocodile who was lying on his back, letting the hose play over his stomach and showing his poor, broken teeth in the first real smile he'd smiled since the cruel Sultan's men had caught him in their nets. And it was marvellous to see how every animal, even the most stupid like the anteaters, or the fiercest like the cougars, or the shyest like the gazelles, found time to thank the yetis with a grateful nibble, a friendly lick or a thankful hiss, before they crawled or slithered or hopped off to freedom.

The dancing bears were the last to go. It was as if they could hardly tear themselves away from the yetis and even when they had shuffled off into the darkness they came back again and again to rub themselves once more against their rescuers.

But at last the zoo was empty and the yetis were

just turning to go back to the lorry when Lucy said: "Where's Ambrose? And what's that splash?"

What that splash was, was Mr Bullaby, the head keeper, whom Ambrose the Abominable had just thrown into the crocodile pond.

"I found him in his house, hiding under the bed," said Ambrose, when the others ran up to him, "and I thought he ought to be punished. Lady Agatha always punished us when we were naughty and this zoo is *more* than naughty, isn't it?"

The yetis stood round solemnly in the moonlight, watching Mr Bullaby in his yellow silk pyjamas, floundering and spluttering in the filthy pool.

"Was I wrong to do it?" asked Ambrose, suddenly growing anxious.

But the others, remembering the pitiful things they had seen that night, said no, he hadn't been.

"If the crocodiles had still been there, you shouldn't have done it," said Lucy, "because it wouldn't have been fair on the crocodiles. But they weren't. So you should've."

And then they all padded quietly out of the zoo and climbed back into the lorry and fell asleep.

Con, curled up in the cab in front, was having a most peculiar dream. He dreamed that a large and rather loopy-looking gnu was looking in at the lorry window.

Making an effort, he opened his eyes, stretched...

A large and loopy-looking gnu *was* looking in at the lorry window.

"Goodness!" said Con. But before he could explore further, Perry came back from the all-night garage carrying the mended pump. "The place's gone mad," he said. "There's a tree sloth hanging from the lamp post, a couple of kangaroos are window shopping in the square and—" He broke off. "Good Lord! Look at the zoo!"

In silence, Perry and the children stared across the little park at the broken fences, the shattered buildings...

"Is it an earthquake, do you think?" asked Ellen, who'd only just woken up and was still rather muddled.

"Or a terrorist letting off bombs?" suggested Con.

But before they could decide how the zoo had got into the state it was in, there was an agitated scrabbling from the container and when Con cautiously opened the door, all five yetis stood looking out at him, beaming with pride and joy.

"We did it! It's a surprise for you! We let out all the animals, every single one!" said Ambrose the Abominable.

There was a moment of total silence while Con took this in. "Oh no! You didn't! Say you didn't!" he begged.

"But we did. All the animals were *sad* so—"

Con's face had turned ashen. He had begun to tremble. "Don't you see, it's a *crime*. Breaking up people's property, smashing things... As soon as the Sultan gets to hear of it, he'll send his soldiers with machine guns. You'll be mown down, you'll be—"

But Perry now came to the rescue. "We're only a hundred miles from the border," he said, "and the Sultan can't touch us once we're across. The pump's mended; no one's about yet – we've a good chance of making a getaway."

And a few seconds later the door had shut on the bewildered yetis and the yellow lorry was roaring out of the city.

A hundred miles in a slow and overloaded lorry can seem like a desperately long way. Every motor horn, every train whistle made the children jump as they imagined the Sultan's men come to round up the yetis or torture them or simply shoot them out of hand.

But the Sultan did not come that day, or any other day. And that was because, by evening, the city of

Aslerfan no longer had a sultan.

What happened was this. On the morning that the yellow lorry left Aslerfan, the cruel and greedy little Sultan woke up in his huge gold and turquoise bed as he did each day, stretched his fat little arms as he did each day, and thought of all the nice things he was going to do, like watching a public execution, having some journalists flogged because they'd dared to criticize him in their newspapers and arranging a hunt in which a herd of exquisite fallow deer would be gunned down from his private fleet of helicopters.

Then, as he did every day, he rang for his servants. But after that, things happened differently. Because what came into the room was not his barber to shave him, or his valet to dress him, or his footman carrying the six fried eggs he always ate for breakfast.

It was a hippopotamus.

"Help! screamed the Sultan. "Help! Help!" He reached for the bell rope and pulled it again. Only it was not the bell rope, it was the tail of an enormous boa constrictor, which now fell in a hissing and annoyed heap on to the Sultan's embroidered counterpane.

"Aaeee!" yelled the Sultan. He leaped out of bed and rushed for the nearest door, which led into his

lapis lazuli and marble bathroom.

Sitting quietly in the middle of the bath was a huge, whiskery and very wrinkled walrus.

"It's a plague! It's a plague of animals! The gods have decided to punish me!" yelled the Sultan, who had read about the great plagues of Egypt, when Jehovah had sent locusts and frogs and flies to punish a wicked ruler who had been cruel to his people.

As the terrified Sultan ran through the corridors of his palace, he saw more and more signs that the gods were out to get him. An orang-utan was crouching on the imperial throne, dreamily cracking

fleas between his teeth; a proud ostrich had just laid
an egg on the grand piano in the music room, and
three armadillos were bulldozing their way across
the table in the state dining hall...

Still in his pyjamas, the fat little man reached the
main courtyard. There was no sign of his servants
or his soldiers, who had all fled when the animals
invaded the palace. But standing by the fountain,
looking at him through golden, serious eyes, were
two very stripy tigers.

The Sultan waited no longer. With a scream of
terror he turned and ran, on and on, through his

terraced gardens, and private parks and pleasure pavilions, on and on, till he came to the brown bare hills that surrounded the city. And there he fell on his knees and beat his head against the earth and asked the gods to forgive him his sins. And the next day he put on a sacking robe and went to live in a cave where he spent the rest of his life gabbling prayers and fasting so that he would get to heaven in the end.

And so the hated Sultan was seen no more, and in the city of Aslerfan there was feasting and rejoicing and dancing in the streets. People hugged each other and let off fireworks and threw open the doors of their cafés so that everyone could eat and drink their fill. The prisoners were let out of their dungeons and the sick were taken off the streets and cared for. But because it was the animals who had brought freedom to the people, the new government made it a law that all the animals that had escaped were to be guests of the city and not to be harmed. So, for many months, while they built a new, model zoo for those animals that preferred to live in town, you could see giraffes dozing in the middle of the road while cars edged carefully around them, barbers politely shaving wildebeests who had wandered into their shops, or old ladies giving lifts to porcupines in their shopping baskets.

Nor did anyone ever find out who had freed the animals. True, Mr Bullaby had gabbled something about furry giants with bedsocks round their necks and Queen Victoria on their stomachs. But when people talk like that there is only one thing to do: take them to some nice, quiet hospital and shut them up till they are better. And that is exactly what the people of Aslerfan did.

7

The St Bernards of Feldenberg

The yellow lorry had passed through the beautiful city of Istanbul and was well into Turkey before Con stopped shivering and peering into the driving mirror to see if anyone was following them. Only when Perry went into a café in a little dusty village where they had stopped for petrol, and heard on the wireless that the Sultan of Aslerfan had fled, did the children relax.

Unfortunately, the news that they had saved the people of Aslerfan from their cruel Sultan made the yetis very smug.

"We did *good*, didn't we?" said Ambrose, his blue eye beaming. "We're sort of *rescuing* yetis now."

"Well, don't be rescuing yetis again, please," said Con, who'd really had a dreadful fright. "Not till you're safe at Farley Towers."

That night Perry found a beautiful deserted little bay on the Sea of Marmara with a track down which the lorry could just go. Lucy and Grandma paddled, lifting the long hair on their legs out of the water like Lady Agatha had shown them, and Ambrose tethered Hubert to a fig tree and told him that he was a big yak now and could eat grass perfectly well if he tried. Con made a bonfire and they sat round it while Perry told them just how he thought the Perrington Porker would look when he had bred it: pink and fat but very strong, with a double-jointed tail and droopy ears, because pigs with droopy ears are more peace-loving than the other kind.

"Can we play the Farley Towers game?" begged Ambrose, as they lay down under the stars to sleep. It was a game that Ellen had invented to while away the journey and the yetis loved it.

"What will we do on our first day at Farley Towers?" said Lucy, because that was the way the game began.

"On the first day you'll have dinner by candlelight with damask napkins," said Ellen.

"What will we do on the second day?" said Ambrose.

"On the second day you'll have tea on the lawn with strawberries and cream in crystal bowls," said Ellen.

"'ird?" said Clarence. "'ird?"

But they never discovered what they would do on their third day at Farley Towers because at that moment Hubert decided he had seen his mother.

Hubert had been seeing his mother ever since

they'd left Nanvi Dar. In fact, when he wasn't swallowing his teat or trying to dig Hubert Holes inside the lorry, seeing his mother was what Hubert did. But up to now his mother, though unlikely, had been *possible*: a stray goat, a distant, browsing sheep, that sort of thing. Whereas what Hubert was now straining to reach, bleating with delight, seemed to be a rusty heap of scrap metal which somebody had left on the beach.

Sighing, the yetis got up again to look.

"No, dear," said Grandma sternly, "that's not your mother. That's a wheelbarrow."

And shaking their enormous heads, the yetis returned to their beds and fell asleep.

They travelled steadily north, through Greece with its ruined temples and its olive groves; through the long, flat plain of the Western Balkans with its storks and fields of maize, until they came to the little country of Feldenberg, in the foothills of the Alps.

And now there were pine forests and clear, rushing rivers and the sound of cowbells from the meadows. The air grew cool, the trim, wooden houses had boulders on the roof to weigh them down against the wind, and in the distance, white as icing sugar, were the glaciers of the Alpine peaks.

"Oh, isn't it beautiful, it's just like home!" cried the yetis when they were allowed to get out for a moment and have a stretch.

"Can I have some leather pants like that?" begged Ambrose, who had glimpsed, in a distant field, a little boy in lederhosen.

But Grandma had noticed something even more exciting. "What's that noise?" she said eagerly, and Con explained that it was yodelling, a sort of cross between calling each other and singing, which people did on mountains.

"I can do that!" said Grandma. "I just know I can." She threw back her head. "Yodel-aaa-eee-ooo," yodelled Grandma. "Yodel-aaa-eee-ooo!"

"Oh, hush, Grandma," begged the children, while all around there was the sound of ear lids thudding shut, "suppose someone hears you?"

But it was no use. Yodelling is like a drug once it gets hold of you and it had certainly got hold of Grandma. And it was with Grandma still going strong that they drove up towards the High Alps, and the pass which ran between the towering crags of the Death Peak to the east and the zigzag range of the Emperor Mountains to the west.

"It's going to be quite a pull with this load on," said Perry. "Cold at the top, too. I think we'll stop off for a proper meal."

So he parked the lorry by a deserted mill on the edge of a pretty village with an onion-domed church, a cobbled square and an inn with carved wooden shutters and a white horse painted on a sign above the door. And when he explained to the yetis that the children ought to have something hot before the next part of the journey, they all promised to be as quiet as mice and keep the peephole tightly shut.

The inn had red-checked tablecloths, wooden benches and nice, old-fashioned paintings on the walls showing brave St Bernard dogs with barrels round their necks saving people from the snow. And while Con and Ellen waded through their huge helpings of liver soup with dumplings, and pickled cabbage with ham, and nut cake with whipped cream, Perry, who spoke a little German, got talking to the innkeeper and his guests.

And what they were all talking about – very angrily – was a mad Englishman called Harry Letts.

Mr Letts was a very rich and very important television tycoon who had come to spend his holiday in the village with his little son, a boy of nine, called Leo. Everybody liked Leo, who was a friendly, quiet, rather dreamy child, but nobody liked Mr Letts, who had gone round telling anyone who would listen that his son was a spoilt, namby-pamby boy ruined by his mother and that he, Harold Letts, was going to make a man of him or else.

So that very morning he had set out with the little boy to climb the Death Peak. And the Death Peak, which towered above the village, was the highest, most dangerous mountain in Feldenberg.

"He is a criminal, a lunatic," said the innkeeper

angrily, wiping his counter clean. "Even an experienced person would not risk the Peak today, with a storm coming up."

"A storm?" said the children, surprised, when Perry told them what had been said. The sun shone; the icing sugar peaks stood out against a pale blue sky.

But the yetis, when they got back to them, nodded their huge heads wisely. "Oh, yes, a storm's coming. A bad one," they said. "We can always tell because the hair on the back of our knees goes tingly."

And sure enough, as the lorry ground its way slowly up the winding road, gradually leaving behind the lush meadows and fruit-hung orchards, the sun vanished behind clouds, the peaks turned mouse-coloured and sinister, the wind freshened...

"Poor Leo," thought Con, looking up at the crags of the Death Peak where the rain that was now lashing their windscreen would, he knew, be falling as drifting, blinding snow. And he thought with a pang of homesickness of his own father, who might sometimes throw bags of flour, but who never came up with idiot ideas like making a man of his son.

About three hundred feet below the top of the pass, Perry gave up. The lorry had started its chicken-with-the-croup noises, and though the windscreen wipers were working at the double it was impossible to keep the windows clear of sleet. To try and make the descent down one of the most dangerous and winding roads in Europe in weather like that would have been madness, even with an empty lorry. As it was...

So he turned off into a deserted quarry, which ran off the curve of the road and provided some shelter. "We'll have to spend the night here, I'm afraid," he said.

The yetis, of course, loved the idea. "Isn't it *fresh*, isn't it bracing?" they said, and for an awful moment it looked as though Grandma would begin to yodel again.

But after a while, Con and Perry began to get worried about Ellen. It was bitterly cold at that height, and though they kept the windows tightly closed, the chill seeped right through their clothes and the thin army blanket which was all they had for covering. Ellen never complained, but she was a frail, slight child and now she had no way of hiding the whiteness of her face or the shivering fits which shook her.

"Listen," said Perry to Con, "do you see that building up there, on the Death Peak? On that rocky ledge?"

Con nodded.

"It's a monastery. The monks that run it are great people – they're always helping travellers in trouble. They train St Bernards too – those mountain rescue dogs. You can reach it in half an hour and the path's perfectly safe."

"You mean I should take Ellen up there and ask if we can spend the night?"

"That's right. But go now, quickly. You've only another hour till dark."

"But what about the yetis?" said Con.

"I'll look after them. They'll be all right, I promise."

Con threw another glance at Ellen, huddled in the corner of the cab and trying to stop her teeth from chattering. "All right," he said.

An hour later, safe from the storm, the children were sitting over steaming bowls of soup and hunks of fresh-baked bread in the monastery dining hall.

It was a beautiful room. Candles burnt on the long wooden table; there were heavy, carved oak settles and a blazing fire of pine logs in which the resin bubbled and sang.

But what Con and Ellen couldn't take their eyes off, was what was lying in a huge, warm huddle of feet and melting eyes and thumping tails across the hearth. Five dogs. Five of the most beautiful dogs they had ever seen: white and brown; gold and liver-coloured; fawn and mahogany, with wrinkled foreheads and slobbery jowls. The famous St Bernards of Feldenberg.

And while the children ate their soup, the friendly monks, clustering round, told them – in a jumble of languages – the story of the dogs.

For a long time, they explained, people had stopped using dogs for mountain rescue work because they were so expensive to train and modern devices like helicopters and radar seemed to make them unnecessary. But a very rich and kind American, an oil millionaire from Texas, who had come to Feldenberg for a holiday, had been so upset to think that those wonderful dogs were no longer bred and trained, that he had sent the monks a litter of five of the most highly bred St Bernards in America – *and* given the monastery a huge sum of money to be used each year for the feeding and training of the dogs.

"How marvellous!" said Con, scratching the ear of an enormous white-and-liver-coloured brute who had fallen asleep across his feet. "And have they rescued anyone yet?"

The monks looked at each other and said, no. Fortunately, the Death Peak was a very dangerous mountain which people treated with respect, so nobody had *needed* rescuing. A silence fell. And then, suddenly, perhaps because Con and Ellen had very *listening* faces, it all came out.

The dogs, said Brother Peter (and all the others nodded to show that they agreed with him) were the most charming, gentle animals that anyone could wish for. The monks adored them; they couldn't bear to think of life without them. There was only one snag. They were absolutely useless at rescuing anyone from anything.

The children found this almost impossible to believe.

"But I thought ... *all* St Bernards..." stammered Con.

The monks shook their heads and sighed. Most, perhaps, but not all. Certainly not Baker or Brutus or Biscuit and quite definitely not Bouncer or Beelzebub.

And one by one, kind Brother Peter, who was in charge of the kennels, introduced the dogs and explained their little troubles.

Baker, it seemed, suffered from chilblains – nasty big pink lumps which came up as soon as he set foot in the snow. Brutus, on the other hand, couldn't stand heights. They had lifted Brutus on to a table once to have his toenails cut and he had very nearly fainted. Biscuit was terrified of the dark and had to have a night light in his kennel. Bouncer, a real bruiser of a dog whose muscles beneath his brindled fur rippled like steel, cried like a baby when he had to wet his feet.

"But that one?" said Ellen. "That huge dark one over there?"

The monks blushed. What was wrong with Beelzebub seemed to be a little different. Then, very shyly, Brother Peter leaned forward and whispered: "He drinks."

And he explained that every St Bernard was sent off with a keg of brandy round his neck so that when the lost traveller was found he could have a healing sip. Beelzebub, however, was driven so mad by the smell of brandy that he simply shattered the keg against the first rock he could find, lapped up the contents – and had to be carried home and put to bed.

And because the monks were good and honest men they had decided that it wasn't fair to go on deceiving the people of Feldenberg and taking the American's money, so they had decided to send the dogs away the very next day. "But it will be like giving away our children," said Brother Peter, and all the monks looked so sad, that for a moment, Con and Ellen, used as they were to yetis, expected them all to burst into tears.

"But if no one ever *needs* rescuing," said Ellen, who couldn't bear anyone to be unhappy, "what does it matter?"

What happened next was just like a play or a film. There was a violent pounding on the door and a man stumbled forward into the room. He was dressed in climbing clothes, his face was badly cut and bruised and his leg dragged as he came forward.

"Help! I must have help quickly! It's my son, my little Leo. He's lost on the Death Peak. Send out the dogs to save him! Please ... quickly ... send out ... the dogs," said Mr Letts – and Brother Peter was just in time to catch him as he fell.

8

On Death Peak

The monks put out the dogs. What else could they do? They pushed out Biscuit, howling because of the terrifying darkness, and Baker, trying to keep his chilblained feet out of the snow. They pushed out Brutus, who got giddy on a kitchen table, and the whimpering Bouncer and boozy Beelzebub with his barrel...

And then, while the younger monks went down to the village for help, the rest of them went back into the dining hall and waited for disgrace and ruin.

Con had known all along, really, what he had to do. When a child's life was at stake you had to take a chance. Even Lady Agatha, he knew, would have wanted him to let the yetis out. Only they could save Leo.

He went over to the fire where Ellen was helping to care for the delirious Mr Letts as he rambled and blamed himself for the accident. Then he slipped out of the monastery and, with his head bent against the gale, ran back downhill towards the yellow lorry.

The yetis when he reached them understood at once. "Don't worry, my boy," said Uncle Otto reassuringly, "we shall find him. Remember, we can see in the dark."

"After all, we are *rescuing* yetis," said Ambrose smugly – and while Perry made his way down to the village to join a stretcher party, and Con set off for the monastery once more, the yetis padded up the steep sides of the quarry and were gone.

Even for the yetis it was bitterly cold on the Death Peak. As they padded across the treacherous glacier, leaped crevasses, peered into gulleys, the snow beat against their faces and the wind scythed like a rapier through their fur. But they let nothing hinder them in their search for Leo. Patiently, clinging with their eight toes on to knife edges of ice, they squeezed down chimneys of rock, dug into snowdrifts, raked the darkness with their saucer eyes...

There was nothing. No answer to their calls. No trace of the boy.

"I don't want him to be dead," said Ambrose in a quavery voice, clambering up a pinnacle of ice. "I don't want anyone to be dead, *ever*."

But things were beginning to look very bad for Leo. And now Grandma was in trouble. She was, after all, over four hundred years old. Shivering fits shook her, her breath came in painful gasps, her legs felt like matchsticks.

"Come on, you stupid old yeti," she scolded herself. "Here's a poor child in trouble and you totter about like an old blancmange."

But though she was cross with herself, she couldn't make her heart pump harder or her muscles pull her up the towering cliffs of rock.

"I'll just rest for a moment," said Grandma. "I'll crawl into this little cave here and then I'll be as right as rain."

She dragged herself into the cave and flopped down on a slab of stone, but still she couldn't seem to catch her breath. Grandma did not often feel old and sad and useless, but she felt it now.

And then, in the back of the cave, she saw

something stir: a fair blur; a faint, small shape. She moved closer, bent over it.

And after that she didn't feel old and sad and useless any more; she felt as happy as she'd ever felt in her life. She had found Leo.

And now a solemn procession wound itself down the Death Peak towards the monastery below.

First came Uncle Otto; path-finding, responsible and serious. Then came Ambrose, beaming with pride because Grandma, who was still feeling rather tottery, had let him carry Leo. Tottery she might be, but not so tottery that she couldn't constantly peer over Ambrose's shoulder and tell him what to do with the boy.

"Gently, now, don't let his neck hang like that, support his head, that's right. Mind that leg..."

Behind Grandma came Lucy, her gentle blue eyes full of pity for Leo, who lay, still as a leaf, with closed eyes in Ambrose's arms.

They were just starting to cross the glacier when Clarence, who was bringing up the rear, suddenly stopped.

"'og," said Clarence firmly.

The others sighed. It was so important to bring the boy to safety quickly.

"No, Clarence, there's no bog here, the ground's as hard as nails," said Lucy soothingly.

"And there certainly aren't any *logs*," said Grandma. "We're much too high for trees."

But Clarence kept on pointing and suddenly they saw what he meant. Wedged between two boulders, lying flat on his back with his chilblained feet stuck in the air like table legs, was a large and frost-covered St Bernard.

They had found Baker.

It was an embarrassing moment for the yetis. They knew that St Bernards were famous for rescuing people and it did not seem right just to pick the dog up as if he were a baby. But Baker, frenziedly wagging his tail, made it clear that he expected just that, and it was with a St Bernard hanging like a gigantic, snuffling muffler round Clarence's neck that the party moved on.

They didn't so much *find* Biscuit as fall over him. He was rolled into a whimpering ball of fur, half-covered in snow, and even when Lucy picked him up and hung him over her shoulders he refused to open his eyes. No one was going to get Biscuit to look into that awful darkness.

Brutus and Bouncer were lying together under an outcrop of rock. Brutus must have got giddy and fallen from it because he had passed out cold. Bouncer was trying to dry his feet in Brutus's armpits.

"This is a very strange mountain," said Uncle Otto, picking up the dogs and tucking one under each arm. "It seems to erupt dogs."

But the mountain had not finished with them yet.

As they came off the glacier on to the last stretch of scree before the monastery, they heard a most unexpected sound.

Somewhere, close by, someone was hiccuping.

Like an old warhorse scenting battle, Grandma lifted her grizzled head. "Wait here for me," she said grimly.

She stumped off down a little gulley. When she came back she was half dragging, half carrying, the large, befuddled and sheepish-looking Beelzebub.

"You disgusting brute," she was yelling at him, "Don't you know what drink does to your liver? Do you want to end up in the gutter?" And all the way down the mountain, Grandma, her grey hand clamped like iron round Beelzebub's collar, threatened him with an Early Grave, an Alcoholic Dogs' Home and a Beating He'd Never Forget.

But now they had arrived at the monastery gates. Very gently, Ambrose lowered Leo on to the ground beneath a clump of wind-gnarled firs. Then the others put down the dogs. This was hard to do because the dogs most definitely did not want to be put down, but the yetis were firm.

There was only one more thing to do and Grandma did it. Filling her scrawny chest with air, she threw back her head and yodelled.

And then, carefully leaping from rock to rock so as not to leave footprints on the snowy ground, the yetis vanished.

And so when Con, with the monks at his heels, came rushing out, they found the five dogs clustered in a warm and sheltering huddle round the little boy – and no one else in sight.

"He's safe! The dogs have rescued him!" cried Con, crossing his fingers inside the pocket of his anorak. "They must have done!"

"No … it can't be," stammered Brother Peter. "It would have to be a miracle."

But the monks were men of God. They were *used* to miracles. If God could make five loaves and two fishes go round five thousand people – well, maybe he could make some of the silliest dogs in the world carry out the most heroic mountain rescue of the century. And as they carried the little boy gently in to the warmth of the fire and put him down beside his joyful father, it was all the monks could do to stop dancing and singing and shouting, they were so happy.

So far from being sent away, Baker and Brutus and Biscuit, Bouncer and Beelzebub became the most famous dogs in the land. Stories were written about them in the papers; they appeared on television; statues of them were put up in the village square. The American who bred them sent the monks even more money so that they were able to build a new chapel with the most beautiful bells that pealed across the valley, and everyone who passed through Feldenberg stopped off and climbed the steep path to the monastery to gaze at the lion-hearted dogs. But after the accident to the Englishman and his little boy, no one was allowed to go climbing on the Death Peak without a proper guide, so there were no more disasters. Which was just as well, because for the rest of their long and happy lives, Baker had chilblains, Brutus got giddy, Biscuit had to have a night light in his kennel and Bouncer refused to wet his feet. Only Beelzebub got a bit better. Sometimes he would take a little Coca-Cola with his brandy. But only sometimes...

As for Leo, there were no bones broken; he only needed quiet and warmth. But the first night in the hospital in Feldenberg he was restless and stirred in his sleep and said: "My ... furry animals ... I want ... my furry things." And the night sister, who knew children who are ill often act younger than their years, went and fetched him a teddy bear from the cupboard in the children's ward. But fortunately by that time Leo was fast asleep.

9

El Magnifico

For two days after they had rescued Leo from the mountain, the yetis stayed quietly hidden in a thick fir wood on the borders of Feldenberg and Switzerland.

The reason for this was Grandma's tonsils. After her last great yodel outside the gates of the monastery, Grandma's tonsils had snapped. At least she *said* they had snapped and Grandma wasn't the sort of person you argued with. Certainly her voice was very croaky; yodelling was out of the question and she seemed frail and tired. So Perry took the lorry down a long, deserted track leading into the forest and parked it by a disused timber mill and they shut up the lorry and took to the woods.

It was beautiful amongst the firs. The grass was soft and mossy; there were red and white toadstools, and bilberries which tasted delicious and made their teeth a rich, dark blue. There was a stream to paddle in and fir cones for Clarence to play with and squirrels to be Ambrose's friends. Grandma rested and Ellen had a Great Combing of all the yetis so that their fur shone again and their silky hair blew in

the wind. She polished Queen Victoria and washed Ambrose's bedsock and she rubbed Uncle Otto's bald patch with resin from the pine trees so that it became the most sweetly scented bald patch in the world. Perry stopped worrying about the insides of the wretched lorry and just lay under the trees smoking his pipe and thinking of his Porker. Even Con forgot to be anxious and when he climbed trees it was more for fun than to see if anyone was coming.

It is always when you are having a lovely and carefree time that the most unfortunate things happen. On the afternoon of their second day in the woods, they were sitting peacefully by the banks of the stream. Clarence was pretending to catch fish; Perry was strumming his guitar. Even Hubert had sensibly decided that a sawn-off tree stump was not, after all, his mother and was making quite a good job of cropping the grass.

"What will we do on the *sixth* day?" said Ambrose, rubbing his head against Ellen's arm.

"On the sixth day you will waltz in the great ballroom beneath crystal chandeliers," said poor Ellen, who sometimes wished she'd never invented the Farley Towers game.

"What will we do on the seventh—"

"AAAAEEEE!"

The terrified scream rang through the forest, sending Hubert head first into a blackberry bush, scattering the birds...

They all scrambled to their feet. Staring at them from the other side of the brook was a fat, apple-cheeked girl in a dirndl, carrying a basket of bilberries. Two flaxen plaits stuck out from her head, her mouth was open and her pale blue eyes were wide with terror.

"*Mutter! Mutter! Mutter!*" yelled the girl and, dropping her basket, she turned and fled screeching through the forest.

"I don't call that a mutter," said Ambrose, who was rather hurt at the way she was carrying on. "I call that a scream."

118

But Perry, his face serious, said *Mutter* was the German for mother. The girl was looking for her parents. And when she had found them...

"Back to the lorry at once, at once!" said Con, all his old worries flooding back. "Oh, quickly, *quickly*."

And gathering Hubert up as they fled, the yetis followed him.

Even Perry was disturbed by what had happened. "If the kid saw the lorry and connected it with the yetis ... and if her parents believe her and don't just think the yetis were wild bears... It could be awkward."

119

"Awkward! It could be a disaster," said Con, sitting pale as death beside Perry and blaming himself again and again for not having kept a better lookout in the woods.

"They could make me open up the lorry," Perry went on. "And even if they don't harm the yetis there's all that business about quarantine. No animal's supposed to come into the country without at least six months in quarantine. If they *are* animals. On the other hand, if they're people they're illegal immigrants, so at best they'd be sent straight back."

"Isn't there *anything* we can do?" said Con frantically.

"Well..." said Perry, his forehead furrowed up. "If they spotted that the lorry is British they'll be expecting us to go north, straight through Germany or France and on to one of the Channel ports. Suppose we turn west instead, and go out through Spain? There's a new ferry boat service from San Vigo which takes heavy lorries. It's a heck of a long way round, but I reckon we'd have a better chance of getting through without any questions being asked."

So the yellow lorry turned westwards towards Spain. Spain is a beautiful country with famous castles, carved balconies, vineyards and chestnut groves.

But there was one thing about Spain that they had forgotten...

*

They reached the little town of Santa Maria in the late afternoon. Flags were flying, a band was playing in the park and the streets were packed with gaily dressed people buying doughnuts and nougat and fizzy lemonade from market stalls.

"Oh, heck," said Perry, "we've hit a bullfight day. It's going to take us ages to get through this traffic."

"A bullfight?" said Grandma, when Con repeated this to the yetis in the back. "But bulls shouldn't be *allowed* to fight. Why doesn't someone throw a bucket of cold water over them?"

Con bit his lip. "It isn't the bulls fighting each other. It's ... people fighting the bulls."

"But that's surely very dangerous? And very foolish?" said Uncle Otto. "Bulls are stronger, and have horns."

So Con tried to explain. "It's a sort of sport. They choose a very strong, fierce bull and lead him into the bullring, which is a huge place a bit like a football stadium. And there are these people called picadors, who ride horses and have spears to jab into the bull and make him angry. And then some other people called banderilleros come and stick arrows into the bull's neck and then when he's very tired, the top bloke, who's called a matador, makes him charge and kills him with his sword."

There was a long silence while the yetis looked at him.

"*People* do that?" said Ambrose at last. "Proper human people?"

Con nodded miserably.

The yetis didn't say anything. But one by one they went up to their bunks and shut their ear lids and turned their faces to the wall. They wanted to have nothing to do with Santa Maria, not even to *see* a place where things like that were done.

After crawling along for another few hundred metres, Perry gave up. People had come in from all the surrounding countryside to see the fight and had just parked their cars and motorbikes and farm carts anywhere they could find, jamming up the roads completely.

"We'll have to wait till it's over," he said, "and people move their stuff."

So he drew up under a poster which announced that this very afternoon, Pedro the Passionate, the most famous matador in Spain, was going to fight El Magnifico, the fiercest bull ever to be bred on the ranches of Pamplona. And when he had convinced Con that the *Mutter*-shouting girl was not likely to turn up with her parents six hundred miles from where they'd left her, he took him and Ellen to a pavement café and they had ice cream and watched the streets empty as everyone was drawn, as if by a gigantic magnet, towards the bullring in the central square.

Meanwhile, back in the lorry, Hubert was feeling lonely and neglected. The yetis were still lying on their bunks with their faces to the wall. Nobody loved him. Nobody *cared*.

His boot face began to crumple. He threw back his head, ready to bleat.

And then he stopped. He had heard a voice. An incredible voice, deep and thrilling and purple. Not a moo. Something stronger than a moo. More of a roar.

Could it be...?

But no, it didn't sound *quite* like his mother.

The noise came again. A low, throbbing sort of bellow. And suddenly Hubert knew what it was. Something even more exciting than his mother. Something he'd had long ago and forgotten all about.

The thing that was making that noise – was Hubert's *father*!

It took Hubert some time to push up the iron bar which closed the back of the lorry, but butting steadily with his little crumpled horn, he did it. The yetis had dozed off with their ear lids closed. No one noticed Hubert jump down, trot across the deserted square and reach the edge of the bullring.

It was made of wooden palings, high and solid and unclimbable. But Hubert didn't mean to climb. Puffing with excitement, he trotted round it looking for a soft place in the ground.

From inside, the bellow came again, filling the whole square with its power.

Hubert hesitated no longer. There was a small gap in the wooden railing patched with canvas, and beside it a pile of rubble where a new water pipe went underground. A perfect Hubert Hole. And putting down his battered head, the little yak began to dig.

The bull they called El Magnifico stood alone in the centre of the ring. Sweat gleamed on the huge hump of muscle which ran down his back; his eyes were wide with terror; blood streamed from a wound in his flank.

A few days ago he had roamed free on the range, feeling the wind between his horns, the good grass beneath his feet. Then men had come and carted him away and kept him for two days in a darkened pen. And now he'd been pushed, half blinded, into this place where men rushed at him on horses and others leaped at him with arrows, and everywhere there were flickering red cloths, and the screams of the crowd, and pain and fear.

But El Magnifico was a great bull. He did not understand why these things were being done to him but he would fight to the end. And he lowered his head and pawed the ground and when the prancing men came with their arrows, he charged.

"Olé!" yelled the crowd. And "Aah!" as a banderillero vaulted to safety over the barrier.

But the bull was growing tired. One of the banderillero's arrows had pierced the muscles of his throat. Soon Pedro the Passionate would provoke him to the charge that would be his last.

"Kill!" roared the crowd to Pedro the Passionate. "Kill the bull! Kill! Kill! Kill!"

Wretched, exhausted, scenting his own death, the great bull lifted his head in a last bellow of misery and pain.

The bellow was answered. Not by an answering *roar* exactly. By a small but very happy bleat. And then the yak called Hubert tottered on his spindly legs into the ring.

He was covered in sawdust and rubble, his left horn looked like a toy corkscrew and a piece of water pipe, dislodged by his tunnelling, had caught in his tail.

Ignoring the murmurs of the crowd, not even *seeing* the picadors on their skinny horses or

the prancing banderilleros with their arrows or Pedro the Passionate standing open-mouthed, his cape in his hand, Hubert tottered forward. Only one thing existed for him: El Magnifico the bull.

"Father!" said Hubert in yak language. "Daddy! It's your son. It's me!"

El Magnifico was completely taken by surprise. He stopped bellowing and pawing and charging and bent his head to look at whatever it was that was blissfully butting him from underneath. He didn't *think* he had a calf like that. His calves, as far as he remembered, were larger and smoother and had a different smell. But with fifty wives one could never be sure. And slowly El Magnifico put out his huge, rough tongue and carefully, painstakingly, began to lick Hubert into shape.

Hubert had never been so happy. No one had licked him since he'd left Nanvi Dar. He trembled with joy, he squeaked with pleasure, he rolled over on his back...

"Aah! The sweet little one," sighed the women in the crowd.

Pedro the Passionate was furious. There are rules about bullfighting like there are rules about boxing. You can't just go up to the back end of a bull and stick him in the behind. To earn his money, Pedro had to *make* him charge.

So he flicked his fingers and the picadors on their poor, skinny horses tried to ride up to El Magnifico again and jab him with their spears and make him fight.

But they had reckoned without the horses. A pawing, stamping bull was their enemy – but a father licking his son was a different matter. They, too, had had foals in distant and happy days before they were sold off to be ripped to pieces in the ring. At first they just wouldn't budge however much the picadors jabbed them with their spears. And then, to show they meant business – the horses sat down.

After that the audience went mad. The men rolled

about in their seats laughing. The women took out their handkerchiefs and began to sob, because it was all so touching and beautiful.

But Pedro the Passionate nearly exploded with rage. He was being turned into a laughing stock. He *had* to kill the bull. He *had* to show them.

So angry was he that he felt no fear, but pranced right up to the bull and flicked him with his cape. Anything to make him charge.

El Magnifico didn't even notice. He was working on a particularly difficult place behind Hubert's right ear. But Hubert had seen the cape: a nasty, swirling thing it was, and it made him nervous. With a worried bleat he rushed forward – right between Pedro the Passionate's velvet trouser legs.

And the last bullfight of the season ended with the mightiest matador in Spain lying flat on his back in the sawdust, a pram-sized yak nibbling the bobbles of his embroidered waistcoat – and the fiercest bull ever bred in Pamplona licking them both.

10

Farley Towers

Bulls who have not been killed in the ring are never used again for fights. So the next day, El Magnifico was sent back by special train to the ranch from which he had come: a beautiful place with fresh, green grass, chestnut groves and cool breezes from the mountains of Navarre. And with him travelled his adopted son, an animal that had become famous throughout Spain – the yak called Hubert.

It was this ranch, in the hills above Pamplona, to which, on a moonlit night a couple of days later, the yellow lorry travelled. Perry had found out where the bull had been taken and they had broken their journey to the coast to say goodbye.

When the yetis had woken up to find Hubert gone, their distress had been terrible.

"I didn't look after him properly," Ambrose had wailed over and over again. "I didn't deserve to have a yak of my own."

"Do you remember his little hooves?" Lucy sobbed. "Just like mother-of-pearl, they were."

"And the clatter of his knees knocking together. I can hear it now," Grandma had moaned.

But now they were trying to be brave.

"After all, every growing person needs a father," said sensible Uncle Otto.

"Look how we miss ours," said Lucy, choking back a burst of tears.

"That El Magnifico animal will be the making of him, I daresay," said Grandma.

But Ambrose didn't say anything. Being brave was beyond him as he faced a yak-less world.

About a mile from the ranch, Perry parked the lorry and while Con went ahead to see that the coast was clear, the yetis crept silently across the fields towards the paddock which housed El Magnifico and his new son.

There had been clouds over the moon, but as they came up to the railings they rolled past and in a shaft of silver light they saw their yak, lying like a shaggy mop-head against the vast flanks of the sleeping bull.

"Hubert!" said Ambrose in a deep and tragic voice. "Are you happy, Hubert? Is this what you wanted?"

Hubert scrambled to his feet and ran forward to the railings. His boot face quivered with excitement, his knock knees clattered together like castanets. Here was Ambrose the Abominable, here were his old friends! He began to butt the railings, making little slivers of sawdust with his crumpled horn.

El Magnifico didn't move. He just lifted his great head, with the wide and curving horns, and waited.

It was a terrible moment. The yetis could have picked Hubert up with one hand and lifted him over the fence and that would have been that. But Lady Agatha had brought them up well. They knew that people – even very young ones like Hubert – have to make their own choices.

So they waited, while Hubert ran backwards and forwards, now butting El Magnifico in the stomach, now rushing back to the railings to stick his nose into Ambrose's outstretched hand.

For a moment it looked as though old loyalties would be the strongest. Hubert even put his head down and started tunnelling a path under the railings. Then with a last bleat of confusion, he stopped, turned and collapsed against the great bull's side.

It was over. Fatherhood had won.

After that, no one tried to be brave any more. Though Con and Ellen travelled in the back to try and console the yetis, there was little they could do. Lucy sat clutching Hubert's rubber teat while her blonde stomach turned dark under a rain of tears. Grandma said they needn't expect her to get over a grief like that at her age and Clarence, managing a whole word for once, said, "Gone," over and over again in a deep and desperate voice. As for Ambrose the Abominable, he lay like a felled log on his bunk, his wall eyes fixed blankly on the ceiling, brokenly murmuring Hubert's name.

After a few miles, Perry stopped the lorry. He needed a short sleep before the last lap which would take them to the vehicle ferry. So he switched off the engine, bent down to pick up his pipe and settled back in his seat. Dawn was just breaking, a pale streak of light on the horizon.

Perry took a puff at his pipe. Then suddenly he leaned forward and peered into the driving mirror.

After that he used Bad Language. Then he looked into the mirror again to make sure that he had seen what he thought he had seen.

He had.

For a moment, Perry was tempted. It would have been so easy to start the engine, release the handbrake, let out the clutch and take off at full speed down the road. Then he sighed, got down and opened the back of the lorry.

So then they all saw what Perry had seen in the driving mirror.

Footsore, knock-kneed, tripping over the tufts of hair that hung from his chest and bleating a frantic, "wait-for-me" bleat – came Hubert.

The yetis being sad had been hard to bear but the yetis being happy was almost as exhausting. By the time the lorry drove into the bowels of the big, white ship that was to take them across to Britain, Con and Ellen were quite worn out.

"I do hope they'll be quiet during the crossing," said Con. "I hate to lock them in – it seems so rude – but with the ship so full, I think we'll have to."

But Con needn't have worried. He could have left the door wide open and none of the yetis would have stirred a centimetre. And the reason for this was simple – they were seasick.

There is always a rough patch of water round the Bay of Biscay and as the boat began to heave and toss, the yetis, unused as they were to the sea, became hideously, horribly, vilely ill. Grandma lay in her bunk groaning and saying that since the ship was going to sink anyway she hoped it would sink *quickly*. Lucy swore that she would never again say "sorry" to so much as a peanut if only her stomach would come out of the back of her throat and go back to where it belonged, and Ambrose, his head in a plastic bucket, was trying to decide who should have his bedsock when he was dead.

There is little you can do for people who are

seasick except leave them alone. So while Perry sat in the bar drinking all the beer he hadn't been able to drink while he was driving, Con and Ellen, who were good sailors, stayed up on deck watching the white spray and the diving gulls and the green wake of their ship in the water. And gradually, as they approached the shores of England, a weight seemed to fall off Con's back, because it looked as though he had really done what he had promised Lady Agatha, and brought the yetis safely to her home.

They landed at Southampton two days later and while the exhausted yetis dozed in the back, Perry set course for the village of Farlingham, now only a couple of hours' drive away.

It was a gentle, misty morning and as they drove past quiet fields and bird-busy hedges, past little copses and peaceful villages, they thought – as people do when they come back to the place where they were born – that there was nowhere quite like it in the world.

"Have you ever thought," said Perry, when they stopped at a transport café for some fish and chips, "that Farley Towers may not be there any more? That it's been pulled down to make a motorway or some such thing? Or that the people who own it have sold it to a hotel or a school or something?"

"I've thought of it often," said Con. "But I don't

see what to do except hope for the best."

All the same, when Perry turned off by a signpost saying "Farlingham 2 miles", Con could have cried with relief. For there, at the end of a most beautiful avenue of lime trees was the house which Lady Agatha had described to him, weeks and weeks ago, in the secret valley of Nanvi Dar.

Lady Agatha had not been exaggerating. It really was one of the loveliest houses he had ever seen. Bathed in sunlight, its mellow brick glowed softly. There were wide inviting terraces which fell away to the rolling meadows of the deer park with its ancient elms. Yellow water lilies studded the lake, and on the wrought-iron gates the Farlingham crest shone proudly.

"All the same, I'll just check at the village shop," said Con. "Make sure the Farlinghams are still there."

So he went into the village shop, which was the old-fashioned kind with sweets in glass jars, and liquorice and bootlaces and apples all jumbled up on the counter. Con bought a quarter of Black Bullets and then, trying to keep his voice casual, he asked who the big house belonged to.

"Oh, that's the Farlinghams' place," said the woman behind the till. "Been in the family since way back."

"Are they nice people?" said Con.

"None nicer," said the shop lady. "I reckon there's no one would have a bad word to say for the Farlinghams. Which is more than you can say for some of these old families."

"Well, I guess we're home and dry then," said Perry when Con came back. "If they don't clap me in jail, that is, for turning in an empty lorry. It's the Perrington Porker for me and back to Bukhim for the two of you, I guess."

Con nodded. "I'd like just to see them safely into Farley Towers, though."

"Of course," said Perry. "Tell you what, I'll book a room for tonight in the pub here. The Farlinghams will probably want you and Ellen to stay with them, but I'd rather be independent. Then tomorrow I can get up to town and see the Cold Carcass people and book your flight home. OK?"

"OK," said Con, and he went to tell the yetis that they had arrived.

When he opened the door of the lorry, he had quite a surprise. Ellen, who had been travelling in the back with them, had worked really hard. Their fur shone, Queen Victoria glistened with polish between the shining plaits on Lucy's stomach and the bedsock was arranged across Ambrose's burnished chest like the Order of the Garter.

"Aren't we smart!" said Ambrose the Abominable. "They'll like us like this, won't they, at Farley Towers?"

"They'd better," said Con in a gruff voice. He'd just begun to understand what it would be like to go back to Bukhim and not see the yetis any more.

And seeing the yetis look so smart made the children suddenly realize how crumpled and dishevelled they themselves were looking after the long journey. You can brush fur, but you can't do much about missing buttons and torn jumpers and socks with holes in them.

"Look, now we know the Farlinghams are still there, I think you should go ahead," said Con to the yetis. "After all, you're sort of family from having been brought up by Lady Agatha, and you've got the bedsock to show who you are. We'll find a field to put Hubert in and then we'll go with Perry to his pub and clean ourselves up and then we'll join you. All right?"

The yetis nodded. "But you'll come *soon*, won't you?" said Ambrose, managing to keep his voice wobble free, but only just.

"Very soon," promised Con.

But when the yetis set off up the avenue of lime trees that led, wide and straight and welcoming, from the main gateway of Farley Towers to the house, they couldn't feel shy and nervous any more. It was so lovely to walk upright and unashamed without being afraid to be seen. Not that there was anyone about in the deserted park, but if there had been it wouldn't have mattered because they were safe now, they *belonged*.

"'ice!" said Clarence in a pleased voice, looking about him.

"Yes, *isn't* it nice?" said Lucy. "It's just like walking into the Farley Towers game. Look, there's the lake where we're going to row and have picnics with lemonade."

"And there's the summer house where Lady Agatha used to read Beautiful Poetry," said Grandma.

"If only she could be with us now. And Father too!" sighed Uncle Otto.

They walked on steadily up the long, curiously empty drive between the lime trees, which made an arch above their heads, and came out on the wide sweep of gravel in front of the great, iron-studded door.

"They will be our friends and tell us stories?" said Ambrose, suddenly feeling rather wobbly and scared.

"Of course they will," said Grandma. "Now come on, ring the bell."

And bravely, Ambrose the Abominable took off his bedsock and, holding it carefully in his right hand, he pulled the big brass handle of the bell. They could hear it peal in the back of the huge house – a deep, long peal. There were footsteps, a creak as of a metal bar being pulled back – and then the great front door swung open and the yetis went inside.

The long journey was over. They were home.

11

The Hunter's Club

While the yetis were walking up the long drive to Farley Towers, a meeting was being held inside the house, in the Gold drawing room, which faced the rose gardens and the terrace at the back.

The Gold drawing room looked much as it had looked in Lady Agatha's day. The beautiful Chinese vases were still there, and the embroidered screen and the harpsichord. The sacred relic was there too: the *other* bedsock, the one that the Earl had brought back from Nanvi Dar and slept with under his pillow until he died.

But there were other things now, hung on the walls or resting on the furniture: things which would never have been allowed in the house when Lady Agatha was a girl. Heads they were, mostly. The stuffed heads of friendly hippopotamuses and gentle giraffes and thoughtful buffaloes, looking down on the room with sad and glassy eyes. There were skins, too – the skins of slaughtered tigers and zebras and leopards lying on top of the lovely, flower-patterned carpet. Sawn-off tusks and antlers were piled above the mantlepiece and in a glass case the bodies of poor, dead fishes hung stiffly.

The meeting was a big one. There were about thirty people sitting round a huge satinwood table, all of them men. And not one of them was a Farlingham.

The lady in the shop had not been lying when she said that Farley Towers still belonged to the Farlinghams. It did. But like many old families, the Farlinghams had become poor. They couldn't afford any longer to keep the acres of roof mended, or pay gardeners to tend the grounds, or servants to care for the ninety-seven rooms. So they had decided to let the house to a school or a club or a hospital who would be able to look after it. And their agent, who looked after things for them, *had* let it to a club. A club that wanted to move from its headquarters in London to a place in the country because it needed more room.

The Hunter's Club, it was called...

*

The members of the Hunter's Club came from all over the world. There were oil sheiks from Iran, film stars from Hollywood, German industrialists, Spanish noblemen – anyone who thought that killing defenceless animals turned you into a "real" man. It cost twenty thousand pounds just to *join* the club and the funds were used to buy aeroplanes and motorboats and snowmobiles so that members could go and kill even the rarest animals in the most distant places without anyone being able to stop them.

In this way the Hunters had gunned down polar bears on the icebergs of Alaska, practically exterminated the Javan rhinoceroses and massacred the gentle, dreamy orang-utans of Borneo. Sometimes they went off on pig-sticking parties in Spain, running wild boars through with spears as they quietly snuffled under the chestnut trees, or they would fly to some African lake and mow down hundreds of gorgeous flamingoes from the comfort of their jeeps.

"Now then, gentlemen," said the club president, a man called Colonel Bagwackerly, who had a boiled-looking face, pop eyes and a sticky moustache which clung like a slice of ginger pudding to his face. "As you know, we are here to discuss a very important matter."

"A very important matter!" yelled the Hunters, banging their glasses on the table. They were already rather drunk.

"As you know," Bagwackerly went on, "next week our great club is going to be one hundred years old."

"One hundred years old!" repeated the Hunters, hiccuping and slapping each other on the back.

"And we are here to decide what kind of hunt we should have for our anniversary celebrations."

"A big hunt! The biggest hunt ever!" cried the drunken Hunters.

"Quite so," said Bagwackerly. "The only question is, what shall we hunt. And where?"

"How about polishing off the rest of the blue whales?" said a black-bearded Scotsman who called himself the MacDermot-Duff of Huist and Carra, and went around in a blood-red kilt and a sporran hung with a dozen dangling badger's claws.

But the others shook their heads. Not enough sport, they said, and it was true. So many of these rare and marvellous animals had already been destroyed by greedy whale hunters that you could travel a thousand miles across the ice-blue waters of the Antarctic and not sight one.

"Vat if ve go schtick-pigging?" said a German member, Herr Blutenstein from Hamburg. But the others shook their heads again. For a big centenary hunt they wanted something bigger than pig-sticking; something with guns in it, and explosions, and blood.

One member suggested a kangaroo shoot in Australia, but so many of the kangaroos had already been turned into steaks that that wasn't any good. Someone else suggested the wild camels in the Andes, but a revolution was going on in South America and the Hunters liked shooting things, not getting shot.

And then a small man with gold-rimmed spectacles and a pinched, pale nose got to his feet.

"I know!" he squeaked. "I know! I've got a great idea!"

"What is it, Prink?" said Colonel Bagwackerly in a weary voice.

They had let Mr Prink belong to the club because he was a very rich saucepan manufacturer and they needed him to buy helicopters and things like that. But everyone despised him: he was weedy and twittery and had a huge wife called Myrtle Prink of whom he was dreadfully afraid.

Now he tried to jump on his chair, fell off and

squeaked: "Yetis! That's what we should hunt! Abominable Snowmen! Fly out to the Himalayas and have a great big yeti hunt!"

There were groans from the other Hunters and the MacDermot-Duff of Huish and Carra swore a dreadful oath. "Don't be an imbecile, Prink," he said. "There aren't any such things."

"Yes, there are, there are!" shouted Mr Prink. "Look!"

And he took out a bundle of newspapers and threw them down on the table.

They were the papers that had been printed after Lucy's footsteps had been found on Nanvi Dar and the headlines said things like: ABOMINABLE SNOWMAN STALKS AGAIN or MYSTERIOUS DENIZENS OF THE MOUNTAIN HEIGHTS or IT'S YES TO THE YETIS.

"Pull yourself together, Prink," snarled Bagwackerly. "A pack of newspaper lies."

"It isn't, I'm sure it isn't," squealed Mr Prink. "We could stalk them in the snow and flush them from their lairs and shoot them with exploding bullets. We could have a yeti skin for the billiard room and yeti tusks in the armoury and—"

"Ein yeti schkalp für die library!" shouted Herr Blutenstein from Hamburg.

"That's *enough*!" thundered Colonel Bagwackerly. "If I hear another word about yetis, Prink, I'll have you thrown out of the club." He broke off. "Drat it, that's the doorbell, and I had to send the servants away. Can't have them prying into our affairs. Go and see who it is, Prink, you might as well do something useful for once."

So Mr Prink got up and went out of the room. When he came back, he couldn't speak. His mouth opened, his mouth shut, but that was all.

"Well, what is it?" said Bagwackerly impatiently. "Who was there?"

"It's ... it's ... what you said I mustn't say another word about," stammered Mr Prink. "With ... bedsocks."

Furiously, Bagwackerly pushed him aside and strode out into the hall. When he came back his bloated face looked as though it had been dipped in flour. "My God," he said, groping to loosen his tie, "my God..."

And then, with a great effort, he pulled himself together. "Shut the door, quickly, quickly," he said. "We've only got a couple of minutes. We must make a plan."

The yetis were sitting in the Blue salon having

afternoon tea. They were sitting very close together though the room was vast – so close that Ambrose and Lucy could curl their seventh toes together like they used to do when they were small.

Polite afternoon tea is not an easy meal for yetis. When they balanced the fragile teacups on their knees, the cups sank right into their fur and couldn't easily be found again, and the biscuits were so thin that they had to say, "Sorry, biscuit," about ten times before they got a mouthful.

But that wasn't why they were sitting so close together. They were sitting like that because of the things on the walls. Lady Agatha had not told them about the things that would be on the walls of the Blue salon and the Gold drawing room and all the other rooms that the yetis had seen. Right above Ambrose, so that his trunk almost dipped into Ambrose's teacup, was the head of a poor, dead elephant. Grandma was sitting next to a large stuffed marabou and Uncle Otto's bald patch had two nasty scratches where a pair of moose antlers had caught him as he bent forward to pass the jam.

And though Lady Agatha's relations had been very nice to them, somehow they had not been quite like the yetis expected. The one with the red face and the gingery moustache who said he was Uncle George had such strange pop eyes and when he spoke it made the yetis feel that they were soldiers on parade rather than members of the family. Uncle Mac, who came from Scotland, had sworn quite dreadfully when he had spilt some hot water on his bare and tufty knees, and though the yetis were used to Bad Language from when Perry changed a wheel, somehow this was different. As for Uncle Leslie, he was such a twitchy, squeaky little man that he made the yetis very nervous. There didn't seem to be any women in the family either, which was a pity. A woman's touch would perhaps have made them feel more welcome.

"'ump," said Clarence sadly. He meant the lump of sugar which, for the third time, had dropped from the sugar tongs on to the carpet.

"I wish Con and Ellen would come," whispered Ambrose – and it was rather an uncertain whisper. "They promised to say goodbye to us."

"Another cup of tea?" asked Uncle George.

But the yetis said, thank you, they had had enough.

"Come, come, just one more cup, I insist. Prink – er, Uncle Leslie, another cup for our visitors. For our *relations*, I should say."

So Uncle Leslie poured out another five cups of tea, keeping his back turned to the yetis, and then Uncle George leaned over and dropped a small, white pill into each of them.

"Let us drink to your happy stay with us," he said.

The yetis were far too polite to refuse a toast. They hadn't wanted any more tea but now, one by one, they tilted their cups into their mouths and drank.

"That ... poor elephant's ... all... swelled up," said Ambrose groggily.

"I feel funny," whispered Lucy. "Not nice funny: nasty funny."

For a moment longer, the poor, drugged yetis struggled against unconsciousness. Then there was a crash as Uncle Otto fell forward across the tea things. Grandma slid off the sofa and came to rest in a grey and crumpled heap on the Persian carpet. Poor, bewildered Clarence keeled over sideways, taking a case of stuffed pike with him as he fell. Then Lucy and Ambrose collapsed into each other's arms – and it was over.

It is easy to trick innocent creatures who trust you. The yetis would not wake for a long time now. And when they did, the fate in store for them was too dreadful for anyone to imagine.

An hour later, Con and Ellen walked up the long avenue of lime trees towards the iron-studded door of Farley Towers.

The grounds were surprisingly deserted. No gardeners bent over the flower beds, no strollers enjoying the golden afternoon.

"Look, an aeroplane! A big one!"

Con tilted his head back at the plane which had appeared suddenly, rising steeply from the fields behind the house. The Farlinghams must have their own airstrip! The thought that they were going to visit people rich and grand enough to run their own aeroplanes made the children rather nervous. They had done their best, pulling the last of their clean clothes out of the battered holdall, but they still weren't exactly smart.

"I'm glad we didn't bring Hubert," said Ellen.

Perry, who wanted to get to the pub for opening time, had lifted Hubert over a low fence into a field of cows. They were the very *best* cows, pedigree Jerseys with soft doe eyes, but Hubert had just turned his back on them and started grazing. After having a famous father like El Magnifico he didn't seem to be interested in mothers any more.

They had reached the gravelled space in front of the house. For a moment they hesitated. The Farlinghams would probably ask them to stay the night, but after that it was goodbye to the yetis, and both the children had lumps in their throats when they thought of it.

"Come on," said Con, "let's get it over," and he ran up the wide flight of steps, and rang the bell.

For a long time, nobody came. Then there were footsteps: slow, heavy ones, and the door was creakingly pulled back.

The first thing the children saw, almost at eye level, was a pair of bony knees with black tufts of hair on them. Then, travelling upwards, they came to a blood-red kilt, a sporran with dangling badger's claws and – much, much higher – a black beard and glittering black eyes...

"Yes," snapped the bearded Scotsman.

"I'm Con Bellamy. This is my sister, Ellen. We've come to see that the yetis are all right and to say goodbye to them. Lady Agatha asked us to—"

"Yetis," snarled the man. "What are you talking about?"

"The yetis who came just now. Ambrose and the others."

"Look, if you're having a joke with me you've chosen the wrong person," said the man. "Yetis, my foot. Now get along both of you. This is a respectable stately home and we don't want any guttersnipes cluttering it up."

"But they *must* be here," said Con desperately.

"Perhaps—" And then he jumped back as the great oak door was slammed in his face.

Feeling suddenly sick with fear, the children turned and went slowly down the steps.

"What *can* have happened?" said Ellen. "Can they have got lost?"

"Hardly, down a dead straight avenue. Maybe Ambrose found a friend?"

But what sort of a friend? Not only were there no people about in the grounds, there were no animals either. No dogs sniffed the moist earth, no cats climbed the rooftops. Even the rooks in the elm trees seemed to have fled.

"Perhaps they've gone to explore the lake or something?"

"We'd better have a look, anyway."

So, fighting down their panic, they searched the woods around the lake, and the Greek temple, and the kitchen gardens behind their sheltering walls. They searched the banks of the stream and the orchard and the stables but there was no sign of the yetis anywhere.

They were searching the topiary, with its yew trees cut into all sorts of shapes, when they saw a second plane come up from behind the house and fly off towards the south.

"There's something very wrong with this..." began Con. Then he broke off. "What is it, Ellen?"

His sister was standing stock still with her hands over her face. He went over to her. Lying at her feet was a cat – an ordinary, tortoiseshell cat.

It had been shot clean through the heart.

For a moment, neither of them could speak. Then: "I'm going to break in," said Con. "I'm going to get into the house *somehow*. Come on, let's try the back."

At first it seemed to be hopeless. The hundred or so windows were tightly shut; the green-painted doors were bolted. And then Con saw one narrow window on the ground floor where the catch had not been pushed completely across the frame. Carefully, levering with his penknife, Con started to work the wood away from the sill. It came slowly, but it came. And then they had climbed through and dropped down safely inside Farley Towers.

They were in the butler's pantry. There was silver waiting to be polished, striped aprons lying on the chair, a big sink... Silently pushing open the green baize door they crept along the stone corridor which connected the servants' quarters with the main part of the house.

There were no footsteps to be heard, no sound of voices. Farley Towers seemed to be totally deserted.

And then, as they reached the hallway which led to the main back door, they stopped with a gasp.

Lying like a blue stain across the flagstones – was Ambrose's bedsock.

"So the man was telling lies. The yetis *have* been here," said Con.

But Ellen had noticed something else. "Look, there's Grandma's shawl, all crumpled up behind that chest. And Queen Victoria..."

"They've been *stripped*," said Con, his teeth beginning to chatter. "Someone has—"

He was stopped by a cry. A weird, strangled, spluttering cry from somewhere below them. "Hublopp!" it sounded like. "Blumph. Haroo!"

"It's coming from the cellar," said Ellen.

They opened one door to a cupboard, another to a lumber room. Then they found it – a dusty, wooden door from which a flight of dank, stone steps led downwards. And there, between cobwebby barrels, the thing that had been making the noises writhed and wriggled.

Con wrenched the gag from its mouth. It was Mr Prink, whom the other Hunters had gagged and bound and thrown into the cellar.

"What's happened?" said Con. "Who did this? *Where are the yetis?*"

Mr Prink became hysterical. "It was just because they talked that I didn't want to join in the shoot. I've never shot anything that talked," he gabbled. "If I'd been able to shoot anything that talked I'd have shot Mrs Prink. Mrs Prink is my wife and she makes me eat mashed potatoes with lumps in them—"

"Shut up about Mrs Prink. What's happened to the yetis?"

"They're on a plane, on the way to the ice floes. There's going to be a great hunt down there in the Antarctic."

Con steadied himself. It was no good giving in to panic now.

"Why there? Why ice floes?"

"So they can run better. They want some sport, you know. This is the famous Hunter's Club. It's no fun shooting animals that just stand still. And everyone in England's so namby-pamby. You can't shoot this, you can't kill that."

"When is this hunt going to start?"

"On Thursday. It's for the centenary of the Hunter's Club. They're all going to fly out and chase them in snowmobiles. The only yetis in the world and all for the club. Yeti skins," raved Mr Prink, "yeti antlers, yeti tusks!"

Con kicked him. "Shut up, you murdering brute. Where exactly are they being dropped?"

"I can't tell you— Ow! Ow! You're hurting me!"

"If you don't tell me I won't hurt you, I'll kill you," said Con, and he meant it.

"A place called Coldwater Straits, near Smithson Island. It's really good hunting country because there's nowhere for them to hide. And I wanted to go too. But I've never shot anything that talked. If I'd been able to shoot anything that talked I'd have shot my wife. Mrs Prink is not a nice woman. She makes me take castor oil even when I'm regular and—"

Con wanted to put his thumbs against Mr Prink's jugular vein and press hard, but there was one more thing he wanted to know.

"How did they make the yetis go with them? What lies did they tell?"

Mr Prink giggled. "They didn't. They put drugs in their tea. And I wanted to go with them, I did really, but I've never shot anything that talked. I've shot a very big rhinoceros from an armour-plated Land Rover, but it didn't talk. If I'd been able to shoot anything that talked I'd have shot Mrs— Help! Help! Where are you going? You've got to untie me!"

"Not a chance," said Con.

It was only when they got out into the fresh air that the real horror of what they'd heard hit the children and then they just clung together in shock, unable to speak.

"It's Monday today, isn't it?" said Con when he could manage words again.

Ellen nodded. On Thursday a plane load of crazy men would set off for Coldwater Straits to murder the yetis.

They had three days to stop them. To achieve the impossible. Just three short days.

12

Coldwater Straits

When the yetis woke they were in the bleakest, most terrible place you could imagine. All around them, stretching to the horizon, was a flat plain of snow and ice, broken only by low ridges like ragged teeth, and here and there a huge frozen block. There was no trace of colour, no blade of grass, no living thing as far as the eye could see – only the shrill screaming of the wind across the sunless waste.

"Oh, where are we? What has happened to us?" cried Ambrose, who was the first to come round after the drugs.

One by one the yetis came to, and stared with wretchedness at the place to which they had been brought.

"I can't remember anything after we drank those cups of tea with the Farlingham uncles," said Lucy.

"Why have they sent us here?" said Grandma. "This place isn't fit for a worm."

"They can't have *meant* to," said Ambrose wretchedly. "Unless we've been bad. Was it our table manners?"

"Pack ice," mused Uncle Otto. "The North Pole? The South Pole? Alaska...?"

"I don't want to be in a pole," wailed Ambrose. "I want Con and Ellen. I want—"

But Lucy had discovered something even more serious. "There's nothing to eat here," she said. "Absolutely nothing."

It was true. Nothing grew on that frozen desert – no moss, no lichen, no grass.

"Wait a minute," said Grandma. "What are those black and white chickens over there?"

"The penguins, do you mean?" said Uncle Otto.

"We can't eat *them*," said Ambrose, shocked. "They're our brothers."

"Don't be silly," said Grandma, "Of course we can't eat *flesh*. But maybe they've laid some eggs."

So they made their way slowly and painfully across the ice, doubled up against the wind. It was dreadfully hard going. The surface looked smooth from a distance, but in fact it was rough, and sharp where floes had been cast on edge by the wind before freezing into the solid mass. The yetis' poor backward-pointing feet were soon bruised and torn.

And it was unbelievably cold. Yetis can stand almost any amount of cold, but this was beyond anything they had ever experienced. The wind whipped the heat out of their faces and hands, and even the almost impenetrable yeti hair was not enough to keep them warm. Soon they were freezing as they had never frozen in their mountain home.

And when they got up to the silent huddle of penguins it was all no good. It's true each of the birds had an egg balanced between its red, webbed toes. But one egg only. *The* egg.

"Sorry, penguin's egg," said Lucy, who was really unbearably hungry.

Then she looked at the father bird standing there quite quietly, not squawking, not protesting, just *suffering,* and she choked and turned away.

"I can't do it," said Lucy. "It's his Little One. It's the only one he's got."

In the lovely, fertile valley of Nanvi Dar, which now seemed just like a distant dream to the yetis, Lady Agatha had taught them always to say "sorry" to only one egg in a nest, so as to leave plenty for the mother bird. But of course in Nanvi Dar there had been no penguins.

Though it had never been properly light, it now became darker and the yetis clung to one another for warmth and comfort. Grandma and Uncle Otto, who were old and experienced, were beginning to give up hope, but for the sake of the children they pretended to believe in rescue. "We must keep moving," said Uncle Otto. "This is polar pack ice. There must be land we can walk to and find some kind of shelter, a cave perhaps. And we will be easier to spot if we are on the move."

"That's right," said Grandma, "and when an aeroplane comes we must shout and wave our arms so they'll see us."

"An aeroplane *will* come, won't it?" said Ambrose. "With Con and Ellen in it?"

"Of course it will," said Uncle Otto. "There has just been some silly mistake."

"What sort of mistake?" asked Ambrose.

"Oh, I expect they wanted to give us a treat so they..." But even Uncle Otto couldn't think of a convincing explanation of how they had come by accident to this ghastly place.

So they started to walk, forcing themselves forward through the gathering darkness, while the wind tore at them, their breath froze and formed icicles in their eyebrows and nostrils and a deathly cold crept slowly but surely through their thick coats, and into their very bones.

After what seemed like many hours of struggling over the treacherous surface, Clarence stopped.

"'oise," he said.

And now the others heard what he had heard.

"An aeroplane," croaked Ambrose. "I knew Con would come." But it was far too dark now for an aeroplane to be out looking for them. It was a strange sound, unlike any they had heard before. It was a deep groaning and creaking, as though some huge monster was turning in an unquiet sleep.

Now Uncle Otto felt despair overwhelming him, for he realized what had happened. Instead of heading for land, the yetis had gone in the wrong direction, and had come to the very edge of the Antarctic ice pack, and what they heard was the sea beating against it, driving new floes into it, breaking others off, sometimes gaining ground, sometimes retreating as the temperature dropped and the sea froze a bit more.

But before Otto could warn the yetis of the terrible danger they were in, there was a sudden booming noise. It was a terrifying sound like the striking of a vast gong under their feet, and the shocked yetis saw a crack open and come rushing towards them, widening all the time. They leaped aside in a panic.

"We must turn back," cried Uncle Otto. They did turn back, wearily struggling over the torn and twisted ice, but they didn't get very far. Utterly exhausted, at the end of their endurance, they collapsed into a miserable huddle, pressing close to one another to preserve a tiny bit of warmth. They could go no further.

As the long polar night dragged on, the yetis told each other stories. They told each other all the gentlest, funniest stories, because they didn't feel like too much adventure. Stories about Mole and Ratty in *The Wind in the Willows* and about Alice and the Mock Turtle and about Henry King who had Swallowed Little Bits of String. And at last, wretched as they were, they fell asleep.

But then a terrible thing happened. Lucy had stopped sleepwalking on the journey from Nanvi Dar. It is a thing you grow out of, like adenoids or sucking your thumb. But now, in her misery and fear, she got up, stretched out her arms and began to totter – eyes open but unseeing – across the cruel ice towards the sea.

She did not get far. A dark gash opened in front of her. There was a splash – a terrible one, like a submerging tank – and then Lucy, who could not swim a stroke, was sucked down into the icy, heaving waters of the coldest seas in the world.

There would have been no hope for her. But though the land of the Antarctic is the most desolate place in the world, there are animals in the sea. And it so happened that two leopard seals had come up to breathe not far away. And when those kind and sensible animals saw that the thing that had fallen into the water was not making the right sort of movements at all – was, in fact, sinking like a stone – they quickly went to help.

It was a hard job, but heaving and buffeting and shoving they managed to edge Lucy's huge bulk on to the ice again.

It was there that the others found her in the morning. A human would have died very quickly. To get wet is the worst thing that can happen to you in those conditions (even sweating in your protective clothing is dangerous) and Lucy was soaked to the skin. But Lucy was a yeti and she was – just – alive. Her long silky coat was stiff and frozen. She was deeply unconscious, but shivering so dreadfully that it seemed as though she was having convulsions; yet when they touched her forehead, it was burning hot.

"Pneumonia," said Grandma grimly.

They made themselves into a shield for her, trying to protect her from the wind, but she went on moaning and shivering. She was delirious too, thinking herself back in the valley with Lady Agatha, saying her lessons, calling to the yaks, singing the rhyming games they used to play...

"Con and Ellen have forgotten us," said Ambrose, trying to rub some warmth into his sister's hands. "They don't love us any more. They couldn't love us and leave us in this dreadful place."

And poor, simple Clarence, who so often summed up for the yetis what everyone was feeling, let a tear drop on Lucy's closed eyes and said:

"'ad. 'AD."

He meant SAD. And it was true, the yetis had never been so sad. Never in all their lives. So sad that they simply didn't want to live. Without a single shot being fired, the Hunters had already done their filthy work.

13

The Round-Up

By the second day after the yetis' kidnapping, Con and Ellen were starting to despair.

Perry, grim-faced and silent, had driven them to London. There, in his bedsit, with its portraits of famous pigs tacked on the walls, he'd developed the photos he'd taken on the journey from Nanvi Dar: photos of Uncle Otto building a campfire, of Lucy saying "sorry" to an outsize tin of baked beans, of Ambrose trying to get Hubert to sit on his knee...

With this proof that yetis really existed, they had gone into action. Perry had visited all the newspaper offices. Con and Ellen had gone with Leo Letts, the boy who was lost on the Death Peak, to the studio of the Metropolitan Television Company, which was run by his father.

"I *knew* it wasn't the dogs who found me," Leo had said, when they'd tracked him down in his smart Hampstead house. "I knew it!" And he was at once as helpful and efficient as anyone could be.

By the time the evening papers came out on that first day all of them carried pictures of the yetis, while the headlines screamed things like: ABOMINABLE

SNOWMEN COME AND GO or YETI SNATCH IN STATELY HOME or MARATHON JOURNEY ENDS IN TRAGEDY. And every hour, from the studios of the Metropolitan Television Company, there was a newsflash announcing the arrival, and kidnapping, of five Abominable Snowmen, possibly the rarest and most valuable creatures in the world.

"*Now* they'll do something, won't they?" said Con, when they came back, exhausted, to Perry's room that night. "*Now* they'll save the yetis."

But "they" didn't. Perhaps it was because no one really knew who "they" were. The police said it was nothing to do with them; they were there to

173

catch people who had broken the law and there was no law against shooting yetis because no one had known that yetis existed. The army said it was not their business – their job was to deal with wars and revolutions and this was neither. And the Minister of the Environment didn't say anything because he was away in the Mediterranean sailing his yacht.

So on the afternoon of the second day, Con and Ellen were sitting wearily on the bed in Perry's tiny flat, while Perry made a cup of tea. All day they had been doing the rounds of government offices and departments. They had been turned away by doormen and security men. They had left messages. They had waited on uncomfortable chairs in outer offices, only to be told that unfortunately the Undersecretary for the Environment, or the Assistant Advisor to the Government Blood Sports Commission, could not see them today.

And there was only one day left. Just one short day before the hunt began.

"There has to be someone," cried Con. "Someone who has power. Someone who would *listen*."

"There is someone," said Ellen suddenly. "One person. The obvious person."

"Who?"

174

"The Queen. She has planes – I've heard of them. The aeroplanes of the Queen's Flight. And she is Commander-in-Chief of the armed forces. *She* could stop the Hunters."

"The Queen!" Con felt like hitting his sister because for a moment he'd really hoped. "That's rich! Two children walking into Buckingham Palace with a crazy story about yetis. Who on earth would take any notice of us?"

"No one," said Ellen. "Of us. Of two children no one would take any notice. But of two hundred – or two thousand – or twenty thousand," said Ellen, and her thin face looked as though someone had lit a lamp inside it. "We must have a demonstration, a March for the Yetis. We can demonstrate outside the palace. They'll have to listen."

"That won't be easy," said Perry, who was stirring three spoonfuls of sugar into each teacup. He knew that when you are tired and depressed sweet tea is just the thing. "I've been on one or two demos in my time, and they take weeks to organize, and you have to have permission from the police or they just come and break it up. And even so, nothing much changes."

They were quiet for a moment, sipping their scalding tea. Then Ellen said, "What else can we do?"

And as usual, she was right.

So Perry went out for fish and chips, while Con and Ellen started making posters. Con's said, ON THURSDAY THE YETIS WILL DIE ... UNLESS YOU COME, and then gave the time and place for the demonstration – Buckingham Palace, two o'clock. Ellen's said, PLEASE, PLEASE, IF YOU CARE ABOUT ANYTHING, CARE ABOUT THIS...

"Right," said Perry, when they had eaten their fish and chips and wiped the grease off their fingers. "It's just before five. I'll go and get these copied. Then you'll have to get to work."

"Aren't you coming with us?" asked Ellen.

"'fraid not," said Perry. "I've got business of my own to attend to."

Con said nothing. What could he say? Perry had brought them all the way from the Himalayas, he had helped them in a thousand ways. If he had had enough, then it was only fair; more than fair. But still, it felt like a nail in Con's heart. Now they really were on their own.

Con and Ellen didn't get back to Perry's flat until around midnight. They let themselves in with the key that Perry had given them, and sank exhausted on to the bed. They had been all over the place with their carrier bags of posters, sticking them on lamp posts and walls, in Underground train stations and bus stops. Sometimes they had been shooed away by irritated shopkeepers and traffic wardens, but sometimes they had met friendly and interested faces. An old lady with a walking stick, making her way slowly along the pavement, had asked Con what it was all about. When he explained, she said that she would tell all her friends. "Not that there are many

177

left," she said. "And how we'll get to Buckingham Palace, I don't know." Ellen had been stopped by a bearded man who was bundled up in an old blanket in the doorway of a posh office building. Beside him sat a small dog that obviously hadn't had a bath either. The man had been mumbling quietly to himself, but when he saw Ellen he shouted suddenly, "That's it, girl, you tell those—" and he used a word that Ellen hadn't heard before, but was quite sure she shouldn't use herself.

And tomorrow was the last day. "Do you think anybody will come?" said Con. He was lying on his back in the dark, staring up at the ceiling.

"Con, I don't know, I just don't know," said Ellen. "In the morning we'll do the schools..." And then sleep took her.

For Con and Ellen, running through the London streets, jumping on to buses, fighting their way through the tunnels of the Underground, the following morning was even more exhausting than the evening before. What they had decided to do was simple enough. To call out all the schoolchildren they could find and get them to join the demonstration in front of Buckingham Palace that afternoon and beg the Queen to save the yetis.

They began in Central London, near the river and the docks, and worked their way outwards.

Sometimes they separated while Con went to a boys'
school and Ellen, overcoming her shyness, tackled
a girls'. Sometimes they came together again before
running on to the next district and the next and the
next...

The first school Con came to was called Bermeyside
Primary and it was a tough one. There was a fight
going on in the asphalt play yard when he arrived,
and children were standing round in a circle jeering
and cheering. There was no teacher to be seen. But
when Con whistled, the fight broke up and the

children advanced towards him. A tall boy with dreadlocks spoke.

"Yeah?"

"Listen, I need help," said Con. "Can you get this school out? The whole school? In front of Buckingham Palace at two o'clock this afternoon?"

"I can," said the boy, spitting out of the side of his mouth. "But why should I?"

Con explained about the yetis and the boy nodded. "I saw it on the telly. But man, the *Queen*. Why not the Mafia or something?"

"The Queen has her own planes. People would listen to her."

The boy stood looking down at Ambrose's photograph, which Con had brought.

"Do we get paid?"

"No. Will you come?" said Con.

He spat again. "OK," he said, holding out his hand. "I'll get them out, and I'll get my cousin Mervyn to bring out Fairfield Junior."

His next school couldn't have been more different – a little prep school inside the gates of a big house where the boys, in white flannels, were already out on the cricket field. There was the sound of clapping and polite voices saying things like: "Well played,

Johnson," and, "Good for you, Smithers!"

Con climbed over the high wall and dropped down beside a dozy-looking boy in spectacles, who was supposed to be fielding at long off but actually seemed to be searching for interesting-looking beetles.

But though he looked dozy, he was very quick on the uptake. "I saw it on TV," he said. "And I'll do everything I can to bring some people. Mind you, there are some pretty grim characters here. There's a boy called Smithers, who pops at nesting blackbirds with his air gun. But I'll do what I can. Oh, heck, there's the ball!"

And to groans and catcalls as the nice boy missed his catch, Con ran out of the high gates and on...

Ellen, meanwhile, was tackling the girls of The Sacred Heart Convent a couple of streets away. The nuns had already shooed the little girls, in their grey pleated skirts and white blouses, into the school and Ellen had to barge her way into the locker room where they were changing their outdoor shoes.

Quickly she grabbed two of them: a fat girl with freckles and a thin one with braces on her teeth, and explained what she wanted. In a minute she was surrounded by whispering, tittering children, some with one shoe on, some with none, all of them wanting to know what was happening. They sighed over Ambrose's picture, said he was just like a teddy bear, and giggled when Ellen asked them to assemble in front of Buckingham Palace. As she ran to her next school, Ellen felt thoroughly disgusted. She was sure she had wasted her time.

Yet it was those same little girls in their white blouses and knee socks who, at two o'clock that very afternoon, locked Sister Maria in the lavatory, shut the Mother Superior in the coal house and marched in an orderly crocodile to Buckingham Palace. What's more, a girl called Prudence Mallory had found time to make a banner with the words SAVE THE YETIS splashed across it in red ink. The banner was made from the calico bathrobe of Sister Theresa which another girl called Betty Bainbridge had "borrowed" when she was meant to be taking a message to Matron. All in all, Ellen had been very wrong to underrate the girls of The Sacred Heart.

Next Ellen visited a ballet school where the girls were doing pliés at the barre, and managed to get past a whistle-blowing games mistress to tackle some cold-looking high school girls stripping for gym, before she met Con again at Newlands Progressive. This was rather an alarming place: very new and fashionable with lots of glass and sculptures in the hall, and the children all seemed to come from very trendy homes. But they were certainly very quick on the uptake when it came to what they called protest. "We're not protesting," said Con, "we're asking for help."

"Of course you're protesting," said a boy of about twelve in bare feet and an Indian shirt, "you're protesting against blood sports."

Con had to agree with this. "But we want to keep it orderly."

"Oh, sure," said the boy. "Trouble with the Bill is just a waste of time."

The teacher came back then – Ellen thought him a bit shaggy for a teacher – but he listened to them, which was more than could be said for some of the others they had met. "This might be a good opportunity for a lesson in practical citizenship," he said. It was an odd place, the Newlands Progressive.

The whole morning, Con and Ellen never stopped to rest or eat as they pounded through the streets of London. They begrudged even the seconds that it took to retie their shoelaces.

Convent schools and prep schools, strict schools and sloppy schools, schools for maladjusted children and schools for little snobs... Jewish schools and French schools and Schools for the Deaf, schools run by bullies and schools run by kind and enlightened head teachers – that gruelling morning, Con and Ellen visited as many as they possibly could. But London is a big city, and there are a lot of schools. They may have broken some kind of record, but they couldn't visit them all.

And by two o'clock, half dead with fatigue, they sat on the steps of the Victoria Monument in the middle of the huge area that faces the Queen's London home. They had bought a couple of meat pies and a banana and as they munched and rubbed their aching feet, they knew they had done everything they could. There was nothing to do now except wait.

14

The Great Yeti Demonstration

"No one's going to come," said Con suddenly, in a flat, bleak voice. "We were mad to think they would. It's all been a complete failure."

"It's only half past two," said Ellen. "Remember, the schoolchildren have got to get out of their schools somehow. That isn't exactly easy. And people have jobs..."

Another five minutes, ten...

Con heard a polite cough, and turning round he saw an elderly couple smiling at him. "Have we come to the right place for the yeti demonstration?" asked the man.

"Our friend Margaret told us about it," said the woman. "She couldn't come herself; she really can't get about much. But we've brought a Thermos and a folding chair for Charles. His knees, you know."

Con said that they had come to the right place, and they set about arranging their chair and getting comfy.

Some more minutes passed.

And then, walking in a neat crocodile down the Mall, their banner torn from Sister Theresa's bathrobe waving in the breeze, came the little white-bloused girls of the Convent of The Sacred Heart. Without fuss, taking no notice of the amused stares of the passers-by and the tourists with their cameras, they bowed their heads to Con and Ellen and then went to stand in a row in front of the tall spiked railings, facing the silent sentries of the Coldstream Guards.

They had hardly got settled when, swinging across St James's Park, came a motley, long-haired crowd of boys and girls from Newlands Progressive. They had raided the art room for posters and the slogans they carried, though not always spelt quite right, were brightly painted and eye-catching. A FARE DEEL FOR YETIS, said one placard and AKTION NOW! said another. They had been singing "We Shall Overcome", accompanied by their teacher on a mandolin, as they straggled across the park, but when they reached the palace they became quiet immediately and went to stand behind the little girls of the convent, their banners pointing so that the Queen could see them.

Then a strange collection of people came shuffling across the road towards the palace. Ellen recognized the homeless man with his little dog who had shouted at her the night before. He had brought some friends with him. It was clear from their appearance that they lacked most of the necessities of life, such as hot water, beds and teeth, but they were in good spirits. Perhaps a bit too good, some of them, thought Ellen. They gathered at the railings, and struck up a conversation with the elderly couple. At first the old gentleman on his folding chair was a bit put out, but the dog soon put an end to that. He wagged his tail, politely, and Con saw the old man reach out to scratch him behind the ear. "It hasn't been the same since Buster went," he sighed. "Can't get another dog now. He'd outlive me."

And now people began to appear from everywhere. The children of Bermeyside Primary came up Buckingham Palace Road, and went to stand beside the Newlands Progressive. The boys of the cricket-playing prep school, in striped caps which made them look like little wasps, marched proudly up Constitution Hill and came to a halt behind the convent girls. Ellen's little ballet students, moving already with the grace of dancers, came in across Green Park.

And so they came. Slowly but surely the trickle became a stream, and the stream a river. There were children from schools that neither Con nor Ellen had had time to visit – and schools that Leo had called out from the north-west of London where he lived. And there were students who should have been at lectures and nannies pushing prams containing babies whose own parents were too rich to look after them. There were mothers and workmen and pensioners.

They had done it. The traffic had stopped and there were long lines of cars with puzzled people in them, hooting. Policemen appeared and looked baffled – was it some kind of rally they hadn't been told about? So many children – and where were the teachers?

"Come along, move along," they said. And people did come along and did move along, but always, quietly and obstinately, to the place they had been told to come, the great circular space outside the stately grey palace of the Queen.

There were perhaps a thousand people there by three o'clock. But an odd thing about crowds is that a thousand isn't very many. Of course in a railway station or a theatre it is a lot. But not in a huge wide concourse like the one in front of Buckingham Palace.

Con and Ellen had done their very best, no one could have done more. But you simply can't get a million people to come to a demonstration in a single day.

And now as Con climbed up the steps leading to the statue of Queen Victoria in the middle of Queen's Gardens and looked out over the crowd, he couldn't help thinking that although it was more than just a puddle of faces gazing up at him, it certainly wasn't a sea.

He raised his arms, and someone started chanting, "We want the Queen, we want the Queen!" Then others joined in, and soon they had all taken up the cry. Then Con lowered his arms, the crowd fell silent, and in his strongest voice, he spoke.

"Thank you all for coming. I shall now present our request to Her Majesty the Queen." Con was an intelligent boy and he knew that the Queen was no freer than anyone else to do what she liked, but was surrounded by officials and red tape and things that it was all right to do and things that it wasn't.

He climbed down, took the scroll of paper that Ellen handed him and began to walk towards the main entrance of the palace. By the huge gates he stopped, not quite knowing what to do. If he walked past the guards he would be challenged and turned back. Boys did not walk casually into the palace, he knew that.

While he stood there hesitating, a grey-haired man in a dark suit came out of a door further on and came towards him, past the guards. He looked pale and stern but he spoke politely to Con.

"What exactly is going on here?"

Con explained clearly and carefully about the plight of the yetis. "It's all in that bit of paper. The place they've been taken to, the latitude and longitude. The people who did it. And the time when..." – he faltered for a moment – "the time when they're going to be shot."

The man took the scroll, which had taken many hours to prepare. "I will see that it goes through the usual channels," he said.

Con didn't know what the usual channels were but he didn't like the sound of them.

"No," he said. "It's for the Queen."

"You must know," said the man impatiently, "that the Queen cannot possibly attend personally to everything that comes her way."

"Not everything," said Con. "But this."

"The Queen is not—"

"I don't know what the Queen is *not*," said Con desperately. "But what she is, surely, is someone that people can turn to when there's trouble."

"I have no further comment," sniffed the man. "You must disperse this crowd immediately, or I shall be obliged to have you arrested for unlawful assembly, disturbing the peace and," he added, as the little dog lifted his leg against one of the stone gateposts, "fouling royal property." Then he turned away and went back into the palace.

"We're staying till something is done," shouted Con to his departing back. But the man showed no sign of having heard.

Half an hour, an hour, and still the crowd stood there, their faces lifted to the great façade of the palace. Newlands Progressive struck up a rousing chorus of "We shall not, we shall not be moved". And then a wave of whispering passed through them.

"Did you see her?"

"It was her, I'm sure."

"A face. There by the window."

"It's the Queen. She's going to come out, I know she is."

But the woman whose face they had glimpsed at the huge first-floor window did not come out on to the balcony.

"She's gone."

"She's not coming!"

"It wasn't her. It was the housekeeper."

"Or a lady-in-waiting."

Suddenly, disappointment swept the crowd. They realized how tired they were, how hungry.

For Con it was worse. It wasn't going to work. The great yeti demonstration was over, and just as Perry had warned, nothing had changed. All this time he had been telling himself that if he worked hard enough, cared enough, he could save the day like some hero in a story. For him it wasn't only about saving a threatened species, about stopping blood sports and meaningless killing. For Con, to fail was to fail his friends; to fail Lucy, Uncle Otto, Clarence, Grandma and Ambrose. They were innocent, and kind, and they had trusted him. He had brought them halfway across the world to certain death. It was unbearable.

Con felt rage rising inside him. He thought he would choke. He ran to the statue, clambered up, and began to shout.

"We've failed. It's useless. Go home. Nobody listens to children and tramps and old ladies, and nobody ever will. Go home. You've heard all that stuff – 'Might is right', 'Money talks'. Well it's true. It's all true. The killing and the hating will never stop. If you say you don't like it, they'll call you a wimp or a wet or a dreamer. If you say there is another, kinder, more thoughtful way, they'll call you a lunatic. If you go on saying it, they'll probably shoot you. Go home." Con paused for breath. Ellen was crying and telling him to stop, but he was just getting warmed up. He had plenty more to say. "And as for the Queen," shouted Con, but nobody ever knew what he was going to say about her, because his voice was drowned by the rumbling growl of a big diesel engine being revved – an engine with a dodgy, clattering water pump. All heads turned, and sure enough, straight up the wide Mall towards Buckingham Palace came a canary yellow articulated

lorry with COLD CARCASSES in large letters on its side. After it, in a long line, came more lorries. There was a low-loader, a giant removal van, a huge-wheeled quarry truck, a spanking new Scania heavy haulage vehicle lit up like a Christmas tree.

The yellow lorry drove up to the palace, and as the crowd parted and cheered wildly, it parked right across the front of the main gates, blocking them completely.

Perry jumped out the cab, looking pleased with himself.

"Oh, Perry, you came back!" Ellen rushed over to him and hugged him. "But it's no good, they're going to arrest us."

"Are they now?" said Perry. "Just give me a few moments to get my mates organized, and we'll have a little chat."

Quickly, he directed the massive vehicles to park across every entrance to the palace. The three big gates at the front were blocked. The other lorries drove round and out of sight, to block the rear entrances.

"Right," said Perry. "That should do it. She won't be taking delivery of any groceries for a while."

When they were ensconced in the familiar cab and Perry was enjoying a well-earned cuppa, Con said, "You're going to get into awful trouble. You can't just lock the Queen into her own palace."

"I haven't locked her in," said Perry, "I've locked everybody else out. It's a picket. Legitimate industrial action. I had a word with some mates about it, and we agreed it was worth a try. I'm not saying it'll work, mind you," he said, directing his words to Con, "but I've learned one thing after all the scrapes I've been in, and that is never give up. And trust your friends," he added.

Ellen blushed. "We thought you'd just gone away..."

"What happens now?" said Con hastily.

"Now," said Perry, "we wait."

They didn't have to wait long. The police hadn't been particularly worried by a peaceful demonstration of children and unimportant people outside Buckingham Palace, but now the wail of sirens was heard and flashing blue lights converged on the scene from all directions. A whole fleet of police cars drew up, and uniformed men started pouring out of them. Perry and the other drivers had formed a line in front of Perry's lorry, with arms folded. They weren't all big and beefy, though the man from the removal van looked pretty fearsome, but they didn't look as though they were going to budge in the face of the massed officers of the law. The policemen stopped at a safe distance from the drivers, and the man in charge produced a loudhailer. His voice echoed over the heads of the crowd.

"You are breaking the law. You must cease this action immediately and remove your vehicles."

Perry didn't need a loudhailer.

"Remove them yourself," he roared back, "if you can." And he held up a handful of wiring. All the drivers had disabled their engines, and it would take many hours to make them work again.

They had a good laugh at that.

"You are all under arrest," came the voice from the loudhailer, "and we are now obliged to take you into custody."

The policemen took out their batons and began to walk forward. A couple of the drivers clenched their fists, and the driver of the removal van produced a mole wrench from his overalls. It was going to get ugly. The remaining demonstrators started booing the police, and chanting "Save the yetis".

Then something made the advancing police stop. A big black car rounded the monument and drove towards the blockading lorries, right between the line of men in their blue uniforms, and the grim-faced drivers. There was a little flag on the bonnet of the car. A young fit-looking man jumped out of the front passenger seat, and ran round the car to open one of the rear doors. Out stepped a tall, well-dressed man with thinning hair and a face which reminded one of a rather sad sheep. Ellen, who had been watching everything from the cab of Perry's lorry, thought she had seen him before somewhere. He walked towards Perry, and stopped in front of him.

"Excuse me," he said, "but one would rather like to drive in and have one's dinner."

Ellen had never seen Perry flustered before, but she saw it now. He actually stammered. "W-well, sir … I'm afraid you can't. The yetis are going to die if we don't stop it somehow."

"Ah yes, the yetis, I read about that, a nasty business."

There was a silence, which seemed to go on for a very long time.

"Coldwater Straits, is that right?"

"Yes, sir."

"Ah, jolly good. That's in BAT, I believe. Now if I can just squeeze past, then perhaps I could have a word with Mother."

Perry stepped aside, and the tall man pressed himself through the narrow gap between the lorry and the railings, and disappeared into the palace.

Everything went very quiet. The police didn't move, the drivers didn't move.

"In bat? Cricketer, is he?" growled the removal van man.

"Why did you let him through?" called Con. "You said it was a picket."

"That bloke," said Perry, "is the only hope we have left."

Time passed very slowly. The few demonstrators

that remained gathered in small groups and talked quietly among themselves. Some reporters arrived, and a van from one of the television networks.

Somewhere in the palace, in a comfortable sitting room with thick carpets and a fire burning in the grate, a delicate hand put down the teacup it had been holding, and reached for the telephone.

For the rest of their lives, there was one moment that Con and Ellen always remembered. As the evening settled down and became night, and all over London the street lights blinked into life, the people outside the palace waited: Perry and the drivers, the remaining demonstrators, quite a lot of them schoolchildren who knew that their parents would be worried sick, the policemen. Only the uniformed driver of the big black car didn't wait. He drove off to put his car in the garage and have his supper.

And then, from one of the doors in the façade of the palace, the grey-haired official emerged and crossed the wide front terrace towards them. They watched him in utter silence as he approached the railings and stopped. He reached into the inside pocket of his suit and brought out an embossed envelope. He poked it rather unceremoniously through the railings into Con's hand, turned on his heel, and departed.

Con saw the royal seal, a magnificent coat of arms with a lion and a unicorn on it. He handed it to Perry.

"You read it, Perry. I daren't."

Perry read it, and in a strange choked voice as though he was getting a cold he said, "All right, Con, up you go. They have a right to hear this."

He gave Con a leg up on to the top of the cab and, from there, Con scrambled on to the roof of the lorry. He didn't need to shout this time for every face was turned towards him, and the only sound was the ever-present thrum of the big city.

"We have an answer," he cried. "I shall read it to you:

"*We have this day in accordance with the petition of our subjects instructed George Ullaby RN, commander of Her Majesty's Research Vessel* Seadog, *stationed in the Weddell Sea, to proceed with all possible speed to Coldwater Straits and in liaison with the staff of the British Antarctic Territory Research Station, there to prevent by any legitimate means at their disposal the unlawful, cruel and inhumane destruction of the yetis.*

"'We thereby require and request, in recognition of the granting of this petition and in anticipation of the successful outcome of this mission, that the vehicles at present obstructing the entrances to our Royal Residence might be removed with dispatch, because the bin-men come on Fridays.'

"We did it," said Con. "Thank you, oh thank you all so very much."

And he started to cry.

It was quite a party. The police gave up any attempt to be proper police. There was so much hugging and backslapping going on, that they really couldn't call it an unlawful assembly. You can't arrest people for laughing and dancing – well, not in England you can't. Some of the constables got straight to work helping the drivers to fix their lorries, sharing jokes about what they had seen on the roads of Great Britain – lorry drivers and policemen are out in all weathers. The Newlands teacher, who had become a royalist, borrowed the loudhailer and started to sing

"God Save The Queen". The old gentleman offered the homeless man a drink from his Thermos, which turned out to contain a pretty decent Speyside malt whisky, and before you could say knife they had decided to set up a kennel in the country to breed Jack Russells, which after a long argument was the only breed they could both agree was a really nice little dog.

There were some unfortunate moments – there always are at a real shindig. Some of the Newland Progressive pupils went skinny-dipping in the Serpentine, and persuaded three girls from the convent school to come along. A small boy from the prep school was violently sick after winning a packet of cigarettes off one of the Bermeyside kids in a hastily assembled game of Texas Hold 'em poker on the flatbed of the low-loader. Still, a party is a party. What can you do?

But before long the celebrations came to an end, and Con and Ellen were on their way home to Perry's little flat, hardly able to keep their eyes open, and still unable to believe that there was real hope for their threatened friends far away on the treacherous ice.

15

The Attack

On the terrible, bleak ice of the Antarctic, the yetis had given up all hope. It was their third night on the ice without food and shelter and it didn't seem possible that Lucy could live through another one. She was quite unconscious; her breath came in shallow, rasping pants and even in that terrible cold she burned with fever. Grandma's teeth were chattering so much that Uncle Otto had had to jam a piece of ice between them to stop her jaw from breaking. Clarence lay beside Lucy, despairing and as still as a stone. Only Ambrose, who had loved people so much, still believed that somehow they would be rescued.

"When an aeroplane comes we must run and shout and wave our arms," he said for the hundredth time.

None of the others answered. They couldn't hear him. Their ear lids had been iced to their ears. The yetis had cried easily but now there were no tears frozen to their furry cheeks. The despair they felt was far too great for tears. And at last Ambrose, too, lay down and waited for the end.

It was their iced-up ear lids that stopped them,

at first, from hearing the drone of engines coming towards them. Five engines. Five snowmobiles: huge, armoured monsters, part tank, part sledge, purpose-built for the hunt, pushing steadily onwards through the desert of snow and ice.

In the first of the snowmobiles sat Colonel Bagwackerly, the president of the Hunter's Club, and the MacDermot-Duff. Their eyes shone with greed and excitement, their automatic rifles were loaded and ready, and on the floor beside them was a sack. Not an ordinary sack. An outsize one, especially made so that it could take the dead body of a yeti.

There were five such sacks, one for each yeti, one in each snowmobile.

"You don't think that mealy little worm Prink'll blow the gaff, do you?" said the MacDermot-Duff. He had stuffed his kilt and sporran inside a quilted flying suit and looked like a large and lumpy liver sausage. "We ought really to have shot him."

"Dash it, man, he is human," said Bagwackerly, flicking the ice crystals from his sticky moustache. And when his companion looked a bit doubtful he added, "Anyway, I was at school with his cousin."

They pressed on, their specially built snowmobiles negotiating the broken surface and ridges of ice with ease. This was going to be the hunt to end all hunts! There weren't going to be many clubs in the world with five stuffed yetis on their walls – perhaps the only yetis in the world! Why one skin alone would be worth a king's ransom!

"Spilt blood is glorious, killing is grand, hunters victorious conquer the land," sang Bagwackerly above the noise of the engine. It was the club song and a perfectly disgusting one, but then the Hunters were disgusting people.

Behind them, in the second snowmobile, was the Sheik of Dabubad with some of his friends. The sheik had murdered all the swift cheetahs and tawny lions and fleet-footed gazelles in the golden plains around his palace and now thirsted for a new kind of slaughter. Behind him came Herr Blutenstein, gibbering with excitement. This was better than schtick-pigging!

"There!" said Bagwackerly suddenly. "Do you see?"

He pointed forward to where some dark shapes could just be made out against the featureless ice.

"It's them all right!" said the MacDermot-Duff, his black eyes popping with excitement.

"Get out the guns," ordered Bagwackerly. And the snowmobiles came steadily on...

"Oh, look! People are coming! In those funny black things. It's Con and Ellen! We're going to be rescued," cried Ambrose the Abominable, leaping to his feet.

The others lifted their weary faces. Making a great effort, they forced their ear lids open. Then, stiffly, without hope at first, they raised their shaggy arms and waved.

"Ambrose is right. It is help after all," said Uncle Otto unbelievingly.

"God has heard us," said Grandma. "It's me singing all those hymns."

Lucy was too weak to move, but for the first time since her illness she opened her eyes and a shy and hopeful smile appeared on her gentle face.

"They've got some sort of stick things in their hands," said Ambrose. "I expect it's bamboo shoots because they're our favourites."

And then it happened. Spattering the ice, the bullets bounced and ricocheted, a hail of death.

"Bullets! " said Grandma unbelievingly. "They're shooting from those sledge things."

The snowmobiles came closer. There was another burst of fire.

"But there's nothing to shoot at here," said Ambrose, peering at the empty, desolate waste.

"Yes, there is," said Uncle Otto, and he spoke in a voice they had never heard him use before. "There is something to shoot at here. Us."

"Damn it, missed," cursed Colonel Bagwackerly. "It's this darned machine jigging about. Can't you hold it steady?"

"I am holding it steady," snapped the MacDermot-Duff.

"Well, I'm not letting those cross-eyed wallies behind us get in first. They're blasted foreigners and I'm the club President. We've got to move in closer."

So the MacDermot-Duff jammed his feet down on

the accelerator and the armoured sledge lurched forward.

"There! Winged one!" shrieked Bagwackerly. "Look, he's fallen, the hairy brute. It's a big one, too! We've done it! The first yeti ever, and I, Cyril Bagwackerly, shot it!"

"It's nothing..." said Uncle Otto, as Grandma and Ambrose ran up to him. "Just ... my leg."

But the wound was a bad one. Blood poured in jagged spurts through the thick fur. An artery had been hit.

Desperately, the others tried to stop the bleeding, closing the wound with their fingers, laying their cheeks against it, but they had nothing. No cloth to make a tourniquet, no bandage.

"They're closing in," said Grandma. "It won't be long now. At least we can die like Christians. Say your prayers, Ambrose, like Lady Agatha would want you to."

But Ambrose was beyond saying anything. If people could do that – if they could come across the ice and shoot kind, good Uncle Otto – then let death come, and come quickly. Ambrose the Abominable was through.

But the men in the snowmobiles did not come on. Their machines had stopped, their greedy, glittering eyes were turned in amazement to the sky.

Aeroplanes. The sky had suddenly filled with planes, skimming low towards them across the ice.

"What the devil?" said Bagwackerly. "Those aren't ours."

"If anyone's trying to get in ahead of us and bag themselves a yeti there's going to be trouble," snarled the MacDermot-Duff. "Those hairy brutes are ours, every one of them."

All the Hunters were sitting back now, looking up through their snow goggles at the sky.

"Schweinehunde!" yelled Herr Blutenstein, shaking his fists. "You schall not schteel my yeti schkinn!"

"Pariah dogs," screamed the Sheik. "Poachers! I'll have you whipped!"

"Quickly, reload, everybody," shouted Bagwackerly, gesturing to make himself heard above the roaring of the planes. "Move in for the kill. We'll get in first. We'll show 'em!"

And in all the snowmobiles, the Hunters, terrified of being done out of their spoils, reloaded their guns and started their machines.

"Ready!" screeched Bagwackerly, and the Hunters gunned their engines and set off at full throttle to finish the job.

But up above them, others were ready too. The aircraft, after circling once, now lined themselves up and flew in low over the snowmobiles. The fuselage doors opened and five long black muzzles emerged.

The Hunters did not have time to scream "Cannons!" or even to notice that it was not the yetis that were being attacked but they themselves before it happened.

"Uuugwaa! Blubble-hoo!" gurgled Bagwackerly. "I'm drowning. I'm choking! Uroo!"

"It's poison, it's ... aauuua gug... I can't see. I can't move! Yak glumph," spluttered the MacDermot-Duff.

"Hilfe! Hulp! I schtuck am," yelled Herr Blutenstein. "I am schtuck." He was indeed stuck. His behind was stuck to his seat, his gloved hands were stuck to his gun, his gun was stuck to his snowmobile, and his nostrils and eyelids were stuck together.

The other Hunters were stuck as well. However, the McDermott-Duff came unstuck again fairly quickly. His hands had stuck to the throttle of his machine, and it careered off at full speed straight into a big frozen ice block. With a cracking sound, the McDermott-Duff was wrenched free and flew like a guided missile before landing with a strange tinkling sound and spinning over the ice for about a hundred metres.

Bagwackerly had been leaning out of the snowmobile to get a clear shot at the yetis, and so much of him was stuck to various parts of the vehicle that even a head-on collision couldn't budge him. The shock of the crash was pretty devastating, however, because it dislodged his nose from the barrel of his gun. Well, most of his nose (it was a long one). The rest of it remained attached to his rifle.

All the other snowmobiles came quickly to a halt as their engines spluttered and died. They had been black and fierce-looking machines, but now they were white and glittery like Christmas decorations. Inside them, the men mumbled and struggled for a while, and then stopped moving entirely. In one of them, the Sheikh of Dabubad was standing like a statue. He was childish and badly brought up, and at the moment of the attack he had been sticking his tongue out at the approaching planes. Now he couldn't get it back in, because it was connected to his right foot by a long column of glittering ice.

The men and women of the British Antarctic Survey had been instructed not to kill and they hadn't killed. But it seemed a pity to waste the latest tear gas or rubber bullets on men as vile and foolish as the Hunters. So they had decided on something much cheaper, simpler, and, in the Antarctic, effective. Water. They were intelligent young people, who knew that the speed of the snowmobiles would make the frozen air even colder, and that water would freeze in seconds. So they had simply pumped a few hundred gallons of water from high-pressure hoses, and encased everything in ice.

The young research assistant who jumped from the cockpit of the Twin Otter as it skidded to a halt on the pack ice found the yetis as still as statues, waiting for death. He walked across the rough ice towards them, his pack of emergency supplies on his back and then, as he saw the blood staining the ice, he started to run.

"It's all right," he shouted. "The Hunters are being rounded up and we have come to take you away."

When he saw Uncle Otto's wound he was white with fury. "Inhuman abominable monsters," he muttered, and he certainly didn't mean the yetis. He bent down and began to unwrap the disinfectant and bandages from the pack he carried.

"I ... expect ... it was an accident," said Uncle Otto, good and noble yeti that he was.

But Ambrose, who had been so loving and trusting all his life, stared at the young man with his wall eyes and said: "It wasn't an accident. They did it on purpose. People are bad."

16

Ambrose Gives Up

The hospital they brought the yetis to was a very famous one in a quiet London square. The nurses were kind and skilful, the doctors clever and comforting and the matron wasn't the starched and stuffy kind but a sympathetic person who let Con and Ellen stay with the yetis all day long, because she knew that people can't get well if they are separated from those they love.

The yetis had become very famous after the children's protest outside the palace and the rescue by the seaplanes of the British Antarctic Territory Research Station, and the nurses were kept busy shooing journalists and cameramen out of the wards. Perry had gone down to Somerset to look for his pig farm, but Con and Ellen had to have a police escort when they went to and from the hospital because of the newspapermen dogging them. And every night on television there was a bulletin about the yetis, and when it was on the streets emptied, as bicycles and footballs were abandoned and children all over the country went inside to watch the news.

At first the news was grave. Lucy was very ill with

pneumonia and Uncle Otto's wound was so deep that he had to have a long and difficult operation to remove the bullet. Both his and Lucy's bed had the curtains drawn round them while doctors and nurses hurried backwards and forwards with syringes and trays of medicine and thermometers.

But slowly they both got better. They could tell that Lucy had turned the corner when she asked the nurses for a mirror and started worrying about the state of her stomach. "It's my pigtails," she murmured groggily. "They're all undone."

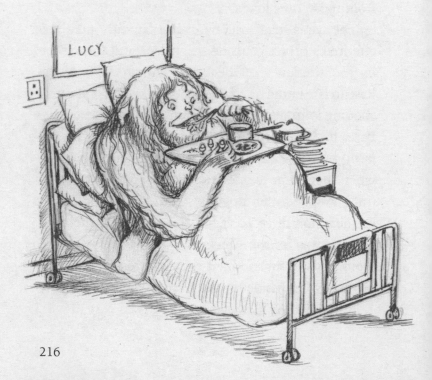

So the nurses, neat as only nurses can be, made her two lovely plaits all ready for Queen Victoria if they found her again. After that Lucy managed to say "Sorry" to a plate of soup which the ward maid brought her. The next morning she said "Sorry" to three boiled eggs, some grilled tomatoes and the bunch of marigolds in a vase beside her bed. After that she was reckoned to be out of danger.

Uncle Otto's wound, too, healed well. Soon he was walking on crutches, looking somehow very manly and distinguished as people on crutches are apt to do, and it was now that something very nice happened to him. The clever doctors had found something to rub into his bald patch which *wasn't* toothpaste or honey or cream cheese but a real medicine which someone had just invented to make hair grow. And almost day by day, as he lay in bed reading the books the kind library lady had brought him on a trolley, they could see the soft, dark down which covered his domed head grow steadily longer and stronger.

Grandma, of course, loved being in hospital. Being old, she had quite a lot of interesting things wrong with her like heartburn and fibroids and wind, which everybody in the hospital took seriously instead of just saying, "We must expect a few troubles as we get older," like Lady Agatha had done.

A lot of doctors came to see Clarence too, and put electrodes on his brain and tried to make him read things. But when the others explained that Clarence's brain had been damaged when he was little and that he was very happy as he was and that they all loved him, they very sensibly left him alone.

With everything going so well, with messages coming in that the Hunters had been turned out of Farley Towers and the proper owner was coming back, with Mr Bellamy phoning to say that the children could stay as long as necessary, Con and Ellen should have been as happy as could be. In fact, they were worried sick.

And what they were worried about was Ambrose.

In the hospital, when the yetis first came, they hadn't taken too much notice of Ambrose. He didn't have pneumonia like Lucy, or a gaping wound like Uncle Otto. He wasn't old like Grandma and bits of his brain weren't missing like Clarence's. A bit of rest and warmth, thought the staff, and Ambrose, who was young and strong, would soon be himself again.

But Ambrose didn't get well and strong, and Ambrose wasn't himself again. When Con pointed out to the nurses that he wasn't eating – wasn't eating at *all* – they told him not to worry. "Young people often go off their food, especially after a shock. Just take no notice."

So the children tried not to make a fuss as Ambrose sent away trayfuls of egg and chips, of castle puddings and banana custard. They tried not to worry when Ambrose lay there with his blue eye dull and sunken and his brown eye glazed and staring at the ceiling. They tried not to worry when Ambrose wouldn't even look up at the telly, though they were showing a Tom and Jerry cartoon.

"Shall I tell you a story, Ambrose?" Con begged.

But Ambrose just shook his great, shaggy head and sighed.

From the first moment she had found him, wall-eyed and crumpled and desperate to be loved, Lady Agatha had known that Ambrose wasn't quite like the others. "I really think you could *kill* Ambrose by thinking unkind thoughts about him," she had said to Con in the valley of Nanvi Dar. Since then, Ambrose had seen people come over the ice with guns; he had seen his uncle shot; he had known hatred.

And now he turned his face to the wall and prepared to die.

In a week or so the doctors and nurses became worried too. There was talk of force-feeding and intravenous drips and things which made the children's blood run cold when they heard of them. And on the news bulletins, now, it was announced that though the other four yetis were improving steadily, there was slight concern about the youngest, Ambrose the Abominable.

After a few more days the "slight concern" was changed to "serious concern".

At night, the doctors made Ellen sleep in a spare room, she was so exhausted from the strain. But nothing could shift Con. He sat by Ambrose's bed murmuring to him, telling him jokes, begging him for Lady Agatha's sake, for Father's sake, to make an effort – to eat something, to get well. But Ambrose just said, "People are *not* my brothers," and grew steadily weaker and more lifeless and ill. Until a day came when the television newscaster looked out of the screen in a very serious way and said: "It is feared that there is little hope for the youngest of the yetis, Ambrose the Abominable, now seriously ill at Park Square Hospital, London."

In the silent hospital, Con sat by Ambrose's bed, trying to believe the unbelievable. There was no hope. It was going to happen. Ambrose the Abominable was going to die.

All day, children had thronged the square outside and stood silently, their faces turned to the hospital windows, waiting for news. Now it was night. Out in the corridor the sister on duty sat in her glass cubicle guarding the white and disinfected room where Ambrose lay.

Inside the room there was no sound – even the soughing of the ventilator had ceased. Ambrose's eyes were closed, his breath would not have stirred a feather. It could not be long now.

Suddenly in the corridor outside there was a scuffle. Then a voice: high and sharp and bossy, saying, "Let me go! Let me go at once!"

The door opened and a girl came into the room. She was about Con's own age, with long, fair hair and grey eyes. She was wearing faded jeans and an old sweater and a haversack hung over one shoulder.

"Is that Ambrose?" she said, still in that loud, high voice, pointing to the bed.

Con nodded, frowning at her to be quiet. Where on earth had he heard a voice like that? And why was her face so familiar?

"Who are you?" he said.

"I'm Aggie. I came as soon as I heard. They'd walled me up in some beastly boarding school in Switzerland and I had to get back."

She went over to the bed and stood looking down at Ambrose.

"He's bad, isn't he?"

"Yes." Con had stopped trying to think where he could have seen the girl before. What did it matter? What did anything matter?

Aggie put down her haversack. Then she bent over Ambrose and still in that high, clear, governessy voice said: "And what, pray, do you think you are doing?"

Con glared at her. No one had spoken above a whisper in that room for days. Yet something held him back from interfering.

"Open your eyes at once!" the bossy voice went on. "*And* your ear lids. You're supposed to have been brought up as a Farlingham. Let's see you behave like one."

To Con's amazement, a flicker passed over Ambrose's face. A chink of blue appeared, then a chink of brown. The left ear lid wavered...

"That's better. And what does one do when a lady comes into the room?"

"Stand ... up," came a thread of a voice from the bed.

"Quite right. So you can *sit* up for a start."

And, unbelievably, Ambrose really did begin to move up on the pillow, almost to raise his head.

"I suppose you realize that dying is Very Bad Manners," the relentless girl went on.

"Is ... it?"

"Certainly it is. What are manners *for*?"

"Making ... people ... comfortable," Ambrose managed to bring out.

"Exactly. Well who's going to be comfortable if you die?" said Aggie briskly. "Sad, that's what they're going to be. What's that by your bed?"

"It's ... my ... milk."

"Your milk! Standing there gathering dust! I'm surprised at you, Ambrose. Drink it up at once," said Aggie, sounding more than ever like an old-fashioned governess.

"I ... can't."

"*Can't*, Ambrose? Or do you mean *won't*?"

She took the glass and put it in Ambrose's hands. Then she raised his head from the pillow and put her own hand under it for support. And Con, who had understood at last what it was all about, looked on, blinking back tears, while Ambrose said weakly, "Yes, Lady Agatha. I'm sorry, Lady Agatha," and drank his milk. Every single drop.

17

Home

As soon as it was clear that Ambrose was going to get quite well again, Aggie went down to Farley Towers to get it ready for the yetis.

Farley Towers belonged to her. Her real name was Lady Agatha Caroline Emma Hope Farlingham and since her father had died in a sailing accident and her mother had married again, Aggie had inherited it. But when Con tried to explain to Ambrose that Aggie was Lady Agatha's great-great-niece, Ambrose just shook his head. "No, she's our own Lady Agatha come back again," he said. "You see, Lady Agatha was awfully tired of her old body, she told us, so she just died and went up to heaven quickly and came down again in a nice new one."

And the other yetis, looking very splendid in their hospital dressing gowns, nodded their heads and said, "You can *see* she's our own Lady Agatha; you can see."

So Con, who knew that people think differently about dying in the place the yetis came from, didn't try to argue any more.

*

It was a golden day in late summer when the hospital ambulances, with a special police escort, brought the yetis, with Con and Ellen, to Farley Towers. Aggie was waiting on the steps to greet them and beside her, getting his front feet tangled in the shoe scraper and bleating like a foghorn, stood Hubert.

The yetis were so happy to see them both that they ran into the house without thinking. But inside the hall they hesitated.

Suppose the THINGS were still on the walls?

But of course they weren't. Aggie had been in such a temper when she saw them that she and her nice old butler had worked from dawn to dusk, stripping the walls and throwing all the stuffed heads and mounted tusks and stretched skins into the lake.

And now Farley Towers was just as Lady Agatha had described it to the yetis in the valley of Nanvi Dar. There were patchwork covers on the four-poster beds, the smell of wax polish on the cedar-wood floors, and bowls of roses on the gate-legged tables. But instead of one sacred relic under a glass case there were now two, because Aggie had found Ambrose's bedsock and washed it and put it with the other one.

Soon the yetis were settled in so happily at Farley

Towers that it was hard to believe that they had not spent all their lives in an English stately home. Grandma took over the housework, vanishing with the Hoover and a packet of sandwiches in the morning, and the sound of her singing "Oh, Happy Band of Pilgrims" would grow fainter and fainter as she hoovered herself away through the Gold drawing room and the Blue salon, reappearing in the evening through the armoury, the banqueting hall and the Spanish dining room.

Lucy tended the flower gardens, and after Aggie had told her which flowers were which, Lucy was most helpful, saying, "Sorry, thistle; sorry, dandelion; sorry, goosegrass," but never – well, hardly ever – saying, "Sorry, dahlia," or "Sorry, lily," or "Sorry, delphinium," so that soon the flower borders looked almost as tidy as in the old days when there had been no less than five gardeners at Farley.

Clarence made himself useful on the farm. All animals like yetis, but simple-minded yetis they really love, and Clarence only had to look at the chickens and they would start laying eggs. As for Uncle Otto, he shut himself into the library and started putting things to rights. The books at Farley had been allowed to get into an awful muddle: Astrology next to Zoology, Mineralogy muddled up with Entomology and Geology absolutely all over the place. Sorting all that out was going to  keep Uncle Otto busy and happy for years.

But it was Ambrose who really saved the fortunes of Farley Towers and he did this by being open to the public. All the yetis had become very famous: people wrote books about them, there was a story about them on the telly and the Queen still sent them hampers of good things from her country homes. But because he had so nearly died, or perhaps because he was the youngest, and wall-eyed into the bargain, Ambrose was, perhaps, the most famous yeti of them all.

And when they realized that it was not having any

money that forced Aggie's trustees to rent her house to the beastly Hunters, they had had the brilliant idea of opening the house to the public once a week and letting Ambrose receive the visitors.

So every Saturday the gates of Farley were thrown open and people came in cars, or on foot, or in charabancs, and paid their money to look round the house where the yetis lived and shake Ambrose by the hand and get his autograph. And when Uncle Otto and Con, who were the best at sums, added up the money at the end of the day, they found that even when they'd paid for food and fuel there was still something left over to make Farley lovelier, like putting new windows in the orangery or buying some peacocks for the terrace.

There was only one person at Farley who did not seem to be completely happy and that was Hubert. Mothers were tame stuff to Hubert now – he had grown out of them. As for fathers, how could he ever hope to find one to compare with El Magnifico? As he dug Hubert Holes all over Farley's velvet lawns, Hubert sometimes had the look of a yak who wonders what life is *for*. And then, not long before Con and Ellen were due to fly back to their father in Bukhim, something happened to change all that.

They were having elevenses on the terrace when a red delivery van swept up the drive and drew to a halt on the gravel. Then two men got out and set a big crate down on the ground.

"'esent!" said Clarence excitedly as they all clustered round. "'esent. 'esent!"

And it *was* a present. Shaken out of its layers of straw it turned out to be – an animal. But an animal unlike anything they'd ever seen.

Its back end was pink and plump and had a corkscrew tail. Its front end was white with black spots, and droopy ears that brushed the ground. In the middle, where the two ends joined, was a curvy, buff-coloured stomach and a forest of tufty hairs.

It was Con who guessed. "It's the Perrington Porker!" he cried. "Perry's done it! It's the Perrington Porker without a doubt."

And of course it was.

The yetis were enchanted. "It's a *lovely* pet for us," said Ambrose, his blue eye shining.

"Let's call him Alfred. A nice, sensible name is Alfred," said Grandma.

But the little pig didn't seem to care *what* he was called. He had eyes for only one person. The yak, Hubert.

Leaving skid marks on the gravel in his eagerness,

the porker slithered to Hubert's side. Then, squealing with pleasure, he began to butt the dishevelled yak in his tattered stomach, to nuzzle him with his pink Hoover of a nose, to stand up on his flea-sized trotters and try to climb up Hubert's tail...

For a moment, Hubert seemed to be completely stunned. Then suddenly it hit him. And as he began to lick the little pig, he seemed to grow taller, his boot face took on a look of dignity and pride, his knock knees straightened.

This was the real thing. Not *looking* for a father. *Being* one!

A week later, a Queen's Messenger arrived at Farley in a black Rolls-Royce to arrange for Con and Ellen's journey back to Nanvi Dar. It was the tired man in the dark suit who had taken Con's petition into the palace, and it was from him they learnt that Parliament had passed a law turning yetis into Very Important Creatures or VICs and that harming them was now a crime which carried the worst punishment in the land.

As for the Hunters, they were still in prison. The police had been forced to let them go at first, because at the time of the kidnapping there had been no law against shooting yetis, because no one knew that yetis existed. But when the Hunters had been freed for a few days they came and hammered on the prison gates and asked to be taken back inside. This was because the people of Britain were so angry at what they had done to the yetis that boys threw stones at them, and old ladies bonked them on the head with shopping baskets, and men coming out of pubs threatened to beat them up.

Mr Prink, however, wasn't in prison. Often he wished he was, because he was somewhere even worse – back with Mrs Prink, who made him gargle with carbolic soap and clean out the budgerigar and eat up the gristle in his mutton fat.

And now the dreaded day came when Con and Ellen were due to leave Farley Towers. They had put it off as long as possible, but though Mr Bellamy had written brave and cheerful letters he had not been able to hide how much he missed them.

Although the helicopter which was to take them to the airport was not expected till midday, the yetis had already put in several hours' hard crying time by breakfast.

"It's not good for people to lose their friends," wailed Ambrose. "It makes them all lumpy in the stomach."

"We'll be back, Ambrose," said Ellen. "You know we will." But she soaked three whole handkerchiefs herself before the drone of the helicopter was heard above the roofs of Farley.

The helicopter landed neatly on the lawns. The pilot opened the door of the cockpit and jumped out. Then he walked round to open the other door. And the yetis stared in disbelief as a tall, strong, marvellously furry figure stepped majestically down on to the grass.

"Father!" they cried, surging forward. "It's Father come back to us! It's our very own Father."

The joy of having him back was so great that they could hardly speak. Uncle Otto had been marvellous but Father – well, Father was Father and they knew now that they need never be afraid again.

Father's first words, however, were grave and sad.

"From the fact that I am here," he said solemnly, "you will know that our beloved Lady Agatha has died. Her end was peaceful and she lies where she wished to lie in the cool earth of our—"

"No, she doesn't," squeaked Ambrose, while Father frowned at him reprovingly. "She doesn't lie, she..."

But Father had stopped taking any notice of Ambrose. He was staring at the steps of the terrace which led down to the lawn.

Aggie had been inside the house when the

helicopter arrived, preparing the yetis' lunch. Now she came down the steps slowly, carrying a tray of drinks. Her long, white cooking apron came to her ankles, her fair hair blew in the breeze, her grey eyes were intent on the brimming mugs.

Father had taken a few steps forward and then stopped. There was amazement in his wise old eyes, and a deep and shining joy.

"That's how she looked when I carried her away from her tent," he said. "Exactly like that!"

Almost unbearably moved, the dignified old yeti walked over to Aggie.

"You've come back to us, Lady Agatha," he said, and bent his head and took the tray from her hands.

And Con and Ellen saw that the story which had begun a hundred years ago in the mountains of Tibet had ended, and that their work was done, and they got into the helicopter and flew away.

One Dog and His Boy

To Milly, Hugo and Hilding,
three very important dogs

ACKNOWLEDGEMENT

I owe a great debt of gratitude to Toby Ibbotson
for the help and encouragement he gave me
in the writing of this book.

Contents

1

Hal's Birthday

All Hal had ever wanted was a dog.

He had wanted one for his last birthday and for the birthday before, and for Christmas, and now that his birthday was coming round again he wanted one more desperately than ever. He had read about dogs and dreamed about dogs; he knew how to feed them and how to train them. But whenever he asked his mother for a dog she told him not to be silly.

"How could we have a dog? Think of the mess; hairs on the carpet and scratch marks on the door, and the smell. . . Not to mention puddles on the floor," said Albina Fenton, and shuddered.

And when Hal said that he would see to it that it didn't smell and would take it out again and again so that it didn't make puddles, she looked hurt.

"You have such a beautiful home," she told her son, "I would have thought you would be grateful."

This was true in a way. Hal's parents were rich; they lived in a large modern house in the suburbs with carpets so thick that your feet sank right into them and silk curtains that swept to the floor. There were three new cars in the garage – one for Albina, one for her husband and one for the maid to use when she took Hal to school – and five bathrooms with gold taps and power showers, and a sauna. In the kitchen every kind of gadget hummed and buzzed; squeezers and coffee makers and extractors – and the patio was tiled with marble brought in specially from Italy.

But in the whole of the house there was nothing that was alive. Not the smallest beetle, not the frailest spider, not the shyest mouse – Albina Fenton and the maids who came and went saw to that. And in the garden there were no flowers – only raked gravel – because flowers mean earth and mess.

Although he knew it was silly to go on hoping, Hal decided he would have a last try. Three days before his tenth birthday he got up early and padded across the deep blue carpet, which was going to be replaced in the coming week because blue, his mother said, was out of fashion. He had said he liked blue but his mother had just smiled at him in that rather regretful way which meant that he had said something foolish.

Now he turned off his night light shaped like a flying saucer and wondered why he seemed to sleep just as badly with the flying saucer night light as he had done with the night light in the shape of a skyscraper.

Then he went into his bathroom and washed carefully, making sure that he didn't miss out any bits, and cleaned his teeth extra hard with his electric toothbrush before spraying his mouth with the high-pressure breath freshener fixed to the wall.

He wanted to have everything right before he wrote the note to his mother because it was important. If she took notice of it everything would come right, but if she didn't. . .

So now he sat down at his specially designed writing desk and found a pen and a piece of headed notepaper, because his parents hated anything to be scrappy, and wrote very, very carefully:

"PLEASE CAN I HAVE A DOG FOR MY BIRTHDAY? PLEASE?"

He wrote it out three times because he wanted the writing to be really good – his parents had moved him from his last school because they said he wasn't making enough progress – and then he padded across the corridor and pushed the note through his mother's bedroom door. There was no point in writing a note to his father because his father was in Dubai, or perhaps Hong Kong. Or even Tokyo. Hal could never be certain, though he tried very hard to keep track of his father's business travels. His father was a "frequent flyer" and more often in the air than on the ground.

Albina Fenton, Hal's mother, was in her walk-in wardrobe, trying to decide what to wear.

"Really, everything's in rags," she muttered, passing along a row of glittering evening dresses, then back along a line of tailored suits, opening drawers of frilly blouses and embroidered scarves. "I'll have to throw most of it away and start again. Some serious shopping is required."

When she came out of the wardrobe, she saw that someone had pushed a note under her door and her heart sank. It would be Hal. She hadn't forgotten his birthday; on the contrary, she had made all sorts of arrangements. She had ordered a gift pack from Hamleys and another from Harrods. They would pick out presents suitable for his age group and deliver them the day before and they had never failed her yet. A well-known caterer was bringing in the food and she had booked an entertainer for the party – but Hal had been difficult about the party because they had moved him from his old school to another one which was more suitable in every way, with the right kind of children, and for some reason Hal had been slow to make new friends.

She picked up the note. If only he isn't on about the same thing, she thought.

But he was, and now she had to explain to him again how impossible it was and had to endure it while Hal turned away and bit his lower lip and looked like a penniless orphan instead of a boy who had everything he could want in the world.

"It really isn't fair," she said to her friends when they came for morning coffee and Hal had been taken to his Activities Club by the maid. "I do everything for that boy and he is never thankful."

Her friends all had names which began with G: Glenda and Geraldine and Gloria – and they were quick to sympathize.

245

"But he does look a bit peaky," said Glenda. "I tell you what, I've read somewhere that they do kissograms for children on their birthdays. Or huggograms, I suppose they would be. They send someone dressed like a chimpanzee or some other animal, and he sings a funny song and delivers a message. Maybe they could get someone dressed like a dog?"

After her friends had gone, Albina rang her husband's office and asked his secretary to get a message through to him in Dubai. "Remind him that it's Hal's birthday on Friday," she said. "He'll be able to pick up a present for him in the Duty Free."

Really there wasn't any more she could do, thought Albina, and she picked up a furnishing catalogue from the pile on the coffee table. Everybody said that beige was the "in" colour this year; she'd have to get rid of the white carpet in the dining room. . . Not that they'd be here much longer: she really felt quite shamed living in a house without a swimming pool.

Right up to the last minute, Hal went on hoping.

He would open his eyes on the morning of his birthday and hear a snuffling noise outside the door and the dog would come running in . . . sometimes the dog was brown and fluffy, sometimes it was white with a smooth coat. Hal didn't mind what it looked like; it would be alive, and it would belong to him, and it would be there when his father was in Dubai and his mother was out with her friends and he was alone in the house with the maid who changed every month and was always so homesick and so sad.

But the phantom dog remained a phantom. Nobody scratched on the door when Hal's birthday came and the sound of barking which made Hal's heart beat fast turned out to be in the street. Hal dressed and went downstairs, where his mother waited beside the breakfast table piled high with parcels. Hamleys was not the best known toy shop in London for nothing; they had sent the latest Xbox game, and a new board game and a laser gun and a radio-controlled metal-detecting car. Harrods had sent an iPod and a giant chemistry set and a Roboquad. . .

"Now are you happy?" said his mother, watching him as he opened his parcels, and he said yes, he was, and she told him that his father would be back that evening and would bring something from the airport.

"Did my grandparents send me anything?" asked Hal, and Albina sighed and produced a small packet wrapped in brown paper.

Her husband's parents were poor and lived in a small cottage on the Northumbrian coast. They had come on a visit once when Hal was small, carrying their belongings in an ancient suitcase tied up with string – and really it had been impossible not to be ashamed of them. They hadn't come again, but they sent the most extraordinary gifts for Hal at Christmas and on his birthday. If one couldn't afford a proper present, surely it was better to do nothing than send a seashell or a piece of rock, thought Albina. Yet Hal always looked pleased with their gifts, and now he gazed at something small and brown and crumbly as he had not looked at any of his other things.

"It's a sea horse," he said, looking at the note that came with it. "It got washed up on one of the rocks. The fishermen say that it brings luck."

So Hal took his presents upstairs and played with them, and in the afternoon the van arrived with the party tea and the birthday cake shaped like a pair of trainers (because nothing that Albina ordered was shaped like itself, and a cake that looked like a cake would have bored her very much). Then the friends came – only they weren't really his friends; he had left those at his old school – and played with his toys and broke the metal-detecting car and tipped the chemistry set on the floor.

But after they had had tea and watched a conjurer there came a surprise.

A van drew up outside; the bell rang – and then the door opened and a . . . thing . . . burst into the room. It was big and dressed in a yellow furry skin, and it had floppy black ears, a lolling pink tongue, and a tail.

For a moment it pranced about on two legs; then it dropped down on all fours and crawled towards Hal and an odd strangled noise came from it which sounded like "Woof, woof."

When it reached Hal, it dropped a big greeting card from its mouth – and in a hoarse voice it began to sing.

"I am your Birthday Doggie,

Your Doggie for the day.

Just pat me and I'll—"

But the song broke off with a splutter because Hal had gone mad.

"Stop it. Come out of there," he yelled, pulling at the creature's head. "How dare you?" He gave a last tug, and the sweaty red face of the man from the Huggograms Agency stared at him. "How dare you pretend to be a dog!" And he began to kick at the man's shins. "You're disgusting. Get out. Go away."

But Alfred Potts, the man inside the suit, had

worked hard at his routine. He hadn't had a fag for a whole hour, and he'd cut down on the beer before he came, and he wasn't going to be kicked by a flea-sized kid.

"Now you just pipe down, will you," he said, gripping Hal's arm. "Here's your mum trying to give you a bit of fun, you ungrateful little—"

But before he could finish, Hal slipped from his grasp and ran sobbing out of the room.

And that was the end of the party.

It was late in the evening before the big Mercedes came up the drive and disappeared into the underground garage. A few minutes later Donald Fenton came in and was greeted by his wife.

"Have you got something for Hal?" she said hurriedly. "You haven't forgotten it's his birthday?"

Mr Fenton clapped his hand over his mouth. He had forgotten. "I was in a meeting till an hour before the plane was due to leave. I nearly didn't make it."

"Oh dear! He kept asking if you'd be back. Well, go and say goodnight to him anyway, he's upset." And she explained about Mr Potts and the huggogram.

Donald went slowly upstairs. He shouldn't have forgotten Hal's birthday, but he hadn't had a minute to himself all day – and the boy would have had tons of presents – Albina always saw to that. When he was Hal's age all he'd had for his birthday was a home-made fishing rod.

Hal was sitting up in bed waiting. He looked small and peaky and there were dark rings under his eyes.

"I've come straight from the airport," explained his father. "I'm afraid I haven't been able to get you a present, but we'll go shopping tomorrow. I can get away early. Is there anything you'd like?"

Hal shook his head. "All I ever wanted was a dog."

But he spoke listlessly; it was all over. That horrible man smelling of cigarettes and beer had somehow destroyed his dream.

Mr Fenton looked at his son – and then he had an idea. "All right, Hal. We'll go out tomorrow and get one."

Downstairs, Albina Fenton heard a shriek of joy coming from Hal's room. "What is it?" she asked her husband when he came downstairs. "What's going on?"

Donald was smiling, looking very pleased with himself.

"I've told him we'll get a dog. Tomorrow."

"A dog! You're mad, Donald. I've told you and

I've told Hal, I absolutely won't have my house destroyed by an animal."

"It's only for the weekend, Albina. They don't rent them out for longer than that."

"Who doesn't? What are you talking about?"

"The Easy Pets people. It's a place where they rent out dogs – it's round the corner from the office. My secretary told me about it. You can get any dog you like for an hour or a day – people rent them when they want to impress their friends or go into the country. They're very carefully chosen – house-trained and all."

"Yes, but what happens when it's time to take the dog back? Are you going to tell Hal it's only for the weekend?"

"Good heavens, no! By the time the dog has to go back, Hal will be tired of him – you know how quickly children get bored with the things you give them. He only played with that indoor space projector we got him for Christmas for a couple of days and it cost the earth."

"Well, I hope you're right. I really couldn't stand any fuss."

"I am right," said Donald firmly.

And anyway, when it was time for the dog to go back he'd be on the way to New York.

2

Easy Pets

The Easy Pets Dog Agency was owned by a couple called Myron and Mavis Carker. The Carkers were greedy and selfish and they liked making money more than anything in the world.

But they were clever. They had realized that nowadays most people didn't want anything to last for a long time. People changed their houses and their cars again and again; they changed their children's schools and the places where they went for holidays – they even changed their wives or their husbands when they looked like they were becoming a bit ordinary and dull.

So why would they want to hang on to their dogs? The slogan "A Dog is for Life and Not Just for Christmas" simply wasn't true for a great many people. Dogs, like children, were a tie; you couldn't do exactly what you wanted with a dog in the household.

On the other hand, dogs were nice. They were fun, and some were very beautiful. To be seen with a graceful, freshly groomed borzoi in the park, or a frolicsome fox terrier, was very agreeable. So what could be more sensible than just to rent a dog – for an hour, or an afternoon, or even a weekend? All the dogs would be pure-bred animals with long pedigrees, and they could even be colour matched with the clothes of the person that was hiring them: a red setter to go with an autumn outfit of russet and crimson, or a snowy Pyrenean mountain dog for a man or woman who liked to wear white.

Of course renting such a dog would be very expensive; the dogs wouldn't just have to be groomed and dewormed and examined regularly by a vet; they would have to have their hair done, tied up in a tuft like a shih-tzu, or shaved in parts like a poodle – and that meant regular visits from hairdressers and beauticians. But people would pay, the Carkers had been sure of that, and they were right. A year after Easy Pets opened, the Carkers were on the way to becoming really rich. And because they had to pay out to so many specialists to help them, they made sure that the kennel maid who did the ordinary work of cleaning out the dogs and feeding them did not have to be paid much. She was a young girl called Kayley, who came in each morning on the tube from Tottenham, and worked all hours of the day because she loved dogs – and as you would expect, the dogs loved her.

The Easy Pets building was in a fashionable street in the middle of London next to a row of expensive shops, but at the back there was a big compound where the dogs slept and a yard where they took their exercise. Kayley woke them early and reassured the dogs who had had bad dreams, like the huge English mastiff who, quite by mistake, had bitten off her mistress's little finger when she was being fed a sausage, and never been punished. Not being punished when you feel you ought to have been is very upsetting for dogs, and the mastiff still suffered in the night. Then Kayley took the dogs out for a short run in the yard and gave them their breakfast.

After that they went to be washed and groomed and have their hair done and their nails polished and their teeth cleaned – and those of the dogs who wore their hair tied up away from their faces were given fresh ribbons, and those like the Afghan who needed extra brushing were taken away to a special dressing room. Then the dogs were sprayed, each with a special scent mixed by a lady who kept a perfume shop, because the smell of dog wasn't thought to be right for the rich people who took the animals out. The St Bernards' scent was called "Mountain Glory", the poodles were sprayed with something called "Dark Dancer" and the collies were covered in "Heather Mist". The dogs disliked these scents more than anything – a dog's smell is as much a part of him as his bark or the way he holds his tail – and they did their best to lick themselves and each other and roll on the ground, but it was almost impossible to get the beastly stuff off.

Then when they were ready for the day's work they were taken to the front of the building, where there were a number of rooms with elegant cages and soft lighting and fitted carpets. Over each cage was the dog's name and above that the name of the breeder he came from. The dogs were not allowed toys – rubber balls or squeaky animals or plastic bones – to chew on because their cages had to be kept tidy to impress the people who came to pick out the dog they wanted. They just had to sit still and look desirable.

When they had first come to Easy Pets the dogs were full of hope. They had thought every time someone came for them it was someone who wanted a companion for life. Someone who was going to give them a home and to whom they would belong. They had gone off with their heads held high and their tails signalling their happiness – but always and always they were brought back, whether it was after an hour or a day . . . back to their cages and to the waiting.

They had each other, and they had Kayley, and they made the best of it, but it was hard.

In Room A there were five dogs. It was the smallest of the rooms and it was rather special because it was next to the little cubbyhole of an office where Kayley worked when she was not out in the yard, and the dogs who spent the day there had become firm friends.

The largest was Otto, a St Bernard with a tan and white face, and deep-set mournful eyes. Otto was wise and strong but gentle. He had had a tragedy in his life: his mother, who was an exceptionally large and heavy dog even for a St Bernard, had rolled over on to her puppies by mistake and squashed them, and only Otto had survived. This was in the mountains of Switzerland in a famous monastery where St Bernards had been bred for centuries to find people trapped in the snow and bring them to safety.

When something like that has happened to you, you don't waste time fussing about small things. Otto had grown into a brave and useful rescue dog, but when a rich young man had insisted on buying him and taking him to England, Otto had made the best of it, though he had been so happy with the monks. Even when the silly young man found that he could not keep a St Bernard in a London flat and sold him on to Mr Carker, Otto somehow managed to stay dignified and calm, and to soothe the other dogs when they complained about the food or the disgusting perfume or the boredom.

Next to Otto was a dog as small as Otto was big – a tiny Pekinese called Li-Chee with golden hair down to the ground and a black scrunched-up face. Li-Chee adored Otto; when they were loose in the compound at night he curled up as close to Otto as he could, and when the St Bernard woke he sometimes felt that he had five legs – four of his own and one

258

that was really a Pekinese. Pekes are lion dogs bred to be the companions of Chinese emperors, and the guardians of palaces and temples – and Li-Chee was as fierce and cross as Otto was silent and calm.

The cage beside the Peke was occupied by a black standard poodle. Francine's coat was clipped and trimmed in the fussy way that people expect of poodles, with fluffy pompoms on her legs and tail and a close-shaven backside, and she was usually rented out by actresses and show people who wanted something glamorous. But inside, Francine was a practical hard-working dog and exceedingly clever. Her family had been circus performers for generations, doing incredibly difficult acts: running up ladders, jumping through rings of fire, balancing balls on their noses. . . Francine had loved the life of the circus – the companionship, the travelling in a caravan between one site and the next. But then someone had said training animals to perform was cruel and the circus had been shut down and now she had to sit still all day in a cage waiting to be chosen.

Across from Otto, Li-Chee and Francine was a rough-haired collie called Honey. Honey was very beautiful, with her long coat of black and white and sable and her soft and trusting eyes. But she was not easy to rent out because she couldn't stop herding things, and because there were no sheep in London she herded anything she could find. She had herded a whole nursery school of little children on to the bandstand in the park, and kept a dozen squawking ducks penned up in a bus shelter.

Honey had been a highly trained sheep dog before she came, but the farmer who owned her had gone bankrupt and had to sell her. All the dogs missed being useful, but for a collie not being able to work is agony. The others worried about her. Mr Carker always sounded angry when she was returned early – and they knew what happened to dogs who had displeased Mr Carker – they simply disappeared and were not seen again.

The last inmate of Room A was an unpleasant bitch who lay on a special satin cushion with a hot water bottle under her stomach. Queen Tilly was a Mexican hairless, a small twitchy dog with a naked spotted skin and legs like sticks. They are a rare breed and most of them are nice, though delicate and shivery, but Tilly had belonged to a wealthy heiress before she came to Easy Pets, and had eaten off silver plates and slept on her owner's silken pillows, and she behaved as though nothing was good enough for her. The other dogs had tried to be friendly when she first came but she just tossed her head and yawned. The only time she spoke was when her hot water bottle cooled down and then she yapped and squealed till Kayley came and heated it up for her. She was the most expensive of all the dogs for hire and actually she wasn't worth the money.

There was one extra cage in Room A which at present was empty.

It had stopped raining and Otto, whose cage faced the window, saw people shutting up their umbrellas, which meant that a borrower would come soon. He sat up very straight in his cage and the other dogs followed his example.

At ten o'clock Kayley brought in a lady dressed in a very elegant black skirt with a purple blouse, and heels so high that she could only totter.

"I think Francine will suit you," Kayley said, going over to the poodle's cage. "She's an extremely intelligent dog and used to restaurants."

"She'll certainly go with my outfit," said the lady. "You see, it's a bit tricky – I met this man at a party last night and he said he adored dogs so I said I adored dogs too and he asked me out to lunch. So I thought I would take a dog along and pretend it was mine – don't you think it's a good idea?"

Kayley didn't. She thought it was a perfectly ridiculous idea, but she was used to the batty ideas of the hirers, so she just smiled and went on stroking Francine's head through the bars of the cage.

"I suppose I could have something smaller, but then it would have to sit on my lap and it might leave hairs on my skirt. Or it would get stepped on by the waiters."

"I think you will find Francine just right," said Kayley again. "She's used to lying under tables. The only thing is, she's very musical – if it's the kind of place with an orchestra playing, she might start to join in. Especially if they were to play a waltz."

But the lady said no, it wasn't that kind of place, it was a very expensive, quiet restaurant, the kind where people talked in low voices, usually about the food.

So Francine was taken away to be fitted with a rhinestone collar and have her ribbon changed for one that would match the blouse of the lady who was going to pretend that Francine was her own dog, and they went away.

When the poodle had been gone for an hour, a thin, worried-looking woman came and said she wanted a very large dog to protect her for the afternoon, because she was going to visit her son, who lived in a district where there were a lot of foreigners and people who were very poor and she was afraid of being attacked.

Kayley wanted to say that people who were poor and foreign did not attack old ladies any more than anybody else – she knew this because the people she lived among were poor, and many of them came from other countries – but she wanted Otto to have an outing so she said nothing and went to fetch Otto's collar and lead.

Some dogs from the other rooms were borrowed, but not Honey or Li-Chee, who spent a boring afternoon dozing in their cages, while Queen Tilly went off to have her body massaged with olive oil because her skin was flaking.

On the following day an elderly woman came for the Pekinese because she had to go and see a friend who was even older, but the visit was not a success.

There is absolutely nothing wrong with old ladies but when your ancestors have been bred to ride on the saddle of the emperor when he gallops off to war, you do not feel like being told that you are an itsy-bitsy little doggie aren't you – and though no dog from Easy Pets ever bit people, Li-Chee growled and showed his teeth and was brought back early.

Honey was hired by a man who had seen all the Lassie films when he was a boy and wanted to be photographed with her on the towpath near his house, and Francine was borrowed again by the woman who had told the man she had met at a party that the poodle was hers.

But on the day after that something unexpected happened.

Kayley arrived early, and came to the compound with her buckets of food and said good morning to the dogs as she always did. But this morning she was not alone. Trotting beside her, a piece of string round its makeshift collar, was a dog.

It was not a make of dog that any of the others recognized. It was white with a brown splodge over one ear and another brown splodge above its tail, and smallish like a fox terrier, and it had bat ears like a corgi whereas its violently wagging tail was a bit like the flagpole tail of a beagle. But it was not any of those things. It was something that had never before been seen in Easy Pets – a mongrel.

Kayley let the mongrel off the lead and he hurled himself joyfully at the nearest dog, which fortunately was Otto. As far as he could see he had been given a present of thirty or so new friends and he didn't know whether to bark ecstatically, roll over, or lie on his back and wave his legs in the air, so he tried to do all these things at the same time.

Kayley took Otto and Francine aside.

"I want you to be very nice to him," she said. Kayley always spoke to the dogs as though they were people and of course they understood her perfectly. "He's a stray. I found him last night outside my house and no one seems to want him."

Kayley lived in a small house in Tottenham with her family. They were very poor and their landlord was a horrible man who wouldn't allow them to keep pets and didn't do their repairs either. The night before she had gone out to the takeaway for the family's supper and found this small white creature, wet through and shivering on her doorstep.

The dogs clustered round, sniffing the newcomer. He smelled of dog and not the nasty scents they had sprayed on them, and though he was a bit enthusiastic and puppyish they were happy to welcome him. Only Li-Chee growled a little because Otto was being very nice to the new arrival and he was jealous.

"I've got a plan," Kayley told the dogs. "I don't know if it'll work, but in the meantime if you could just play with him and make it seem as though he belongs."

She let them out into the yard and ran round with them while they had their exercise, and with such a crowd of dogs the little stray did not stand out.

When it was time for the dogs to go to their cages, Kayley slipped the mongrel into the empty cage in Room A. There was nothing to do now except wait for Mr Carker to come on his daily inspection, and hope for the best.

He came as soon as the dogs were settled, wearing the white overall he wore to impress the clients, and carrying a clipboard, on which were his notes. For Mr Carker kept notes on everything: how often a particular dog had been borrowed, whether the client had been pleased with him, and the exact profit the firm had made. Dogs to Mr Carker were just machines for making money and any animal that did not look like it was earning its keep was sent away at once.

"Well, how are we doing this morning?" asked Mr Carker, and Kayley said that everything was fine, and that the headmistress of a primary school had rung up and wanted to rent Otto for a whole day as an end-of-term treat for the children.

Then he stopped at the cage with the little white stray which Kayley had brought in.

His face darkened. "What on earth is going

on here? Are you mad, girl? This is a mongrel. Who brought him in and what is he doing here?"

"Please, sir, I brought him in but he's not a mongrel." Kayley was a truthful girl but if a life could be saved by telling lies, then one just had to go ahead. "He's a new breed. They're just going to register him at the Kennel Club. I got him for my birthday but our landlord won't let us keep dogs."

Mr Carker scowled at the newcomer who was wagging his tail and giving little barks of greeting.

"It's true," said Kayley. "Honestly. He's a . . . Tottenham terrier. They're becoming quite fashionable. I saw one at a dog show in Brighton."

Mr Carker hesitated. Kayley was very knowledgeable about dogs, and it wouldn't do to be ignorant of a new breed, but he was suspicious.

"I've got his pedigree at home," said Kayley. "Couldn't we try him? Maybe we could charge a bit less as he's new."

"Well, perhaps." A Tottenham terrier. It had a good ring to it. "But mind you, if he hasn't been hired by the end of the week, then he goes. If you can't take him there's always the cat and dog shelter. I won't have an animal here that doesn't earn its keep." And as Kayley bent down and stroked the dog through the bars: "Did you hear me?"

"Yes, sir."

At the door Mr Carker turned. "You'd better find a name for him and get it put on his cage."

"Yes, sir," said Kayley again.

But she already had a name. She had found it when she looked into the mongrel's eyes. They were dark and trusting and full of intelligence – but they were not completely equal. On one eye was a splodge, a single fleck of gold.

"He's called Fleck," she said.

But Mr Carker had already gone.

3

The Tottenham Terrier

Left alone in Room A, the dogs looked at their new roommate. They were kind and caring dogs and they were worried.

The Tottenham terrier, or whatever he was, was altogether too hopeful and too excitable for life as a rental dog with Easy Pets.

"Calm down," Otto wanted to say. "Take it easy. Just sit in the front of the cage; don't throw yourself at people."

But Fleck could no more calm down than he

could fly. He was here with new friends, at the beginning of a great adventure. He wasn't quite certain what the great adventure was, but it would be to do with someone who would come for him, and who would love him and whom he would love. The little mongrel didn't understand that Mr Carker would send him away if he had not been borrowed by five o'clock on Friday and if he had done he would not have worried because he was absolutely certain that somebody would come.

A mongrel and a cross-breed are not the same thing. A cross-breed is a mixture of two breeds only, and is considered quite respectable – like a labradoodle – but a mongrel can have six or more different strains of dog in him. And in Fleck's case the six strains, whatever they were, all seemed to be breeds that were used to serving people and looking after them and belonging.

At ten o'clock, Otto stopped trying to calm Fleck and all the others dogs fell silent because that was when, outside the window, a guide dog called Grace came past, taking her blind mistress to the shops. Grace was a golden retriever, and while all the others admired Grace for her skill and her hard work, Otto did more than that. Otto really worshipped Grace.

Soon after that Mr Carker brought in a man in

a chauffeur's cap and Queen Tilly was taken away to have her special jacket put on – one with press studs down the back so that people could open it to see that she really was hairless all over – and then the chauffeur carried her to a waiting Rolls-Royce, where a lady who was going to show her off at a coffee morning in her mansion was waiting.

Renting out Queen Tilly always put Mr Carker in a good humour because he got so much money for her, and when he passed Fleck's cage he laughed.

"No one's come for the Tottenham terrier, I see," he said to Kayley. "And no one will, if you ask me – I've never seen such an ugly little brute."

He was one of those people who think that dogs can't understand anything that humans say and Kayley had to stay behind and pet Fleck before he was his old self.

It was a long day for the small white dog. Otto was taken away in the middle of the morning by the headmistress of the school whose children had asked for a dog for the day as their end-of-term treat, and Honey was borrowed by a man who was meeting a rich friend at a country club and wanted to look sporting. Then Francine went off with the lady who was still hoodwinking her new boyfriend, making him believe that the poodle was hers.

271

Early in the afternoon a couple came who had been told to lose weight and go for walks and they thought taking exercise might be less boring if they did it with a dog.

"This is a nice dog," said Kayley, showing them Fleck, "he's got a lovely nature."

But the man said he was an odd-looking creature and if they had to go to the park they might as well take something with a bit of class, and they went through into Room B and picked out a Saluki with long silky ears and an arched back.

Then Li-Chee was taken away to have his ears syringed and only Fleck was left. He tried hard to amuse himself but it was very lonely without the other dogs, and though his cage was comfortable it was still a cage, and without meaning to, he began to howl softly.

In a second, Kayley was in the room.

"Oh hush, Fleck. Please be quiet. Mr Carker really hates dogs to howl."

She fondled his head, and he stopped at once — but there was no hope now that anyone would come for Fleck that day; the hiring stopped at five. And that meant there were only two more days for the Tottenham terrier to earn his keep and become an Easy Pet.

*

It was always late when Kayley got home. Mr Carker did not live in the Easy Pets building – he and Mrs Carker had a very elegant flat a few streets away – and it was Kayley's job to make sure that the dogs were safely in their compound, and the building was locked and the burglar alarm put on at the end of the day. And even when all that was done she had an hour's journey on the tube.

But she did not come home to an empty house – far from it. Kayley lived with her mother, her grandfather, her twin brothers, who were still at school, and her ten-year-old sister, Pippa.

The O'Brians were poor. Kayley's father had been killed in an accident on a building site, and though her mother had a job sewing for a wealthy lady called Mrs Naryan, and her grandfather had his pension, money was very short. The little house was shabby, the carpets were threadbare, greasy smells from the burger chain next door wafted through the window, but when Kayley came home she was hugged and petted, and when her family asked how she got on, they really wanted to know because they thought that her job as kennel maid to the Carkers was the most interesting you could imagine.

And the person who hugged the hardest and

wanted to know the most was ten-year-old Pippa.

"Did your plan work?" she asked now. "Has Mr Carker let him stay?"

Fleck had spent the night at the O'Brians' and all of them wanted to know about the stray.

"He's given him till Friday night. If nobody borrows him by then he's going to send him away."

Pippa was a sturdy, cheerful girl – but now her face puckered up.

"To the cat and dog shelter?"

Kayley nodded.

"Well, I think it's wicked. He knows perfectly well they can only keep the dogs for three weeks and then if no one's given them a home, they have to have them put down. It's just a sneaky way of getting other people to do your dirty work."

Pippa knew all about the dogs that Kayley looked after. On Sundays she went along to help Kayley with the cleaning and the feeding; and she was determined, when she was old enough, to follow in her sister's footsteps.

"He's got to let Fleck stay," she said now.

"If only he'd see. . ." said Kayley. "Mind you, Fleck shouldn't really be a rental dog – he's a bit mad, the way he goes on about people. He's like Snow White when she sings that song. You know:

'One Day My Prince Will Come'. He's convinced his prince will come – or his princess. You should see his eyes every time someone comes into the room." She shrugged. "Anyway, we've got to make up a pedigree for him before the morning. Mr Carker wants one to put over his cage."

Supper was ready then, and the twins needed help with their homework, and after that Grandfather had to be wheeled down to the shop to buy his lottery ticket.

But at last everything was cleared away and Kayley and Pippa went into the little bedroom they shared and started to work on Fleck's pedigree.

"Pedigrees are always complicated and a bit ridiculous," said Kayley. "The bitches are called things like Wilhelmina Bossyboots of Kilimanjaro. And the more highly bred the dogs are, the longer the names."

They spent a long time thinking, but in the end they decided that Fleck's mother had been called Rodelinda of Mersey Drive because that was the name of the street where they had been for a takeaway on the night they found Fleck.

"And his father could be Frederick the Fifth of Fillongley," said Pippa. "It might bring him luck if he was called after the farm."

Fillongley was the name of the farm which had belonged to the O'Brians till their great-great-grandfather went bankrupt. There was a painting of it above the mantelpiece, and whatever else occasionally got pawned or sold, the picture of Fillongley Farmhouse stayed where it was.

They went on making up pedigrees, getting wilder and sillier till it was time for Pippa to go to bed.

When she came to tuck her sister up for the night, Kayley said, "You'd better pray for Fleck. Pray that there's someone out there who wants him."

"Yes, I will," said Pippa.

And she did. But Pippa wasn't a gentle and accepting girl like Kayley. Pippa was a fighter. She wanted to go out into the world and do battle for the rights of stray dogs everywhere to have a decent home. And not just stray dogs. Everyone who was poor and treated unfairly by life. When she was six, she had dragged a girl called Myrtle to the school toilet and flushed her head down the pan because Myrtle had been bullying an infant in the reception class.

When later Kayley slipped into the bed beside her sleeping sister, she could hear, quite distinctly, the sound of Pippa grinding her teeth.

*

Back in the compound at night, Fleck cheered up again. Though he was careful not to take up Li-Chee's place by Otto's left foot, he slept with his roommates. Otto was tired – there is nothing more exhausting than being petted by twenty-five small children – but he had time to give Fleck a goodnight lick before everybody slept.

But the next morning, and the morning after, which was the fateful Friday, the waiting began again. Fleck now had his name above his cage, and his pedigree, which Kayley had inscribed on a serious-looking piece of paper, and he had a number – Number 51. If only someone came and rented him out, just one person, just for a short time, everything would be all right.

But the day crawled on, and again nobody came for the little dog. The other dogs became more and more concerned; they understood full well what happened to dogs that never left their cages. They were taken away by two men in brown coats and bundled into a travelling crate and never seen again, and they could hardly bear to watch as Fleck pressed himself against the wire and looked up with his unequal eyes as the borrowers came – but not for him. He knew better now than to howl, and

Kayley came whenever she could to stroke him – but as the minutes ticked away the atmosphere in Room A became more and more tense, and when Queen Tilly started one of her squealing sessions because her hot water bottle had cooled down, the others forgot themselves and started to growl.

Then at three o'clock Mr Carker came in with his clipboard.

"It seems there isn't much call for Tottenham terriers," he told the little dog. "We'll have to get rid of you. Can't have you eating me out of house and home."

And he told Kayley to expect the men from the Canine Transport Company, who were coming to take the dog away.

He went out and shut the door and Fleck was left cowering in the corner of his cage. He recognized Mr Carker's tone all too well. He had heard it often in his hard life as a stray.

Then at four thirty, a large Mercedes drew up in the street outside, and a man got out, holding the hand of a small boy.

4

Hal Chooses

Mr Carker always saw important clients in his office before he took them round, and Mr Fenton, who was head of International Power Inc., was clearly important.

"I believe you know our terms," he said, "they're laid out in the brochure. Twenty-five pounds an hour, and a deposit of three hundred pounds, returnable when the dog is brought back to us in good condition. Now, for a weekend borrowing we have a special rate—"

"Yes, yes," said Mr Fenton hurriedly. Hal had been looking out of the window and hadn't been listening. He lowered his voice. "Perhaps you have someone who could show my son round while we deal with the business." He gave Mr Carker a meaningful look and Mr Carker caught on quickly. He was very used to people who lied to their children, and he went out into the corridor and shouted for Kayley.

"Will you take the young gentleman through the rooms and show him the dogs?" he said when she came. "He's going to pick one out."

Kayley smiled at Hal and he smiled back. He thought being a kennel maid must be the most wonderful job in the world; and she was so pretty with her wavy dark hair and her deep blue eyes. . .

"I'm allowed to pick out whichever one I want," Hal told her. "I hope it'll be a young one because dogs can live for fifteen years, can't they, or more, so I'll have him till I'm grown up."

Kayley drew in her breath. She knew that Easy Pets were never rented out for more than three days. So they were tricking the child; she'd seen it done before. "Have you got any special breed in mind?"

Hal shook his head. "No. I just want to look – when I see the right one, I'll know." He looked up at her trustingly. "I'll know at once, I'm absolutely sure."

"Yes," said Kayley. "It's often like that. One just knows."

She took him first to Room E, at the back of the building, and stopped by a basset hound, wheezing mightily in the corner of his cage. He was a most attractive dog, and Hal scratched him through the bars of the cage, but he did not say anything. The dog next to him was the mastiff who had bad dreams, and Hal listened open-mouthed while Kayley told him the sad story of the swallowed finger.

"She's over it now, but the other dogs are very gentle with her; it's as though they know."

Nobody could help loving the mastiff but Hal was a sensible boy. It was nearly half-term now but later he would be at school part of each day; such an enormous dog would not get enough exercise. Next to the mastiff was a beautiful Cavalier King Charles spaniel who obediently lay down on his back with his paws in the air ready to be scratched or stroked – or even kicked, because these spaniels are such good-natured dogs that they will do anything to give their owners pleasure.

"He's had a bad time too," said Kayley. "The couple he belonged to split up and they sent him backwards and forwards on the train between Edinburgh and London, from one to the other. If he sees a train now, he just sits down and howls."

"Oh, I wish I could have him," said Hal. "He's a marvellous dog." And Kayley nodded, for the spaniel would have been a perfect choice.

But Hal went on to the next cage, past a corgi, past a schnauzer . . . and then through into Room D.

The first dog they came to there was a Dalmatian, and Kayley half waited for Hal to say, "That's the one," because since the famous film about Dalmatians every child in the world seemed to want one. But again, though Hal scratched him through the bars, and sighed a little – he did not stop. They passed a Lhasa apso, so hairy that it was hard to tell which end was which, and a pug. The dogs were tired now, it was the end of a working day, but when they saw Kayley come with a visitor they did their best to sit up and greet them politely. A chow . . . a beautiful Tibetan lion dog . . . a Labrador. . .

Hal was looking a little strained now. He had been absolutely certain that he would know when he came to the dog that was for him – yet they had passed so many marvellous dogs and no voice had spoken inside his head and said, "Stop! This is the one."

Suppose he had been mistaken? Suppose there wasn't one dog waiting for him which he would instantly recognize? And Kayley, seeing his anxiety, put her arm round his shoulders and they moved on into the next room, Room C, where she pointed out the special things about each of the dogs they came to: the markings round the eyes of a deerhound, which in the old days had made people think they could tell the future . . . the tight woolly coat of the Irish water spaniel which meant they could swim in the coldest water.

And still Hal marvelled at the dogs, and still he shook his head, and still they went on.

Hal's father had come to join them now and he tried to give Hal some advice. "That boxer's got a nice smooth coat – he wouldn't make too much of a mess," he said. Or, "I dare say your mother wouldn't mind that little dachshund too much?"

But Hal, with his forehead crumpled up, scarcely heard what he said. With Kayley beside him, he walked from dog to dog – and looked . . . and did not say the words that everybody waited for.

Room A now. They passed Otto, and Hal stopped to give him an extra scratch between the ears. The beauty of his character shone through; this was a very special dog, and he saw how tenderly Kayley smiled at him. Francine too; Hal could see through the fussy poodle clipping to her hardworking, steady soul. Then the collie . . . Hal had seen every Lassie film ever made – but still he did not stop. Nor did he stop for the Peke, or Queen Tilly lying on her hot water bottle.

But this was the last room. There was one cage in the corner but it was empty. There were no more dogs.

"I was wrong," he said in a small voice. "I thought I would know."

It didn't matter. Every dog in the place was worth having. He would get Kayley to pick one out for him, but his confidence was gone.

It was at this moment that two men in brown overalls came through the door which led from the street into the cubbyhole.

"We've had a message from the shelter," one of them said. "They've got a burst pipe – the floor's awash and they can't take in any more animals tonight, so we've brought him back. Number fifty-one."

"Where is he?" asked Kayley.

"He's still in his crate out at the back. We were just going to load him up when we got the message. Where do you want him?"

"Bring him in here," said Kayley.

"Oh, we can't do that. Mr Carker's signed him off – he wouldn't want—"

"Bring him in," repeated the kennel maid.

There was a short pause; then the men shrugged and went out again.

Kayley followed them. There was the sound of a crate being prised open, and something small and white appeared in the doorway. For a moment, Fleck stood still and looked about him. Then like a bullet from a gun he shot across the room and hurled himself at Hal. Almost at the same time, Hal dropped to his knees and held out his arms.

"I told you!" he cried. "I told you I'd know. I told you both of us would know!"

Mr Carker came in at that point and took everything in.

"Ah, you have found the Tottenham terrier," he said with an oily smile. "We were just about to take him to . . . to a dog show . . . but there's been a delay." He turned to Mr Fenton. "Of course for a dog like that we'd have to charge considerably more. The breed is still very rare."

Mr Fenton was about to complain, but then he looked at Hal. Or rather he looked at the bundle that was Hal and the dog, seeming to merge into a single thing – and he shrugged and followed Mr Carker to his office.

"He's called Fleck," said Kayley, when the men had gone. "It's because—"

Hal looked up at her. "I know why – it's because he's got a gold fleck in his left eye."

"Yes," said Kayley. "That is exactly why."

5

First Day

Hal woke feeling . . . unusual. He was warm – but that wasn't so odd. What was odd was that he felt happy. Comfortable. Safe. Not as though he had had bad dreams – not as though he had had dreams at all.

On the other hand his bed was hard. It was surprisingly hard. Then he realized it wasn't a bed at all. He was lying on the floor with his duvet over him, and then he remembered. He had promised not to let Fleck sleep on his bed, and he had kept his promise. But he wasn't going to leave his dog alone on his first day in his new home.

And at this moment a cold nose was thrust into his hand – and Fleck exploded into the glory of a new day. Like his owner, Fleck woke to safety and happiness and warmth. He leapt on to Hal's chest, he licked his ear, he jumped off and rolled over so that Hal could rub his stomach.

But Hal was remembering his mother's words the night before.

"If he makes a puddle on the carpet he's going into the garage and staying there."

There was no time to lose in getting Fleck out of doors.

Getting dressed was not easy because Fleck had good ideas of how to "help" – putting Hal's socks in interesting places and herding his shoes . . . but when Hal was ready he allowed him to slip on his collar and lead and followed him down the stairs like a model dog walking to heel.

Hal let himself out of the front door and down the drive. The garden, which wasn't really a garden but a lot of raked gravel, stretched away to either side but they reached the road before Fleck lifted his leg. Opposite the house was a private garden belonging to the people in the street but there was a notice on the gate saying No Dogs or Unaccompanied Children.

But past the end of the road, where the houses were smaller and not so elegant, there was a park, open to everybody. His mother didn't like taking him there; the children who played in it could be rough – but Fleck thought it looked good. He steamed ahead, looking back at Hal every so often, and then they were through the gates.

It was a very ordinary city park but Fleck behaved as though he was in paradise. He put his head down and sniffed the whole history of the dogs that had been there recently. He tried eating a tuft of grass and sneezed. He found a fascinating pile of raked leaves. And all the time his ears twitched with eagerness, and his face turned back to Hal, making sure that Hal too could smell the smells and feel the earth on his paws, and share.

Hal let the dog lead him – and because of that found himself face to face with a girl of about his own age with masses of fair hair and bright blue eyes. She was sitting on a bench reading and was the sort of pretty, self-assured girl that usually frightened Hal, but Fleck liked her immediately.

"He's got a lot of breeds in him, I'd say?" she said, stroking his back, but Hal shook his head.

"He's a Tottenham terrier," he said.

"I've never heard of that," she said. "It must be a new breed. He looks really intelligent. Why don't you let him off the lead?"

"I've only just got him. I'm going to take him to dog training classes next week but I don't know if he'd come back."

"Of course he'd come back. He loves you."

Hal looked at her. Her words made him feel ridiculously happy. He bent down and unclipped the lead. Fleck shook himself, then took off like a racing greyhound – and disappeared behind a clump of trees.

There was a moment of panic as Hal and the blonde girl looked at each other. Supposing he disappeared for ever? Then with as much speed as he had raced off, the little dog returned, a streak of white on his way home.

"Told you," said the girl.

But Fleck was now ready to play. He led Hal to a large tree, and raced round it, chasing whatever was in his head – imaginary squirrels, rabbits, rats even. Hal followed him going the other way and they met in the middle. The girl with the blonde curls came too and a long game of chase followed. It was an oak tree; last year's acorns lay on the ground. Fleck tried one, didn't care for it, spat it out.

Behind the tree was a large hole – obviously the other dogs who had helped to make it were the right kind, because Fleck was delighted with it. He dug his share, with yelps of pleasure. The earth was rich and dark and damp – it must have rained in the night.

Two boys who had been kicking a football came over. Remembering the boys who had destroyed his birthday toys, Hal was apprehensive, but they were friendly – and let Fleck chase their ball a few times before they wandered off.

"I'd best take him back now," Hal told the blonde girl. "I haven't had breakfast yet and my parents will be wondering where I am."

She nodded. "See you tomorrow maybe," she said. "I'll walk with you to the gate."

But the path they took led past a pond – and on the pond were half a dozen ducks.

Fleck stood for a moment taking stock. The hair on his back rose, growls worthy of a Steppenwolf came from him, and before Hal realized what was happening, there was a mighty splash and Fleck was swimming strongly towards the ducks.

The birds squawked indignantly, then took off

with a flutter of dripping wings. Fleck swam to and fro for a few minutes, pretending he had only gone in for the exercise; then, as Hal called him, he scrambled out through the reeds.

"Run!" said the girl. "Don't let him get near you." And she took off along the path. But Hal had only been a dog owner for a day. He waited, and Fleck came as close to him as possible and then, most mightily, he shook himself.

"That's a plucky little brute you've got there," said an old man leading a Great Dane. "They're good swimmers, these cross-breeds."

Hal was about to explain that he was a Tottenham terrier – but he was almost as wet as the dog and he put Fleck on the lead and set off for home.

As they came up the drive to his house, Hal began to worry. He had promised his mother that he wouldn't let the dog make puddles, but Fleck was practically a walking puddle all by himself. He decided to go in through the back. Olga, the new maid, was surly; she came from Kazakhstan and hardly spoke a word of English and Hal was afraid of her sulks and her tears. But when she saw him with the soaking little dog she pulled him into the kitchen, and found a towel and rubbed Fleck till he looked freshly washed rather than bedraggled. Then she found some dry clothes for Hal and pushed him forward into the dining room.

"Mother eats already – go quick. . ." she said.

But she was smiling.

"If I didn't know it was going to be over the day after tomorrow, I couldn't stand it," said Albina. "I found a white hair on the carpet – and another on the footstool. And I nearly fell over the creature's drinking bowl. I do so hate mess!"

Albina's friends – the ones with names beginning with G – were having morning coffee with her and they were very sympathetic.

"I had a friend whose husband brought home an Irish wolfhound," said Glenda. "Imagine it – one swish of his tail and a whole table full of precious ornaments were swept to the floor. And all the husband could say was, 'The dog is saying hello.' She divorced him, of course – nothing else to do."

Hal came in then, carrying Fleck for safety, to greet Aunt Georgia and Aunt Glenda and Aunt Geraldine.

"I thought you'd like to see him," he said.

Fleck wanted to get down and say hello properly, with sniffing and rolling over and all that kind of thing, but Hal held him firmly. Aunt Glenda was wearing very full purple harem trousers and pumps with a big tassel on the toe and he had already discovered how fond Fleck was of anything attached to shoes.

"He's not completely trained yet, though he does sit for quite a long time when you tell him to," he told the ladies.

He carried the dog round to each of them as though he was offering them a wonderful present. Geraldine patted him gingerly, Glenda just smiled nervously, and Georgia said, "Does he bite?"

"Well, I hope Donald knows what he's doing," said Glenda, when Hal had carried the dog out again. "It doesn't look as though he's tired of him yet."

"Donald is sure he will be by tomorrow evening. Hal had to get up early to exercise him – it's a lot of work looking after the things. And frankly, whether there's a fuss or not, I really couldn't go on with this. Suppose he scratches the new coffee table?"

And all of them shuddered at a thought as dreadful as that.

That night, lying on the floor again covered by his duvet, with Fleck curled up beside him, Hal was thinking. Often and often when you wanted something and then got it, it was a disappointment.

He had looked forward to going to the Seychelles for a holiday – his parents had said there would be snorkelling and scuba diving . . . but when he got there he developed a horrible rash from some tropical bug and couldn't go into the water at all. And it was the same with skiing – they'd all gone to Davos and then there wasn't any snow and the hotel was full of people having parties and drinking too much and being sick and they'd come home early.

But having a dog was completely different. He'd wanted it and wanted it and when it happened it was even better than he'd thought it would be. He'd imagined some of it – the companionship and the warmth – but he didn't realize a dog would make you laugh so much, nor that he would help you to make so many friends.

It was extraordinary too how much a dog made you see. The hollows in the oak tree . . . and the way the acorns sat so neatly in their cups . . . how the earth clagged together, so dark after rain. . . Hal hadn't even noticed that it had rained.

And how much he made you think. Fleck had found an iron grating over a drain when they went out in the afternoon. The drain had interested him so much that he'd lain down on his stomach, just looking and smelling and investigating, and Hal realized that he'd never before thought about what might live down there, in the black and evil-looking water. Perhaps ancient river spirits, driven from their homes . . . or strange animals washed down through bath outlets . . . there might be a whole drain underworld that no one knew about.

He reached up to turn on his night light, but Fleck was lying across his feet and Hal didn't want to disturb him. Anyway, he didn't need a night light now he had a protector and a friend.

Early the next morning, which was Sunday, Hal wrote a postcard to his grandparents in Northumberland. He had never had anything interesting to tell them but now he did. He knew how pleased they would be for him, how glad that he had a dog. There was a dog, of course, in their cottage by the sea. Then he addressed the card and took it to the letter box, with Fleck following at his heels.

They went on to the park and though they did not meet the girl with blonde hair, they met the man with the Great Dane and the big dog stood patiently while Fleck went round and round him, admiringly sniffing at each leg. Then they ran to the tree and found the hole and the pile of leaves and it was as though the park was already home.

Sunday was Olga's day off but today she stopped Hal as he came in and showed him a bone which he could have for Fleck. It was the right kind of bone, not splintery, and Fleck thanked her very beautifully. She had stopped being silent and surly, and Hal realized that she had just been lonely and sad, another thing the dog had made him understand. Apparently she had had a lot of animals at home in Kazakhstan and whenever she couldn't think of the name for whatever the animal was in English, she made the right noise – mooing and bleating and barking and hissing, till both she and Hal were doubled up with laughter.

"What on earth is going on here?" said Albina, coming in just as Olga was pretending to be a goat trying to swallow a bicycle tyre. Then she caught sight of Fleck, chewing his bone. "Oh, Hal, he'll make a mess on the floor. Don't bring him into the drawing room whatever you do."

In the afternoon Hal's parents had been invited to have tea with Sir Richard and Lady Dorothy Graham, who lived in a beautiful house in Richmond near the river, and had three children roughly Hal's age. They were perfectly behaved children, the kind that made Hal want to be sick.

"Only there's no question of taking the dog,"

said Albina. "Lady Dorothy's house is absolutely spotless – and anyway he'd make marks on the leather of the car."

Albina's Mercedes was upholstered in snow-white Moroccan leather and was the apple of Albina's eye.

"I'm not going without Fleck. Absolutely not," said Hal.

"Well, you can't stay here alone," said Albina.

But to everyone's surprise, Olga, who always had Sunday afternoon off, said she would take Hal to the shopping mall so that he could buy a ball and some toys for Fleck.

So Hal stayed, and had a lovely afternoon. He had not spent any of the birthday money from his Australian godmother and he and Fleck studied squeaky rubber ducks and balls of various sizes and plastic bones and clockwork mice. There were other people there choosing Sunday treats for their pets, and the girl with fair hair Hal had met in the park was buying hamster food.

"We have tea!" said Olga, to Hal's surprise, taking the girl by the arm. "You go ask mother – I have much cake."

So the girl, whose name was Hilary, came to tea and they played with Fleck and threw the squeaky toys for him and he rushed all over the house retrieving them. But when Hilary had gone, and he settled down for a nap in Hal's room, Fleck was not lying on the rubber duck which had been his favourite, but on Hal's blue face flannel which had slipped from the side of the washbasin on to the floor. And later, when Hal tried to take it from him, he produced his first attempt at a growl and fastened his teeth more firmly round his treasure.

This flannel, Fleck was saying, is now mine.

6

The Trick

Hal was in bed, his father was in his study – but Albina was on her hands and knees on the stairs, searching for dog hairs. Hal had promised he would clean up after the dog wherever he went, but now she could see a hair on the half landing, and something – possibly a speck of mud – on the bottom stair.

She gave a squeak of irritation and reached for the dustpan and brush she had brought. Olga could do it properly in the morning but the wretched maid always went to bed so early.

Thank goodness this was the last day of having a messy animal in the house. Tomorrow Fleck was going back to where he came from. She really couldn't have stood any more dirt and annoyance.

Going back into the house, Albina stored her dustpan and went to say goodnight to Hal. He was usually very quiet before she came in – but tonight there was the sound of running footsteps and shouting. He was having a game with the dog – and then came a crash as something fell to the floor.

She opened the door

"Oh Hal, not the night light! You know how expensive that was. It's a special design and the pieces are hand-made to go with the carpet."

She picked up the lamp. It was definitely ruined, the pieces bent. "I don't know how I shall ever replace it."

But Hal didn't seem to be sorry.

"You won't have to," he said cheerfully. "I don't need a night light any more. I don't care how dark it is now that I've got Fleck."

Going downstairs again, Albina went in search of her husband.

"I thought you said Hal would be bored with a

dog after two days. You promised me."

Donald was in his study. A small earpiece which connected him with head office in New York hung out of one ear. He hadn't heard a word she said.

Albina repeated her words. "Will you listen? I'm telling you, he isn't sick of the dog and you promised me he would be."

Donald switched off reluctantly.

"Well, whether he's sick of the dog or not, the animal goes back first thing. Make sure you get him there by ten o'clock, otherwise I have to pay for another day's rental. And see that you get all the deposit back. The chap who runs the place is the worst sort of shark."

Albina stared at him. "I'm not taking him back. You're taking him back."

"No, I'm not. I told you, I'm catching the six o'clock plane from Heathrow in the morning. I'm going to New York. I'll be halfway across the Atlantic before the Easy Pets place opens."

"Well, I think that's a bit much. What am I going to tell Hal?"

"Tell him anything you like – but not till the dog's safely back."

Albina was very angry. "It's all very well for you – having ideas and then flying off and leaving me to pick up the pieces. You do it all the time and I'm tired of it."

"If you think I like flying all over the world, you're mistaken. It's very exhausting. I do it so that you can have a beautiful home and all the clothes you need. If you weren't so extravagant. . ."

They began to quarrel. They were so used to quarrelling that they almost forgot what the quarrel was about. This one went on till it was time to go to bed – but by that time Albina had decided that she would get the maid, Olga, to take Hal to the dentist on the following morning – and while he was gone she would bundle the dog up and take him to Easy Pets. By the time Hal got back everything would be over. He would be upset, she could see that, so perhaps it might be an idea to take him shopping in the afternoon. Perhaps a new Scalectric set . . . or one of those miniature radios shaped like a piece of fruit. She had seen them in the Hamleys catalogue and they looked really cute.

The appointment with the dentist was at ten o'clock.

"Olga will take you," said Hal's mother on the following morning.

"Can I take Fleck? The receptionist is very nice;

she'll let me put him in the garden at the back."

"No, Hal, definitely not. No animals are allowed in the surgery, you know that."

"But—"

"That's enough, Hal. Go and clean your teeth and get ready. You can give Fleck a bone to eat while you're away."

Hal shook his head. "We've only got the kind left that splinters, but I'll stop off on the way back and get a good one. Marrow bones are best. Olga'll help me, she said." His eyes lit up. "And we could go and see if Fleck's basket has come in. The man in the pet shop said it might be in today."

He bent down to the dog and put his arm round him. "I won't be long, Fleck – and then we'll go into the park and go and see the tree and the drain . . . and maybe Hilary will be there."

Fleck wagged his tail and tried to lick Hal's face, but when Albina spoke sharply to him he whimpered and went to fetch his flannel. His eyes, as he watched the door close behind Hal, were dark pools of anxiety.

Something was wrong.

Hal came running in an hour later, already whistling for the dog as he opened the door. "Fleck," he called. "Fleck, I'm back!"

He waited for the yelps of welcome, the sound of toenails skittering over the marble floor of the entrance hall.

Silence.

Olga went to look in the kitchen. Hal raced through the house.

"His lead's gone. That must mean that Mummy's taken him out for a walk. I knew she'd get to like him. I knew it!"

Olga's face was grave.

"I make cocoa," was all she said.

It was nearly an hour before they heard the sound of the car, and then Albina got out. She had no lead, no small white dog . . . only some parcels.

Hal ran towards her. "You've got Fleck, haven't you?"

"No, Hal, I haven't. Fleck's gone back to where he came from."

Hal did not speak, but something had happened to his face that made Albina step back a pace.

"You mean you've taken him back to Easy Pets?"

"Yes, that's right. You see your father just rented him for the weekend. We could never put up with the inconvenience of a dog for longer than that, but we wanted to give you a treat."

"You're not going to fetch him back?" said Hal in a toneless voice. "It was just a trick you played on me?"

"Not a trick, Hal. We just wanted you to have a dog for a little while. You know how I feel about animals in the house. And I've bought you a present."

She handed him a gaudily wrapped box. The next second the box flew across the room and crashed into a vase on the ornamental chest.

"Oh Hal, look what you've done," shrieked Albina.

"It's what you've done," said Hal in a strange, grown-up voice. "That's what you want to think about."

And then he turned and went up to his room and shut the door.

7

Sorrow

The dogs in Room A were doing their best. They understood what had happened to Fleck: how he had felt about the boy who came to fetch him, and how the boy had felt about him, and now they did everything they could to cheer him up.

All of them had known sorrow. Francine still dreamed of the circus and the busy useful life she had led there. Honey, in her sleep, still raced over the heather-clad hills at the sound of her master's whistle. Otto had never stopped yearning for the peace of the monastery and the silent dignity of the monks. Li-Chee still waited for someone who would look into his fiery soul.

They had all hoped, as Fleck had hoped, that they would find a master worth serving – and had found only borrowers who came and went and did not care – but they were older and wiser than the little mongrel and they knew that one had to pull oneself together and make the best of things.

Fleck, in his cage, tried desperately to take in what they were telling him, but he was overwhelmed by grief. He lay with his head between his paws. His coat looked dead, his eyes were dull and he had eaten almost nothing since his return.

Kayley was working in the cubicle next door and whenever she could she came in to look at the Tottenham terrier. She had saved the blue flannel that had been clamped between Fleck's teeth when he was returned. Mr Carker did not allow it in the cage but fortunately the Carkers were away at a dog show looking for exotic dogs to buy and now she dipped it in Fleck's water bowl and moistened his mouth.

"You must try and drink," she told him. "You're still a young dog. This isn't the end of the world."

But she was lying and she knew it. Fleck's world had ended when the door of his cage shut behind him and Albina Fenton hurried away on her high heels.

"Please, Fleck, for all our sakes," said Kayley, stroking his weary head.

But Fleck only looked at her with his unequal eyes, and gave a desolate whimper which he quickly tried to repress, because he knew that Mr Carker did not approve of unhappiness.

Yet the daily round had to go on. Kayley went to hose down the yard, Otto was led away by a weedy man who wanted to impress his friends. Li-Chee went off to sit on the lap of yet another ancient lady . . . and Fleck rolled himself up into a dismal ball at the back of his cage and escaped into sleep.

"Is he any better?" asked Pippa, as soon as Kayley had taken off her coat.

Kayley shook her head. She was very tired.

"But that's ridiculous," said Pippa. "He can't go breaking his heart after only three days with someone. It isn't what happens."

"It has happened," said Kayley, and flopped into a chair.

She wasn't usually like that and Pippa, who thought the world of her sister, was angry.

"I expect the boy's forgotten all about him," said Pippa.

"No," said Kayley. "He won't have done. Some boys would have done but not this one. It was just one of those things."

Ralph, one of the twins, looked up from his homework and said it was like Romeo and Juliet. "They only saw each other for a moment on a balcony or something and that was it."

"How did it turn out?" asked Pippa.

"Badly," said Ralph. "Everybody died."

"Idiot!" said Pippa. She could see that Kayley was at the end of her tether. She poured her sister a cup of tea, but she was scowling. Things did happen that were over the top. There was the story of Greyfriars Bobby – a Skye terrier who wouldn't leave his master's grave and lay on his tombstone every night for eight years till he died too. It was supposed to have really happened – one could go to Edinburgh and see the grave.

"Well, if the boy hasn't forgotten about him, then he's just feeble. It's because he's rich, I suppose. Rich people are always wimps. I wouldn't let someone give me a dog and then take it away again. Not on your life."

"What could he do?" asked Kayley. "He's only a kid."

"He could steal Fleck," said Pippa. "That's what

I'd do. It wouldn't be proper stealing. It would be taking back what belongs to one."

But Kayley, remembering Hal, so small and well behaved beside his overbearing father, didn't think there was much likelihood of that.

"We'll have to leave for work very early on Sunday," she told her sister. "The Carkers will still be away. I must say I'll be glad of your help."

But Pippa meant to do more than just help. She meant to investigate.

"I'm going to ask Dr Rutherford to come and see Hal," said Albina, to her husband. He had just come back from Beijing, where he had done an important deal, and looked surprised.

"Is he ill?" he asked.

Albina looked annoyed. "I told you – he's off his food and he looks thoroughly peaky and he hardly speaks to me. School begins again on Monday. We can't send him back looking like something out of an orphanage."

"Oh well, I suppose it can't hurt to get him checked out," said Donald. "There's been a nasty flu bug around. I sat next to a man on the plane who kept sneezing. I hope I haven't caught anything."

When ordinary people want to see a doctor they

go to the surgery and wait for their turn, but Albina was too rich to be ordinary, and she had a private doctor who would come and see patients in their houses.

Dr Rutherford was elderly, with white hair and a pleasant face, and when he had examined Hal he asked Mrs Fenton to leave him to talk to Hal on his own.

"I can't find anything wrong with you physically," he said to the boy, "though of course if you don't eat you're going to get steadily weaker."

Hal shrugged. "It doesn't matter," he said. "There's nothing I have to do."

Dr Rutherford waited. "Nothing?" he said.

"No. Not now."

"But you did have? You did have something to do?"

"Yes."

But he wasn't going to talk to the doctor about Fleck, or the way his parents had betrayed him.

"Well, I'll leave you a tonic," said Dr Rutherford. He smiled. "That's what doctors do when they can't think of anything else. I think that what's the matter with you is in your mind, but if you don't want to speak about it, I won't force you."

Dr Rutherford went downstairs and found Albina waiting.

"Well? Did you find anything?"

Dr Rutherford put on his coat. "No. There is nothing physically wrong," he said. "But there is something wrong just the same. The boy is deeply unhappy. Perhaps you know why this might be so?"

Albina flushed. "No, I don't. Hal has everything a child could possibly need." Then, as the doctor looked at her steadily, "There was some fuss about a dog – we rented one for him, and he thought it was here to stay and when we took it back he became quite unmanageable."

"Ah. That would explain it," said Dr Rutherford. And suddenly there came into his mind the memory of a white bull terrier bitch he had owned as a boy. She had run up the sides of trees and hung off a branch with her teeth, like a piece of washing. When she died of old age he had hidden in the attic and cried for a week. "Well perhaps there is a way of undoing the damage," he told Albina. "You will have to look into your mind."

But Albina, when he left, did not look into her mind; she looked into the kitchen, where she had to prepare her own lunch because Olga the maid had had the nerve to give notice on the day that Fleck was returned.

"You do bad," she said to her employer. "You do bad thing. I go."

And she had left, even though she had no job to go to and Albina offered her more money if she stayed. Fortunately that afternoon, the three G aunts came to tea, and were shocked to hear of the uselessness of the doctor, coming on top of the impertinence of the maid.

"You know, Albina, I was wondering," said Geraldine. "Have you ever thought of sending Hal away to boarding school? I know you'd miss him but a change of scene is always a good idea."

"And he does seem to be getting rather spoiled. I mean he's been sulking now for nearly a week," said Glenda. "I tried to tell him that the dog would have forgotten him completely but I don't think he heard me."

"Of course you'd find it difficult without him," said Georgia. "But it's his good you want to be thinking of. And unless you mean to have another baby to keep him company. . .?"

Albina shuddered. "Oh no! No, I couldn't go through all that again. The nappies . . . and the screams. . ." She pondered what her friends had said. "I suppose he does need companionship. I'll talk to Donald."

Her husband said it would be very expensive. "Boarding schools cost the earth. But I suppose it would help to build his character. The fuss he's made about this silly dog business doesn't make one very cheerful about his future. If I gave way to my feelings every time I had an important deal to do, where would we be now?"

"Of course I'll miss him," said Albina. "I'll miss him very much. But he's so moody at the moment – and anyway I think we'll be moving house again soon. I've seen a place with a swimming pool in the basement – and a billiard room. Not that we play billiards, but you never know – so that'll keep me very busy."

Donald was not interested in Albina's plans for moving. He was used to shifting house every couple of years, just as he was used to changing his car, and his firm was expanding in the Far East. He'd be away even more, but he was glad that Hal would be somewhere settled.

Every man worth his salt wanted his children to have the best.

8

The Cottage by the Sea

"There's a postcard from Hal," said Alec Fenton, coming into the cottage and stamping the mud off his boots. It was only a few steps to the shore where he kept his dinghy but it had rained in the night and the path easily turned to mud.

His wife, Marnie, who was kneading bread at the kitchen table, wiped her hands and smiled with pleasure. "Let's have a look, then."

It was a long time since they had been to London

to visit Hal's parents, but they thought the world of their grandson.

Marnie read the card over her husband's shoulder.

"Well, that is good news! He's got a dog all for himself! I always said that was what Hal needed."

Alec nodded. "Growing up in that museum – it's no life for a boy."

He looked out of the cottage window. The tide was out, and the sand stretched in a golden curve to the water's edge. It was a quiet day and the islands were distinct: the big island, Farra, where the monks had lived in medieval times, the smaller low-lying island where their neighbour grazed his sheep, and the rocky outcrop where the seals came to breed. A cormorant dived from a rock and came up with a fish in his beak. The gulls circled. Alec's own boat, the Peggotty, was pulled up on the shore, ready for the evening's fishing.

"It looks as though Albina's seen the light," said Marnie, "if she's let him have a dog. Maybe we were hasty, thinking ill of her."

The visit that they had paid to Albina and their son had been such a wretched business that they had never gone back. They had been made to feel like the crudest peasants. Albina had raised her eyebrows when she saw their luggage, and said

"Really?" in a surprised voice when they said they'd prefer to sleep together in the one room rather than have the separate rooms she offered them.

"We've been together for thirty-five years," Alec had said. "We've no call to change now."

She had looked pained when Marnie went to the kitchen to thank the maid for the nice meal she had cooked, and pointed out that the maid was paid to do the cooking.

And their own son, Donald, had hardly been there. He was endlessly flying about, and driving about, and when he was at home he had things dangling from his ear the whole time so that he could talk to Moscow or New York instead of the people in the room.

Donald had been a nice, ordinary little boy. He'd helped his father with the lobster pots, and worked in the fields, and they had hoped he would take over the land and the boat when the time came.

But after he'd got a scholarship to a posh boarding school, Donald had changed. He'd made remarks about the cottage, how shabby it was, and how small, and asked why they didn't get a proper car instead of the wheezing old truck they used for everything – and he'd gone off to make his fortune in the south.

And he had made it all right. If living in a house

where the bath taps glittered so much that they gave you a headache, the food looked as though it was waiting to be photographed for a magazine and there wasn't a living thing in sight was what he wanted, he'd made it all right.

But Hal . . . Hal was different. He was the most loving, funny little boy. He and Marnie would have gathered him up and taken him away on the spot if they'd been allowed to. Even then they'd seen how lonely the little fellow was.

But now he'd be better. There was nothing like a dog for company. They only had their old Labrador now but they couldn't imagine life without a dog.

"Let's write him a letter and ask him if he can't come up to visit us and show us Fleck. Albina must have changed if she's let him have a dog. If Donald's too busy to bring him, there might be someone coming north and we could meet him."

So they wrote a letter to Hal, not just a postcard. It said they hoped he could come now he was older, and bring his dog. They said it wasn't a difficult journey. If he could get a train as far as Berwick they would meet him, and after that it was only half an hour's drive in the truck.

Hal got this letter on the day he went off with his mother to buy the clothes for boarding school.

9

Dog Rescue

Mr Carker put an advertisement for his Easy Pets business into the papers every month. The advertisements were very glossy and there were pictures of the particularly beautiful or rare dogs which could be hired. In the latest advertisement there was a mention of the Tottenham terrier, a new breed of which there were very few specimens in England, and it said that Easy Pets was the first rental agency which had such a dog on its books.

This advertisement was read by a Miss Gertie

Gorland, a tall, thin woman who lived with her brother Harold, who was also tall and thin.

The Gorlands ran a hotel by the seaside which was doing badly, and a steam laundry which was doing badly, and a delicatessen which was not only doing badly but had actually gone bust, and when they saw the advertisement they had a brainwave. "We could breed Tottenham terriers," said Gertie. "Set up a puppy farm. If they're so rare, people will pay fortunes for them."

So they went round to Easy Pets and arranged to hire out Fleck for a couple of hours. They wanted to make sure that this new breed was not fierce or liable to attack strangers.

When they saw Fleck they quickly stopped worrying about his fierceness. He was curled up in his cage and scarcely looked up when they came in – there is nothing like misery for making one tired – but when Kayley put on his collar and lead, he followed them dutifully out into the street. To tell the truth, he didn't care who he was with or where he was going.

The Gorlands hadn't gone far when they decided that the Tottenham terrier was not likely to catch on as a fashionable pet. No one stopped them and asked them where they had got that dear little dog, no heads turned – and out in the strong light they had to admit that the terrier was an odd-looking creature with his short legs and bat-like ears.

When they had walked for a while, Gertie said she was hungry, and Harold said he was hungry too. Tall, thin people need a lot to eat.

"We could see what he's like in crowded places," said Gertie, looking down at the dog.

So they turned into a well-known department store where there was a grand restaurant which permitted one to bring in dogs. The owners had been forced to do this because a lot of famous people ate there who refused to be parted from their pets.

When the waiter had shown them to their table, the Gormans put the loop of Fleck's lead under the leg of Gertie's chair, and when he had smelled the hundred or so pairs of uninteresting feet and the over-rich smells of the food, Fleck crawled under the table and went to sleep.

"I'm not being difficult," said Hal. "It's just that I don't mind whether I have a blue tuck box or a brown one. I would mind if I could, but I can't. It doesn't make any difference."

Albina sighed. "I don't know what to do with you. I'm spending a fortune to make sure you're properly kitted out for your new school, and you just stand there like a dummy."

They were in a famous department store, buying Hal's school uniform for Okelands. They had already bought four pairs of navy blue trousers, six white shirts, two striped ties and a cap with the Okelands motto on it. The motto was in Latin and usually Hal would have asked what it meant but now he didn't care. If it said, "Go Out and Kill People With a Hatchet" it wouldn't have mattered. Nothing mattered to Hal any more.

After the tuck box came the scarf and the blazer and the socks. . .

When everything had been paid for, Albina decided to go round the store. Although she didn't need a wedding dress she took Hal through the bridal department, and though she already had eighteen nightdresses she took him through lingerie, and though she never gardened, only got the maid to hose down the gravel, she went through the gardening department, fingering wheelbarrows and tubs of artificial roses.

In the jewellery department she bought herself a diamond bracelet, and after that she was in such a good mood that she said she would take Hal out to lunch in the restaurant which was famous for its exotic and unusual food. Hal had eaten there before and been sick afterwards but he followed his mother and the waiter to a table covered in a pink cloth, with a vase of lilies in the centre. The smiling waiters wore tailcoats and an orchestra played softly on a dais.

"Now isn't this nice," said Albina. She took the huge menu the waiter offered her and became absorbed in it.

"I think we'll have—" she began.

But she didn't go on.

Three tables away, Gertie was just dipping her spoon into her tomato soup when a kind of earthquake hit the store.

The Tottenham terrier who had been lost to the world leapt to his feet and pulled so hard at his lead that Gertie's chair fell over and she went crashing to the floor, followed by the plate of soup, which landed upside down on her blouse.

And as she lay kicking and screaming, Fleck took off.

This exhausted little dog who had hardly been able to put one foot in front of the other raced across the room like a bullet from a gun, passed the first table – felling a waiter who was carrying a tray of glasses and a bottle – and the second table, where a man tried to catch him and toppled over backwards, and crashed violently into the third . . .

. . . where a boy had jumped to his feet, knocking over the vase of flowers, which rolled on to the floor and tripped up a lady making her way to the toilet.

The head waiter, hurrying in through the double doors from the kitchen to see what had happened, found everyone screaming and complaining and mopping at their clothes. Everyone except a young boy and a small dog, who saw nothing but each other.

"It's absolutely extraordinary," said Albina to her husband when he came home that night. "They had to send for a security guard to carry the wretched dog away, howling and struggling, with his head twisted towards Hal. And yet Hal just sat in the taxi on the way home without any fuss. He didn't cry or anything, and he seems quite resigned to going away to school. He's asked if he can spend a night with Joel tomorrow to say goodbye. That was the friend he made in his first school – do you remember? Rather a common little boy, but I've said yes."

"Well, it looks as though he's growing up at last," said Donald. "We've obviously done the right thing, not letting him wear us down. I'll go and say goodnight to him."

Going up to his son's room, Donald saw that

Albina had been telling the truth. Hal seemed calm and quiet, he hardly mentioned having met Fleck in the restaurant, and said he was looking forward to going to school and that he was glad to have a chance to say goodbye to Joel.

And indeed Hal was calm and quiet, because he now knew exactly what he was going to do. One of the things which people had told him was that Fleck would have forgotten him. Well, they had been wrong about that, and it seemed to him that they were wrong about most of the things that mattered.

Hal was tired of living in a grown-up world. It was time to make his own world where things were right and fair and as they ought to be.

Mr Carker was in a towering rage. He stamped through his office, cursing and swearing. The restaurant had sent in a huge bill for the damage that the little dog had done. Gertie Gorland was suing him for the price of her blouse, which had been entirely ruined by soup. The businessmen whose suits had been damaged when the waiter's tray fell on them were asking for hundreds of pounds to buy new ones, and the lady who had fallen on her way to the toilet was going to send him her medical bills.

"I won't have it," raged Mr Carker. "I'll fight everyone. I won't pay a penny to those rogues! As for that blasted dog, he's out of his mind. It's probably inbreeding – you get that in these pedigree animals."

He sent for the vet and told him to give Fleck an injection which would keep him quiet till he had decided what to do with him, after which he and Mrs Carker set off for a nice weekend in Brighton to get over the strain of the last few days. Kayley would see to the dogs on Sunday. She always did.

But on Sunday morning, Kayley woke with a temperature, a sore throat and a splitting headache.

"You've got flu," said her mother. "And you're not going to work."

"I have to," said Kayley. "Pippa can't manage everything on her own and she's got all her stuff to get ready."

Pippa was going off to spend a week at school camp on the following day.

But when Kayley tried to sit up in bed, the room spun round and she was forced to lie down again.

"Of course I can manage on my own," said Pippa, looking mulish. "I know exactly what to do and you know it."

"It's too much," Kayley repeated.

But by this time, Pippa was halfway out of the door.

All the same, Kayley was right. There was a terrible lot to do.

On Sundays there were no rentals; the dogs spent the morning in the compound while the rooms were cleaned, the cages swept, the water bowls rinsed out and the carpets hoovered. In the afternoon the dogs were taken back to their cages for a couple of hours while the yard was hosed down and the bedding in their sleeping quarters changed and the food prepared.

By four o'clock Pippa was exhausted. There were only the dogs in Room A now to be taken back, and the burglar alarm to be put on and she could go home. Otto and Francine and Honey and the little Peke sat quietly in their cages, but Fleck was stretched out barely conscious after his injection. Pippa had had to carry him in from the compound and she felt such rage that if Mr Carker had come in then she would have throttled him. It was for being loving and faithful that the little dog had been punished.

As she bent down to his cage, Pippa heard a noise coming from the office next door. It sounded as though the door from the street was being opened, and by someone who did not want to be heard.

The alarm was not switched on yet. Pippa waited

till the sound came again. Then she pounced.

"Got you!" she said, bursting through the door.

The boy she had surprised was about her own age, a slight, fair boy wearing a rucksack and carrying a canvas holdall.

Pippa stared. At the same time from next door came the sound of Fleck whimpering in his drugged sleep, and suddenly Pippa knew.

"You're the boy who had Fleck," she said. "Hal, is that your name?" She looked more closely. "Have you come to steal him?"

Hal wasted no time.

"Yes," he said. "And you're not going to stop me."

"I never said I was. But have you got a proper plan?"

Hal nodded. "My parents think I'm staying with a school friend but I'm going to take the night train to the Scottish border. You can buy a ticket for a dog. I've got money. My grandparents live there. They'll take us in, I know they will."

"Well, that sounds all right. But I warn you, you'll have to carry Fleck at first."

Hal's face went white. "Is he hurt?"

"No. But that charming Mr Carker ordered him to have an injection to keep him quiet. Come on, we'd better hurry. I've got his flannel – you'd better take that. Thank goodness my sister's not here. She's one of those good people. She can't help it; she thinks you mustn't break the law."

"I used to be like that," said Hal.

He followed her into the room and bent over Fleck's cage. Hal had no eyes for anyone except Fleck, but the other dogs got to their feet, quivering with curiosity and excitement . . . and then with despair.

For they knew what was going to happen. Fleck's story was going to end happily. His master had returned and was gathering him up to take him out into the world. Fleck was going to be free.

Otto was as devoid of envy as any dog but his whole body trembled with longing. Francine had pushed her muzzle right up to the bars and her black eyes were full of grief. Grunts of frustration came from the Peke.

Hal, lifting up his sleeping dog, saw none of this. But Pippa saw it. She had grown up with these dogs and she knew them like she knew her own brothers.

"Let me know when you get there," she said. She scribbled her name and phone number on a piece of paper and Hal put it in his pocket.

"Thank you," he said. "I won't forget."

It was very quiet when Hal had gone. Time to take

the other dogs back to the compound and put on the burglar alarm. Time to go home.

But Pippa did not move. She was looking at Otto, still trembling with longing, at the anguish in the collie's eyes. . .

And she was their jailer. Hal, whom she had despised as rich and feeble, had freed his dog, but not she. She was dooming them to imprisonment, to sitting there like toys, day after day, waiting to be claimed.

The dogs expected nothing. They only looked. Then Otto moaned once softly – and suddenly Pippa went mad. She marched over to the cages and one by one she undid the catches and threw wide the doors. Then she opened the door into the office and the one out into the street.

"You can go," she told the dogs.

And they understood her. Otto waited for a moment to lick her hand; Honey rubbed her head against Pippa's skirt, saying thank you.

Then they were gone.

Only Queen Tilly stayed in her cage, though the door was open. Freedom did not interest this spoilt creature. Later she began to complain because her hot water bottle had gone cold, but there was nobody left to hear her. Nobody at all.

10

And Then There Were Five

Hal's arms were getting tired. He had not expected to have to carry his dog to King's Cross station. He had bought a map and learnt the route from Easy Pets and it shouldn't have taken more than an hour to walk, but that was when he thought that Fleck would be trotting at his heels.

To begin with the little dog was just a dead weight, but now he was beginning to stir in Hal's arms. His back leg twitched once, then again, and

Hal turned into a small park with a fountain and sat down on the rim. It was dusk, and the people were all leaving. Soon the street lights would be lit.

The panic Hal had felt when he found Fleck stretched out in his cage had died down. Pippa had told him that he would recover, and Pippa knew about dogs. Now he laid Fleck down across his lap and began slowly, steadily to stroke his back.

"Please wake up," he begged his dog. "Please."

And it worked. The injection was wearing off and now Fleck turned and opened his eyes – and then he looked at Hal. Looked and looked with his dark right eye and his gold-flecked left eye, trying to believe what he was seeing. He gave a ghost of a whimper and then another. He was still too weak to do more than faintly move his tail, but as he took in that he was really there, where he needed to be, he began carefully to lick Hal's wrist. He licked it steadily, thoroughly, making sure that everything was as clean as it ought to be.

Then he began on the other one. No piece of skin was left unwashed; every inch was cared for. Only when he had made certain that everything was as it should be did his tail start to wag, slowly at first, then fast, and faster . . . and from his throat came a burst of ecstatic barks.

333

And Hal held him close and told him that he would never leave him again. Never.

"I swear it, Fleck," said Hal to his dog. "No one will come between us ever again, do you hear me?"

Fleck heard him. He became very quiet, and sighed, and buried his head in Hal's chest and slept once more.

At first the four dogs Pippa had let out simply ran. They bounded down the long straight street which led away from Easy Pets, feeling the strength in their legs and the breeze blowing through their coats. Li-Chee had to take four steps to one of theirs, but even with his bandy legs he kept up.

They were free! No one tugged at their leads, shouted at them, pulled them away from whatever it was that they wanted to see or smell or touch. They had dreamed of running like this so often as they slept, their limbs twitching – and woken to face another day of sitting in their cages.

When they had run the length of the shopping street, they came to a row of houses with gardens. One of the garden gates was open. The patch of lawn was messy and rough; there were no flowers in the flower beds. It was exactly right for what they needed to do.

Francine went first, rolling and rubbing and rolling again. Then Honey followed, and Otto and Li-Chee. They rolled and turned and crawled on their stomachs, rubbing themselves as hard as they could against the scratchy grass. They pushed their faces into the earth. From time to time they stopped, their tongues lolling from the effort, and grinned at each other.

And it worked! Gradually the loathsome scents that had been sprayed on the dogs at Easy Pets disappeared, blotted out by earth and grass and mouldy leaves and comforting compost. The last whiffs of "Mountain Glory" left Otto's thick coat, the vile odour of Francine's "Dark Dancer" coiled up and was wafted away. Honey's horrible "Heather Mist" and Li-Chee's "Lotus Blossom" were extinguished. They sniffed each other blissfully, making sure that they smelled as they should smell once again: of dog. But now someone came out of the house shouting and shooing.

"Get out!" he said. "Get out of my garden at once."

The dogs looked at him. They would have liked to thank him for the use of his garden but he didn't seem to want to be thanked so they trotted out of the gate and into the street.

Now that they were rid of the ghastly, gooey scents which had plagued them, they could really enjoy the smells they came across. Spices from a distant kebab shop . . . pigeons on the roof . . . worm casts in a tub . . . an old shoe caught in a drain . . . dust and the sour smell of spilled milk from a doorway . . . cats which had passed by, of course . . . tom cats, kittens . . . a dead mouse in a gutter. . .

They had never been allowed to spend long enough at a lamp post, with its whirligig of amazing odours, before someone had yanked them back.

Then suddenly Otto stood stock-still and called the others. They came at once because what Otto had discovered was obviously important. They had caught the smell of a hundred pairs of feet, and of more dogs than they could count, but the smell which now came to them was familiar. It belonged to the boy who had come to Easy Pets to take away his dog. Now, as they put their noses together, they could smell the dog. It was Fleck, the small white mongrel who had been their friend.

They waited no longer. Their noses down, their tails up, they set off down the road, across a zebra crossing, and into a small park with a fountain.

*

Everybody now felt fine except for Hal. Fleck had greeted his friends with enthusiasm, barking and wagging his tail from the security of Hal's lap. The four dogs who had been freed from Easy Pets felt fine too. It was good to see the little terrier again, and though roaming free through the town had been interesting, it was comforting to find a human whom they could trust. They settled themselves at Hal's feet, ready to do his bidding, and Li-Chee, who was really very tired, closed his eyes and had a nap.

But Hal was desperate. He hadn't been able to believe his eyes when the Easy Pets dogs came bounding across the park towards him. What should he do now? The dogs must have escaped after Pippa left, which meant she would get into trouble, but he couldn't think of that now. Nor could he take the dogs back. The risk that there would be someone there who would make him give Fleck back was far too great.

"Go home," Hal said, trying to sound firm. "Go on – go home!" and he waved his arms in the direction of the street.

The dogs just looked at him. Otto's ears twitched; Francine blinked. Humans did make odd remarks like that sometimes. It was best to take no notice. Where was home? Certainly not the place they had come from. Not one of them moved.

And why should they? thought Hal. What kind of "home" was Easy Pets for a self-respecting dog? But he had to get Fleck to King's Cross. The train left at nine-thirty and it was the last one of the night. Surely if he began to walk they would make their own way back?

He put Fleck down on the ground, and clipped on his collar and lead. It was awful to leave the dogs to fend for themselves but he had to get Fleck away before anyone noticed that he was gone.

He began to walk towards the gates of the park. Fleck could walk quite well now, with only a slight drunken lurch. The effects of the injection were almost gone. And a few paces behind, quietly and without fuss, came Otto and Francine, Honey and Li-Chee. A drunk carrying a bottle came towards them, and Otto's hackles rose. He growled in his throat, and the drunk retreated. Not only was Otto accompanying them, but he had set himself up as a bodyguard.

Following his map, Hal walked the streets of London with his Tottenham terrier – and a few paces behind, correct and obedient, came the four dogs who had broken free. Every so often Hal stopped and said, "Go home, go on. Go!" and they looked at him politely, waiting till he should set off again. They were no trouble; stopping at zebra crossings, talking to any other dogs they met only briefly before catching up again with Hal. Fleck's tail was high with pride, for not only was he reunited with his master, but he was enjoying the company of his friends.

They reached King's Cross at last. Fleck was overwhelmed by the throng of people, and Hal picked him up as he made his way to the ticket office.

"Go home, please," he said for the last time to the four dogs who were following him, but they only pressed closer on his heels because there were smells and sounds there that were most unappealing to self-respecting dogs. Someone was being sick; a group of people in funny hats were shouting and hiccupping and singing stupid songs. The dogs looked at Hal with their innocent eyes, wondering why they were there, but they trusted him to do his best even in this loathsome place.

Hal was desperate. He carried Fleck to the queue for the ticket office, and the four dogs queued also, silent and well behaved. Even if he'd had the money to buy tickets for the four escapees, he couldn't have done it. The regulations said a passenger was allowed to bring only one dog on to the train.

"Yes?" said the ticket clerk impatiently.

"A single to Berwick on Tweed and one for the dog," said Hal, laying his money on the counter.

He took his ticket and the one for Fleck. The train was on platform seven. There weren't many trains now. He made his way along the almost empty platform, and the dogs, full of trust, came after him.

Hal knew there was only one thing to do. Getting Fleck away safely was a matter of life and death. He would get on the train and shut the door quickly and then – he was sure – the other dogs would go away. In the morning, when he reached Berwick, he would ring Pippa and tell her what had happened and she could organize a search for the dogs. Nothing terrible could happen to them in one night.

He got into his carriage and put Fleck down on the floor. Then he climbed in after him and turned to shut the door. The four dogs were still on the platform, looking up at him trustingly, but he hardened his heart.

"Come on, Fleck," he said, and made his way to his seat.

"The nine-thirty service for Berwick and Edinburgh is now ready to depart from platform seven," said a voice over the loudspeaker.

Doors slammed shut. The guard gave his signal. The train began to move.

The phone went at six o'clock in the morning and Pippa ran into the hall and lifted the receiver. It would probably be from Alison, the friend she was meeting so that they could go to school together. Everybody was assembling there to wait for the bus which would take them to the camp in the New Forest.

But it was not Alison.

"Is that Pippa?" said a faint voice.

"Yes. Who's that?"

"It's Hal."

"Goodness! Have you got to your grandparents' already?"

"No, I haven't." Hal's voice sounded strained and worried. "I'm still here. I'm in London because an awful thing's happened. All the dogs that were in the room with Fleck have escaped, and they caught up with me and won't go away. I'd got on the train, I was all ready to go, but they just sat on the platform and looked and waited. They were sure I was going to take them too. I tried to ignore them but I couldn't, so I got off the train again and spent the night in a freezing shed at the back of a building

341

site. It was horrible. There was a Rottweiler guarding it but Otto just talked to him and he let us in. Only you've got to come and take the dogs back, Pippa. You've got to."

Pippa's mind was racing. "Where are you? Tell me exactly."

"I'm in Mortland Square. There's a patch of grass and a war memorial. I can wait here for a while but people are beginning to stare. It's off the North Road."

"All right. I know it. Just stay there. Don't move, whatever you do. Tell them you're waiting for their owners or something."

She put down the phone. Kayley was still asleep. She'd been asleep the previous night too when Pippa came back. Pippa's rucksack was packed, there was only her toothbrush to put in and the packet of sandwiches her mother had made the night before. She crept to the kitchen and took it from the fridge and added some cold sausages and half a loaf of bread. Then she hurried to the sitting room and turned on the computer and printer and wrote a note to her teacher to say that she had flu and would be unable to come to camp, and signed it with her mother's name. Her mother's handwriting was easy to copy.

"Did I hear the phone?" said Mrs O'Brian sleepily as Pippa crept in to say goodbye.

"Yes. It was Alison to say we're to meet half an hour earlier. I'll have to be off."

She hugged her mother and let herself out of the house. When she reached Alison's house she dropped the letter in and hurried on to the bus stop. She was sorry to miss the camp but Hal was obviously going to make a thorough mess of things if she didn't get there to put him right.

Hal looked cold and peaky and there was a smutty stain on his cheek, but the dogs seemed to be in fine fettle. They greeted her rapturously, tails rotating like windmills. Francine gave her a paw; Honey rubbed her nose against Pippa's leg.

Pippa opened her rucksack.

"We'd all better eat something," she said. "Cold sausages aren't good for dogs, but they'll have to do."

The sausages did very well, wolfed down by all five of the dogs, and Pippa and Hal shared the sandwiches. Hal was beginning to feel a bit better. The night on the filthy floor of the hut had taken it out of him.

"We'll get a hot drink in a minute," said Pippa.

And then: "I think I better tell you what happened to the dogs. They didn't escape. I let them out. On purpose."

Hal stared at her. She went on. "Suddenly I couldn't bear to see them in their cages like that, when Fleck was going to be free. It was a sort of brainstorm, I suppose. Really stupid. Anything could have happened to them, but it didn't. They found you so that's all right."

"But it isn't all right," said Hal frantically. "I must get away. I think I may be able to change my ticket – I'm not sure – but I can't take the others. You simply have to take them back."

"Well I'm not going to," said Pippa firmly, zipping up the rucksack, "so you can forget that absolutely."

Fleck was in his usual position on Hal's lap and Hal gathered him and held him very close.

"My parents will find I'm gone in a few hours and then it will all begin. And I tell you if they try to take Fleck away again, I'll kill them, and no one wants to kill their parents."

"Never mind your parents," said Pippa. "What about your grandparents? The people you're escaping to. What are they like? Describe them."

"They're very kind and . . . quiet but not soft at all. They're like . . . it sounds silly, but like trees, or earth . . . things that are just there and you don't think about them but it would be awful if they were gone."

`"And you're sure that they'd take you in, you and Fleck?"

"Yes. They've always thought I should have a dog and they live by the sea in Northumberland where there's lots of space. They wouldn't just send us back, I'm sure."

Pippa was fiddling with the strap of her rucksack. Otto had come to sit beside her and was resting his head on her shoulder. "And what about the others?" She waved her hand at the four dogs sitting round in a companionable silence. "Would they take them in too?"

This was difficult. "I don't know," said Hal slowly. "They live in a small cottage and my parents are always saying how poor they are . . . but I don't believe they'd send the dogs back to Easy Pets once they knew what it was like. I don't know, but I don't believe they would."

"Well, that settles it," said Pippa. "We'll come with you. We'll all go to Northumberland."

Hal stared at her. "But how? I've hardly any money left and they won't let us take all the dogs on the train."

"Then we won't go by train. We'll walk and get

lifts on lorries or on anything we can get to take us. You'll see," said Pippa, getting to her feet. "We'll get a map as soon as the shops open. But it can't be too difficult. After all, one thing is certain about Northumberland. It must be in the north."

11

Hal Has Gone

Albina was sitting by the telephone. She was as pale as death and every so often she let out a little moan. Gloria sat beside her, ready to take over when Albina had to go to the lavatory so that the phone was never left unattended. Geraldine was manning the coffee machine in the kitchen.

The Fentons were waiting for word from the kidnappers who held Hal. Any moment now they would ring and demand an enormous ransom for the boy – and then Hal would be returned. Donald had sent out for thousands of pounds in cash. It was in a pouch in the hall guarded by Glenda so that they could drive it instantly to wherever the kidnappers wanted to meet them.

If they were willing to pay enough, Hal would be returned, they told themselves again and again. Everything would surely come right, if the money was there. Even in their distress and fear for Hal, the Fentons found it hard to believe that money wasn't the answer to everything.

It was three hours now since they had rung Joel's parents to tell them to send Hal home, and heard that Hal had not been with them – that they had no idea where he was.

Albina's terrified shriek had brought Donald running, and half an hour later the house filled with policemen. Donald had been angry because they were ordinary constables, not high-ranking detectives, and he'd made so much fuss that a second squad car arrived with an inspector and a sergeant.

The police had searched the house, examined Hal's belongings, taken photographs and removed items from the bathroom for DNA testing.

And they had asked questions, some of which had annoyed the Fentons very much.

"Is there anything that was upsetting your son?" they had wanted to know. "Anything that might make him think of running away?"

Even in the midst of their grief, Hal's parents had been very angry.

"Certainly not. Hal had everything a boy could want," said Albina.

"You say he was going away to boarding school. Could he have been frightened of that?"

"No. Definitely not." Both Hal's parents were certain. "He said only yesterday how much he was looking forward to it. And you can see," repeated Albina, waving her hands at the heaped-up toys in Hal's room, "he had everything a boy could want. He wouldn't run away."

"I tell you the boy's been kidnapped," said Donald. "Everyone knows we're well off. You must get a lead on that – and make it clear that we'll pay any ransom. The sky's the limit."

But the infuriating policemen had insisted on going through the routine procedures and getting the names of all the people they wanted to question: Joel's parents, Hal's school friends, people in the shops.

"Was there anyone else working here in the house?" asked the superintendent.

"There was a maid, a foreigner. But she won't

know anything. Unless she's in league with the kidnappers. She was a most impertinent woman."

A policeman took down Olga's address. Their slowness infuriated Donald.

"For God's sake! Surely you know how to track down kidnappers? They're probably a well-known gang. They could be hacking off his ear." He broke off and turned his head away. All the ghastly things he had seen on television swam before him. "I'll offer a hundred thousand pounds' reward for any information," he went on. "Make sure you put that up everywhere."

"Best hold on a minute, sir. We don't want everybody coming in with cock and bull stories. Not till we've finished our enquiries."

So now they had gone, leaving Donald desperate and fuming.

"They're hopeless. You can tell. It's all plod, plod. I'm going to hire a private detective. Mackenzie had one when his wife lost her jewels. He said he was very professional. Cost the earth, but that's all to the good. You can't get the best on the cheap."

Donald went to look up the names of private detectives, and poor Albina sat by the telephone, weeping and waiting for word from the kidnappers while Gloria and Glenda and Geraldine made coffee and brought her clean handkerchiefs. But the hours passed and no word came.

The first thing Kayley heard when she came down the street towards the Easy Pets building was Queen Tilly screaming.

"Oh heavens, what's happened?" said Kayley and began to run.

She was still ill and shouldn't have been coming to work at all. Her mother had tried to stop her but without success: there was no one else to see to the dogs.

The side door which led into her office was unlocked. The burglar alarm was off.

Kayley's heart was thumping now. What was Queen Tilly doing in her daytime cage when she should have been asleep with the others out in the compound at the back? And why were the doors of the other cages wide open?

Queen Tilly, seeing her, screamed even louder. Her hot water bottle had been cold for hours and she had an itch on her back. Tilly never scratched her own back; she waited till somebody came and gave her a body rub.

But today, Kayley, who always spoke so gently to the dogs, just said, "Shut up, for goodness' sake," and hurried out to the yard. What had happened to the other dogs in Room A? Where were Otto and Francine and Li-Chee and Honey? And where was Fleck?

It didn't take long for her to find out that the dogs were gone. She searched the sleeping quarters, the other rooms, every nook and cranny of the Easy Pets building, whistling and calling, but there was no sign of them.

An hour later, Mr and Mrs Carker sat in their office, scowling at the policemen who had come to investigate, and scowling at Kayley.

"It's a tragedy. An outrage," said Mr Carker. "Five of my most valuable dogs stolen! What do I pay for if not the protection of the police, eh? Tell me that!"

Kayley sat scrunching her handkerchief into a ball. She had been crying and looked completely exhausted, and the youngest of the policemen glanced at her and shook his head.

She had answered their questions as truthfully as she could, but she had not told them everything. It was clear to her that Pippa had forgotten to put on the burglar alarm and as a result the thieves had been able to get in and steal the dogs. And she would not give Pippa away. Her sister was too young to be in that kind of trouble.

"I must have forgotten," she said when she was questioned about the alarm. "I wasn't feeling very well." The police could see that this was true. The girl shouldn't have been at work at all.

But Mr Carker was busy telling the superintendent how valuable the dogs were.

"The St Bernard was bred specially for me in Switzerland," lied Mr Carker. "He must be worth a cool three thousand pounds. And the poodle won best in show in Paris. I've refused a fortune for her. Every dog in that room is priceless. One of them was a new breed, a Tottenham terrier. He's just been registered by the Kennel Club. I've had a stampede of people trying to buy him off me, but I wouldn't sell."

The policeman who had been recording what Mr Carker said looked up. "What about that bald little yelper?" he asked. "The Mexican hairless? She was in the same room as the others, wasn't she? Is she worth anything?"

"I'll say she is," said Mr Carker. "She's the most valuable one of the lot."

"I wonder why they didn't take her then," said the inspector – and the youngest policeman, who had met Queen Tilly, grinned and said under his breath, "I could guess why not."

Routine investigations took up the next couple

353

of hours – fingerprints, paw marks, door locks, statements. . .

"We'll let you know, sir," the superintendent said to Mr Carker. "And we could take the young lady home. She obviously isn't well."

"Oh no, no," said Kayley. "I've got a lot to do."

But when the police had gone, Mrs Carker turned to her. "I'm afraid you'll lose your job over this. We can't have someone so careless in charge of thousands of pounds' worth of dogs."

Kayley looked at her with brimming eyes. She could not imagine life without the dogs.

But Mr Carker gave his wife a look. Kayley was paid half of what they would have to pay anybody else. And all the stolen dogs were heavily insured. He wasn't going to lose any money, and that was all that mattered.

"You can stay till we find someone to take your place," he said.

So Kayley went on working though she was ill, though her heart felt like breaking when she thought of the five dogs who had been her friends, and though she was worried sick about Pippa, who would be in such terrible trouble if the truth came out.

Just as the awful day was coming to an end,

Donald decided to ring his father and mother up in Northumberland. After all, they were Hal's grandparents. They had a right to know.

Alec and Marnie were already in bed when the phone rang, but Alec padded downstairs, stepped over old Meg, the Labrador, and picked up the phone. He hated the telephone, and a call late at night could only be unwanted news.

But it was worse than he could have imagined.

"Hal's been kidnapped?" he repeated – and took a deep breath because the room was spinning round.

Donald told him what had happened.

"The police think he might have run away, but that's complete nonsense. I've got the name of a detective to put on the case. He's supposed to be very good. He ought to be at that price."

"How's Albina taking it?"

"Badly, of course. She won't go to bed, just sits by the phone."

"Poor lass. You'll let us know the minute you hear anything, won't you?"

"Of course."

Donald was about to hang up when his father asked one more question. "Was the dog with Hal when he disappeared?"

"What dog?"

"Fleck. He wrote to tell us he had a dog."

"No, no. That was days ago. We took the dog back. It was only out on hire. Hal didn't mind. He made a fuss at first and then he forgot all about him. He was excited about going away to school."

Alec went upstairs very slowly. He thought about saying nothing to Marnie but he'd never been much good at concealing things from his wife.

"What is it?" she asked. "Come on, it's bad news I know."

Alec told her.

"Donald is sure the boy's been kidnapped, but I wonder."

They sat up in bed, very close together, trying to bear what seemed to be unbearable – that Hal was missing and in danger.

"What exactly did Donald say?" Marnie wanted to know.

She listened carefully while Alec repeated his conversation with his son.

"Well, there's one thing in all that that's nonsense," said Marnie. "There's no way Hal has forgotten about the little dog."

"That's what I thought," said Alec.

After a while they gave up all attempt at sleeping and went downstairs and made a pot of tea. They sat with it while the night turned gradually paler, thinking about the boy they saw so rarely and loved so much. And old Meg lay with her head resting on Alec's feet and kept watch also.

12

The Murgatroyd Family Wedding

The children had walked for several hours and it seemed as though London would never end. They were no nearer a road where lorries might slow down and give them a lift. Hal had had no sleep and very little food. He was completely exhausted, and even Pippa was secretly wondering if they should give up.

They reached a big petrol station with a café attached. It was part of a concourse and was completely jammed with a row of cars and lorries and caravans which seemed to belong together.

The children flopped down on a bench by a messy ornamental pool and the dogs had a drink. From the lorries and caravans came unexpected noises – the stamping of hooves, the sound of a parrot squawking, snatches of music. On some of the caravans were red circles and a picture of a clown's head. Scrawled on the sides were the names of the places they were going to: Todcaster, Berwick, Aberdeen. . . And above them, in big letters: Henry's Circus for Today.

"Why is it a Circus for Today?" Hal wondered, and Pippa said it was because they were only allowed to have animals that did tricks anyway, like dogs and horses, not lions or tigers or sea lions.

"They tried having circuses without any animals at all but no one went to them so they brought back all the animals that are tame already."

Wandering between the caravans were gaily dressed people, and mechanics in grease-stained overalls. A woman in a red shawl carried a baby in her arms. Now there was a sort of stirring and everyone began to go back to their cars or caravans. The circus, it seemed, was getting ready to move on.

It was at this moment that they noticed that Francine was missing.

It was an awful moment. The dogs had kept together throughout the journey; the children had hardly needed to check where they were. Now, though they called and searched, the poodle was nowhere to be seen.

"Find her," said Pippa to the other dogs. "Come on, Otto, you're a rescue dog. Find Francine."

The dogs put their heads down. It was difficult with so many smells coming from the parked vehicles, not to mention fumes from the petrol pumps. Then Otto took off towards a trailer parked near the end of the row and galloped round to the other side. They all followed him – and stopped dead.

At first they just thought they were seeing double. There was not one black poodle on the grassy verge, there were two. The second poodle was black like Francine and clipped in the same way – he could have been her twin – but as they stared they saw that he was slightly bigger, and a male.

But it was what the two dogs were doing that made them gaze with open mouths.

The dogs were dancing. Not tottering about on their hind legs as dogs sometimes do, but properly, beautifully dancing to the sound of an accordion played by a tall man in overalls. They pirouetted, they turned, they looked into each other's eyes, held by the music. The big male poodle was absorbed, but Francine was transformed; her eyes shone, her head tilted to catch every drop of sound. They could see how happy she was, how exactly where she wanted to be.

The man put down the accordion and picked up a hoop that had been lying on the grass and held it up. He was a big man; the hoop was high. The male poodle went first, flying through it effortlessly. Then, without a moment's hesitation, Francine followed.

Even in mid-air, with her ears blown back by the breeze, she seemed to be smiling with pleasure.

But now the man had caught sight of them.

"Well, well," he said, "that's one of the best trained dogs I've seen. She's got the measure of Rupert all right. I didn't have to tell her anything; she just took off. Looks as though she was trained by Elsa. You can always tell Elsa's dogs; they've got that natural look."

Pippa nodded. "Yes, that's right," she said, to Hal's amazement.

"And this'll be her new act?" said the man, looking at the other dogs. "Trust Elsa to train a St Bernard; they hate the noise and fuss of a circus usually.

But Elsa could train a brain-dead earthworm. You travelling with her?"

"Yes. She's our aunt. Well, sort of. . ." said Pippa, while Hal continued to stare at her.

The man grinned. "'Sort of' is right – she must be on her fifth husband. But what's she doing here? Last time I heard she was doing the season in Bournemouth."

"I'm afraid that fell through," said Pippa.

"Oh it did, did it? Well that's a piece of luck for us. We need a dog act. Petroc's Poodles have let us down – Petroc's had to go to hospital. I'm just looking after Rupert here till he gets back." He gestured to the poodle standing very close to Francine. "But where's Elsa's van? I didn't see it come in."

"It broke down," said Pippa. "There was a sort of horrible scraping noise. Elsa wasn't at all pleased."

"I bet she wasn't. Swearing fit to bust, I'll wager."

"Yes, she was. She told us to come on ahead and tell you."

"Did she then?" said the man, whose name was George. "Well, we're just off. You'd better jump in that lorry over there for now. There's plenty of room and it's full of hay. We'll sort you out when we get there. Wait till I tell Mr Henry – he'll be over the moon, Elsa's dogs falling into his lap like that."

He had a word with the driver and let down the tailboard. The children climbed aboard and so did the dogs – except for Francine, who stood still and looked at Rupert, while Rupert looked at her.

"Come on, Francine," called Pippa.

But the two poodles just stood very close together and did not move.

"All right, you can go with them," said George to Rupert, and the two dogs jumped in together and lay down side by side.

"How can you tell all those lies?" asked Hal when they were under way. "You must be mad."

"They're not lies," said Pippa. "They're stories."

"I can't see the difference," said Hal.

"That's silly! If you're reading a book with people having adventures you don't think you're reading a lot of lies. You're just glad there's something going on."

Hal was not reassured. Elsa with her five husbands and her bad language sounded absolutely terrifying.

"I expect she carries a whip and cracks walnuts with her teeth," he said.

But, as Pippa pointed out, they were driving steadily in just the direction that they wanted to go.

"Todcaster's only thirty miles south of Berwick. You said nothing mattered except getting Fleck to your grandparents and that's exactly what we're doing."

And she leant back against a hay bale and closed her eyes and went to sleep.

It was almost dark before they reached Todcaster, the first town in which the circus was to perform. It was an industrial town surrounded by moorland and as the children tumbled out of the lorry they could feel the slight chill in the air which meant that they were truly in the north.

George was with them almost straightaway.

"Haven't heard anything from Elsa, have you?" he asked, and Pippa said no.

"Aunt Elsa doesn't believe in mobile telephones because she read somewhere that they give you canker of the ear."

George shook his head. "Daft as a brush; she always was. Still, we need a dog act and hers will be the best. I suppose we'd better fix you up with somewhere to sleep in case she doesn't make it till morning. The dogs can sleep in the lorry, but you'll want somewhere a bit more comfortable."

He went off and came back with a nice round-faced woman whom he introduced as Myra.

"She's got a big caravan. You can kip down with her just for one night."

"That's right. There's room for two little ones," said Myra. "We brought up four kids in our camper."

It turned out that Myra was a fortune teller. When the circus came to rest she smartened up her caravan and put on her hooped earrings and her purple headscarf and told people what was going to happen to them. She called herself Mystic Myra and was very popular because she never told people anything nasty.

"It's not that I believe in it," she told the children. "It's a load of codswallop if you ask me, but it does no harm and every little helps where money's concerned."

Myra's husband was called Bill. He'd been a sword swallower, but one day when he was doing his act, two swords had become crossed in his insides and he'd been rushed off to hospital to have an operation. Now he helped George, who was the chief mechanic.

Bill and Myra couldn't have been friendlier. They cooked a lovely corned beef hash for the children and showed them where they would sleep and even found enough scraps for the dogs, who settled down for the night in the lorry. All except Fleck. The Tottenham terrier had tried to keep quiet, but when he realized that Hal was not coming he began to whine and then to shiver – and even though the others looked at him reproachfully, he couldn't stop himself from howling dismally. Ever since Albina Fenton had tried to tear the flannel from his mouth and carried him back to Easy Pets, Fleck lived in a world where nothing and nobody was safe.

In the caravan, Hal heard him and put down his knife and fork.

"I'm sorry," he said, feeling embarrassed. "He's very young. . ."

"Oh well, you'd better bring him in then," said Myra good-naturedly. "I reckon he's not much more than a pup. Though what Elsa would say, spoiling him like that. . ."

So Fleck was brought in and curled up at Hal's feet with his flannel and fell instantly asleep.

The following day was a Sunday and it was spent getting everything ready for the performance on the following day. To Hal and Pippa, who had never seen a circus, let alone travelled with one, everything was exciting and amazing. The Big Top seemed to go up in an instant. . . One minute there were great folds of canvas lying on the ground, and the next moment the huge dome went up, the flag on the top unfurled to say "Henry's Circus" – and they were in business! They had borrowed leads for all the dogs so that they could wander about without getting in the way, and wherever they looked there was something going on. The liberty horses, coming out of their vans and stepping across to the stables, the acrobats warming up on mats outside, the clowns unpacking their gear. . .

They watched and wondered, trying to keep out of the way. Otto alone didn't care for what was going on. He was descended from the great Barry, a St Bernard who had saved so many people from the snow that when he died he had been stuffed and put in a museum. When you have an ancestor like that, the noise and glitter of a circus is hard to bear, and he plodded along with a weary look in his bloodshot eyes. Li-Chee snuffled along behind him, his long hair brushing the ground, and from time to time he sneezed the fringe out of his eyes. But Francine's feet scarcely touched the grass. She almost danced; her eyes shone. If ever there was a dog who was exactly where she belonged, it was the poodle – and Rupert never left her side.

But now George called them into his camper and asked again if they had heard from Elsa.

"Mr Henry's waiting for his dog turn. Can you get them to do something without her?"

"We could try," said Pippa. "But it's always Elsa who sets them off. We just watch."

"Well, you think," said George. "We open tomorrow, and if there's no sign of Elsa, we'd better be sending you back. Can't have children gallivanting all over the countryside on their own."

"Could we have a little time to think about it?" asked Pippa. George said yes, they could.

"What are we going to do?" said Hal, as he and Pippa made their way back to the caravan. "We can't possibly make them do tricks."

"We've come such a long way," said Pippa. "If they send us back now, you know what will happen. The dogs back in their cages for ever – Fleck too – and the police probably. . . I don't think I can bear it. There must be something we can make them do."

Myra was tidying the caravan, getting it ready for people who wanted to have their fortunes told. "Petroc's poodles used to do a turn jumping on and off the backs of the liberty horses as they galloped round the ring," she said. "But I suppose your dogs wouldn't do that."

And the children, remembering the lordly horses with their silken manes, said no, their dogs probably wouldn't do that.

"Well, what's Elsa's show then? Is it 'The

Murgatroyd Family Go to Their Wedding'? I always liked that, with the dogs in their cart on the way to the church. People may say it's old-fashioned but it always goes down well, especially with a bit of business from the clowns."

"Yes," said Pippa, "that's what it is . . . sort of."

"That shouldn't be too difficult, then. If Elsa doesn't get here in time you could borrow some of Petroc's stuff. He left it all in his van. There'll be a cart of some kind you can use and a hamper full of costumes. I'll look it out for you."

An hour later, the children and the dogs were standing at the entrance to the circus ring. Two of the clowns, Tom and Fred, had found Petroc's cart and Myra had dragged out his dressing-up hamper and gone back to her caravan.

"Well, we'll leave you to get on with it," said Tom. "Just call us when you're ready and we'll fit our business in with you. Then we can have a proper run-through."

They went off. Hal opened the hamper and looked at the gaudy clothes with disgust.

"What gives people the right to dress up animals and make them look as silly as they are themselves?" he asked.

Pippa did not answer, and when Hal looked at her he saw that her face was rigid and she was as pale as death.

"I can't," she gulped, staring at the empty expanse of sawdust, and the rows of tiers stretching upwards. "I've absolutely no idea what to do. I must have been mad."

"But we've said—"

"I can't," said Pippa again. "I absolutely can't." She was almost crying. "We'll have to come clean. I'm very sorry."

The dogs had been waiting patiently, wondering what was going on. Now Francine stepped forward. She dived into the hamper, picked up a wreath of white flowers in her mouth and laid it on the ground.

"She must have done this before," said Pippa.

They put the wreath over the poodle's head and she sat up on her hind legs, every inch a bride. If Pippa did not know what to do, Francine quite clearly did.

After that, somehow, they managed to carry on. They found a tiny bonnet for Li-Chee, who was to be the baby, and a frilled hat for Honey, who was to be the mother. But Otto took one look at his hat and turned away.

"We can't make him dress up – not Otto," said Hal.

"We won't have to," said Pippa, "not if he's just pulling the cart."

Rupert, of course, was the bridegroom. There was no trouble about getting him to put on a bow tie and a silk waistcoat. He, like Francine, knew that dressing up was part of the job.

They decided that Otto should pull the cart round the ring twice, with Francine and Li-Chee and Honey on board. They would stop at the church, which the clowns would set up, and Rupert would be sitting there, waiting for his bride. The wedding would take place out of sight behind a curtain, and then the bridal party would come out again and drive to the wedding banquet in another part of the ring and the show would end with the two poodles dancing together.

"That part will work at least," said Pippa. "There can be a spotlight on them, and then it can go out suddenly and everything will be over."

But even such a simple routine was unbelievably difficult for the dogs to learn. Getting Otto to pull the cart round the ring took ages. He trembled with outrage, but Pippa was patient. Gradually he went round; his eyes were full of despair, but he went.

Li-Chee grumbled in his throat but when Pippa said, "Please, Li-Chee, please," he sat still in his seat. Honey looked round from under her frilled hat as if asking why this was happening to her, but she too sat where they put her. Francine, standing straight on top of the cart, kept the other dogs in check.

But Fleck wouldn't leave Hal.

"It's no good. He'll have to stay with you," said Pippa.

Hal agreed, but sadly. "He was such a joyful dog when I first got him," he said. "But now. . ."

"He'll be joyful again, you'll see," said Pippa. "He's just lost his confidence."

They rehearsed for most of the morning, and then the clowns came back. Whatever they thought privately about "The Murgatroyd Family Go to Their Wedding", they kept it to themselves.

"We'll come on first, getting the feast ready, trying to blow up balloons and all that," said Tom. "There's plenty of chance there for a bit of business – that'll loosen everybody up. And we'll have a word with Steve about the music. You'll want the Wedding March where they go into the church, I expect, and then a waltz when the poodles do their dance."

"Yes," said Pippa. "Thank you. I hope it'll be all right."

Fred looked at her worried face.

"Of course it'll be all right," he said. "And anyway, with a bit of luck Elsa'll be here in time to put in the finishing touches."

The children looked at each other.

It wouldn't need a bit of luck for Elsa to come and do that – it would need rather a lot.

13

The Detective Agency

Curzon Montgomery sat in his leather armchair leafing through the pages of Yachting World. There was a hundred foot ketch for sale which he had his eye on. They were asking a ridiculous price but if the morning's interview went as he hoped, he'd be able to make a bid for it. Not that he liked being at sea. All that roughness and choppiness could really get you down, but you couldn't beat a yacht as a place for giving parties.

The room he sat in did not look like an office.

It was furnished like a very expensive sitting room with deep upholstered sofas, a thick-pile carpet and the kind of pictures on the wall which might be absolutely anything. All the same, it was from this room that Curzon ran his Media Management and Manhunting agency – or MMM for short.

Curzon did not accept just any sort of client, as he made clear. He was very particular – but actually only very special clients could afford his fees. Not that he was greedy, not at all, but his uncle, Lord Featherpool, had invested a lot of money in MMM and he expected results.

Now Curzon rang for his receptionist, and a beautiful girl with a bandage round her ankle came teetering in. Fiona Enderby-Beescombe had been at school with Lord Featherpool's niece and in need of a job, and Curzon had been glad to take her on. It was true that her habit of wearing ten-inch heels meant that she was frequently injured, and she spent so much time painting her fingernails that she did not always reach the phone in time, but Curzon had been pleased to hire her because as soon as she opened her mouth people knew that she came from the right background.

"I'm expecting an important client at ten, Fiona. A Mr Fenton. We shall want coffee. You'd better turn on the infrared detector and the digital decoder and all that stuff. He might want to have a look. And tell Sprocket to keep out of the way."

Ten minutes. Was there time for a small snifter? A whisky before an interview often made things go smoothly. But before he could open the drinks cabinet, the bell rang and Donald Fenton was shown in.

Donald and Albina had had a sleepless night. The kidnappers had not rung and the police were useless – plodding and slow. But the head of the MMM agency was a reassuring sight. The office was in the most expensive block in the city, the sign outside the door in gold letters so small and discreet that it had taken Donald several minutes to find it. Everything, in short, was of the best.

Curzon rose from his chair. His large red face was amiable. As they shook hands he said, "Now, how can I help you? I gather your son is missing."

"Yes. Yes." Donald was a sorry sight. There were dark rings under his eyes; his hands shook. "We're sure he's been kidnapped but there's been no word. The police had the nerve to suggest he might have run away, but that's nonsense. Hal had everything he wanted in the world. My wife and I tried to gratify every whim of his. You should see the toys in his nursery."

"Quite. Quite so. Now if you'll just tell me the whole story."

So Curzon switched on the recorder and Donald told of the night they thought Hal had gone to stay with his friend and the awful discovery that he had never turned up there, while Curzon nodded his head in an understanding sort of way.

"I came to you because I heard how you found Mackenzie's wife's diamonds. It was an amazing piece of work," said Donald.

Curzon smirked modestly "Yes . . . yes. That took a bit of doing. A very tricky case . . . but it came out all right in the end."

Actually what had happened to Mackenzie's wife's diamond necklace was not quite what Curzon pretended. A few days after the necklace went missing, Curzon went round to a cocktail party at the Mackenzies' house and drank so much that he wandered out into the garden to look for a place where he could be sick. He had decided on the compost bin and was just lifting the lid when he saw the glint of diamonds inside. (Mrs Mackenzie was a keen gardener and had been cutting roses before she set off for the opera.)

So Curzon slipped the necklace into his pocket and two days later he rang Mackenzie and told him that after a very difficult and secret piece of detection he had managed to find it.

"I've brought the photos of Hal of course and. . ." here Donald's voice faltered, "his toothbrush for DNA samples and a few clothes. . ." He turned away to gather himself together.

"Good man. Good. . . Now perhaps you'd like Miss Enderby-Beescombe to show you round the laboratory. As you'll see, we have all the latest equipment. Meanwhile I'll get on to my team."

Although Miss Enderby-Beescombe was a little vague about some of the gadgets she showed him, the hum and whirr and flashing lights in the adjoining room were impressive. But what impressed Donald most of all was the fee that MMM charged.

It was six hundred pounds an hour, Curzon told him, and then a fee of fifty thousand once the boy was found.

Donald, returning home, was able to reassure and comfort Albina. At that price MMM had to be not only good, but the best.

When Donald had left, Curzon picked up the internal phone.

"Sprocket?" he barked.

"Yes, sir, it's me," said a high voice.

"Of course it's you, you idiot," said Curzon. Sprocket was in fact "the team" about which he had boasted to Donald Fenton. "Now listen. We've got a missing boy case. I want a hundred flyers and a photo in the usual dailies. There's a twenty-thousand-pound reward for news of the boy. Fiona'll bring everything down."

"Yes, sir. I'll see to it straightaway."

Milton Sprocket was a thin, pale young man who was never allowed upstairs because he had a local accent and had not been to the right school. MMM had the use of a basement room and a garage and it was there that he was to be found.

He was a man who took his work very seriously. After rather a sad childhood being bullied at school and failing his exams, Sprocket had taken a correspondence course at the College of Surveillance and Technology and got a Diploma in Detection and Tracking (or DDT for short). It was a first-class diploma because the college didn't give out any seconds or thirds, and after this his life had changed.

Sprocket was hard-working and neat. In his cubbyhole in the basement was a cabinet with a number of drawers, all carefully labelled, in which

379

he kept his disguises. There was a drawer labelled: moustaches, eyebrows, nose hair. Another said, scabs, wounds, pimples and boils, and another read, spectacles, monocles, ear trumpets. There was a wig stand in a corner, and a compartment for false teeth, and in a locked cabinet on the other wall lived a row of bottles labelled spit, blood, pus and phlegm, which had been a special offer on the Internet.

But though being in disguise and stalking people was what Sprocket liked best, most of the room was given over to the latest technology. The gadgets upstairs were only for show; it was down here in the basement that the real stuff was to be found. There were fibre-optic cables for looking round corners, and underwater cameras with fins, and sat navs which told you where you were going and where you had been, and binoculars with night vision, and ultraviolet heat-sensing devices . . . and because some of these things were not very easy to understand, Sprocket had a tall pile of instruction manuals over which he pored for long hours, trying to work out exactly what went where.

Not only that, but Sprocket was also a poet. In the MMM garage next to his room was a white van which he used when he was detecting, and on the side of the van was a verse he had written quite by himself.

Have you lost it or misplaced it?

In a jiffy we will trace it!

The poem was written on a board which could slide out and be replaced by others if he was on a secret mission and both he and the van needed to be in disguise. For example, there was one for when he wanted to pretend to be a greengrocer, which went:

When your appetite's on edge,

We will bring you fruit and veg.

He was also working on a completely new verse which he meant to use when pretending to be a plumber, but it was giving him trouble. A poem like that had to be strong and powerful, but of course none of the words in it could actually be rude.

He pressed the repeat button on his phone and listened to the last part of Curzon's message once again.

"This is a big one, Sprocket. Go to it! No hanging about."

Sprocket smiled and rubbed his hands. He was just in the mood for an important and tricky case.

14

Nini

Greystoke House was a big stone building on the outskirts of Todcaster. From the street it looked forbidding and grim, but inside the walls had been painted in bright colours. There was a nursery full of toys, and a room where the older children watched TV. Mrs Platt, the house mother who was in charge, was a fat and friendly lady who did her best to be motherly. All the same, to the children who lived there, waiting to be placed with foster parents, it was still "The Home", a place in which no one wanted to stay longer than they needed.

The small girl who sat up in bed on the morning that the circus opened in Todcaster had no interest in being fostered. She seemed to have no interest in anything. She was a beautiful child with huge dark eyes, thick jet-black hair and golden skin, but she lived in a closed world which nobody could reach.

She had come from an Indonesian island, a place of great beauty with lush forests, crystal rivers and mountains shaped like big green cones, but a place too of sudden earthquakes and terrifying landslides. Nini's family had died in one of these, and she had been taken to an orphanage to be cared for by nuns.

It was a peaceful place set in the grounds of a temple where the monks prayed and chanted, and the little dogs who guarded them sat on the stone steps keeping evil spirits at bay.

Then one day a rich businessman and his wife had come to the island for a holiday, seen the little girl playing quietly under a jacaranda tree and decided to adopt her and bring her back to England.

For the first few months that Nini was with them they were delighted with their pretty daughter and dressed her beautifully and showed her off to their friends. But then they found that the little girl did not learn to speak English as quickly as they hoped – in fact she did not speak at all. They took her to a doctor and another and another and were given a lot of names for what might be the matter with Nini, but no one could tell them what to do. She was not deaf, and she could see perfectly well, but she was enclosed in a world of her own.

Then one day when she had spent the whole day being tested in a hospital, Nini had a terrifying tantrum.

"They do that in the East," a friend had said. "It's called running amok."

This was too much for the couple who had wanted a pretty, prattling doll, and they took her to the Children's Welfare Centre and said they couldn't keep her. Since then she had been in Greystoke House, not misbehaving, not being difficult, just not really being there at all.

Now she got out of bed and ran along the corridor, moving as lightly as a little ghost, and into the room where the older boys slept, and pulled at the duvet on the bed nearest the door.

Mick woke, saw who it was, and sat up.

"Today's the circus, Nini. We're going to the circus," he repeated.

He was a tough Geordie with ginger hair, freckles and a cheerful open face. His grandfather had been a coalminer till the closure of the pits. For some reason Mick had become Nini's protector and the only person of whom she took any notice. "It'll be good," he went on. "There'll be horses and acrobats and clowns."

But Nini did not answer, only looked at him. He might have been telling her about a visit to the dentist. Mick sighed and reached for his clothes.

Greystoke House was not far from the common where the circus was encamped. The children walked there, shepherded by plump Mrs Platt and a nursery assistant called Doreen. They danced along, excited by the treat to come. Only Nini, clutching Mick's hand, walked along in silence.

The circus was gearing up for the start. On a platform outside the big top a small man with a moustache was juggling a mass of coloured balls. Another man in spangled tights was beating a big drum.

"Come and see Henry's Circus, the eighth wonder of the world!" he shouted.

The Greystoke children were early. They filed into the front row. Mick sat down next to a boy of about his own age, with a white dog on his knee. Nini was beside him. Her legs, too short to reach the ground, stuck out in front of her.

"It's going to start," Mick told her.

But nothing moved in the beautiful mask-like face.

Hal, holding on to Fleck, was sick with nerves. In half an hour The Dog Family Murgatroyd would do their turn, and if it went wrong they would be banished from the circus. All the same, he turned to smile at the boy who had just come in with a group of children and was sitting next to him. He had ginger hair and looked friendly.

The house lights dimmed, the band struck up. Mr Henry, in his ringmaster's clothes, cracked his whip.

The procession came first. The horses, the clowns, the tumblers and acrobats, Pauline's Parrots all sitting on her shoulders. There was a burst of clapping – and the show began.

The Texas Terrors galloped in first – a string of horses ridden bareback by three men who leapt from one gleaming back to the other. . . The Dainty Danielas – a group of girls in shining costumes who climbed on one another's shoulders and threw each other up in the air. . . The Comedy Horse, a pony who followed his master round the ring trying to get sugar lumps out of his pockets. . . A stupendous display on the high wire with men and women pretending to push each other off. . .

Hal was holding his breath. The time had come. Fleck whined once and Hal shushed him.

"And, now Elsa's Fabulous Dogs in 'The Murgatroyd Family Go to Their Wedding'," announced the ringmaster.

The clowns came on first. They wheeled in a huge bath filled with water, and carried buckets and a ladder. They were trying to get ready for the wedding feast, but everything kept going wrong. The legs came off the table they were scrubbing; the balloons they were trying to blow up burst in their faces or floated out of reach; one of the clowns fell backwards into the bath. . .

A tent with a big notice on it saying "The Church" had been put up near the entrance, and Rupert appeared and sat in front of it in his bow tie and silk waistcoat. Another lot of clowns came in on stilts, carrying trays of wobbling jellies and coloured streamers in which they got entangled, and they threshed about and pretended to cry.

And now, to a fanfare from the band, the cart pulled by Otto made its entry.

Otto was wretchedly nervous but Francine had

given him a good talking-to and he managed to trot steadily three-quarters of the way round the ring. Li-Chee in his little bonnet and Honey in her frilly hat sat in their seats, but Francine was standing up on her hind legs. With her white wreath and the enthusiastic little yaps she gave, she was obviously an eager bride.

But now something happened which the children had not bargained for. The audience broke into a storm of clapping and as the sound grew louder, Otto began to tremble. He had faced all sorts of dangers in Switzerland, climbing up rock faces and plunging into dangerous crevasses to rescue trapped climbers, but this noise was horrible; it was not to be borne. His eyes rolled and he stopped dead.

And Li-Chee, who would have done anything for Otto, jumped down from the cart with his bonnet askew and reappeared beneath Otto's legs. He meant only to reassure his friend, but it looked as though he was trying to pull the cart, and everybody laughed. Not at the clowns now, but at the gallant little dog.

It was at this moment that Mick turned in amazement to the little girl beside him. Nini was leaning forward intently, her whole face alight, her eyes fixed in wonder at the Peke.

In the ring, no one, for a moment, knew what to do. Otto was standing stock-still, his head hanging. There was no way he was going to pull the cart as far as the church.

And once again it was Francine, that old trouper, who took over. She leapt from the cart but she did not run towards her bridegroom. She charged in the other direction, making noises of terror. She had changed the plot and become a dog who did not want to be married, who wanted to be free – and Rupert caught on at once. He jumped to his feet and gave chase, barking angrily – a bridegroom who wasn't going to be done out of his bride.

The two poodles rolled over together, but Francine escaped and ran up a ladder, and took a flying leap into the arms of one of the clowns. Rupert followed her. But now the clowns understood the game. They pretended to catch Francine; they grabbed her and lost her and hit their foreheads in despair. Round and round the ring went the fleeing bride, between the legs of the clowns, flying over the table, hiding behind the bath, yelping in mock terror – and round and round went Rupert, the thwarted bridegroom, following her trick for trick.

The slapstick grew wilder and wilder. The clowns stepped into the buckets, fell on the balloons and burst them. . . Li-Chee left Otto and joined in, yapping at the top of his voice.

Meanwhile, Fleck, on Hal's lap, had been getting more and more excited. All his friends were down there and he wanted desperately to be brave and join them but he couldn't quite do it. Then, in a sudden burst of courage, he jumped off Hal's knee, leapt over the barrier – and landed in the bath of water. For a moment he paddled up and down, then he scrambled out, shook himself, and joined in the chase.

But now came Honey. She was, after all, the mother and she couldn't bear the mess and muddle any longer. She leapt from the cart, still in her frilly hat, and began trying to herd the clowns, the dogs, the balloons – everything she could see – towards the exit.

Round and round they went, Francine and Rupert in the lead, then Li-Chee, Fleck and Otto with the cart. And round and round went the clowns.

But they still hadn't left the ring and Honey now called on all her old sheepdog skills. She turned and ran in the other direction to meet Francine, her runaway daughter, head on. The music grew to a crescendo, everyone disappeared through the exit – and the lights went out.

And the audience roared and stamped and clapped and cheered, while behind the scenes, Mr Henry and George looked at each other and grinned.

Performing dogs are valuable, but dog clowns are pure gold.

"Well, we did it," said Pippa triumphantly. "I reckon we can stay till Berwick and then it's hardly any distance to your grandparents'. Even if they do something quite different next time, Mr Henry won't send us away."

They had taken the dogs back to the lorry and were helping out in the tent where the performing animals were housed. For a small sum the audience could visit them in their cages after the show.

"Excuse me." Hal turned to find the ginger-haired boy who'd been sitting next to him.

Clutching his hand was the tiny girl with jet-black hair. "I was wondering if there was any chance of seeing the little dog that tried to pull the cart. The Peke. She's nutty about him."

Nini looked up. "Small dog," she said.

"I think she's seen dogs like that where she came from. Temple dogs they were, guarding the monks and chasing away evil spirits and all that stuff. But it's amazing because she's never taken notice of anything up till now. I've got permission from our house mother, as long as we're not too long. She's taken the others to look at the liberty horses."

"Small dog," repeated Nini, who never spoke.

"He's in the lorry with the others – just across the grass," said Hal. "Come on, we'll show you."

They were greeted by a chorus of friendly barks. Mick lifted Nini up on to the hay bales and she disappeared into the huddle of dogs. When they looked at her again, they saw something unexpected. Nini had not picked up Li-Chee or hugged him. She was sitting cross-legged in front of him, not touching him, murmuring to him in her own language while Li-Chee stood very still, his face lifted respectfully up to hers. It was obvious that he understood every word.

"You can't imagine what a thing this is," said Mick, and in a few words he gave them Nini's history.

The children had moved a little way away, giving Nini as long as they could. They were talking quietly, beginning to make friends, when two stable lads came past.

"Look at this," said one. "Here on page two." There was a rustle of pages being turned. "That's the spit an' image of the boy with the white dog. The one that's staying with Bill and Myra. Don't tell me it isn't."

The children, hidden by the side of the lorry, froze into silence.

The other lad whistled through his teeth. "'Twenty-thousand-pound reward for news of him,' it says. It can't be the same boy."

"Maybe not. But it looks like him and it's worth a chance. The phone number's here."

The men moved away out of earshot. Mick, looking at Hal and Pippa, saw the shock on their faces.

"I don't want to pry, but if there's anything I can do to help?" he said. "I mean if you're on the run or something." And as the children exchanged glances, he said, "You don't have to explain, I'll help you just the same. It makes no odds to me."

Hal only hesitated for a moment. The red-headed boy was probably quite as much in need of twenty thousand pounds as the circus lad. But Hal felt certain that Mick was to be trusted, that he was honest and truthful and brave. He said, "Yes, maybe you could help. We'll have to leave here at once, but we don't really know where we are or anything. We ought to hide somewhere overnight, I suppose, and then start off at dawn."

Pippa looked at him, frowning. It was usually she who made the decisions — and they knew nothing about the boy.

"You can spend the night at our place," said Mick. "There's a big boiler room in the basement. No one goes there. I know where the key is. I'll get it and get some food down there and blankets. There's only Mrs Platt at night and she sleeps like a top."

"Would you really?" said Hal. "I think that might work. But how do we get to you? Did you come in a bus?"

Mick shook his head.

"We walked. It's only twenty minutes from here. I'll draw you a map."

"What about the other children?" asked Pippa. "Can you trust them not to give us away?"

Mick said, "Yes."

They left a note for George. It was hard lying to someone who had been so helpful but there was nothing else to do. The note said that Aunt Elsa had got in touch and told them that she couldn't manage to get north because her brother-in-law was in hospital, so they were taking the overnight bus back to London. Fortunately Bill and Myra had gone out to the cinema, so the children were able to say goodbye by letter, and to thank them for all they had done.

Then they gathered up their belongings and went to fetch the dogs.

At first all went well. The dogs liked the idea of a late-night walk. They noticed that Pippa had strapped on her haversack and Hal carried his holdall, and both of them wore their anoraks. For Fleck and Otto and Li-Chee and Honey this meant that they were off on another adventure and they were ready for it.

But not Francine. Francine knew that they were leaving. Leaving the circus – and leaving Rupert.

She sat down where she was. She threw back her head and she howled. It was the most desperate and forlorn sound the children had ever heard. And from George's camper where he now slept, Rupert replied and came to her.

What followed was almost unbearable. The poodles stood together in the dusk; their bodies so close that they might have been one thing. They did not bark or complain; they only shivered as sorrow gripped them.

Hal and Pippa watched, and the other dogs too. Could they force Francine away? She loved the life of the circus, and she loved Rupert. It was a proper enduring passion, they knew that.

Yet could they go on without her? This flight was an adventure they all shared.

The two poodles still stood like statues. No one else existed for them. Otto took a few steps towards them and then stopped. He and Francine had been friends for a long time, but he did nothing. Francine would have to decide this for herself.

"Come on, Hal," said Pippa, who could bear it no longer. "We have to get on. She's got a right to stay."

They turned and made their way slowly over the trampled grass. They had reached the entrance to the circus when Francine gave a last, heart-rending howl. Then she turned away from Rupert and raced after them.

15

Greystoke House

Mrs Platt was snoring – a great juddering noise that sounded as though it would rattle the window frames. One of the boys whom Mick had put on guard leaned out of the landing window and signalled to Mick in the shrubbery to say that all was clear.

In the girl's room, Nini lay silently in her bed, but she was not asleep.

It was almost dark now. They would be here soon – and Mick settled down to wait.

*

The dogs walked slowly. They had had a hard day and their performance in the ring had tired them. The last dog, as they made their way through the unfamiliar streets, was Francine. She was usually so light on her feet, but now she could hardly put one paw in front of the other, and her head was down. Every step was taking her further from where she wanted to be and she looked as though she didn't care whether she lived or died.

Hal was trying to read Mick's map, hastily scribbled on the back of an envelope. In the failing light they took a wrong turn – but at last they came to the iron gate of Greystoke House.

There was no time to be anxious – Mick was there in a moment.

"You must be absolutely quiet," Pippa told the dogs. They understood, and followed as Mick led them round to the back of the building and down a short flight of stone steps.

They found themselves in a boiler room with a bare stone floor, coiled pipes round the walls, a big heater humming in one corner. The windows were shuttered and a faint blue light hung overhead. It was dry and warm, and in a corner they found blankets and pillows which Mick's friends had "borrowed" from the storeroom and brought down in secret. A big bowl of water, and plates piled with meatballs and rice, pinched from the children's supper, were laid out on the floor.

"Did you have to go without your meal to give us this?" asked Pippa.

Mick shrugged. "The girl who serves supper is pretty sloppy. It isn't difficult to get stuff off the table, and we don't go hungry here. The food's dull but it's perfectly OK." Then he said, "Nothing happens, that's the worst of living in a place like this. We'd do worse things than going without meatballs to know we can help."

The dogs were too well trained to start eating without permission, but they looked hungrily at the plates, and then at Hal and Pippa, and when they got the signal to begin, they put their heads down and ate.

All except Francine. Francine looked at the food and turned her head away and walked to a quiet corner of the room, wanting only to be alone with her grief.

"Come along, Francine," said Pippa, fondling her head. "Try just a little."

But Francine wouldn't eat. She gave her paw to Pippa a few times to say she understood that Pippa was sorry for her. Pippa wasn't to worry, she was saying, but right now she couldn't swallow even the smallest mouthful.

"We'll be keeping watch," said Mick. "Someone will wake you first thing in the morning so that you can be off in case the boiler man comes – though he's not due tomorrow."

Hal and Pippa looked at him. There was nothing to say except thank you, so they said it, and several times over.

"We won't forget this," said Hal. "Not ever. And if there's anything we can do for you, well, you know. . ."

Now that they were temporarily safe, Hal and Pippa had time to wonder what the stable lad would do, and how likely they were to be pursued. It was not so far to Hal's grandfather overland, but it couldn't be done in less than two days' hard walking, across moorland and fields, towards the coast.

But soon they stopped whispering and curled up on the blanket, and although the stone floor was not exactly comfortable, they slept.

The dogs slept too. Otto lay close to Francine and his reassuring bulk did something to calm her. Once or twice she woke up briefly and whined, remembering what she had lost, but then Otto would move closer to her, and she was quiet again. Fleck lay across Hal's feet, his flannel beside him.

Upstairs, Mrs Platt still snored, the breath wheezing in and out of her great bulk, and while they heard the steady, unpleasant noise she made, Mick and his friends knew that the fugitives were safe.

But in the room she shared with the other little girls, Nini sat up in bed. She had been waiting, and now she pushed back the bedclothes and fetched the brush and comb from her locker and crept, silent as a wraith, along the corridor.

At the top of the stairs she ran into Mick, who was keeping watch.

"See small dog," she said. "See Li-Chee."

Mick stared at her. How did she know? Had she overheard something when he was talking to Hal and Pippa or did she have some other way of knowing things? Whatever it was, he couldn't take any risks. Even Mrs Platt couldn't sleep through one of Nini's tantrums.

He took her hand. "You can see Li-Chee but you must be very, very quiet or they will take him away. Do you understand? Absolutely silent."

Nini nodded, and he led her down the cellar steps to the door of the boiler room.

The little girl knew about moving silently. She opened the door of the cellar so quietly that the huddle of dogs hardly stirred and the children did not wake. Only Li-Chee, who was on the edge of the circle because he had given his place beside Otto to Francine, raised his head.

He was surprised to be woken and at first he wondered if it wasn't one of the other dogs she wanted because he was used to being small and unimportant and only suitable for old ladies. But as Nini knelt down in front of him he realized that it was really him she wanted, just as it had been him in the lorry, and though he was very sleepy and would have liked to close his eyes again, he made himself stay awake and began to lick her wrist.

Once again, Nini did not hug him or try and pick him up. Instead, she took up her brush and comb and very slowly, very carefully, she groomed the long, silky golden coat and smoothed back the hair that had tumbled into his eyes.

And as she brushed and combed and tidied him, she was back in her homeland, helping the girls who danced in the temple to prepare the little guard dogs that they worshipped for the festivals.

Everything came back to her – everything she missed so terribly that she had shut it out completely:

the scent of jasmine, the temple bells, the quiet voices of the nuns in the orphanage . . . the warmth, the sun on her skin . . . and her own language.

Steadily, quietly, Nini brushed and combed and murmured. And as she worked, the homesickness which had crippled her and turned her into a mute came out, and the tears she had not been able to shed ran down her cheeks.

And Li-Chee stood trustingly in front of her. Already he loved her. She had chosen him and he had chosen her, but as the grooming went on, there came from his throat a low rumbling . . . a kind of gargling sound – and Nini put down her brush. She recognized the noise Li-Chee was making. In his polite way he was telling her that he did not want to be groomed. He did not want to be worshipped.

He wanted to be understood. To go forward. . .

For a moment Nini sat still, thinking. Then she gave a small shake of her head, and let it all go out of her; her memories, her sadness. She looked round the dimly lit room at the other dogs. She thought of the very small girl in the nursery who had tugged at her skirts, wanting to be her friend. She thought of the games they played in the garden of Greystoke House, the squirrel they had tamed, the cartoons they watched at bedtime. She thought of Mick.

It was time to move on.

"Wait here," she said to Li-Chee.

She crept out again and made her way to Mrs Platt's sitting room. The scissors were where she remembered, at the bottom of the sewing basket. Nini took them, being careful to carry them with the points down as she had been taught, and made her way downstairs again. It would not be easy, but she would do it. She would be brave.

Li-Chee was waiting where she had left him.

"I won't hurt you," she said. "Just stand still."

Then she began to cut, and to snip and to cut again, and as she did so, the golden silky coat which had imprisoned Li-Chee fell silently to the floor.

Pippa was the first to wake, and it was all she could do not to let out a cry of horror.

"What have you done?" she said. "For heaven's sake – oh, the poor, poor dog!"

Nini did not answer; she only smiled.

"He's ruined," said Pippa. "He'll never be in a show again. Nobody will want a dog like that."

But now Li-Chee got to his feet and shook himself, making sure that it had really happened. And then he went mad. He raced round the cellar, he rolled over and over waving his paws in the air, he let out high-pitched yelps of sheer delight.

He could see, he could move, he was revealed as the dog he really was. A lion dog, a fighter, the guardian of emperors, not a pampered plaything for old ladies. His little squashed face looked out at the clear, clean world, and his pop eyes glowed in the morning light. Someone had understood him; someone had found out who he really was!

Hal woke then and saw what had happened, but before he could say anything Mick came in and said it was time to go.

16

Sprocket Gets a Call

The stable lad lost very little time. As soon as the horses were bedded down for the night, he made his call.

Curzon, of course, was no longer in his office. He often did not return after a long lunch, and Fiona never stayed once he had gone. So it was in Sprocket's little cubbyhole that the phone rang, and he seized it eagerly.

"MMM here. Milton Sprocket speaking."

He listened, getting more and more excited, trying to take notes with one hand.

"I'm pretty sure it's him," the voice at the other end was saying. "Looks just like the photo. You did say twenty thousand pounds? No funny business?"

"Yes, yes," said Sprocket eagerly. "Now just tell me exactly where you are. Give me your coordinates."

But the stable lad had not heard of coordinates.

"Don't know what they are, mate. We're in Todcaster with Henry's Circus. And you better get up here quickly because we'll be on the move again soon."

When he put the receiver down, Sprocket was in a state of feverish agitation. It was clear that he had to act straightaway and not wait for Curzon's instructions. What's more, it seemed that the boy had not been kidnapped as everyone thought, but had run away. Children did run away to join the circus, Sprocket knew, and that meant he would not want to be recaptured and taken home. And this, in turn, meant some serious disguises while the boy was being stalked and cornered and brought back. The van would have to be disguised too – probably best to put on the greengrocer poem. They'd like the idea of fresh vegetables up in the north.

Sprocket hurried to the cabinet and opened the

top drawer. He was a fair man and tried hard not to have any favourites among his moustaches, but there was one that he did love particularly. It was a rich nut-brown colour and wonderfully bushy, and it settled against his upper lip like the softest fur. He put it on and immediately felt ready for a great adventure. Then he packed up a couple of wigs, an ear trumpet and some pimples and boils, but not the scars – you couldn't have everything. At the last minute he added the bottle of blood but left the one labelled saliva – there would be places up there where one could spit if necessary.

Running backwards and forwards, Sprocket loaded the van, putting in the new sat nav, the infrared heat-sensing device, the binoculars with night vision. . . The little packet containing Hal's toothbrush and his handkerchiefs went in the secret compartment behind the driving seat. And of course he had a case ready packed with pyjamas and a change of underclothes. Sprocket's mother had always been careful to see that her son understood the importance of being fresh and clean not just on top but all the way through.

He was removing the board which said, Have you lost it or misplaced it? In a jiffy we will trace it, and sliding in the one which said, When your appetite's on edge, We will bring you fruit and veg, when he remembered that he had not left a message for Curzon. So he went back into the cubbyhole and sent a coded message from his computer to Curzon's computer upstairs, telling him where he had gone.

Then he eased the van out of the garage and set off for the motorway. As he passed a row of shops he saw a big notice in one of the windows in which a light still burned.

Easy Pets, it said. Pedigree Dogs to Rent.

Sprocket drove on without a second glance. He was not fond of dogs.

The light should not have been burning at Easy Pets so late. Kayley had been due home an hour ago. She still had flu and should have been in bed. But one of the dogs, the mastiff who had eaten her mistress's finger by mistake, was running a temperature. Her nose was dry and she was off her food and Kayley sat with her, wondering whether to call out the vet so late. The Carkers never came to the dogs after hours.

She was feeling wretched. She went on missing the dogs in Room A more than she would have thought possible, and she was terribly worried about Pippa. The police had been back asking a lot more questions and she felt that it was only a matter of time before they found out that it was Pippa who had been in the building on Sunday night.

She was putting on her coat when Queen Tilly started up again. The Mexican hairless was disgusted. She was a dog who in a way was born disgusted, but since her roommates had disappeared, life at Easy Pets had become impossible. The five dogs who had replaced Otto and Francine and the others were simply not fit to associate with a Mexican hairless who had belonged to an heiress and eaten off silver plates. There was an Airedale who suffered from hairballs, a dachshund who dribbled, and some others that it was better not to think about. So she twitched and screeched and yelped and grumbled, till Kayley came to her in the compound and put another cushion in her padded sleeping basket and gave her a drink of milk.

When she got home at last, Kayley was so exhausted she could hardly put one foot in front of the other. But one of the twins was stuck with his homework and needed help, and Grandfather had to be wheeled out to the shop. Nothing could convince him that he wasn't going to buy back the family farm with his winning lottery ticket.

Mrs O'Brian was still out, working late for Mrs

Naryan. For a moment Kayley wondered whether to go and fetch her. The Naryans were always so friendly and welcoming, and the warm house with its wonderful silks and perfumes seemed very tempting on this miserable night. Once when it was raining badly, Mrs Naryan had sent her mother home in her husband's silver Rolls-Royce, a car so silent and so beautiful that it was hard to believe that it was just an ordinary machine and not something out of a dream.

But she was too tired to go anywhere. When she had finished her chores, Kayley picked up the phone meaning to ring Pippa – she had an emergency number for the school camp and perhaps it was best to warn her. But then she thought better of it. It seemed cruel to spoil Pippa's holiday, and she put the phone down again and climbed wearily into her bed, and tried to sleep.

At MMM the phone rang, and rang, and rang again as Donald tried desperately to get news of his son, while upstairs, Albina, wearing no make-up for the first time in her adult life, wept over the beige carpet which had arrived that afternoon to replace the blue one in Hal's room.

17

Honey on the Hill

Mick had told them the quickest way out of Todcaster. They had walked steadily along quiet streets, which turned into country lanes as they came closer to the moors. Li-Chee had started off very full of himself. He had been a small dog before but now, shorn of his golden pelt, he was a very small dog indeed, not much bigger than a well-fed rat. Inside, though, he was a lion, and when Pippa tried to carry him part of the way, he yelped with outrage. But after a few hours everybody needed a rest. Now they were leaning against a low stone wall, and around them were fields and low hills. A curlew called, a soft wind blew. Mick had managed to find some bread and butter for them and a few biscuits which they shared with the dogs.

"I don't know why he did all this for us," said Hal. "I hope I get a chance to repay him some day."

"You could do it by going on being his friend," said Pippa – and Hal looked at her, surprised. He hadn't been brought up to think that friendship was enough. You had to give people something solid: a present or money. But of course Pippa was right.

They were thinking of moving on when they heard a piercing whistle from the hill behind them. The dogs pricked up their ears, as they did at any sound, and flopped down again.

Except for Honey. One minute Honey was beside them. The next second she had jumped the wall – and was gone.

Old Selby the shepherd had come out of his cottage in a gloomy mood. His back ached, his knees were stiff, but that wasn't what was making him feel wretched. His niece had found a place where he could spend the rest of his life in comfort: a room in a block of flats called Rosewood, built as sheltered housing in the town. Rooms like that were hard to find and she had showed him round proudly.

"See how warm it is," she said, pointing to the radiators. "And there's a warden here all the time. If you want anything you just have to press the bell."

It was very kind of his niece, but when he thought of Rosewood his blood ran cold. He had not found it warm but unbearably stuffy. The people looking out of their rooms to give him a friendly greeting as he went down the corridor made him feel stifled, and out of the window you could see nothing but houses and still more houses.

Selby had been a shepherd on these hills for fifty years. He'd lived in the same stone cottage, run the same breed of sheep, woken each day to the sound of birdsong and the soughing of the wind. But old age had overtaken him, as it had overtaken his dog, Billy. Billy had been one of the best sheepdogs in the country but now he limped and wheezed when he had to run fast.

Well, it was no good fighting against what had to be. His niece was right. He couldn't really manage any longer. He'd have to sell the flock and find a home for Billy, and with luck both he and the dog wouldn't last too long.

Meanwhile, the sheep had to be gathered from the hill and brought down into the fold for dipping. The dog had done it a thousand times, and now he waited, ready for the command. He would go on till his lungs burst, but Selby knew how much it cost him.

Selby fetched his crook and sent him off. Billy ran up to the flock and lay down behind the sheep. He was panting pathetically but he waited, ready as always to do his job.

Old Selby put his fingers to his mouth and whistled, the sign that Billy was to start the gathering. The sheep were widely scattered today, and as obstinate as only sheep can be and they knew that Billy was no longer the threat he had once been. He began to round them up, but a couple of ewes broke away and went off to the left. The dog chivvied them back but now the rest of the flock was separating again. One old ewe, a thoroughly bad-tempered animal, had begun to graze.

Old Selby, watching, shook his head. It was no good hoping. He was too old to train another dog. There was no escaping Rosewood.

But now, when Selby was feeling so wretched, there was worse to come. A honey-coloured blur streaked up the hill and headed straight for the flock. A fox? No, a stray dog. A sheep worrier as likely as not.

"Blasted townies, letting their dogs off the lead," he grumbled.

He began to struggle up the hill, waving his stick, knowing there was nothing he could do if the dog was a killer.

Then he stopped dead and stared.

The new dog had come round behind the unruly flock in a wide run and now, head low, totally concentrating – sometimes darting left or right to check breakaways – she was gathering the animals into a tight bunch. Then she dropped down behind them, ears pricked, with Billy at her side.

She was waiting for instructions. A trained dog? Was it possible?

Half wondering if he was dreaming, Selby whistled again, giving the signal to start the fetch.

And slowly, expertly, the unknown dog began to move the flock down the hill towards the fold. Any stragglers were immediately brought back. She seemed to know what the sheep were going to do before they knew it themselves. She could run like the wind when it was needful, but there was no hassling, no snapping at their heels. With Billy helping as best he could, she sent them steadily to where they needed to be.

For Honey, as she worked, the miserable months

she had spent at Easy Pets fell away. It all came back to her – how to anticipate the movements of the flock, how to prevent trouble. . . She could feel the wind blowing through her coat. Her eyes shone. She could have run like this forever.

Within minutes the sheep were streaming like a white river into the fold, and Selby moved forward to close the gate.

"That'll do," he said to both the dogs, and Honey, who had flopped down beside him, looked up, her plumed tail waving, for she remembered those words from her former life, and knew what they meant. That the job was over, and had been done well.

Ten minutes later Selby sat in his kitchen, drinking a cup of tea. Honey was lying on the hearth rug beside Billy, who had made room for her, and as he looked at her, Old Selby allowed himself to dream.

What if it really was a miracle? What if this wonder dog had come to save him and his flock? With a dog like that he could last another five years, and then they'd know what they could do with Rosewood.

He was interrupted by a knock at the door and he opened it to find a small girl, breathless and looking very worried.

"I'm sorry to bother you but you haven't seen a dog – a rough collie, white and black and sable? She just took off and vanished when she heard a whistle."

Selby let her in and pointed to the rug.

"I thought it was too good to be true," he said as Honey got to her feet, tail wagging, and came to greet Pippa. "You know she's a proper sheepdog, don't you? One of the best. You should have seen her on the hill."

"Yes, I know. She was trained somewhere not far from here but the man who owned her had to sell his farm. She was bought by a family with small children who teased her and—"

Pippa broke off. She had nearly been stupid enough to mention Easy Pets.

Honey was still welcoming Pippa, rubbing her nose against Pippa's legs. It was Pippa who had set her free. She remembered the other dogs, she remembered the journey they were taking.

But then she ran back to Selby, and looked up at him. Here was her true master; it was here that she could do her real work and be herself. And she sat down between Selby and Pippa, in a moment of confusion and despair.

Old Selby bent down and pulled her ears. He

knew he could keep her. If he said "sit" she would sit. If he said "stay" she would stay, and she would do this till the day she died.

Pippa was silent, remembering Francine. Honey would have to choose, but was it fair to make her? She was a different kind of dog. There had been a girl in Pippa's class whose parents had decided to get divorced. The girl had managed all right till she was asked to choose which of her parents she wanted to live with, and after that she had simply fallen apart.

If it was so hard for a person to decide, could one ask it of a dog?

In the end it was old Selby who did the choosing. He had never taken another person's dog, and he would not do so now, but the next moments were the hardest he could remember.

He raised his stick and spoke to Honey.

"Go on. Be off with you," he said in his gruffest voice. "Get out of here."

Honey whined, and looked up at him and licked his hand, but his stick was still raised, and slowly, very slowly, looking back over her shoulder, she followed Pippa out of the door.

Selby stood on his porch and watched them go. Miracles occurred all right, but not, it seemed, for him. His eyes were watering, and angrily he wiped them with his sleeve.

"Blasted wind," he muttered.

Then he turned back into the house, and went to phone his niece.

18

The Dumper

Kevin Dawks was a kind man. One knew this because he was always helping people. He helped the manager of the supermarket in the town with the pile of rotting vegetables and plastic bags and oozing paint tins which wouldn't go in the bins, and he helped the owner of the pub with the old telly and the bicycle his son had written off – and he helped the man in the garage with the oil cans and bottles of poisonous liquids which were cluttering up his shelves.

He helped them by taking these things away and finding a place for them. The places he found were some way out of towns and villages, in quiet parts of the countryside. It might be in a bluebell wood or a river valley or a freshly planted field. Kevin didn't mind, as long as it wasn't overlooked by anyone and he could tip out his load of filth without anybody seeing.

Of course, he charged quite a lot for this service. Being a dumper is a dangerous business, and he always had to look out for the police or busybodies who said that what he was doing was illegal and disgusting. And because he didn't make as much money as he deserved to, he had other jobs. He stored things that had fallen off the back of lorries, like cartons of cigarettes and bits of jewellery, or tools that had been nicked and needed to be kept before being sold on – and he hid these in a lock-up shed on the edge of the moor.

The children had kept up a steady pace after they left the shepherd, and by early afternoon they were on a quiet country road leading up to the moors. Beside them, in a dip sheltered by birch trees, ran a crystal stream.

"My grandfather says you can drink from all the

streams up here. The water comes off the Cheviots and it's the cleanest in the country," said Hal. "If you go on ahead I'll just go down and fill my water bottle."

"All right, but don't be long," said Pippa.

She went on with the other dogs, while Fleck and Hal scrambled down the steep sides of the little valley. It was a beautiful place. The bracken fronds were uncurling, bluebells flowered between the birches . . . they were magical, these sheltered dells.

Fleck had been running ahead, but now he came back to Hal and stopped in front of him, holding up a front paw.

"What's the matter, Fleck?"

Fleck whimpered, and Hal saw a piece of rusty wire caught between his toes. Hal took it out, and it was then he noticed the smell.

It was a smell that seemed completely unreal in this lovely place. A vile sick-making stench of decay and rottenness.

Then he saw it: a pile of rubbish spilling down to the edge of the water. There was a torn mattress; half open tins of oil oozed on to the grass. A heap of rotting food burst out of a plastic bag, and an old sofa lay on its side, its rusty springs sticking up from the stained upholstery. Some of the refuse had been tipped into the stream itself; foetid bubbles of gas broke the surface of the water. A twisted electric fire was wedged against a boulder. A young birch sapling had fallen across the stream, broken by the weight of an iron bath.

And over everything, this unspeakable smell. . .

Hal hardly remembered how he got back up the bank. He was in a state of shock. Who could do this; who could turn this wonderful place into a hellhole? He was still getting his breath, tying up his shoelace at the edge of the road, when a pick-up drove past him, braked, and backed towards him.

Kevin had just finished dumping his load by the stream before Hal came, and had had a rest, dozing in his lorry, as people do when they have done a good morning's work. He was setting off again, bound for his lock-up on the moor, when he saw a boy sitting on the side of the road. The boy had fair hair and was wearing a blue anorak – and for some reason he seemed familiar.

The hair began to rise on the back of Kevin's neck. He braked and reached for the newspaper.

Yes, it was what he'd thought. He'd seen the advert when he was having his breakfast and now he peered at it again. This was the boy for whom they were offering twenty thousand pounds' reward! He peered again but there was no mistaking it. Hardly able to believe his luck, he leant out of the window of the cab, and in his oiliest voice, he said:

"Want a lift?"

Hal shook his head.

"Thanks, but I'm with a friend. I'm just going to catch her up."

Kevin grinned. The boy was obviously lying. There'd been no mention of a friend in the advert, but he'd go along with it.

"Well, I'm going that way. I'll pick her up and give both of you a lift to the village. It's not far. My name's Kevin, by the way."

Hal hesitated. But it was true he'd been longer than he intended. He'd trusted Mick and it had been all right. People in the north were known to be friendly.

"All right," he said. "Thanks."

He climbed into the cab and pulled Fleck in after him, but Fleck was behaving badly. As the engine revved up again he began to growl and show his teeth.

"Quiet, Fleck," said Hal.

But Fleck, usually so obedient, took no notice. Hal was looking down, trying to soothe him, and at first he did not notice that the van had swerved sharply to the left, up a rutted track.

"Stop," he said. "That's not the way. We should be going straight on," and as Kevin took no notice, he said loudly, "Where are you going?"

"You'll see soon enough," said Kevin. His voice was quite different now, harsh and ugly.

They drove uphill towards an isolated shed. But Fleck was going crazy. He jumped off Hal's lap and tried to clamber on the steering wheel, all the time barking at the top of his voice.

"Shut up, you little tyke," said Kevin. And he seized the dog by the scruff of his neck and threw him out of the window.

Hal screamed and tried to get out too, but Kevin put out one arm and held him in a grip of steel. He wasn't going to let twenty thousand pounds get away.

While Fleck yowled in anguish on the path, the pick-up drove up to a stone hut with a corrugated iron roof, standing by itself on the edge of the moor. Pulling the struggling Hal out, Kevin dragged him to the door and pushed him in.

"Fleck!" screamed Hal.

Then the door was slammed shut, the bolts pushed across, and it was padlocked.

Kevin walked away, thoroughly pleased with himself. Now for a phone call to the number in the advertisement and then – twenty thousand pounds!

The wretched dog was still yowling and whining, trying to get to Hal in the shed. Kevin picked up a stone and threw it hard, and it hit the cur on the side. Then he took his mobile out of his pocket and went a little way up the hill to get a signal.

Fleck was absolutely beside himself, trying to reach Hal. The stone hadn't drawn blood but it had bruised his shoulder. He could hear Hal's voice inside, frantically shouting his name.

For a few minutes Fleck ran uselessly round and round the hut, trying to find a way in. Then quite suddenly, he took off and raced like the wind down the hill and along the road.

Pippa was getting annoyed. What on earth was Hal doing? It shouldn't take so long to fill a water bottle. The dogs had been sitting round her obediently, waiting, but now they got to their feet and stared at the road, their noses twitching. Something was coming towards them – a white streak which, as they watched, turned into Fleck. But this was Fleck as no one had seen him. Not a wistful mongrel but a messenger bringing unspeakable news.

He raced up to the dogs, panting terribly, but he wouldn't rest. He jumped up at them, he shoved his nose into their sides, all the time talking in frantic barks.

"Where's Hal?" asked Pippa, her heart beginning to pound. "Where is he, Fleck?"

Fleck ran up to her, then back to the dogs. He started off up the road looking back over his shoulder but at first they did not follow. Then quite suddenly they understood, and a change came over these gentle domesticated pets. As one, they tore off up the track, with Fleck in the lead, and Pippa saw something which she was to remember all her life – the hunting pack, its blood up, closing in for the kill. Even Li-Chee, bouncing over the heather in the wake of the others, felt the blood of the grey wolf pounding in his veins. For wolves these dogs had been in the distant past, and wolves they had become again.

Kevin had made his phone call and, feeling very pleased with himself, he stretched out on the grass. The boy was still hammering on the door but he'd get tired of it soon enough. There was nothing to do now except wait till he could hand him over.

And then, all the things he had promised himself –

a new lorry, the deposit on a little bungalow, a trip to Las Vegas. That snooty girl in the checkout would go out with him fast enough when he was loaded, thought Kevin, going off into a doze.

He woke to find two huge paws on his chest and an enormous pair of jaws, with a row of terrifying teeth, salivating into his face.

Then he felt both his legs being worried and bitten, his trousers ripped, as Francine took one leg and Honey the other.

"Stop!" screamed Kevin in agony. "Let go. Let go!"

And now Li-Chee, who had not been able to keep up with the others, came panting up, leaped on to Kevin's stomach, disappeared under Otto's chest and fastened his needle-sharp teeth on Kevin's nose.

This was too much. Kevin struggled to his feet and in a welter of furious dogs, he staggered towards his van. Managing to shake off the Peke, blood pouring from his nose, he reached for the door handle.

But now it was Fleck's turn. Before Kevin could open the door, the Tottenham terrier raced up to him, sprang up – and bit him savagely in the behind.

And Kevin stumbled, fell forward on to the foot plate, and passed out.

It was there that Pippa found him, and after that everything went very quickly. Hal's thumps from inside the hut grew louder. Pippa ran up to the door and saw the padlock. Searching the lout's trousers, she found the key. Within minutes Hal was free and trying to calm his ecstatic dog, while Pippa relocked the door.

"We'll have to go up on to the moors," she said when she heard what had happened. "We can't risk the road now. While the sun's up we ought to be able to navigate all right. It's practically due east to the coast."

They set off up the hill, the dogs still excitedly circling them. The going was hard over the rough ground but they did not dare to slow down till they were sure that Kevin was not following them. After a couple of hours the children were exhausted.

"I'm going to get my breath back," said Pippa when they came to a patch of grass and scrub on which a few juniper bushes grew.

She flopped down and Hal sat down beside her.

"Here, Fleck," he said, feeling in his pocket. "You can have your flannel for a bit. I reckon you've earned it."

Fleck mouthed the flannel and wagged a polite tail. But just then the dogs heard something interesting in the bushes and in a flash all five of them were off in pursuit.

"Was it a hare?" asked Hal.

Pippa shrugged. "I didn't see. But they must be very hungry. Maybe they'll catch something they can eat. They'll be back in a minute."

Pippa was right. The dogs returned presently. Whatever it was had been too fast for them. But when Hal patted Fleck he saw that Fleck had lost his flannel.

"Where is it?" he asked his dog. "Where's your flannel?"

Fleck looked down at the ground, then up at Hal, ran back a few paces and returned, while Hal looked at him, worried. Was there going to be a fuss? Up to now he had guarded his flannel with his life.

But after a moment Fleck sat down and began contentedly to lick his paws. It didn't matter any longer where his flannel was. When he bit Kevin, Fleck had tasted buttock blood, and a dog who has done that has moved a long, long way from flannels.

19

Tracker Dogs

It was Curzon himself who took the call from Kevin on the hillside, and he hung up feeling extremely excited and pleased. What a breakthrough! The boy not only sighted but actually caught: imprisoned in a shed and only waiting to be picked up.

For a few moments Curzon, in his mind, spent the reward money which Donald Fenton would pay him. He wasn't so sure now about the yacht. A friend of his was building holiday homes on a Pacific island. Incredible houses they were, with five different swimming pools as well as the sea. Come to that, why wait till Fenton came up with the cash? Why not put down a deposit now? Leaning back in his chair, Curzon imagined himself standing on the top diving board, about to do a swallow dive into the turquoise water, while a cluster of beautiful girls in bikinis watched him from below. Then he remembered that Sprocket had to be sent north at once to bring the boy back, and he picked up the phone again.

"Sprocket?" he barked. "I need you straightaway. You've got to go up north – the boy's been sighted."

"Yes, sir. I know. But I am up north already."

"Eh? What? What are you talking about?"

Curzon was completely confused. It was true he hadn't seen Sprocket all day, but he often didn't see him all day, and as a matter of fact he liked it better that way.

"I'm in Todcaster, sir," came Sprocket's patient voice. "I left you a message."

"Oh, you did, did you? I'm afraid the computer's down."

Actually what had happened was that Curzon had found what seemed to him a load of gobbledegook on his screen and simply erased it. He could never remember codes.

"Now listen carefully," he went on. "The message is from someone called Kevin Dawks. He's on the road between Hilldale and Grant End." He read off Kevin's instructions. "'No policemen,' he said. He won't talk to anyone in uniform. Do you understand me?"

"Yes, sir. Absolutely. I'll make my way there at once."

Sprocket had had a miserable time in Todcaster. After driving through the night, he arrived at the circus to find the stable lad who had phoned him in a raging temper.

"He's done a bunk," he told Sprocket. "Must have pushed off last night, but it was him all right, so I want some of that reward."

After that, Sprocket had questioned various people in the circus, who told him that the boy had gone back to his Aunt Elsa who had sent for him because her brother-in-law had to have an operation.

Anyone else might have given up then, but not Sprocket. Ferreting around, he learned that some children from a care home had come to the circus, and been seen talking to the boy. So he drove to

Greystoke House and parked his van opposite the gates.

He had just got out his binoculars and was getting ready to do some serious investigating when a woman knocked on the window and asked him for a cauliflower.

"A nice firm one," she said, "but not too big. There's only the two of us now, with my daughter having gone off to London."

It was quite difficult to get rid of her, and in a way Sprocket blamed himself. If he had disguised the van as belonging to a plumber instead of a greengrocer, there would have been no bother. But though he had worked hard on his plumbing poem as he drove through the night, he hadn't been able to find a suitable rhyme for toilet. There was "oil it" of course, but if there was one thing people didn't want near their lavatories it was a lot of oil.

But there was worse to come. No sooner had he fixed his binoculars to his eyes than a fat woman burst through the gates and started threatening him.

"How dare you, you dirty old man!" she yelled. "I'll have the police after you, spying on innocent children."

As he drove away, Sprocket had been very upset. He was only twenty-six, and being called old was hurtful.

So when his phone rang and he heard Curzon's message, his spirits soared. Stopping only to adjust his moustache and consult his road map (because the instruction book for the new sat nav seemed to be in Finnish) he set off for the village of Hilldale.

Kevin had come round to find his trousers torn, and both his backside and his nose still painful, but the knowledge that he would soon be a rich man consoled him. And the wretched boy had gone quiet at last; there was no sound from inside the shed.

His first sight of the white van coming up the track made him start to his feet angrily. He didn't want any bloomin' vegetables and what did the bloke think he was doing, trespassing like that? But Sprocket's first words allayed his fears.

"Milton Sprocket, from MMM," he announced. "I gather you have the boy."

"I've got the boy, but have you got the money?'

"The money will be forthcoming," said Sprocket grandly. "As soon as I deliver the boy."

"All right," said Kevin. "Come on. He's in the shed there. I had a devil of a time keeping him in."

"Is he violent?" Sprocket asked anxiously. Children grew up very early these days, he knew, and they were strong. It was all that healthy food they were given to eat, and the exercise they took.

Kevin threw him a contemptuous glance. He unlocked the padlock, loosened the bolt, and stepped back.

Nothing happened.

"Come on out. I know you're in there."

Silence. Kevin made his way into the shed – and came out again.

"He's done a bunk, the little. . ."

The language Kevin used surprised Sprocket. Some of the words he simply did not know, although he was a poet.

"He was in here," said Kevin when he had sworn himself to a standstill. "It was him all right."

"I don't doubt it. He was seen in Todcaster last night."

"I won't be beaten by a squirt of a boy," said Kevin. "But it's all right, I know a friend who'll help us find him. Come on. You can leave the van here."

"Where are we going?"

"We're going to see Colin. He'll put Darth and Terminator on the job. The boy won't get away from them, I promise you."

Darth and Terminator were dogs. Sprocket had to tell himself several times that that was what they were. They were not hellhounds, not monsters out of a hideous dream, but as the beasts growled and slavered and threw themselves against the wire fence of their enclosure it was hard to believe. When Kevin had explained that they were going to get hold of Colin's tracker dogs, Sprocket had been nervous but excited. He hadn't taken the course on tracking with animals at his detecting college because it cost extra, but he knew all about bloodhounds, with their wrinkled faces and melancholy eyes, who could follow the scent of any human being.

But Darth and Terminator did not have wrinkled faces and they did not have melancholy eyes. They were grizzled, short-haired beasts, squat and barrel-chested with small ears and slightly bandy legs. And they were vicious. The pit bull in their ancestry was easy to see, but there were other strains there, and the whole animal, as Colin explained, was a high-powered machine for tracking anything in flight and running it to the ground.

As Colin let them out of their enclosure and snapped on their leads, Sprocket allowed himself a question.

"They wouldn't harm the boy, would they? I don't, think the reward will hold good if he's damaged at all."

"Na, they're trained to a tee," said Colin, spitting

on to the grass. "They'll hold a runaway down but they wouldn't bite him. Unless I told them to tear him apart."

While the terrifying animals were loaded into the back of the pick-up, Kevin put Sprocket in the picture. "There's no one knows more about tracking with dogs than Colin," he said.

It seemed that Colin had brought the sport of urban hunting to Todcaster. With Darth and Terminator, and a gang of friends with similar dogs, he went out at night after foxes who had come into town to raid the dustbins. Having no coverts to hide in, the foxes were easy prey.

"People wrote in and made a fuss," said Colin. "Didn't like their children finding headless foxes on the way to school." He laughed – a deep rumbling sound that shook his swollen belly. "Darth won't eat the back legs. He's a picky eater, is Darth."

They reached Kevin's lock-up and the dogs bounded out. Sprocket gave Colin Hal's handkerchief and the dogs sniffed round the shed. Then suddenly they burst into excited cries and raced off up the hill.

"Told you," said Kevin. "He'll have taken to the moors."

The next hours were a nightmare for Sprocket,

panting after Darth and Terminator as they strained at the end of their leads. The dogs kept up a steady pace and as they ran there came from their throats an eerie, half-crazed baying – a sound to freeze the blood.

"You're sure they won't harm the boy?" Sprocket repeated from time to time, remembering the headless foxes.

"Gentle as lambs they'll be, when they've got him," said Colin.

And Sprocket could only say again that for a boy brought back in pieces in a bin bag nobody would pay a penny.

The hunt went on. They stumbled through bogs, and over piles of last year's bracken. The weather was changing. A sharp wind had blown in from the sea, followed by the first spots of rain, and it was now that Sprocket felt a chill on his upper lip and realized that the worst had happened. Somewhere on the way he had lost his deeply loved moustache.

And still the terrifying beasts raced on.

Then, when Sprocket thought he could not go another step, the dogs checked, sniffed hard, circled . . . and suddenly took off in a different direction with a series of wildly excited yelps.

"They're getting close," shouted Colin over his

shoulder. "I'm going to let them go."

He slipped off the leads and the slavering beasts were off at speed, their noses down, sounding off in triumph.

"This is it! They've found him! There – behind those trees," shouted Colin. "Come on!"

He ran after the dogs and Kevin and Sprocket followed him. As they came into the copse, they saw that Colin was right. The hunt was over.

Darth and Terminator stood opposite each other, both tugging at something they held in their teeth, each dog claiming whatever it was as his own.

The men came closer and saw what it was. A blue face flannel.

It was not a good moment. The dogs showed no wish to go on with the hunt. As far as they could see they had done their job. They went on playing tug-of-war with their trophy while deep growls rumbled in their throats. Then when the flannel came away in two halves, they settled down to devour their prize.

"It's going to be a rough night," said Colin, turning up his collar against the rain. "We'd better get some shelter and try again in the morning. They'll pick up the scent again soon enough."

"What sort of shelter?" asked Sprocket nervously.

He was right to be nervous. Half an hour later they came to a bothy that Kevin knew about. It was nothing more than a rough, windowless hut with an earthen floor covered in sheep droppings. The wind roared through the cracks in the building. Water trickled down the walls.

Kevin and Colin did not seem to be bothered. They took out their hip flasks of whisky, belched, told a few stupid jokes, and were soon in a drunken sleep.

But for poor Sprocket, huddled in his jacket and as far away from the dogs as he could get, there was no sleep. He had never been so wretched in his life. He had put a few biscuits into his pocket before he set off – the plain kind with no disturbing raisins or nuts which might scratch the lining of his stomach – but whenever he tried to put one in his mouth either Darth or Terminator came and fastened their teeth round his wrist till he had handed it over.

As the miserable hours passed and the rain beat down on the roof, Sprocket did his best to console himself. Perhaps if he brought the boy back safely, Curzon would allow him to come upstairs sometimes. Perhaps he would even let him have an office next to the beautiful Fiona. And perhaps too the awful writer's block which had attacked him would lift and he would be able to write his plumbing poem.

But it did not seem likely, and as the wretched night wore on there was worse to come. In a corner of the hut he heard the sound of one of the dogs being extremely sick. Shining his torch on to the ground, Sprocket saw – in a pool of vomit, the remnants of the blue flannel, and beside it, covered in slime but still quite recognizable, his much-loved and sadly missed moustache.

Hal and Pippa, as they stumbled through the wildness of the night, would have been grateful even for a leaking, windowless bothy in which to shelter. They were in the middle of the moor and hopelessly lost.

At first they had made good progress, navigating by the sun. Hal had even hoped that they might get to the coast that day. But very quickly the weather changed, the sun disappeared, and then came the darkness and the rain.

Both children had been brought up in town. The blackness of the night overwhelmed them. It was not just an absence of light, it was a malevolent force, and the rain did not come down only from the sky. It came from all sides, blown by the ceaseless wind. It ran down inside their anoraks; it drenched their shoes. And Hal was also suffering from delayed shock. That hour spent locked up in Kevin's shed had shaken him more than he realized at the time. He began to think that they would never reach the cottage by the sea – that they were doomed to fail.

"If we stop now we'll probably die of exposure," said Pippa. "I never understood what that was, but I do now."

"We'll probably die of it whether we stop or not," muttered Hal.

They stumbled on, over boulders, across streams that were hardly wetter than the ground beneath their feet, and the faithful dogs followed. From Li-Chee, shorn of his pelt, came noises that were not very lion-like. He gave small snuffles of distress, and when Pippa picked him up he buried his nose in her jacket. The others padded on resolutely. Fleck was keeping up well; he seemed to have grown up since he had saved Hal from Kevin's clutches. And the dogs looked out for one another. If one of them for a moment vanished in the darkness, the others waited.

When they first saw a glimmer of light they hardly dared to believe it. They knew that people in the last stages of exhaustion see things that are not there. But the light was real. It grew stronger – and as they beat their way towards it they saw that it came from a tall, imposing building.

"It looks like a castle," said Pippa.

"Probably belongs to an ogre," murmured Hal. "Who else would live in the middle of nowhere?"

But whoever it belonged to, they had to go forward, and with the dogs pressing close behind them they made their way towards a great door. Even if whoever lived there was going to turn them in – even if he was going to eat them – they had no choice except to beg for shelter.

The bell clanged inside the great building and they waited. They were going to press it again when a slit opened in the door and a face appeared.

The face vanished and for a while nothing happened. Then slowly the door drew back and they saw a tall, hooded figure who stood there in silence.

"Please—" began Pippa. But she got no further because an awful thing now happened. Otto, the wise and gentle dog whom they would have trusted with their lives, had gone mad. A rumble came from his throat, and before they could stop him he reared up and with the full force of his weight, he landed with his paws on the shoulders of the hooded man.

The children started forward, horrified. This was the end of all their hopes of sanctuary. Then they saw what Otto was doing. He was licking the man's face. The rumble in his throat had become a kind of purring, and his tail went so fast that it had become a blur.

The hooded man allowed himself to be greeted like this for a few moments. Then gently he removed Otto's paws and came towards them.

"You are welcome, my children," he said.

"Can we bring the dogs in?" asked Pippa.

The tall man smiled.

"If you could not bring dogs into this place it would be strange indeed."

20

Otto Remembers

They had come to the monastery of St Roc. The tall
man who had greeted them was the abbot, in charge
of the monks who lived there, and now he led them
along a corridor hung with paintings of various
saints. It was warm and very quiet and there was a
smell of beeswax and lilies. To the frozen children it
seemed like paradise.

Otto did not follow the abbot. He walked beside
him, his nose within inches of the abbot's robe.

"Of course," whispered Pippa. "Otto came from a

monastery in Switzerland. The abbot there bred him himself, Kayley told me."

They were put in the charge of a round-faced monk with a friendly smile who introduced himself as Brother Malcolm and took them into a room where a fire burned brightly. Their wet clothes were peeled off and taken away and dry clothes brought in all sorts of shapes and sizes into which they fitted themselves as best they could. In a corner of the room, another monk was busy towelling the soaking dogs.

Then they were led into the refectory, where the monks were sitting at a long table, eating their supper. The abbot was in a carved seat at the top, while a very old monk, perched against a kind of high desk, was reading aloud from The Lives of the Saints.

The children slipped on to the end of a bench. Two plates of soup were put before them, and two hunks of bread, and as they began to eat they saw that five bowls had been put down on the floor beside the wall, and the dogs, with their heads down, were eating hungrily.

After the soup came a dish of fruit. Hal managed to make out the shape of the apples and pears; then they became blurred, and he could only just stop himself from falling forward with his head on his plate.

At the head of the table, the abbot made a sign, and Brother Malcolm came up to the children.

"You must be ready for your beds," he said.

He led Pippa and Hal out of the room, and Li-Chee, Francine, Honey and Fleck followed close behind them. But not Otto. Otto gave an affectionate goodnight lick to his friends, then padded over to the head of the table and flopped down with his great muzzle across the abbot's feet.

They followed Brother Malcolm up the stairs and along a silent corridor with a number of identical doors. They were hardly surprised any more when he opened the first of the doors and they found a number of dog beds and a water bowl.

"It's like Goldilocks, only with dogs instead of bears," whispered Pippa, and Hal nodded.

There was no need to persuade Li-Chee and Francine and Honey to lie down. They had already chosen their beds and begun to turn themselves round and round, getting ready to settle down for the night. But Fleck stood beside Hal, waiting. He did not seem pathetic or frightened as he had done before when he expected to be separated from his master. It was rather that he felt that it was necessary

449

to look after Hal, and Brother Malcolm picked this up at once.

"Perhaps he'd better stay with you tonight," he said.

Ten minutes later, Pippa was in bed in one of the small, whitewashed rooms which the monks kept for their guests, and Hal was in another, with Fleck on the floor beside him.

Hal fell asleep at once, but after an hour he was woken by a thump and found Fleck preparing to settle down on top of him.

"No, Fleck, get down," Hal ordered, looking at the spotless white cotton bedspread and remembering Albina's agitation about dogs on the coverlet. And as Fleck did not move: "You heard me. Dogs don't sleep on beds, it's not allowed."

Fleck got down, but reluctantly. The door was ajar, and he went out into the corridor, then back into the room, then out again.

"All right, if you want to go and sleep with your friends, I'll take you back," said Hal, getting out of bed.

But as they passed the next door, which was ajar, Fleck stopped.

"What is it? What's the matter?"

Hal followed Fleck's gaze. Lying on the bed of

what must have been a fairly portly monk were three retriever puppies. The monk was snoring gently, the bedclothes going rhythmically up and down, and the dogs lying across him rose and fell also, soothed and lulled into the deepest of sleeps.

"OK, Fleck, you win," said Hal.

In less than five minutes Hal was asleep again, and his dog lay curled up at his side.

It was not until the following morning that Pippa understood about the place they had come to.

She had been too tired to take in anything much the night before, but now as she woke, she looked eagerly round her room. It was very plainly furnished, but there was one oil painting on the wall above her bed. It was of a man in sandals wearing a robe and carrying a staff. Round his head was a halo, and at his feet sat a dog holding a piece of bread in his mouth. It was a very nice dog, white with big black patches and concerned eyes. The bread was not for him, you could see that. It was for the man with the halo.

Underneath the picture, in gold letters, were the words "St Roc".

"Of course," said Pippa aloud. "I've been an idiot."

Her grandmother had been very devout and told her the stories of the saints. St Roc had been a healer who looked after people with the plague until he caught the illness himself and went into the forest to die. But he didn't die because a dog brought him food from his master's table until he recovered. Saints usually have a bad time, being shot full of arrows or broken on wheels, but this dog, who did not even have a name, had saved him, and since then Roc had been the patron saint of dogs. He was the patron saint of other things too – surgeons and people with knee problems and tile makers – but dogs were what he was famous for.

And this monastery was dedicated to his name!

Brother Malcolm, when he brought their dry clothes, told them more. "There is a picture of him in stained glass in our chapel window. As you will see, we try to carry on his work," he said.

The monks had already had their breakfast, but two places were laid for the children, with glasses of milk and home-baked bread and honey from the monk's own hives. And the dogs' breakfast too was waiting in their bowls.

But there was no sign of Otto, who had eaten earlier.

When they had finished their meal, Brother Malcolm took them through a door in the building and out into a walled garden. The weather had cleared; the air was soft and gentle after the storm. They walked between neatly kept herb beds and rows of young vegetables into an orchard full of blossoming apple trees. Under the trees stood a dozen beehives, which the dogs respectfully avoided.

"Is it true that you have to tell bees all the important things that happen?" asked Pippa. "Like when somebody dies."

Brother Malcolm turned to her. "Yes, it's true. Bees are messengers. They will carry anything you tell them straight up to God."

Hal had almost forgotten that they were on the run. He felt completely safe and contented. Perhaps he could be a monk when he grew up, he thought. It was true that monks couldn't get married, but from what he'd seen of married people that might be no bad thing.

The dogs had been snuffling about peacefully, but now they began to bark excitedly, while the whole of Li-Chee's back end quivered with pleasure. The children looked up to see the abbot coming towards them. Beside him, as though he had been there all his life, was Otto.

The abbot spoke quietly to Brother Malcolm, then turned to the children. "We've something to show you which you'll find interesting, I think," he said.

He led them to a low building standing by itself, and opened the door.

The floor of the room they entered was covered in a thick layer of straw and in the straw, playing and squealing and rolling over and over, was a host of puppies. The straw was golden in a shaft of sunlight and the puppies were golden too. Retrievers with dark brown eyes and the softest of milk-filled stomachs.

"We breed guide dogs for the blind," said the portly monk who was in charge of them. "This litter is from a mother who comes from a long line of working dogs. We keep them till they're ready to go off for their training. Not all of them are suitable but we've learnt to pick out those who should go forward and the rest go to good homes."

He scooped up a very energetic puppy who was trying to make friends with Fleck.

"This one is very promising," he said. "Alert but not nervous."

The abbot nodded. "Brother Ambrose can tell when they're just a few weeks old."

"There's a guide dog who comes past the place where my sister works," said Pippa. "Grace, she's called. She's incredible."

The puppies were becoming overexcited, scurrying about all over the place as they tried to make friends with the visiting dogs. But now Otto took a few paces forward and sat down.

At once the puppies went to him, and began to clamber over his legs, to play with his tail and dig their noses into his fur. Then carefully the huge dog rolled over on to his back, giving them even more places to climb, and with squeals of delight they crawled over his stomach, hung on to his ears. He had turned himself into a warm and living climbing frame and the abbot looked down at him with a glow in his eyes. It was almost as though Otto knew that each of these little creatures would one day be responsible for a person's safety and life.

But the time had come for the children to hear their fate and the abbot led them to a bench under the apple tree.

"Now," he said. "Tell me your story."

Hal turned anxiously to Pippa. She was usually the one who spoke for both of them, but though he was proud of Pippa's ability to make things up, he hated the idea of telling lies here in this place.

Pippa moved closer to the abbot and began to speak.

"It really started with Hal. His parents got him this dog and he thought it was for good but after two days they took it back to Easy Pets and he was desperate and so was Fleck. I knew about it because my sister is the kennel maid there. . ."

She went on to tell the abbot about her own brainstorm in letting the dogs go, their determination to reach Hal's grandfather in his cottage, what had happened in the circus and their mishaps with Kevin the Dumper. And Hal listened in amazement, for every word she spoke was true.

When she had finished, the abbot turned to Hal.

"Your grandfather's cottage is near here?"

Hal nodded. "It's down on the shore opposite Farra Island. He's a fisherman and he has a smallholding there. If I could get to him before there's a fuss with my parents he would understand."

"And you think he would take you in?" asked the abbot.

"Yes, I do. He's always thought I should have a dog."

"But five dogs? Has he always thought you should have five?"

Hal hung his head. It was true that all he and

Pippa had thought of was getting safely to the cottage, but he could see how it would look to the abbot. Was it possible that they were going to be sent back or turned over to the police? They'd come so far, but even now a single phone call could end it all.

The abbot was silent, occasionally pulling one of Otto's ears. The minutes passed.

When he spoke, the words were solemn and slow.

"Since you're so near your journey's end I'll let you go on your way. But if I haven't had a telephone call within twenty-four hours to say that you have arrived safely, I shall straightaway call the police. Now go and find Brother Malcolm. He will give you some sandwiches and make sure you know the right path."

As they reached the building, the abbot went up the stairs with Otto, but the relief the children felt was mixed with anxiety. What of Otto, who had found his true place and his true master? Remembering Francine and Honey and what those two had suffered, they were very much afraid. Would Otto refuse to come? And what would it be like to finish the journey without him?

"It isn't for us to decide," said Hal. "The abbot will know."

When they were ready, the children and the other dogs waited at the front door. The abbot came downstairs with Otto at his side. He laid his hand on the great head.

"If God wills, we shall meet again," he said to him.

Otto made no fuss. He knew that his job was not yet done. He only moaned once, and pushed his muzzle against the abbot's robe. Then he turned and followed the children out of the door.

21

The Last Lap

Colin had been right to boast about his dogs. Darth and Terminator did pick up the scent again. When they were taken back to the place where they found the flannel, they circled for a while and then took off at speed, running out of the copse across the open moors.

Colin still held them on the lead, and Kevin ran beside him, but poor Sprocket lagged badly behind. He was cold and hungry and tired, and his hand was wrapped in a handkerchief because Terminator had bitten him.

"Call that a bite?" Colin had jeered when Sprocket had cried out. "You wouldn't have a hand left if he'd bitten you. It's just a little nip, playful-like."

It had happened when Sprocket put his hand in his pocket to get out an indigestion pill, and Terminator thought he was reaching for a biscuit which didn't seem to be coming his way.

I ought to get myself to a doctor and have an injection, thought Sprocket as he panted after the others. I could be in danger of getting tetanus, or even rabies.

And what was this mad runaway boy doing? He seemed to be heading towards the coast – but why? Was there a boat waiting to take him off? Was he part of an organized gang? The picture Curzon had shown him had been of a small, ordinary boy, but he seemed to be turning into a maniac.

The children left the monastery in high spirits. The sun was shining, larks sang, the heather was green and fresh after the rain. A well-made track led them gradually off the moor and down towards farmland. Hal knew that in a few hours he would be sitting in his grandfather's kitchen.

They passed a few isolated cottages and a farm, and then, at a place where the road curved round the hillside, they saw it at last – the sea! The North Sea can be grey and forbidding, but today it was like an ocean in a dream, blue-green and glittering with light, the white horses curling on to the golden sand. Hal had never visited his grandparents, but they had told him so much about where they lived, had drawn so many maps and pictures, that he felt as though he was coming home.

"Do you see that bay – the far one?" said Hal. "That's where the cottage is. Behind those dunes. I think we can take a short cut across country."

They left the track and started to walk over rough pasture towards the coast.

But the dogs had become restless. They stopped with their noses in the air, sniffing and listening. And then the children heard what the dogs had already been aware of: the baying of hounds.

At first they took no notice. It was probably some kind of local hunt, people chasing after hares. Then they looked back and saw, rounding the bend on the road, three distinct figures. Two of them were in front, leading a couple of dogs. Now they stopped at the place where Hal and Pippa had left the track, while the dogs sniffed the ground, trying to pick up a scent.

Then suddenly one of the figures shouted and pointed while the other bent down and slipped off the leashes. The next moment, two dark, squat shapes leaped the low stone wall, and howling like creatures from the netherworld, they began to streak off down the hill.

Even then the children could not at first believe what they were seeing – it seemed impossible. Then suddenly they understood. It wasn't hares or foxes that these hellhounds were chasing.

"It's us they're after," shouted Pippa. "They're hunting us!"

Terrified, they began to race and slither down the steep slope and all the time the baying became louder. There was no moment when they dared to look behind them, so they did not notice that Otto was no longer there.

He had stopped at the edge of the last steep scramble down to the beach and was standing as still as if he were Barry, his stuffed ancestor in the Natural History Museum, his silhouette outlined against the high blue of the early summer sky.

The two hellhounds ran straight as arrows towards him, ignoring gorse, cowpats, a clump of barbed wire. The muscles in their chests and forelegs were bunched, their upper lips curled back, showing even more of their fearsome teeth. Their eyes were red, saliva streaked down their necks and they had stopped barking. The shouting was over; the tearing and rending was about to begin.

Otto waited, perfectly still.

The pursuing beasts were only a few feet away from him now. With an immense effort they managed to stop themselves and adjusted their legs for the leap which would finish Otto and allow them to continue their headlong race for the boy. But for a moment they hesitated. The pit bull in them was ready for murder, but the bloodhound part wanted to get on with the chase.

And in this moment of indecision, Otto spoke. The growl started from somewhere in the lower abdomen and when it finally reached his voice box and emerged into the outside world it was like the sound of a mighty river swollen by rain as it thunders over great falls to the plain below.

At first nothing happened. The furious attacking dogs slavered and rumbled and grimaced. Then as Otto's endless growls rolled out over the grass, their attitude slowly changed. Their upper lips covered the ghastly fangs, their breathing quietened, their brows wrinkled in puzzlement. A small nervous yawn escaped them and slowly their gaze dropped to Otto's feet.

And then the two satanic beasts sank first their buttocks, and then – with their forepaws pushing gingerly forward – their bellies to the ground. They tried a last tremulous growl but it had more than a touch of squeak in it.

As if to say, "No. Not a single word more," Otto finally lowered his head, took a step forward and opened his mouth. And at the other end of these two terrors of the night, something odd occurred. A small tremor seemed to affect their stumpy tails. Could it be a nervous twitch? But no. It came again, and it was getting stronger . . . and stronger still.

For the first time since they were puppies playing happily at their mother's side, Darth and Terminator were wagging their tails.

Down on the beach, Hal and Pippa and the other dogs raced along the sands, burst through the doors of the cottage and tumbled in a heap into the hall.

22

The Sea, the Sea!

Hal's grandmother was crying. She wasn't pretending not to as she bustled round making tea, buttering bread and opening biscuit tins. Throughout the ghastly week in which they had waited for news of Hal, Marnie had been brave and hopeful for her husband's sake, but now she let go.

The kitchen of the cottage seethed with dogs and children. Otto had padded in quietly when his job was done, and Meg the old Labrador had come out from under the sofa and was doing her best to be polite to the newcomers.

In the middle of the throng sat Fleck, looking very pleased with himself. Hal's grandfather had greeted him by name as soon as he had stopped hugging Hal.

"Hello, Fleck," he had said, picking him out as the dog who mattered, whose place this was. "Welcome to our home." Already Fleck had taken charge of one of Marnie's slippers and was keeping it safe.

Hal, perched on a stool by the kitchen table, was completely happy. It was all as he had hoped. His grandparents, so warm and understanding, the crackling fire, the view outside the window of the sea and the islands and the scudding clouds. . . Only it was even better than he had imagined because he had saved not only Fleck but the other dogs, and he had found Pippa!

But when the children began to speak of their adventures, the horror of the last hour came back in full force.

"We were chased by tracker dogs," said Pippa. "Honestly. We couldn't believe at first that it was us they were after."

"It was as though we were criminals," said Hal. "You never saw such animals. If it hadn't been for Otto—"

466

He broke off, because the back door of the cottage had opened and in the threshold stood a large, uniformed policeman, looking very much at home.

"Afternoon," he said, removing his cap.

The children froze. Had they been betrayed? Were they going to be packed off to London and the dogs imprisoned again? Was it possible that Hal's grandparents were going to turn them in? For a moment, Hal's whole world seemed to topple.

But the policeman had begun to speak.

"I just called in to see if you'd had any news of the boy," he said, "but I see that all's well."

"Yes, thanks, Arthur. Hal's safe and sound and so is his friend Pippa. It was what we thought. He came with Fleck here. But the children have just told us they were chased by tracker dogs. Can you believe it?"

The policeman nodded. "We've had a message from one of the farmers out on the moor. I've sent a couple of men up there now. We reckon we know who they are. Chap called Kevin Dawks and his friend. Kevin's a dumper and they're nasty pieces of work, both of them. They're breaking the law, of course, tracking without a licence."

He put his cap on again, shook hands with the children, and left.

"He's been such a comfort," said Marnie. "Came in every day to see if you'd turned up. The police never thought you'd been kidnapped. They always thought you were on the way to us."

But now it was time for the telephone. The call to the abbot didn't take long, but Pippa's call home was not quite so simple. It was Kayley who answered the phone.

"We've been expecting you back from camp for an hour. Is the bus late?"

"Actually, I'm not at camp," said Pippa. "I'm in Northumberland."

"You are what?"

"I'll explain. Only it's a long story."

There was a pause. Then, "Is it a story about dogs?" asked Kayley.

"Yes, it is." Pippa took a deep breath. "That's exactly what it is. I've got them here with me and. . ." She launched into an explanation.

When she hung up, she looked distinctly shaken.

"My sister's coming to fetch me," she said. "I hope that's all right. She's a bit cross."

Actually, considering how good-tempered Kayley usually was, she had not been a bit cross. She had been very cross indeed.

"Now you, Hal," said his grandfather.

*

In London, Albina picked up the phone and shrieked.

"Oh, thank goodness! Thank the Lord! Oh, Hal, we've been so worried, I thought I would die! You must come back at once – at once. Is there an aeroplane you can get? Or perhaps the train's faster. No, what am I saying? Of course we'll come up and fetch you in the car. We'll be with you in a few hours."

Hal's voice cut in, quiet but implacable.

"I'm not coming home," he said.

"What? Oh, Hal, darling, what are you saying? Hal. . ." She began to sob down the telephone but her son did not relent. He was reliving the moment when he had come back from the dentist and found Fleck gone.

"I'm here with Fleck and I'm not going to give him up. Not ever."

"No, no . . . of course not. I'm sorry. It'll be all right, we understand."

"You tricked me," said Hal. "I don't trust you any more." Albina was still crying but Hal was seeing Fleck, lying unconscious on the floor of his cage. "I'll never trust you again."

He was about to put down the receiver when his

grandfather came and took it out of his hand.

"Albina, I'd like to speak to my son, please," he said. "Is he there?"

"Yes, he's here. Oh, what shall I do?" Albina was beside herself. "Donald, it's your father."

Donald took the phone.

"You've got the boy?"

"Yes, he's safe and sound and he's got his dog. But he's very tired and at the end of his tether. Give him a few days to rest up before you come."

"But that's ridiculous. You can't expect us not to—"

His father's voice was different. Not the voice of someone who had decided to stand aside and not interfere. This was his father's voice as he remembered it from his childhood.

"The boy needs time. Come up at the end of the week. And remember this, Donald: if you try to take his dog away, you'll have lost him for good."

Returning to the kitchen, Alec found his wife and the children with their faces pressed to the window.

"We saw them," said Pippa gleefully. "In a police van. The dumper was there and another man and two dogs. And there was someone else with them sort of cowering at the back. He looked terrified."

She spoke the truth. Milton Sprocket, arrested by the police, hemmed in by Darth and Terminator, cold and bitten and disgraced, had sunk to the very depths of his being.

23

Return of the Dogs

On the following day Hal was out in the garden helping his grandfather weed the vegetable bed when he saw an enormous silver car drive up to the cottage. Immediately he was furious. His parents had promised not to come up before the end of the week. What's more, they had bought another car they didn't need – a Rolls-Royce gleaming with newness.

The car stopped, and out of the driving seat came a calm-faced Indian gentleman who stood for a moment looking at the view. Then a second door opened, and out stepped Kayley.

When she had finished talking to Pippa on the telephone, Kayley had hurried round to find her mother, who was sewing with Mrs Naryan. It was no good trying to shield Pippa now, so she explained exactly what had happened.

"I'm going up to fetch her straightaway," she said. "Goodness knows what else she'll get up to. There's an overnight bus to Berwick, I can catch that. I've got enough in my savings for the fare, just about."

But at this point Mrs Naryan put down her needle.

"That is not a good idea, I think," she said in her soft voice. "This bus will not be pleasant."

She walked out of the room and came back with her husband. Mr Naryan, like his wife, was small, soft-spoken and gentle. He was also one of the richest men in England, having built up a flourishing import-export business in the years since he had left Rajasthan.

"I will drive you to Northumberland," he said.

And when both Kayley and her mother said no, no, it was out of the question, it was impossible, he only smiled. "There is a man in the north whom I would like to see," he said. "I will come to your house at six tomorrow morning."

Now he shook hands with Hal's grandparents and then took his leave. He was going to spend the night in a hotel further up the coast and come back for Kayley and Pippa on the following day.

The dogs remembered Kayley. They remembered her so well that she was nearly knocked over, and Kayley petted them and talked to them as only she could talk to dogs.

But her greeting to her sister was not so enthusiastic.

"Come outside," she said to Pippa when she had been welcomed by Hal's grandparents and said hello to Hal.

The first ten minutes as they walked along the beach was spent by Kayley giving Pippa a piece of her mind.

"You must have been mad," she said. "We've had the police round, and the Carkers are spitting blood. I thought you'd forgotten to set off the burglar alarm, but letting the dogs out on purpose. . ."

"I know," said Pippa. "I sort of saw red. The way they looked when Hal took Fleck away . . . I couldn't bear it."

"That's all very well, but what now? Hal's grandparents can't keep five dogs. What's going to become of them? If we take them back to Easy Pets it'll come out that you let them go, and—"

"We can't," Pippa broke in. "We absolutely can't take them back to sit in those awful cages again."

"Well, how can we find homes for them?"

Pippa looked at the four dogs who had followed them on to the sands.

"They've got homes, Kayley. All four of them. They found homes for themselves, but they came on with us to see Fleck safe. They've found homes and work and masters that they want to serve."

"What do you mean?" asked Kayley.

So Pippa told her.

They left early the following day. Mr Naryan was a Buddhist and didn't seem to mind dogs piling into his beautiful car. The Buddha held all life to be sacred, and whether it was a businessman or a St Bernard lolling on his spotless cream upholstery made no difference to him.

Fleck said goodbye again and again to Otto and Honey and Francine and Li-Chee, and they said it to him. But the little mongrel was not worried or upset. He had known at once that he and Hal belonged to the cottage in a special way, and when the others got into the car, he turned and went back into the house and flopped down contentedly beside old Meg.

For Hal it was more difficult. He and Pippa hadn't been together long but those days on the road had changed him. He'd be able to write to Pippa and phone her, but seeing the dogs go was hard.

It was Kayley who comforted him.

"You'll see them again, Hal," she said. "When you've shared so much with someone, whether it's a dog or a person, they don't just go out of your life."

They drove to the monastery first. As the car slowed down, Otto, who had been looking out of the window, began to moan and gargle deep in his throat, and to press his nose against the glass. They stopped outside the gates to let him out, and Pippa and Kayley went with him. Pippa was putting up her hand to ring the bell, but before she could do so the door opened and Brother Malcolm stood there, smiling his welcome.

But now it all went wrong. She had expected Otto to rush inside and up the stairs, but he wouldn't go. Instead he turned and raced away round the side of the building and out of sight.

"He is in the garden," said Brother Malcolm.

"We'd better go and see," said Kayley.

The girls walked past the herb beds and into

the orchard, where they saw an unusual sight. The abbot of St Roc lay on the grass, felled like an oak tree. And over him and beside him and round him was Otto, now licking, now barking, now simply sitting on his chest.

"Is it all right?" shouted Pippa.

The abbot did not reply. He merely raised one arm – perhaps in blessing, perhaps in greeting, perhaps just because it was the only one of his limbs that he could free.

The girls did not repeat their question. If ever anything was all right, this was. They turned and walked back to the car.

Old Selby, the shepherd, was getting ready to load his possessions on to the removal van. There weren't many of them. His room in Rosewood was small, and everything was built in and fitted. He'd set the bonfire, ready to burn the stuff he wasn't taking, and now he picked up his crook and laid it across the top. Billy was going to a farmer in the neighbouring valley. He padded miserably behind his master, his eyes clouded with anxiety, and from time to time he lifted his head and howled.

All the same, it was Billy who first heard the

car purring down the track. His ears went up. He yapped once as the door opened.

"Go, Honey," said Pippa. "It's all right. You can go now."

Honey bounded out, came back once to her friends, and then was gone.

But Pippa, following her, stopped in dismay, seeing the removal van, the bonfire.

"Oh dear," she said. "You're leaving! We'd hoped you'd be able to have Honey, but if—"

Old Selby was bending down, rubbing Honey's head.

Now he straightened himself. "No, I'm not," he said. "I'm not leaving now. I'm staying right here where I belong."

He walked over to the bonfire and picked out his stick. Then he went over to the driver of the van.

"I've changed my mind," said Selby. "You'll have to take the van back."

The driver looked at him, ready to argue. Old people had fancies, he knew. The shepherd probably didn't know what he was doing.

But then he looked at Selby again. When he first saw him he'd taken him for a man near the end of his life, but he seemed to have changed. He didn't really look old at all – and the driver shrugged, and got back into his cab.

"Come on, Honey," said Selby. "We've got work to do."

They caught the circus in Todcaster on its last day. The big top had come down; lorries were being loaded. Francine was out of the car, streaking away the moment it stopped. Kayley and Pippa, following her, heard her yapping outside one of the caravans. Then a black shape bounded out and in a moment Rupert and Francine were dancing round each other in a frenzy of joy.

Now a thin man in a beret followed Rupert out of the caravan and introduced himself as Petroc.

"This must be the dog that George told me about. Francine, is it?" he asked in a slight foreign accent.

"Yes, it is. We wondered if she could stay with you?"

Petroc sighed. "It would have been good. She could have joined my act, Petroc's Poodles. It is the best dog act in the world," he said modestly. "But a dog like that is worth a lot of money and I am a poor man, so I'm afraid—"

"We don't want any money," said Kayley quickly. "We just want her to be happy."

Petroc looked at Francine, rolling over and over

with Rupert on the grass. His thin face creased into a smile.

"She is happy, I think," he said. "Yes, I know dogs and this one is happy. She is very happy indeed."

But Francine did not forget her manners. She gave a paw to Kayley, then to Pippa, then to Kayley once again, before she followed Rupert into the caravan and her new life.

The car was empty now and Li-Chee was getting worried. He had whimpered pathetically when Otto left, and now he sat on Pippa's knee, his pop eyes anxiously searching her face. Where was everybody? Had he been forgotten?

Kayley and Pippa too were nervous. This last stop was going to be difficult. What if there was a rule against having pets in the care home? Mr Naryan, driving steadily, said little, but he was a comfort.

"He has a big heart, that one," he said. "It will be well with him."

As they turned into the drive of Greystoke House, they saw that the garden was full of children. They stopped and Li-Chee jumped out – and then from the group of children one little girl came running like the wind.

"Li-Chee," said Nini, and now she did not kneel

to him, but scooped him up in her arms.

Then Mick came over and Pippa gave him the note that Hal had written.

"We made it all right, thanks to you, and your friends," she said, and Mick said it was nothing, and that Nini had been quite different since the night they came.

"She talks now and she sort of fits in. It's great."

But the difficult part was still to come. Mick took them to Mrs Platt's office, but they had to be careful because the house mother knew nothing about the night in the boiler room.

Pippa said they were looking for a home for the Peke.

"We remembered that Nini liked him so much when she came to the circus. But perhaps there's a rule against having animals here?"

Mrs Platt said no, there wasn't. In fact, at the last meeting of the committee it had been suggested that the children might have a dog. "There was a very nasty character in a white van out there the other day," she said. "Sat there for hours. I thought then a dog might see him off." She went to the window. "My goodness, that's not much of a watchdog, though. It looks like a little rat. Is that the one in the circus act? What's happened to his hair?"

481

Kayley looked at Pippa, who was the family liar.

"A horrible boy cut it because he was jealous," said Pippa. "Our dog act was better than his."

Mrs Platt was shocked. "People don't know how to discipline children these days." She looked out of the window again. "But really, I don't think—"

She broke off. Li-Chee, who had been sitting on Nini's lap, suddenly raced down the steps, barking at the top of his voice.

"It's the newspaper delivery boy," said Mrs Platt. "Well, I reckon I was wrong about him not being a watchdog."

"Pekes are amazing like that," said Kayley. "They're lion dogs, bred to protect emperors and give notice of danger."

"Are they then?" said Mrs Platt, looking at the newspaper boy, who had dropped the paper and run back to the gate. "Well, well – I guess he can stay."

The last thing Kayley and Pippa saw as they drove away was Li-Chee sitting on the top of the steps. Nini was on one side of him and Mick on the other, but Li-Chee's paws were stretched out in front of him and he held his head high.

Just so had his ancestors sat and guarded the palaces of emperors. And just so sat Li-Chee now, protecting Greystoke House.

24

Albina Grovels

Albina was on the floor on her hands and knees, making odd noises, clucking noises, then cooing noises, then wheedling noises. The floor was not the carpeted floor of her London house, it was the rough-boarded floor of the cottage, covered in a worn old rug.

"Please, Fleck, please. I'm sorry," she said. "I didn't mean it. Please come out and let's be friends."

Hal's parents had arrived an hour earlier. Hal had allowed himself to be embraced, but only politely.

And Fleck had taken one look at Albina, growled horribly, and vanished under the sofa.

"It's no good," said Hal. "He'll never forget what you did."

"Can't you make him come out?" begged Albina.

"No. And if I could I wouldn't," said Hal.

Donald had gone out with his parents to look at the boat and Hal and his mother were alone.

Albina tried again. Marnie had given her a bone and she waggled it back and forward under the sofa but Fleck ignored it. Grovelling on the floor, she went on making what she hoped were wooing noises. Then she put her hand under the sofa and pulled it back with a cry as Fleck's teeth fastened on her fingers.

"Oh, what shall I do?" she cried, getting to her feet. "Look at my tights, they're ruined. And my skirt." She went over to the table and sat down. Then she let her head fall forward on to her hands and began to sob.

For a few moments Hal, sitting opposite, just let her cry. Then something horrible happened. The anger he had felt with his parents began to get weaker . . . and weaker still. He missed it badly, this rage which had kept him going on his adventure. But there was nothing to be done about it; it was gone. His mother had done a wicked thing; she was foolish and misguided – but she was his mother.

He put an arm round Albina.

"It's all right," he said. "It's over. It's all right."

And at that moment Fleck came out from under the sofa and trotted over to the table. It was "forgiving time", it seemed, and he flopped down between Albina and Hal, and yawned, and went to sleep.

Later that afternoon, Hal went for a walk along the dunes with his father. The last week, when he'd not known whether his son was dead or alive, had changed Donald Fenton. It was as though Hal's love for his grandparents made him see his old home as he had seen it when he was a boy. He no longer felt like sneering at the shabby cottage, the old boat with its temperamental engine. While Hal was with his mother, Donald had been out and emptied the lobster pots, and helped Alec fix the pump on the Peggotty. It was a screwdriver which Donald now wore behind his ear, not a gadget connecting him with New York.

"You really like it up here, don't you?" said Donald.

"Yes, I really do. And so does Fleck."

Donald sighed. Fleck was here to stay, but he was not going to make life easier.

"What about Okelands? We took a lot of trouble getting you in there."

"I'm not going to boarding school," said Hal. "I told you, I'm not leaving Fleck. What I'd like to do is stay here and live with my grandparents. There's a school in Seaville."

"Yes, I know. I was there for seven years."

Hal looked up at his father. He was staring out at the sea and he looked stern – or was it sad?

"You like it so much better here than being with us? Than being at home?" asked Donald, and Hal could not help hearing the hurt in his voice.

"It's not exactly like that," said Hal. "I wouldn't like never to be at home again." He thought of the blonde girl in the park, and Joel, the school friend he'd been pretending to stay with, and now of course there was Pippa. And his parents, who had got everything so wrong but who were trying now. Perhaps in their own way they had always tried.

"Could I stay here for another month? I've missed so much school anyway. Then I'll get Fleck trained."

Donald turned to his son and smiled with relief. There wasn't going be a battle. Hal was going to come home.

486

"I don't see why not," he said. "I'll come and fetch you, and spend a few days. It's time I had a break."

But people do not change completely, however hard they try.

"I'd like to buy you something really nice, Hal. It can cost as much as you like. I mean it – the sky's the limit."

Hal looked at him for a long time.

"All I ever wanted was a dog," he said.

But as Donald's face fell, Hal had an idea. "Actually, there is something I'd like. I'd like it a lot, but it's not exactly for me. It's for Pippa's family. I'd never have made it here if it wasn't for Pippa. They're really hard up. If you could help them, then perhaps they could start up something for themselves. Kayley shouldn't be working for Mr Carker anyway. He's an awful man. Maybe they wouldn't have to know where the money came from?"

Donald nodded.

"Consider it done," he said, and they turned and made their way back to the cottage.

25

What Happened to the Carkers

Kayley sat in her little office at Easy Pets. She had been working since seven in the morning, making a register, alone and without pay in the deserted building, and she was absolutely exhausted.

Just a week after she brought Pippa back from Northumberland, Kayley had come to work as usual and found that the Carkers had disappeared. They had put in such a ridiculous insurance claim for the missing dogs that the accountants had started to look into their affairs, and it was found that they had been cheating on their income tax for years and years.

So the charming couple had fled to Spain, owing Kayley her wages and leaving only enough food for a couple of days for the dogs.

Fortunately, a charity which cared for animals in distress had stepped in to try and find homes for the abandoned dogs. Because the Easy Pets dogs were highly bred and had been well looked after, plenty of people had come forward to offer to have them, but Kayley had absolutely insisted on inspecting every single home to make sure that it was suitable for the dogs she had cared for and knew so well. Now she only had to check the list of new owners and the job was done.

Well, almost done. All the dogs were happily housed, except for one. No one had come forward offering to have Queen Tilly. She sat now on her hot water bottle, shrieking and twitching and shaking with ill temper, the only dog left in the huge building that only a week ago had been full of life.

"Oh, what on earth shall I do with you?" Kayley asked her.

She would have taken her home herself if it hadn't been for her landlord, who forbade all pets. Kayley had pity even for this most unattractive dog.

It was as she was standing by Queen Tilly's cage that the doorbell rang.

Outside on the steps stood a rather forlorn-looking young man.

"The name is Sprocket," he said.

A lot had happened to Milton Sprocket since he had followed Darth and Terminator across the moors and been picked up in a police van.

The disgrace, for a detective, of falling into the hands of the force was overwhelming, but even worse was the terror he had felt at being cooped up with the two tracker dogs, slavering and frothing and showing their teeth only a few inches away from him. Darth and Terminator wanted to make it clear that though Otto had stopped them in their tracks, they were still killing machines, and whenever Sprocket tried to move his cramped limbs, their lips curled back over their incisors and they growled like the hounds of hell.

Though Sprocket had been released almost straightaway and been able to get back to his van and drive to London, he had been left with a serious trauma. It was a kind of mental illness: a terror not just of dangerous dogs but of all dogs. Even a dog walking along on the other side of the road brought on an attack, causing him to shake all over.

This was obviously very inconvenient for a detective. A man with a false moustache shaking like a leaf was apt to attract attention. Nothing could be done about the tragic block over his poetry, thought Sprocket, but surely he could find somebody who would help him to overcome his fear of dogs? So he had consulted a doctor, who had sent him to another doctor, who told him that the only way to be cured was to have a dog of his own.

Sprocket had never been a dog lover. There was too much chewing and slobbering involved for a neat and careful man like himself. On the other hand, his work was suffering. Then he had a brainwave. He would rent a dog from an agency, just for an hour or two. If it brought on an attack he could always bring it straight back. Perhaps he could start with half an hour, then an hour. And the dogs could gradually get bigger. It would be expensive, but he was no longer so hard up. His aunt had died and left him some money and he hoped one day to set up on his own.

And thinking about dog hire agencies, he remembered passing one on the way north, and drove to Easy Pets.

The girl who let him in was pretty and gentle and nice. Sprocket took to her at once, but she had sad news to give him.

"I'm afraid we're closed down. The owners have left, and we've had to find homes for the dogs. I wish we could help you but you see. . ." She waved her arm at the empty cages, the bare floors, the bin bags waiting to be collected.

"Oh dear. Well, I'll just have to try somewhere else."

He was turning to go when a high-pitched and angry yapping broke the silence.

"She's the last dog left," said Kayley. "We can't find a home for her, I'm afraid. I don't know what will happen. . ."

She led Sprocket into Room A where the Mexican hairless in her cage was screaming and twitching and shivering with loneliness and rage.

"Goodness." Sprocket had never seen such an unappealing dog.

"I'm afraid she gets the gripes from time to time," said Kayley.

Sprocket stared at her and his mouth dropped open because an absolutely amazing thing had happened. The dreadful block that had stopped him from writing poetry had disappeared. It was the word gripes that did it. For what was gripes except the perfect rhyme for pipes. And, as if it had been lowered down from heaven, the completed couplet came to him.

> If your toilet's got the gripes
> We will come and fix your pipes.

It was pithy, it was exact, and there was nothing in it that his mother would think was rude.

In her cage, Queen Tilly was still twitching and shivering and screaming, and Sprocket, looking at her, wondered what she reminded him of. Then suddenly it came to him. Of course. Himself. He had been like that all through his school days, shivering and twitching and wanting to scream. Unwanted. Unloved.

He took a deep breath. He couldn't do it. It was impossible.

But in his mind he had already done it. After all, this revolting little creature had given him back his gift for poetry. Perhaps she would turn out to be his lucky charm.

The relief of having found a home for Queen Tilly kept Kayley going on the long journey on the underground, but when she got home she flopped down on the sofa, thoroughly miserable. She'd lost her job and the dogs who had been her friends, and the loss of her wages would make things really hard for the family.

"It's all right, love," said her mother. "I've got my sewing with Mrs Naryan, and you'll find something else to do. A girl like you won't be out of work for long."

But jobs were hard to get, and Kayley didn't have a lot of paper qualifications. When she'd phoned about a vacancy in a boarding kennel they'd asked her if she had a Diploma in Domestic Canine Management. Without it, the lady thought, she would find it hard to muck out the dogs' cages or take them for a walk!

Pippa came in then from school, followed by the twins, and everybody did their best to cheer Kayley up, but what had happened at Easy Pets had shaken them all.

They were sitting down to their supper when a black car drew up outside the window. An expensive-looking car, out of which stepped a smartly dressed man with a briefcase.

"What does he want, I wonder?" said Mrs O'Brian, looking worried. "We've paid our rent."

"They'll be inspecting something," said Pippa gloomily.

The doorbell rang.

"I'd like to speak to Miss Kayley O'Brian, please," said the man with the briefcase. "Is this the right house?"

"Yes," said Pippa, who had opened the door. "I suppose you'd better come in."

Albina was shopping. It was her favourite occupation and she was entirely happy. The three G aunts were with her. Hal was coming home in a week's time and she was getting ready.

The shop was called The Pampered Pooch and it sold everything that a well-turned-out dog might need. A famous dress designer had just produced a new range of tartan jackets and matching booties for afternoon wear, and for more athletic dogs there were jumpsuits of mink or ermine. Displays of jewelled collars were arranged on satin cushions. There were diamond studs for dogs to wear in their ears, and gold ribbons to plait into their moustaches, and inflatable ham bones which played "Silent Night" for dogs who found it difficult to sleep. Kennels shaped like paddle steamers or railway stations or giant boots stood on the floor, there was a stand of motoring goggles for dogs with sensitive eyes, and the shelves groaned with bubble baths and scents and deodorants for dogs who worried about their personal hygiene.

"Oh dear, I don't know where to begin," said Albina. "There's so much. Do you think Fleck would like a pillow shaped like a frankfurter sausage?"

Georgina had found a cashmere bonnet for cold days with a ribbon to tie under the chin, and Gloria had fallen for a blanket which played "Hush-a-bye Poochie" when you picked it up.

The ladies ran hither and thither, getting more and more excited.

"Look, here's a collar with real garnets," said Glenda. "I think garnets would suit him, don't you? And it would go with your bracelet, wouldn't it?"

Albina took it from her hand.

"Yes, it would. Though there's an even better one over there. Look! It's in alligator skin with a double row of rhinestones and the clasp is sixteen-carat gold."

They picked up a bottle of scent called "Doggy Delirium" and put it to their noses.

"It's heavenly. He must have some of that," said Georgina.

She looked at the price and gave a little shriek, but really the expense didn't matter. Spending a lot of money was what it was all about.

"There's some canine mascara here," said Glenda.

"I seem to remember his eyelashes were rather pale."

They were piling up their purchases, ready to take them to the counter, when they saw an object that stopped them in their tracks. For a moment they could not even speak, it was so beautiful and wonderful and strange. A platinum pooper scooper set with opals and amethysts.

Albina reached for it with a shaking hand.

"It's copied from a design that was used by the Russian royal family," she said, reading the label. "Oh, I must have that, I absolutely must!"

But just as she was about to add it to the other objects they had chosen, something happened. Albina straightened herself. She stood stock-still and a kind of judder went through her. A sort of twitch. . . And then slowly, very slowly (because it was so difficult) she put back the bottle of "Doggy Delirium", and the blanket which played "Hush-a-bye Poochie", and the garnet collar, and last of all, with a stab of real pain, the pooper scooper made of platinum.

"No," said Albina, being nobler than she had ever been in her life. "I've decided. I'm not going to buy anything till Hal comes home. I'm going to wait. It is for Hal to choose."

And with the G aunts following, she marched out of the shop.

*

Hal was reading a letter. He sat on an upturned boat on the shore. The sun was shining and the North Sea was on its best behaviour, silver near the shore, shading to pale blue and then a deep azure. The tide was out and the sands stretched for miles, empty and golden, as they do on the Northumbrian coast.

Fleck sat at his feet, but the letter was a long one.

"All right, Fleck, you can go and explore," said Hal – and Fleck looked up at him and then trotted off along the beach.

The letter was from Pippa, and as he read it, Hal smiled, for his father had done exactly what Hal had asked of him. And done it secretly.

. . . It's absolutely extraordinary because it happened just when Kayley came home after she finished at Easy Pets and she was feeling really rotten. Apparently one of the people who used to rent dogs noticed how good Kayley was with animals and he put her name down for a grant from a charity that looks after animals. It's a huge sum and of course it's all tied up with endowments and things. I don't really understand the details but it means that Kayley can do what she's always wanted to do: start an animal rescue place where the animals are cared for properly and never have to be put down even if they're sick and can't find homes. We've looked

at a patch of land not too far away and there's a little house – it's not much more than a hut at the minute, but we're all going to pitch in and make it habitable. Isn't it fantastic? You'll come and help, won't you? And maybe that nice maid Olga you told us about? We're going to call it Fillongley after the family farm. Grandfather's over the moon. . .

Hal looked up. He'd go and phone his father and thank him.

But where was Fleck? There was no sign of him on the long, deserted beach. For a moment Hal was overcome by panic. Had he got lost, or drowned, or stolen? It wasn't like him to go so far on his own.

He put his fingers in his mouth and whistled – and a white speck appeared, grew larger, and flopped down at Hal's feet. Fleck's tongue lolled, his tail thumped on the sand. He seemed to be smiling. . .

A dog who belongs to somebody forever is a dog who is free.

Sharon Rentta sent us lots of drawings for
ONE DOG AND HIS BOY. We couldn't
use all of them but they are too good to
leave out completely.